Praise for t
CURTISS AN

"Matlock's down-to-earth characters and comforting plot will please many."
—*Booklist* on *Recipes for Easy Living*

"Once again, Matlock delivers a gentle, glowing tale that is as sweet and sunny as its small town setting. Readers will be delighted by this deft mix of romance and…slice-of-life drama."
—*Publishers Weekly* on
At the Corner of Love and Heartache

"This is a delicious read for a lazy summer day. It's not overly sweet, and it has enough zing to satisfy readers thirsting for an uplifting read."
—*Publishers Weekly* on *Cold Tea on a Hot Day*

"Ms. Matlock masterfully takes readers into a world full of quirky characters and small town simplicity where they will wish they can stay."
—*Romantic Times* on *Cold Tea on a Hot Day*

"With realistic characters and absorbing dialogue, Matlock crafts a moving story about a woman's road to self-discovery."
—*Publishers Weekly* on *Driving Lessons*

"This is simply a great read."
—*Romantic Times* on *Driving Lessons*

"This one will warm you."
—*Romantic Times* on *Lost Highways*

Sweet Dreams at the Goodnight Motel

Curtiss Ann Matlock

MIRA®

MIRA®

ISBN 0-7783-2091-X

SWEET DREAMS AT THE GOODNIGHT MOTEL

www.MIRABooks.com

Printed in U.S.A.

First Printing: October 2004
10 9 8 7 6 5 4 3 2 1

ACKNOWLEDGMENTS

My deep gratitude to my editor, Leslie Wainger, who has supported me for many years now with her calm confidence, and for always believing in me, and in life.

Special thanks to Susan Pezzack, who came up with the delightful title to this book, and to Dianne Moggy and all the MIRA team, for giving me a home where I can write true to my heart and Southern voice.

Thank you, Meg, for your creative ideas, gift of encouragement and cheerful voice that always delights me.

I am eternally grateful to my sisters on the journey, who prayed me through: Cheryle, Mary Ann, Darlene, Beverly, Carol, Carolyn and Melanie.

To my dear Barb—there is no gratitude large enough.

Thank you to my dear husband, James, for hanging in there.

And to all the dear readers who write to tell me how much you love Valentine—Thank You!

"I know this about life: it goes on and on and on, nothing new under the sun, yet somehow we all have to learn our own lessons by feeling around in the dark and doing the best we can with what we've got."

—Vella Blaine

From: Vella Blaine
To: <haltg@mailectric.com>
Sent: May 20, 1997, 6:30 p.m.
Subject: Hello from Valentine

Dear Harold,

I want to say that you pay me a lovely compliment to take the time to let me know of the good that the sore gum remedy I posted on the caretaker list has done your wife. My husband, Perry, was a very fine pharmacist for fifty years and invented the tooth powder for his own uncle's sore gums. We have used that powder on our teeth for thirty years, and we still have every one of them—teeth, not years, although I guess we have those, too.

Of course now, after Perry's stroke, I am the one to use it on his teeth. I guess he'll have his teeth, even if there isn't much left of the rest of him. It worries me that with him like he is, I may not know if he has a toothache, so I like to keep up with his dental hygiene.

And yes, I live in a real town named Valentine. It's in Oklahoma. Some people think the name is romantic, but there was no romance intended; it was simply the name of one of the early families. The town might have ended up being named Blaine, from my husband's family, who were most prominent, but the Valentines were always a pushy bunch and got their way.

Valentine certainly isn't much compared to your Newark,

I'm sure, although I have not seen Newark. I have never traveled all that far and wide. I used to go with some regularity to the Dallas-Fort Worth area to buy for our drugstore—Blaine's Drugstore and Soda Fountain, providing a young, up-to-date pharmacist an extensive selection of health and beauty aids, and drinks, ice cream and sandwiches. Our store is a town landmark, seventy-five years old, seventy of those in the same place on Main Street, and still going strong. It's harder for me to get away from the store these days, since I have both it and Perry to handle.

One place I went years ago was Galveston. Oh, my, I loved the beach, but Perry wanted to get home, so we didn't get to stay more than three days. That used to be Perry's limit anywhere, three days, and then he quit going at all, even to see his mother after she married for a fourth time and went off to Tulsa. Perry always used to say that Valentine was his home and there was no place like home.

I can agree with that. There likely isn't, or else why would one ever want to get away and see someplace else?

Well, thank you again for letting me know the sore gum remedy helped you and your wife. What is her name? I know your struggle as a caretaker, and it pleases me to think that I helped you in some small way.

Vella, in Valentine.

She pressed the send button, then sat there for a few seconds, staring at the silvery screen of the computer monitor. She always had the odd feeling of wondering where her message went and imagined it disappearing into thin air. She imagined typed words floating out into space. Maybe her message would be stuck with thousands of other messages on one of those countless satellites that she had heard of on CNN, ones that didn't even work anymore but were just space debris.

Who knew what alien might read her message from Valentine and look down on it, a small town in a great big world. It kind of made her wary of what she said.

Wish Me Well

Chapter One

Shreveport, Louisiana

Sometimes a person sees or hears something at a particularly pivotal moment. Behind the moment, though, is a lot of time, years maybe, where all manner of unfed desires and dashed dreams have been jammed down and compressed, very much like packing in an explosive. Then comes that particular moment that ignites the fuse. The lid is blown off, and all those desires and dreams come spewing forth, which accounts for all manner of both passionate crimes and daring new lives.

This is what happened one evening to Claire, a lonely but mostly reasonable woman, when she read the words on the bathroom wall: *On my way, just passing through, looking for real life—wish her well, this Lily Donnell!*

It was on the inside of the stall door of the ladies' room at the truck stop out on I-20, where Claire and R.K. had ended up coming for supper because R.K. loved their ribs and no one bothered him. R.K. was a television weatherman of long-standing for the prime-time news hour—the weatherman with the highest ratings in the market—but most people at the truck stop restaurant were travelers and thus didn't recognize him, and those regulars who did had seen him eat ribs often enough to no longer be impressed by him.

Inside the bathroom stall, Claire studied the comment as she adjusted her black thigh-high panty hose. It was written in blue marker, right between *Call Heather for a good time* and the phone number, and *I love Johnny Deland in Bossier City* in a big lipstick heart.

Just passing through…looking for real life.

"My, Lord, aren't we all? I wish you well, Lily Donnell," Claire muttered.

Her mind went into a buzz as she almost slammed out of the stall, washed her hands at the sink and applied lipstick in the mirror.

She paused and looked at herself. A blank face gazed back at her.

Oh, she was attractive enough. She caught the eye of many a man, and both R.K. and her ex-husband Andrew termed her a good-looking woman. Had she not been, neither of them would have been interested in her; such was their nature, and that was not criticism but truth.

She took the paper towel to the mirror, wondering if it were filmy. It wasn't. The woman looking back at her was gray. She needed something. A new hairdo. A new shade of lipstick.

A life.

She went back to the table, played with her napkin, and broke things off with R.K. She waited for him to finish his ribs, though. After the lengthy months of feeling like she needed to break off with him and not doing it, she didn't see any point now to hurry and ruin his supper.

After she told him, as gently as possible, R.K. looked at her a long minute in which he laid down the knife he had been using to butter each bite of biscuit. Then he said, "You mean it this time, don't you?"

"Yes." She looked him in the eye. She had almost broken off with him countless times in the past two years, since her divorce, when he had started after her like Sherman after the South.

"I'd thought with Andrew gettin' married to Nina—" he gave her his best teddy bear expression that was as sweet as it could be "—well, that maybe now you could really see me."

"I care for you…you're a good friend. You're a handsome, wonderful and good man." She had about torn her napkin to shreds. "I'm just…I just can't go on lettin' you think there's gonna be more." She stopped short of saying how hard she had tried to make more out of it, because that seemed like kicking a poor dog.

When he said, "I don't mind waitin', Claire," she almost put her head down and cried, she felt so badly. What was there to say back to that?

"Oh, I just can't let you do that. You are too wonderful to waste a minute holdin' your life back on account of me. You deserve a wife and family, R.K. I can't ever give you children, and you will make a wonderful father."

"I don't want any children," he said with earnestness. He was determined to make this hard.

"Not now, but you might later…and I'm goin' to go away, R.K. My therapist says it's imperative that I go with no strings attached. I don't have anything to give you right now…not you or anyone. I have to get myself together before I can consider a relationship with a man. I'm possibly going to Riverbend, for a month."

It was a bald-faced lie, but she told herself it was possible. She knew that this sort of line would touch R.K., who had, before weatherman school, set out to be a psychologist, which was what had possibly drawn her to him, because of her mother's history of emotional instabilities, and R.K. knew a bit about her mother, too.

And now that she had started lying, she couldn't seem to stop. "My therapist really thinks that I'd better take a rest. These last years have just added up…gettin' divorced…losin' Mama…and now Andrew and Nina."

Making the list, she began to truly depress herself. She began to believe that she had better pack her bags straight away for the psychiatric hospital.

He nodded and looked sympathetic. They sat there in silence for a long minute. R.K. broke this by, in his typical thoughtful fashion, asking if she was up for the apple pie and ice cream.

"I think I'll skip it tonight. You go ahead, though."

He said he'd skip it, too.

While he paid the check, she walked outside. The night was cool and smooth. She looked upward, trying to see stars, but there were too many lights, from the restaurant, the gas station, the semitrucks rumbling this way and that. The sky just looked black, yet she knew that up there stars did twinkle.

For an instant she was a girl, ten, maybe, who had just stepped out the back door of the old house, while inside, with her grandfather and aunt gone, her mother entertained a man friend. Dreamy country music floated out into the night, accompanied by the squeak and thump of feet dancing over the living room floor.

She couldn't see the stars, because of the light from the house, but she knew they were up there. Even though barefoot and fearing to step on a snake, she padded farther and farther out into the backyard, until at last she could see them—stars twinkling like spilled diamonds. It was the grandest sight in the world.

Funny how some moments that seemed rather ordinary but weren't, for some reason stayed in memory.

It came in memory, too, her mother's call after her friend had left. "Claire, honey, it's lonesome in here. Come sit with me for a bit, please?"

Her mother's plaintive and desperate voice echoed so long and so loud in her mind that she didn't hear R.K. come up behind her; she about jumped out of her skin when he spoke.

"You ready?"

"Oh. Yes…"

He held the car door for her, then paused before closing it, saying, "What is it that you want, Claire? What are you lookin' for?"

And, still feeling her mother around her, she replied, "I guess if I knew, I wouldn't be lookin', would I?" She smiled. "The best I know is real life, whatever that is."

He drove her home and walked her to the door, where he just had to say, "If you change your mind when you come back from Riverbend, you call me."

She could not believe he would say that. She felt embarrassed at her past behavior that led him to say it, and annoyed with him that he would let her treat him in such a manner. She made herself slow down enough to touch his cheek in a tender gesture, then she slipped through her front door, closed it and leaned against it, eyes squeezed closed for a full minute.

Opening her eyes, she looked around the small entry hall that glowed in the low light of a lamp on the side table.

Alone…alone…alone. *Just like your mother.*

Pushing from the door, she walked quickly to the kitchen and turned on the light, stood there blinking, then turned and hurried back to the door, put her hand on the knob. But R.K. was gone.

In that instant, she decided that she had made a terrible

mistake. She went to the phone on the hallway table. She would call R.K. and make up with him. She would set a record. He wouldn't even be to the boulevard.

She lifted the receiver, thinking up what she would say. But then, all of a sudden, her mind and hand stopped. She stood poised, then hung up the phone and strode back to the kitchen and through it to the garage. She got into her car and drove with purpose the fifteen minutes to Andrew's apartment in an old restored brick warehouse down near the river, which he, as the successful architect that he had become, owned and had renovated.

So late at night during the week, the street was all but deserted. She stopped the car at the opposite curb and lowered the window, looking up at the lighted windows of the second story across the street for thirty minutes, in the nature of the desperate woman she felt herself becoming.

Several times she caught sight of Andrew's shadow, and once Nina passed near the window. It was a swift passing, but enough that Claire saw her clearly and knew well it was the younger woman.

Her heart felt as if it had been stabbed. Of course, it was not strange for Nina to be in Andrew's apartment. The two were engaged. Likely they had slept together often. But in the way of a longing woman, Claire thought that there was no proof of this, and, indeed, that perhaps Nina would be leaving at any moment.

She could wait for the woman to leave. Or she could go up and boldly ask to speak to Andrew with the woman there. Or—she reached for her cell phone and punched the number for Andrew's apartment.

But she did not call. She sat holding the phone, until a patrol car had cruised past twice, and she saw it turning to come back. With a great, painful sigh, she laid the phone aside, started the car and drove home, where she threw off her clothes and took to her bed. Her collapsed state was retribution for the lying she had done with R.K. All that she had described was coming true, she thought, wallowing in her depression. She would be turned over to a therapist and sent to the psychiatric hospital, and likely she would end up becoming the image of her needy and uncertain mother.

Claire Wilder was forty years old, childless and divorced, and had spent the better part of the past two years waiting for her ex-husband to wake up and come home.

Only Andrew had not come home, and was, in two weeks, to marry a woman twelve years younger than Claire, who now didn't know what she would do without either her husband or her dream of reconciliation.

Claire did not know how she had gotten into this life she was living. At a young age, somewhere back when she had begun to work to get herself and her mother up out of the tumbling down old house on the dusty back road, she had determined that she would not turn out like her mother, who had spent much of her life going through boyfriends, psychiatric wards and long stretches confined to bed.

For the most part, Claire had succeeded well. She had gotten an education, and searched out and landed a handsome, stable but ambitious young man with whom to fall madly in love. They had been a perfect match. Everyone said so. She had expected to find with him everything that she had missed out on in her childhood—a place to belong in a loving family, noisy kids and a pretty home, maybe one with a picket fence and flower gardens, where she enjoyed living all of her days and ended up sitting out on a porch in the evening, holding old hands with her husband.

Yet, somewhere along the way of their eighteen years of marriage, they had gone wrong. Everything had fallen apart, and here she was, alone in a way that her mother had never been alone, because Claire did not have a daughter as her mother had enjoyed, to comfort and take care of her.

She just didn't know what to do now. She didn't seem to have any dreams. When she tried to have dreams, it was like she was looking down into a dry well. She tried to want things. She tried to want R.K. He was such a kind, adorable man, and he desired her. She simply couldn't work up any return desire, though. In fact, she didn't seem to have any desire for anything at all, except possibly to stay right in her bed forever.

These thoughts occupied and in a hundred ways tormented her for four days, which she spent sleeping for hours on end, and when not sleeping, she cried while looking through the albums of pictures taken during the early happy years of her marriage, where she was a sunny blond beauty and her husband a handsome man on the rise. She also watched reruns of *The Andy Griffith Show* and *The Brady Bunch* and chick-flick movies on the Lifetime Network and cried more. She drank the one bottle of wine in the refrigerator and pots of darjeeling tea, and ate every already cooked thing in the house, down to the cans of Vienna sausages left over from her mother's final visit. Her mother had loved Vienna sausages.

During this dark time, the only persons Claire spoke to were the pizza delivery boy, who stepped back a pace when she opened the door, and Gayla Jean, her ex-sister-in-law and co-worker in the legal department of Tri-State Food Distributors, who called to find out why she wasn't at the office.

"Claire, honey, what is wrong? Is your answerin' machine broke? Melody called you three times this week, and I called you last night, and Mr. Dupree himself called you today. He's real upset not to hear from you."

"I've got a terrible toothache. I had to have emergency oral surgery," Claire said, which she thought explained why she sounded so strange. "I didn't hear the phone last night. I thought I called yesterday, but I guess the pain medication has me really messed up."

At that moment she came face-to-face with an error of her ways. She saw that she lied and, in that one instant, it was like seeing into the past and future at once, seeing her marriage, her divorce and her life. And the person she lied to the most was herself.

Chapter Two

The old cypress souvenir box sat on the shelf beside the brass urn that held her mother's ashes. Claire had not seen the box ever in her life until her mother's death, when she found it tucked into the drawer of the nightstand in her mother's bedroom. The contents had been a surprise then, and now, taking it in hand, she sank to the edge of the bed and opened the box on her knees, lifting the items and looking at them one at a time, in the manner of an inspector looking for clues.

The box held several photographs of her parents, one of herself as an infant, and an astonishing love letter from her father—astonishing mostly because her mother had kept it—and several other trinkets that Claire fancied her father had given her mother: a tiny plastic heart bracelet, a gaudy souvenir handkerchief from New Orleans, and a tiny serviceman's issue *New Testament Bible* from the Gideons.

The photograph of her father, the only one she had ever seen, was faded black and white, and her father's face was in shadow, telling her very little. She could not tell if she resembled him at all, and if she passed him on the street, she wouldn't know him.

From his stance and the Army uniform, she guessed him to be around twenty or so. He had his arm around a shorter, older man, whose face was also made indistinguishable by a straw cowboy hat. On the back of the picture was written in pencil: John & his father.

Oh, Daddy…Daddy.

Claire did as she always did, peering even more closely, trying to see the smaller old man beside her father—the man who had been her grandfather, and at whose home in the wilds of Oklahoma, to hear her mother describe it, Claire had been born. Her birth had taken place almost three weeks early and was induced, so her mother had said, because of eating some unidentifiable food made by Mother Tillman. Her mother had hated it there with her father's people—"They still had an outhouse and no electricity, for heaven's sake"— and within weeks had brought Claire home to her own family in Louisiana.

Also in the box was a snapshot of her mother and Claire. It was the only photograph she'd ever seen in which her mother was truly smiling. Her mother was holding Claire, who appeared to be about a year old. Directly behind them was a brand-new, two-toned Ford, and Claire always imagined her father having snapped the shot, very pleased with both his beautiful wife and his new car.

Then there was a photograph of her mother with her father, and they looked in love. Maybe it had been right after they were married. In the photograph, her mother wore a belted suit with straight shoulder pads and smart, three-quarter sleeves. Her mother had never worn pants a day in her life, but neat shirtwaists or slim skirts and blouses with pearl buttons, and low-heeled pumps that unfailingly matched her purse, white, black, navy or taupe. Her hair and appearance were such that she could have been a stand-in for the Breck girl.

How a woman of her mother's careful and fragile sort had gotten paired up with a rough man who worked as a roustabout on oil rigs, and who Claire vaguely recalled as being all baggy clothes topped by a permanently tanned face and shaggy dark hair, was one of those mysteries explained only by her acceptance that people often made senseless choices.

With a sigh, she closed the box, sitting for nearly five thoughtful minutes considering what her father and his people would have looked and been like, before she gently returned the box to its place on the shelf beside the urn.

Claire opened the refrigerator door and looked inside at an almost empty jar of mayonnaise, a couple of wilted celery stalks, and tuna salad that was likely a week old. After staring at this pitiful sight for another thirty seconds, she closed the door, deciding to choose going to the Piggly Wiggly over slicing her wrists.

In the bathroom, she wet her face, then caught her reflection in the mirror. *Oh-my-Lord.*

She dressed in capri sweatpants and a sweatshirt with the sleeves cut off. She tried but did not succeed very well in doing anything with her hair. In the end, she dug a ball cap out of a drawer and stuck it on.

The beauty shop she frequented was in the strip mall with the Piggly Wiggly. Her regular beautician wasn't in, but another stylist agreed to take her.

"I want a different look," she told the woman. "I want to cover the gray."

"Uh, uh, uh," said the stylist, with a studying gaze. She had a turban on her own head, and Claire suddenly thought that might not be a promising sign.

The stylist said, "We're not gonna cover you up, honey. We're gonna re-*veal* you."

The comment startled Claire. Had she possessed energy to leave, she would have. Instead she sat there and watched as the woman began whacking at her hair.

Two hours later Claire emerged from the beauty salon and headed for the Piggly Wiggly. She kept looking at herself in the store windows as she went along. An unidentifiable woman in sweat clothes with short, bouncy blond hair gazed back at her.

The middle of the day was when mothers shopped with their children. Claire pushed her cart up and down aisles where she heard women, with overflowing shopping carts and crying toddlers, shouting, "Stop that runnin'! I'm gonna get a'hold of you!"

Claire's cart contained bananas, a small box of instant oatmeal and a six-pack of single-serving fruit cans.

She stood staring at the meat in the cold shelf display. She thought about getting a leg of lamb. She used to just love lamb stew. She made it quite well, and Andrew liked it. But an entire leg, just for herself? She could have the butcher cut it up and package it separately for freezing.

Just then a woman stepped in front of her. "Excuse me." She took up the leg of lamb and dropped it into her overflowing cart.

Claire moved down the aisle and picked up a package of bologna and tossed it into the bottom of her cart.

A very round and beautiful baby in the seat of a cart smiled at her in the dairy aisle. Claire winked, and the baby giggled. The mother gave Claire a small smile and pushed the baby on, as if to put some distance between them.

The childless state at her age was, even in this modern era, an oddity. People could be cruel about her not having a child. Very often the first thing someone said was, "You don't have any children?" and with it came the look of incomprehension, as if she were some odd breed of woman.

Another often-said comment was, "Well, you don't know what it's like to have children tuggin' on you, Claire. You're lucky."

Sometimes people said, "Didn't you want any children?"

The truth—that she had lost two babies—was not only hard to say but made things awkward. Everyone would then feel sorry for her and not know what to say and move away as fast as possible.

It seemed that childless women of her age were expected to either be deep into their careers—possibly an attorney or doctor, or perhaps an artist, or at least a wise professor—or deep into charity work. This went double for women without children who were not married, and really older women with no children were supposed to have retired from high-powered careers and do major charity work, like getting hospitals, cancer wings or colleges at universities built.

Claire was a legal secretary, in the same position for the past sixteen years, with no room for advancement and none particularly desired, either.

She sat in her car in the parking lot and ate a banana and a rolled up piece of bologna, and thought about the state of her life as she watched women push carts and children out of the store from the shelter of her large dark sunglasses.

Finally she started the car and drove to the corporate offices of Tri-State Food Distributors. At the elevators to the second floor and the legal offices, she caught sight of herself in the mirrors. Full color.

At first she didn't recognize herself with her new hair, but then she did recognize the sweats that she still wore. She thought of turning around and returning when she had cleaned up and was wearing more appropriate clothes. But the elevator opened, and she got on.

"Is this about John Montgomery? Did he offer you more money?" said Herbert Dupree, her boss and general counsel for the Tri-State Corporation.

She told him no, that she just needed a change in her life, and she did apologize for not offering a two-week notice, but she believed Melanie or any one of the other secretaries could fill in nicely. It was as if she were standing in the corner and watching herself speak to him, and she was quite approving of, even a little amazed at, her confident and polite demeanor. She knew her mother would be approving of the politeness. Her mother, even in her worst emotional state, would speak politely, because God forbid there be any sign of unpleasantness.

Herbert Dupree, who was often unpleasant, was a little frothy. "Well, I don't have time for your female craziness. If you come back in a week, you can have your job back. Other than that, don't expect any unemployment benefits."

No "I'm sorry to lose you. Is there anything I can do to help?" or "I appreciate your hard work and loyalty for the past five years," or even, "You made the best damn coffee in the state."

Claire said nothing more, just turned and left, hearing a drawer slam behind her.

While she was getting her private belongings from her desk and office, Gayla Jean came in. "Claire? My gosh—your hair! It looks so great."

"Thanks," Claire said, rifling in the top drawer of the desk, dropping things into the box she had gotten from the closet.

Gayla Jean came over and touched her hair. "Did you get it frosted?"

"Yes."

"Melanie said you're quittin'. Are you really?"

"Yes."

"Ohmygod. What's happened? Is there some problem with your teeth? Do you have oral cancer or somethin'?"

This brought Claire's gaze up to see Gayla Jean staring at her with wide eyes. Then she remembered the lie she had told. "No. My teeth are fine. I'm just goin' away for a bit." She took the nameplate off the desk, had a second thought and dropped it back. She wouldn't be needing it.

"Claire, what in the world is goin' on?"

"You know what I started out in college to do?" Claire said as she gathered up her favorite fingernail file and three bottles of polish. "I started out to be either an interior designer or an anthropologist. But then I married Andrew, and we needed money, so I dropped out and went to work. The plan was for me to work for a few years and support us while Andrew finished school, and when he became an architect, then he was going to support us while I made our home and had babies. Somehow I ended up a legal secretary here and never moved on, and now Andrew's gone and marryin' a bimbo, who will be havin' his babies."

Gayla Jean stared at her. "Honey, you are beside yourself."

"I know, but that does not change the fact that I really hate bein' a legal secretary. I have always hated it. And I never even got a decent vacation the entire time I was married to Andrew. We always had to go someplace to *schmooze* with *Somebody*. Bermuda...Cancun...Hawaii...while I really wanted to go to a cabin in the mountains or a cottage down t' the gulf, just someplace to be quiet and be together." She paused, staring into space, thinking of it.

"I doubt Nina is gonna jump in there and have Andrew's babies," Gayla Jean said, interrupting Claire's reverie. "I just can't see that."

"Okay, so they're goin' to build an architecture dynasty.

Whatever, I just don't want to be here when they get married. I just can't be here anymore, period." She picked up her collection of dog Beanie Babies. "Take these for your kids."

The phone on the desk rang. Melanie, a young all-round assistant who had appeared to stand in the door, said, "I need to get that, Claire."

"Yes, you'd better." She moved out of the way, and the younger woman lunged for the phone.

"Look, Claire. Stop just a minute and calm down." Gayla Jean took Claire's arm and pulled her aside, speaking in a lowered voice. "I wasn't gonna say anything to you. I didn't want to speak out of turn. But yesterday Andrew came over to talk to Lamar. Lamar didn't want to tell me, because he was afraid I would tell you, but I promised I wouldn't. Only now, I think that God would want me to drop that promise." She paused for emphasis. "Andrew is havin' second thoughts about this marriage to Nina."

Claire gazed into Gayla Jean's golden eyes.

"Claire, honey, he's most probably gonna break up with Nina."

After a moment of taking this in, Claire said, "Well, I hope she doesn't kill him," and picked up the box of her belongings.

She remembered her umbrella in the closet. "Melanie, anything I left is yours. The *p* sticks on the keyboard, I have the clock set five minutes fast, and Mr. Dupree will scream obscenities at you if you don't tell him to cut it out. And don't go into his office without knocking, or you'll never get some things out of your mind. And be smart—after you get some time in here, look for a nicer guy to work for. Money can't buy everything."

"Th-thanks," the young woman said in a faint voice. "I'll miss you, Claire."

Claire, who was almost out the door, went over and gave

the young woman a hug, then strode out, with Gayla Jean following and saying, "Claire, honey, are you listenin' to me? Andrew is turnin' around. I thought that was what you have been waitin' for."

"I don't know anymore what I was waitin' for," Claire said and punched the elevator button.

She hesitated, then awkwardly kissed Gayla Jean on the cheek. "I'll call you. I'll keep in touch," and went for the stairs rather than wait for the elevator.

Gayla Jean came after her. "Well, where are you goin'?"

"To get a life…to see where I was born…maybe I'll find my daddy."

"When will you be back?"

"A month, maybe two. I don't know."

"You have lost your mind."

"Wish me well!"

"Well, honey, I do. You know that."

Gayla Jean, staring over the railing, heard her own voice echo down the stairwell. Then she pivoted and hurried back to her desk in a cubicle that sported a window and pictures of her children pasted alongside of it.

She jerked up the phone and dialed her husband. Waiting for him to pick up, she stepped over to look at her image in the small round mirror hanging on the partition.

Her husband came on the line. "Lamar, you need to call Andrew and tell him that Claire has up and quit her job, and not only that—she is leavin' town. She's talkin' crazy about gettin' a life and seein' where she was born." That gave her pause. "Isn't she from here? I always thought she was from here."

Lamar said he had thought Claire was from some suburb of Shreveport. Then he gave her a lecture about butting in. "You need to stay out of their affairs, Gayla Jean."

"I have stayed out of it, and we see where it has gotten. Just call him, Lamar."

He said what he always said when he didn't want to do something. "I will, if I have time. I'm really busy."

"Honey, how do you think you would like me as a blonde?" she asked before hanging up.

He said the correct thing. "I'd love you if you were bald-headed, sweetheart."

Good Lord, what *had* she done?

The hot sultry air blew in the car window. It felt odd on her short hair.

"You will be okay. You will. You are totally alone, but not without attributes."

Her mother used to say that to her: "Claire, you have so many attributes. If you play your cards right, you will find a well-fixed man who will take care of you."

"Right, Mama."

She had not been an idealistic fool. Her mother's life had taught her that life without a man could be hard, and she had always been good with money. Andrew had so trusted her that he had relied on her managing their finances. She had established a rule of having enough money in savings to pay bills for six months. This was where not having children did improve her life. Without children, who needed new shoes every six months, new clothes, dental work and the latest toys, one could achieve quite a good financial situation.

And if she really needed to do so, she could go right to John Montgomery over at Montgomery, Lawrence and Eleazar and get a job.

"It is okay. Quitting a job is not a sin. God is not going to strike you dead." Although she rather held her breath, waiting.

Coming to a stoplight, she glanced over to the flashy pickup truck beside her, with country music blaring out its open windows. The man in the passenger seat gazed down at her. "Hey, beautiful." He was young.

A little surprised, she looked straight ahead. The light changed, and the truck took off.

Going more slowly, Claire glanced at her image in the side-view mirror. In her dark glasses, she looked young. And her hair was very blond.

It wasn't as if she never received male attention. She did. But she had not received it so openly for a long time. Usually those who showed interest were older, studious types. Even R.K.

She had been born a blonde. Her mother had told her, and it showed in her elementary school pictures. She thought back, remembering that she had been blond until around thirteen, when she had quit riding her bike a gazillion hours in the sun. When she had married Andrew, she'd had long straight hair that she had highlighted blond, like a Beach Barbie doll. Andrew had loved it.

When had she quit highlighting her hair?

Stopped at another red light, she flipped down the visor and popped open the mirror there, peering over her sunglasses at her image. An impatient honk sounded from behind, and she threw up the visor, jammed her sunglasses in place and hit the accelerator.

Somehow, with her new bleached-blond status, she felt like a woman capable of speeding.

Chapter Three

She took the contents of the cypress box, along with her important papers and put them into a manila envelope, then stuck the envelope into a large canvas tote. From a kitchen drawer she added a road atlas and handful of colorful travel brochures that she had been accumulating for all the years she had tried to get Andrew to go on a vacation that didn't involve putting on the dog and hobnobbing with business clients, followed by the years she had kept trying to work up the courage to go on vacation by herself.

She paid all of her bills ahead for two months. She canceled the newspaper and arranged to have her mail held at the post office. She gave her houseplants to her neighbor on the right, and the perishables from her refrigerator to her neighbor on the left.

In an intent, obsessed manner, she went through the house, pulling out things that she couldn't bear to leave behind. She tucked the photo albums of her wedding and early years with Andrew into the suitcase, pulled them out, and an hour later put them back in again. She wrapped her mother's urn of ashes in a T-shirt and found space in a corner of the car trunk. She found the sleeping bags she had purchased with great hopes and never used and threw one on the back floorboard.

Andrew always had said that she took more stuff when traveling than any one woman he had ever seen. Just for a week in Jamaica once, she had taken two large cases, a weekender, an overnighter and two tote bags. She never wanted to need something and not have it.

In the end, she had suitcases and bags and crates crammed into every nook and cranny of the trunk and rear seat of the car. She looked, she thought, like a vagabond.

She left before eight in the morning, when the sun was bright but the air still held a freshness. She checked her telephone just before leaving. Somehow she had thought Andrew might call. That Gayla Jean would tell him about her leaving, and he would call, just to wish her well.

But he didn't. And she would not call him.

She was on her way, she told herself, backing out of the garage into the golden rising sun. Her neighbor on her right, Joie Lagere, was setting out her trash. Claire waved at her.

Joie called, "Have a good trip!"

"I will. Thanks."

She could hardly believe that she was going. That she was driving right on through the gates of the exclusive community and heading down the road.

She wondered how Lily Donnell was making out.

Then—*good Lord, there was Andrew's silver Jaguar convertible coming toward her!* He veered over to her side of the road, causing her to brake hard.

Holding the steering wheel, attempting to catch her breath, she watched him get out and stride toward her.

His hair was a mess—he had always had such a head of hair—his shirttail was out and his pants wrinkled, as if he had jumped up and come in a rush, and before she could scold him about recklessly endangering their vehicles, he said, "I'm glad I didn't miss you."

Ohmygod.

He gazed down at her, and she gazed up at him there beside her car.

"Your hair looks great," he said.

"Oh." She touched her hair. "You really think so?" She bit her lip and wondered what was taking place in her life.

"Yes." His expression said that he did. "Gayla Jean told me about you quittin' at Tri-State and goin' away on vacation. Goin' home, she said? Up to Oklahoma?" He raised his eyebrows.

"Yes, I am."

They looked at each other for half a minute.

Claire wished she could think of something really witty to say. And then he asked her if she had gotten the oil changed in the car and had the whole thing checked over for the trip.

She was relieved and proud to be able to tell him that she had gotten that chore done only the previous week.

"Well...good." He looked a little disappointed, and she almost felt badly about being so capable with the car. Then he brightened and lifted two brown paper bags that he had obviously just remembered. "I brought doughnuts and coffee."

He was like a Prince Charming, bringing her favorites— jelly-filled. He gave her the entire bag, too, then handed her one of the foam cups of coffee. She passed him back a doughnut.

He stood drinking his coffee and eating the doughnut in the middle of the street.

"Looks like you are plannin' to be gone a while," he said, gesturing at her back seat.

"Maybe a month." She spoke with her mouth filled with doughnut.

"You always like to have everything you might need," he said.

"Yes." She tried to figure out how she could ask about Nina.

He said, "I can check on the townhouse while you're gone."

"I think it will be fine. It's safely locked, and the Green-leafs and Joie Lagere and her husband—they moved into Conrad Horner's place last month, didn't I tell you? Well, they both will keep an eye out. Pretty hard for anyone to bother it, really."

"Where did Conrad go?" he asked.

"Died. Right after New Year's."

He didn't recall her telling him. She said that she had. This was the oddest encounter in the entire world, she thought, finishing her doughnut.

Quite suddenly, he tossed out the rest of his coffee and leaned down, propping his hand on her open window.

"Nina and I broke it off. We're not gettin' married. I just thought I should tell you, before anyone else did. You don't need to worry about hurryin' back for the wedding." He gave a wry smile.

She came out with, "I wasn't comin' to the wedding. In fact, I was leavin' so I wouldn't be in town for the wedding."

She was surprised at her own directness, and Andrew appeared surprised by the statement, too.

He said, finally, "Then I've saved you the trouble. You don't have to go. You can stay."

She gazed at him for several long seconds, and then turned her head and looked out the windshield. "I'm all packed and already started."

"You could turn around."

She kept looking out the windshield, feeling as if she could hardly breathe.

"Look, Claire...could you spare me a little time? Maybe we could go somewhere for breakfast. We could talk."

"No, I can't. I want to get on up to Oklahoma this afternoon. Look around before dark." She could not believe she had said that. She stared at him with wide eyes, wondering how he would take it.

"Okay." He sounded and looked disappointed. "When you come back, I'd like us to talk."

"Yes...me, too," she said quickly.

They gazed at each other a minute more, questioning.

He stepped back. "You call me if you need anything. Just keep in touch, okay?"

"I will."

Then he stepped forward and bent quickly to kiss her. She didn't move but accepted his kiss, then kissed him back, before breaking breathlessly away.

With a fumbling hand, she put the car in gear and drove in an arch around his Jaguar. *Good Lord, she had lost her mind.* She was leaving him. How could she do that?

Andrew, watching the Mercedes drive away in the early-morning light, didn't quite know what to do. He felt a sort of panic, thinking of her leaving. He had meant to stop her, and he couldn't quite comprehend that he had not been able to do it.

And then he saw the Mercedes backing up.

In fact, it was gaining speed. And heading right for his Jag.

With alarm, thinking that maybe Claire was really mad at him and was going to smash his car, he ran toward the Mercedes.

She stopped with a squeal of tires just short of his car. "Do I get my weddin' present back?" she asked.

His reaction was one of confusion, as he looked at where her car bumper just missed his. "Well, I don't know."

"I really liked them. Silver goblets, from Tiffany's…in New York. I sent them last week. Did you see them?"

"Well, I guess not. And I guess Nina's in charge of the presents. Do people usually get their gifts back when a wedding is called off?"

"I don't know. I've never known anyone who called off a wedding."

They gazed at each other again, each sort of waiting, holding their breath, a maybe sort of attitude.

"Which one of you called off the wedding?" she asked, and he knew this was the real reason she had returned.

He would never look good in this thing. "Well, it was a mutual thing. I guess you could say that I brought up the subject, and Nina made the final decision when she threw the glass of ice water in my crotch and told me that she would have her uncle fire me."

She nodded thoughtfully. "What was *your* reason, then?"

He took a deep breath. "She didn't know who C.C.R. was."

"You could have bought her an album."

"I knew it wasn't going to work. I knew I'd been an idiot." The truth and humbleness…that was always the way to go with Claire.

She half smiled, a smile that made hope pop into his chest. She then chewed on her bottom lip as she gazed up at him.

"Call me," he said. "We can talk when you come home?"

"Yes," she said, with a nod.

He thought for a moment that she was going to stay. He saw her hesitancy, and he had a little panic, because he suddenly wasn't certain of what he would say to her and how everything would go.

But then she put the car in gear and drove off.

He watched the rear of the Mercedes, seeing how slowly she drove and thinking that she might stop again and return.

When she didn't, his hope slipped only a fraction. He knew how she had looked at him, how she had kissed him. He wasn't too late. She would take him back.

Suddenly mindful of his car and the way it was sitting there in the road, he strode to it and succeeded in jumping over the door and into the seat. With satisfaction, he punched the stereo button, and the rocking blues sound of Creedence Clearwater Revival came blaring out at him.

He wished he had told Claire how beautiful he had thought she looked. He wished he had said a lot of things to her.

Chapter Four

A mile down the road from leaving Andrew, she whipped into the lot of a convenience store to turn around and go back. She was just going all to pieces with aggravation and happiness. She wasn't certain if she wanted to go back and throw herself into his arms, or to smack him for putting her through all that she had gone through since he had been engaged to Nina.

As if a hand came down on her head, though, she stopped before entering the road. With her foot on the brake, she looked left in the direction of Andrew, then right in the direction of the interstate highway.

Gripped suddenly by what felt like immense gumption, she took a deep breath, turned right and hit the accelerator. *On her way…*

She was definitely in quite a state. She was actually so discombobulated that she took a wrong turn getting onto the highway and almost ended up in Bossier City. She got hold of herself and made the circle to get going back west, and soon Shreveport and the rising sun were receding in the rearview mirror, while George Strait played on the radio and the road rolled ahead into Texas, which was a very big state and could no doubt occupy her for hours.

Once she was well along and had completely conquered the urge to turn around and run back to Andrew, she stopped at a busy truck stop, with eighteen-wheeler semis, travel buses and campers seeming to loom around her. She fueled the car and used the rest room, where a large board for writing messages hung on the wall. This ploy had not altogether saved the walls, but since they were mostly tile, the board was easier to write on. Claire was digging in her purse for a pen, when a tough-looking woman in leather pants came out of a stall and said, "Here," and handed her a red marker.

"Thank you."

She wrote, "On my way, looking for real life—all those who care please wish her well, this hopeful Claire."

The tough-looking woman squinted to see what she had written, then said in a highly skeptical tone, "We-ll, I wish you well, honey."

Welcome to Valentine

From: Vella Blaine
To: <haltg@mailectric.com>
Sent: May 28, 1997, 11:30 a.m.
Subject: Our Town

Dear Harold,

It was a delight to get such a long letter from you. I obviously got things mixed up with thinking that you were from Newark. I must have interchanged Newark and New Jersey. I looked on the map—it's this year's Rand McNally, we're selling them at the store—and found Cherry Hill outside Philadelphia, like you said. I'm not certain how I would feel surrounded by so much town.

I have lived in Valentine all of my life. You can find it on the map just a little below Lawton, which is the home of an army base of historic distinction. Valentine is officially five miles long, from one Welcome to Valentine sign to the other, and approximately three miles wide. We're actually spreading far beyond that now. We have a new Dairy Queen built out on the highway.

Main Street, where our drugstore is located, is the hub of town, and the neighborhoods spread out from it. We have a population of near twenty-five hundred now. We are growing as a bedroom community for retirees from the army up in Lawton. This is good for our drugstore. It's the only one in town, and retirees need us.

I saw on the Weather Channel just the other day mention of that big hurricane—I forget the name—that once went all the way to New Jersey. We get bad storms here, let me tell you. We're in what they call Tornado Alley. I swear it's the worst I have ever seen it this season. From the beginning of April until now, our city work crews have been kept busy from morning till night, clearing streets from downed tree branches and sewer drains from stuff. You could not imagine the stuff they find. Last month one of the city workers thought he found a dead body, but it was just one of those inflatable girls from the sex shop up in Lawton. Well, we think it was from up there. We don't have such a shop around here, although obviously there might be a market.

We're a farming community, and this weather has taken a chunk out of the spring calving, and the wheat harvest is looking threatened. Both the FFA fair and auction and the annual Fix-up and Paint-up campaign by the Baptist youth were postponed so many times, they finally canceled them. There's a few senior citizens who are really hurt by that. The Girl Scout cookie campaign has made about half its usual amount, and the sales of gardening supplies at MacCoy's Feed and Grain are down fifty percent.

The bold truth of it, as much as I'm a bit ashamed, is that our business here at the drugstore has increased. Stress contributes to all manner of ailments, you know. We're selling aspirins and St. John's Wort at an amazing rate, and then there's our soda fountain. Really, all the places in town that sell food and drink do pretty good in hard times, because people are comforting themselves with barbecue and ice-cream sundaes. I put in a latte machine way over a year ago, and that has sure been a moneymaker. People come in here to chat and get their worries out, and then we all find out what's going on with everyone else.

We were in the drugstore when a tornado came over us at

treetop level a couple of weeks ago. It never did touch down, thank goodness, but it ripped the tornado siren off the fire station and snatched the steeple off of St. Luke's Episcopal church. Neither the siren nor the speaker that broadcast St. Luke's virtual bell were ever found.

High winds and possibly a tornado picked up a train car of sugar and threw it over into a pasture at the Ford ranch. The cattle went right to it and ate themselves sick. Half a dozen of them liked to have died.

One of the storms brought five inches of rain in less than twenty-four hours. I think that's like your hurricanes, isn't it? Water flooded creeks and ditches to dangerous levels and almost drowned a dog and her pups who had dug under the back porch of my neighbor's house. I looked out my kitchen window and saw their boy—Willie Lee—coming around the side of the house with what looked like a box, and I thought what in the world, so I called down, and it turned out that he had sneaked out to save the dogs. His mother Marilee went out after him, and it was a miracle that the both of them were not electrocuted, because my daughter was almost a victim right down at the beauty parlor.

Belinda—that's my daughter—was getting a perm and sitting under the dryer when lightning struck the building with enough of a jolt to blow the switch plate off the wall and across the room, passing right by her head. It shocked everyone, and they screamed, and this scared Belinda, who didn't see the switch plate and didn't really know what was going on, but she smelled that electric burning smell, you know, and the way everyone was staring at her, she thought that the hair dryer might be on fire, so she jumped up to get out from it, but a roller got caught on the hood and pulled the whole thing out of the wall and she about got herself electrocuted.

Well, there's a peek into my little world. I would love to hear more about yours. What do you do?

Maybe I should tell you that I'm 66 years old. I'll send you a picture, if you will send one to me.

Write when you can.

Your friend in caretaking,

Vella, in Valentine.

She wondered if he would write again after reading her age. She didn't think shaving off two years was a sin, but why did she bother? Once a person neared the big 7-0, well, one was old and nothing could hide it.

That unsettling thought was quickly dismissed as not a consideration at all, and she hit the send button.

Chapter Five

It was midafternoon when Claire turned down the exit ramp of the toll road and came to a stop at the intersection with a state highway. The green sign read Valentine 10 Miles, with an arrow pointing to the right.

She turned right. Martina McBride's singing from the radio gave her courage, and she pressed the accelerator, enjoying the way the car sped over the ribbon of blacktop that snaked through rolling hills scattered with cattle, mesquite and clumps of trees. Now and again sunlight broke through the thick, patchy clouds and glimmered on the car, as if someone up in the heavens was keeping track of its progress.

Claire had now been on the road for going on eight hours, nearly two hours of that crossing Dallas and Fort Worth in rain so hard and thick that she was certain she was about to be run over by a semi. She had been scared to pull off and scared to keep going, and had only kept on by default of not being able to make up her mind.

Thinking of this in that particular moment, she had the

clear and sharp insight that she lived much of her life in like manner. Right then she felt she should pull over and look at the map, but she could not seem to decide on an appropriate stopping spot, so she kept going, while moisture gathered between her breasts and her cotton shirt stuck to her back. Even with the air conditioner going at half-blast, the air was stuffy. Lowering the window, she breathed deeply of the humid spring breeze.

As she had been doing since leaving Andrew standing in the road, she found memories flooding her. Things she had not thought of in years. She recalled how her preference for driving with the air conditioner blowing and window open had driven him nuts. He would get all sharp about it and accuse her of wasting fuel.

For the first half of their marriage, when she had thought everything that Andrew said was gospel, Claire had been afraid to roll the windows down until she first carefully shut off the air-conditioning, thinking that this was the way it had to be done and almost afraid of making an error that would cause the car to break down or explode or something, and that her recklessness with both money and a natural resource would elicit a bolt of lightning from God.

Finally, though, the ludicrousness of her worry about it dawned on her. There was Andrew making sure every pair of his jeans and every one of his shirts got starched at the laundry, all the way through college and not worried one iota about wasting money or energy. She worked up to sneaking driving with the windows down and the air-conditioning going, figuring what he didn't know saved her from hearing about it.

Since she and Andrew had divorced and she got custody of the car, she drove around with the air-conditioning on and windows down all the time. Several times during her marriage she had even driven Andrew around with it like that. Once he had pointed out to her that the air conditioner was on, and she simply said that she liked it that way. He had not said another word, and in fact, she rather thought he had enjoyed the ride, which brought to her mind the question of why in the world she hadn't spoken up for herself from the very beginning.

Now, leaning forward slightly, she peered hard through her dark sunglasses. Had she taken a wrong turn and missed the town?

She was flapping her hand around to grab the map in the passenger seat when a ringing startled her. It was her cell phone, which she found underneath the map.

"Where are you?"

She was a little disappointed that it was Gayla Jean and not Andrew. "On a highway in Oklahoma."

"Oh." Gayla Jean sounded a little disappointed.

"I've only been gone since this mornin'."

"I know. Lamar said that Andrew talked to you this mornin'."

"Yes, he did. Just as I was leavin'."

"That's what Lamar said. I thought maybe you wouldn't go once Andrew told you about him and Nina breakin' up, but he said you went ahead and went."

"Yes." The entire conversation seemed rather pointless.

"I was surprised that you went ahead and went."

"Well, I was all ready. And I need this vacation."

"I understand that. Once you get all started on a trip, it's almost impossible to stop. But I thought you might want to know that Andrew was really excited to have talked to you. He told Lamar that things are promisin' between you two."

"Well, we're goin' to talk when I come home." Claire felt a little annoyed. She felt pressed, as if her own plans for vacation and time to think were being diverted, and yet she felt guilty about leaving Andrew, especially after kissing him as she had. She didn't want him to feel unwanted. And in fact, in that moment, she really missed him. She suddenly realized that she was tired and wished she was back with him.

This all went through her mind, but the best she could get out was, "I think maybe I'll only be gone a couple of weeks. And he can call me. We'll be talkin' on the phone." Her mood perked up, thinking of talking to him from a distance. That might be the best way to start.

Gayla Jean said, "Well, honey, I wanted to tell you, too, that if you need anything, you call me. Although Lord knows what I could do. Call the police I guess. Make sure you are careful when you get out of your car. Stay in well-lit areas…."

While Gayla Jean went on at some length about safety precautions for a woman traveling alone, Claire peered hard for road signs that would say she was coming to the town. She was thinking of maybe getting something quick to eat, possibly visiting her grandparents' graves, then turning right around and heading back for Shreveport and the man she had left there. Those were the actual words she thought to herself—*the man she had left there*—like a country song.

Just then a horn blared behind her so loudly that she jumped and dropped the cell phone, almost veering off the narrow pavement in the process.

A faded blue car came roaring around her with another loud blast of the horn and headed away down the highway with a plume of black exhaust. She stared through billowing haze at the driver's arm out the window in a rude gesture and then the Chevy emblem cockeyed on the trunk.

Denny Rhodes, the driver of the Chevy—a vintage Impala—cast a glance in his rearview mirror and swore again. He got so mad at the Mercedes-Benz driver for blocking his path, and for being a stupid, rich woman driver, and even for having such a fine car, that he would rather have rammed into it and pushed it off the road. In fact, for a split second he played the scene all out in his mind, backing up and ramming the white luxury vehicle—*pow!*—right off the road and sailing into the pasture. He could do it, too. The Impala was like a tank, and he didn't care what happened to it.

His girlfriend, Sherrilyn Earles, was embarrassed to death and rode hunched over in the passenger seat, hoping the driver of the white car hadn't seen her but mostly concentrating on keeping her legs squeezed together because she was about to pee her pants.

Seeing the Welcome to Valentine sign flash past, she thought, *Oh, thank God,* and struggled for the courage to tell Denny to stop at the first place with a bathroom. The reason she was in such a state was that Denny didn't like making what he considered random stops.

In the pasture across the road from the Welcome to Valentine sign, where he and his son were rebuilding cattle loading pens, Larkin Ford had witnessed the old junker careen around the gleaming white car, then come speeding past, leaving fumes and the smoke of burning oil in its wake.

A few feet away, his son Travis flipped up the shield on his welder's helmet and said, "That engine ain't long for this world."

Larkin responded with a grunt of agreement as he watched the gleaming white car, a Mercedes, come down the road, gathering speed, only to slow down as it came abreast of him and Travis, where it stopped as if on sight of them. Larkin, wondering why the driver would be looking at them, then realized she was looking at the dirt road there beside them.

The car turned onto the dirt road and stopped. The tinted window came all the way down, and a woman leaned out and called over the distance, "Is this the road to the Valentine cemetery?"

Travis, who had radar for any female within a mile of him, had already ripped off his welding helmet and was hotfooting it to the fence, "Yes, ma'am…"

Larkin watched his son's strong muscles move beneath the shirt that was wet with sweat. His son pointed in the direction of the cemetery, obviously giving directions, which couldn't much be needed, as all the woman had to do was go on down the road and she'd run into the cemetery, just like the sign pointed.

The car headed on, and Travis returned to say, "She was lookin' for the cemetery."

Larkin didn't say that he had perfect hearing. He watched the white car go down the dirt road.

After a moment, Travis added, "They really need to have the sign read *Valentine* cemetery for folks who come from out of town."

Larkin gave that thought, then said, "How many out-of-town folks do you suppose come to the Valentine cemetery?"

"Might be more if they put up a decent sign," said Travis.

Farther down the road, at the edge of town, Frank Goode was putting a new announcement on the mobile sign that he had rented for his Goodnight Motel. He had thought all morning to come up with a clever idea. He finished rearranging the letters, changing *Motel for Sale, Free Continental Breakfast* to read:

Own where Patsy Cline slept
50s Vintage Motel For Sale

He was running out of letters, but it was always important to keep the word "free" in there, and best to use red letters. He found enough to put off to the side: *Free Breakfast*.
The sound of a car slowing caused him to look around

with a spark of hope that maybe his sign was already working. To his disappointment, he saw it was an old beat-up job, not at all the sort driven by any prospective buyer.

His spirit slumped slightly, but he consoled himself that the people in the car had at least been looking at his sign.

"What do you mean, advertisin' 'Own where Patsy Cline slept'?" his wife, Gertie, asked him with an attitude when he reentered the office. "Just because your folks bought that scam, doesn't mean anyone else will."

"I am not scammin' anyone. I just want to get some attention, and if someone wants to see the register, I'll show it and let them decide for themselves. And besides that, Wanda Jackson and Hoyt Axton did stay here. Their names are there," he said, as if that bolstered his supposition about Patsy Cline.

The old register card had an entry for what looked to be Patsy Cline, although there was a water stain over the name. The Patsy was in doubt, while the last name was most definitely Cline. The original owner of the motel had claimed it was Patsy Cline, and as devoted Patsy Cline fans, his parents had bought the motel back in 1977. They would display the register, which not only had the water-stained name, but also the names of a number of celebrities, from country singers to rodeo cowboys, and one flamboyant politician who was charged with all manner of illegalities.

His wife gave him one of her nail-him-to-the-wall impatient looks, and he added, "Do you want to retire early to Florida or don't you?"

Her reply to this was to tilt her head in halfway agreement and turn her attention to perusing the many Florida brochures they had accumulated.

Chapter Six

Vella Blaine had propped open the front and rear doors of the drugstore, and a fragrant spring breeze floated past where she sat on the edge of the chair at her desk in the back room and checked her e-mail on the computer for the third time that day.

Going on four days, and she still had not received an answer to her last e-mail to Harold.

Disappointed and annoyed, she reached for the pack of long dark cigarillos in the top drawer of her desk. She lit up and blew out a long stream of smoke, just waiting for Belinda to holler from the front and tell her to quit with her stinking cigar.

Vella had been hoping that the few exchanges she had enjoyed with Harold might lead to more, but obviously that wasn't going to happen. It hadn't even led to learning his last name. Obviously he was another washed-up old man. There were so many of those in her life; she didn't need another one.

Just then a young woman—a girl, really, of the low sort

who wore a ratty big T-shirt and blue jeans and flip-flops, came running in, looking around in a frantic state.

Vella pointed the way to the ladies' room around the tall utility cabinet, and the girl tossed a "Thank you," of which Vella approved. So many people these days didn't know how to say thank you. The skinny thing had real pretty red hair, too.

She remembered how her own hair used to be black as night but was the color of steel now. Men used to look at her and desire her. Everyone in town had thought for years that she was having affairs all over, probably a reasonable assumption, given her and her husband's natures, but she never had. She had been true blue to Perry. At least until a few years ago, when she had almost had an affair with the landscaper she hired for their lawn. Still, it had been an *almost* thing, which probably did count in heaven, though.

Sometimes, God help her, she regretted not having that affair.

"Mama! We got two banana splits to go."

With a sigh, Vella tamped out the cigarillo and left her small desk and thin hopes of clandestine e-mail.

Out front, her daughter stood at the cash register, with her attention directed at the shopping program on the television up on the wall. Belinda, like her father had been, was big on television. She did not "do food," as she said. She would serve coffee or tea, and she handled the pharmacy and gift counters, and that was her boundary, a word she'd learned from Oprah. They had counter help, but it was hit and miss, and this afternoon was a miss, so Vella was the counter-girl.

It being midafternoon, the soda fountain had little business. As he always was at this time of day, Winston Valentine was ensconced at a table doing the crossword puzzle from the newspaper, which he also read a bit to Perry, who just sat there staring up at the television, too.

They had a nurse for Perry at home, but Vella liked to

bring him to the drugstore for a few hours several times a week, in order to try to stimulate him. Although, she had tried to stimulate him for all the years of their marriage and had not succeeded very much, so she couldn't understand why she kept at it. Possibly the effort had become a habit too strong to give up.

She was grateful to be diverted from this dismal thought by the customer before her. This one was a stranger and no doubt a match to the low sort of girl who had raced into the rest room. He had a stringy ponytail hanging over his shoulder and long sideburns growing down his face.

"Two banana splits?" she confirmed.

"Yeah," he said.

Yes was a perfectly good word.

The hoodlum fellow pulled out a wallet that was attached to his pants with a chain, and Vella figured he was going to pay for the banana splits; however, he tossed several bills on the counter and said, "Two packs of Marlboros. She'll—" inclining his head to indicate the girl who had run into the bathroom "—pay for the splits when she come out."

Vella laid the packs on the counter, then returned to making the banana splits. She kept glancing at the hoodlum, wondering if he might attempt to rob the store. There had been two robberies of the store, both times in the seventies. She saw his eyes move over Belinda and the counter as he played a minute with the packs of cigarettes.

Oh, he thought he was something cool, entering a dated, small-town drugstore with its door propped open. He sauntered away and then stopped at the open door, where he slowly tore the cellophane off one cigarette package and deliberately let it fall to the floor. He lit up while doing a good pose of some tough hoodlum type, with T-shirt sleeves rolled to show his biceps in the style of the late 1950s that was making a comeback. He probably thought he invented tough-cool, Vella thought, seeing him cast a glance to her, as if expecting her to complain about his tossing down trash.

She turned away to take up the can of whipped cream and saw his reflection in the mirror in front of her. She imagined herself saying, *Buddy, when I was sixteen, I was runnin' with boys who would make hamburger of you.*

And where had the time gone? What had she done with her life?

She wished the young hooligan *had* robbed them. It would have been something, some excitement to carry her through.

When the young woman came out of the rest room, Vella was setting the banana split containers on the counter. "Your friend ordered these for you and said you would pay."

"Oh."

Vella watched the little thing dig into her purse. She was pale as buttermilk. Young people these days existed on hamburgers and fries and thought they were never going to need their bodies after the age of thirty.

Just then, at the same moment that Julia Jenkins-Tinsley, the postmistress, came through the door with her rolling mail cart, a car horn honked loud and hard.

"Good Lord!" Julia whipped around to cast a glare at the street.

The girl fumbled with her money and finally got it handed over on the counter just when the insistent car horn sounded again.

Belinda said, "My gosh, what is that person wantin'?"

"Oh…it's for me," said the girl in an apologetic manner, sticking out her hand for her change while at the same time frantically attempting the impossible of gathering up the dessert containers with the other hand. Vella told her to wait a minute, she'd put them in a bag, but the girl, stuffing the change into her purse, said, "Oh, no, I can get them.

"Thanks," she flung over her shoulder as she scurried out like a mouse with its tail on fire.

"They aren't from around here, are they? I don't recall seein' them." Julia Jenkins-Tinsley was craning her neck to inspect the couple and their car.

"Well, if you don't know 'em, we can rest assured they are not from here," Winston put in, coming up from his crossword puzzle.

Julia, intent at the window, didn't hear his sarcasm. "Oh, it's a Texas tag. Likely just passin' through." She returned to sit herself at the counter, parking the delivery basket close at her knee, where she could put a hand on it, if she felt the need. Julia took her responsibility of handling the mail with extreme seriousness.

"I'd just as soon that sort keep on goin' through town," she added. "They remind me of some poor characters out of a trashy movie about killers run amuck across the rural South."

"Why do you suppose they never make movies about killers run amuck across the rural Northwest?" Winston said, his expression turned pondering. "Or the rural Northeast? Or have you ever seen a movie about pervert killers run amuck across the rural Midwest? No, it's always the South, with big-bellied mean sheriffs."

To this, Julia said, "You know, Neville's gone on a diet. He's lost ten pounds."

"Has he looked behind him?" Vella asked, placing sundae glasses on the shelf and seeing Winston, in the mirror, toss his newspaper in the air. They had not fully appreciated his clever comment. Her heart pricked, and she thought to speak to him, but somehow she didn't seem to have the energy to deal with Winston's sensitivities.

Belinda was just then saying to Julia, "Well, that guy was behind the times. Only older men lost from the sixties keep their hair long like that. No modern men wear long hair any-more. Well, except for Indians. They are the only ones it suits, anyway. White men just look grubby, especially old men…like Joe Miller. I always want to ask him why doesn't he cut his hair? He could be a nice lookin' man, and just be-cause he lost his legs doesn't mean he shouldn't make all he can of his appearance. No wonder he's got to take antide-pressants. And he doesn't set his granddaughter a good ex-ample, either."

Joe Miller was fifty-five, Vella thought. *Old* was definitely relative.

Julia said emphatically, "Joe Miller is a Vi-et-nam vet, and with what he's given this country, he can wear his hair any way he wants." She never put up with criticism of anyone who served the country, whether in a military or civil ser-vice position.

"I didn't say he couldn't. I just said he'd look and feel bet-ter with his hair cut off. When people look neat and tidy, they feel better, and then they act better, and then others around them act better and start feeling better, and pretty soon everything is nicer all the way around," said Belinda, with the staunch attitude of a reformed slattern who had found style and taken it on as a religion and the answer to everything wrong in the world.

"Well, I don't think cuttin' his hair is gonna make Joe Mil-ler feel like he has legs," Julia said.

Belinda didn't argue that point and instead asked Julia why she was delivering the mail. "Did Norris go on vaca-tion? He didn't say anything yesterday."

Vella could tell that Belinda felt slighted not to know the goings-on of their regular mail carrier. Her daughter and Julia were neck-in-neck with knowing the activities of everyone in town.

"No. He broke his toe last evenin'. Dropped a refrigerator on it when he was helpin' his son move." Then, as if suddenly realizing she was sitting at the soda fountain, she said, "I'd like a cup of latte, Vella, with whipped cream. I'll be walkin' that off doin' Norris's route for the rest of this week, at least, until I can get people shifted around."

Vella, who experienced a slice of satisfaction every time she used the latte machine, which had proven to pay for itself despite a number of people's initial skepticism of the idea, filled a fat stoneware cup with the brew, added a dollop of whipped cream and set the concoction in front of the postmistress. Taking up the packet of mail on the counter, she went over to check on Perry and sit at the table with Winston, who had returned to his crossword puzzle.

"Know a four letter word for work?" he asked.

Wanting to smack him for inattention, she just sat there.

When she didn't answer, he looked at her and got a very uncertain expression, which was gratifying. She had wanted him to see her state. After all the years of their friendship, he should at least recognize her state without her having to say it aloud.

"You look like you need a quiet nap," he said.

"I need a lot of things." She spoke in the way of desperate-eyed women from movies who were about to take poison.

Winston blinked and looked more uncertain. His expression helped her a little.

He said, "Well, don't go lookin' at me. I'm too old for almost all of it."

"I know that."

The truth of it caused her spirit to sink like a rock. There was no one in town her age who could keep up with her. Winston had tried once, and she thought of it, of their one hot kiss several years ago, and how that had been ridiculously stretching it then on both their parts—her for believing him capable, and him for even trying—and now he was ninety years old. *Good Lord 'amercy.*

Winston sat there watching Vella's face grow haggard. He tried to come up with something of a boosting nature to say. In fact, in those seconds of watching her face, he became a little frantic to boost her, because if Vella sank, what chance did the rest of them have to stay afloat? Vella was unsinkable. She was the last unsinkable woman in his life.

Before he could come up with anything worthwhile, though, she called Belinda to help her get Perry out to the car to go home. Grabbing the handles of Perry's wheelchair with strong hands, she headed away without so much as a so-long.

Knowing he had somehow failed her, Winston sat there and watched the two women disappear into the back room of the drugstore. He felt totally helpless and useless. Perry couldn't even say goodbye to him, because Perry no longer talked.

People didn't think Perry knew anything, but Winston, well acquainted with the man since boyhood, was confident that he did. He saw the spark and flash in Perry's eyes from time to time, and when Perry wanted something, he was adept at letting it be known.

Winston suspected that Perry had chosen to give up on talking, something the man had never liked to do anyway. Winston was fairly certain that Perry was pretty happy, finally. The man didn't have to carry on a conversation with anyone nor do anything but watch television and be taken care of, which, as far as Winston could tell, had been Perry's only ambitions for years. And finally Perry had women fawning all over him. The man had it the best of his entire life.

Winston turned his inner eyes on himself and saw an old man alone. His wife had died years ago, and the past winter his girlfriend, Franny, had died in her bed in the night, leaving him flat. Thinking of this caused his throat to swell up.

His wife and girlfriend had both been unsinkable women, women he had counted on to be there, and yet they had gone on before him and left him alone. He couldn't stand for another woman to leave him, and now Vella was dying inch by inch in her heart.

He was sitting there with this dismal fear all over him when a woman came through the door. He spared her a glance, blinking through his bleary vision and being irritated at the intrusion into his misery.

Nevertheless, he was a man with principle, especially with women; he roused himself enough to offer, "They stepped out momentarily, if you're wantin' somethin' from the fountain."

"Oh."

He saw her completely then, from the feet upward, as his gaze traveled up a lush female body wearing tight denim jeans and a crisp white blouse. She was an attractive blond woman who was removing her sunglasses and turning her luminous eyes on him.

Instantly, age forgotten, he began coming up from the chair. "Can I help you? If you need a prescription, you can call the druggist from the back over there…but if you'd like somethin' from the fountain, I can get it for you."

"Oh," she said again, looking uncertain.

He forced straightness into his spine and moved to the counter, forgetting all about his cane and asking her if she wanted a cold drink.

She said, "Yes, thank you. I'd like a Coke."

"One Coca-Cola comin' right up."

He grabbed a glass, but she said, "Oh, I think maybe I'd like a milkshake, if that will be okay. I see there's a strawberry milkshake on the menu."

"Ah…yep, there it is. Let's see…" Hopefully, he offered, "I could make you a nice Coke float with vanilla. Would that do?" He really didn't know how to make a milkshake. As many years as he had been coming in the drugstore and help-ing himself and others, he had never made a milkshake.

She said she would love a Coke float.

"Good choice!" Happily, he grabbed a tall Coke glass.

He was making comments about the weather to the woman when Belinda came in and looked surprised to see him there. He didn't bother with explanation, just finished with the float and wiped the glass carefully before handing it across to the woman, who had sat herself on a stool and flashed him a million-dollar smile.

Oops, forgot a straw. She gave him that gorgeous smile again and played the straw around in the drink. Ice cream was good on a warm, humid day, he said, and she agreed to that. He asked her where she was from, and she said Shreve-port. He said he had guessed that she was from somewhere down there by her lovely accent.

Extending his hand over the counter, he introduced him-self and took her hand in a firm shake. "I'm Winston Valen-tine, very pleased to make your acquaintance."

"Claire Wilder," she said, her eyes on him with high curiosity.

"Welcome to our town, Miss Claire," he said, holding her gaze as he did her hand.

Chapter Seven

The old man asked what had brought her to town, and she told him that she had been looking for her grandparents' graves, but that she had not found them in the Valentine cemetery. Was there another cemetery in town?

"Yes, ma'am. There's Little Creek cemetery out east of town. And who are your grandparents, if I might ask?"

She told him, and he said, "Oh, yeah…I knew Grover Tillman. I imagine he's out there at the Little Creek. He lived out that way."

Gazing at his aged face, she felt odd feelings. He had known her grandfather, her father's father. This old man was the first person she had ever heard speak of knowing her grandfather, a man of her own blood.

He said, "I'll show you the cemetery. Belinda, put Miss Wilder's cold drink on my ticket," and came out from around the counter to get his cane before Claire had really assimilated his stated intention.

Glancing back, she saw the woman, Belinda, staring at

them with avid eyes. Out of the store, she saw the woman through the window glass; she had picked up a telephone.

As they left town, Mr. Valentine launched in with memories and said that he had traded a few horses with her grandfather.

"Oh, Grover, he grew some good runnin' horses, and he made fine whiskey. Bootleg. Oklahoma was dry till '58. Lots of farmers and ranchers made fortunes running bootleg up from Texas, down from Kansas."

Her grandfather had been a bootlegger? That would likely explain much of her aunt Agnes's attitude.

He went on about this colorful history as they drove to the Little Creek cemetery, and when they went through the grounds, searching the headstones for Claire's grandparents, he made comments about many of the people buried there, things such as, "Oh, he made a bundle on runnin' hooch," and, "She was so ugly she needed to stay home," and, in a sad, pained voice, "Liked to killed that little one's mother when she died."

While an entire family of Tillmans took up a section of the small cemetery, they appeared to have no connection with Claire's grandparents, Grover and Martha, whose separate graves she found, along with their children's, clear on the other side, located between a couple of Smiths and a large family of Lowenthalls. There was a headstone for a child, marked Baby Girl, with a date that indicated the child had lived a week, and a headstone for Rodney Tillman, who had died at fourteen.

"They also had my father," she said, looking around as if she might have missed his grave.

"I seem to recall Grover havin' a boy. What was your father's name?"

"John."

The markers sat unadorned and forgotten looking. Of

simple and cheap concrete, the letters wearing away. She crouched to run her eyes over the names and dates recorded for Grover Tillman and Martha Overton Tillman.

A wave of disappointment and confusion washed over her. Was this all there was? Hard lifeless concrete stones carved only with names and dates, with nothing more than a space in between where their lives had been.

Whatever had she hoped to find? Evidence of the man who had become her father? A man who had walked out of her life.

Where are you, Daddy? She had wondered that for just about all her life.

Slowly straightening, she turned and found Mr. Valentine sitting on one of the Lowenthalls's sparkling granite head-stones. He told her that Marty Lowenthall had died owing him $200, so he felt justified in taking it out in rent of a seat.

"You know, Grover was only a year behind me." He gestured to the headstone. "I don't recall him in school much, but I'll take a look around my house for a yearbook. I used to have a couple. Will you be stayin' in town long?"

"Oh, no. Tonight, I guess. I saw a sign for a motel." She had not planned much beyond this point, and suddenly, looking again at her grandparents' graves, she thought of the senselessness of her trip. There was nothing here beyond names that she already knew. An overwhelming urge struck her to get out of the cemetery, so strongly that she started for the car and had to slow herself down to wait for the elderly man.

On the drive back to town, he invited her to his home for dinner, and when she declined, he suggested taking her to dinner at a local café. "People come from fifty miles just to eat at the Main Street Café."

She asked him if he was making that up, but what she was

thinking of was a smooth way to decline. It had just then begun to dawn on her that he seemed admiring of her. She didn't want to hurt his feelings.

The elderly man swore that he was not making anything up, that the café made things like raisin pie and peanut butter and jelly sandwiches and prizewinning meat loaf.

"You need to eat supper, darlin', no matter what else you do…and I might remember more about your grandparents and daddy." He gave her a decidedly flirtatious grin. "And you wouldn't want to disappoint a feeble old man after I have been so generous to help you find your family's graves, would you?"

"You are anything but feeble, Mr. Winston."

"Winston will do. I'm glad you don't think I'm feeble, but I *am* ninety years old."

She looked at him, and he looked back at her, before she returned her attention to the road that was flying beneath the wheels of the car.

He said, "Darlin', I'm in my very twilight, and I think I've fallen in love for the last time in my life."

Startled, she glanced over to see that his eyes were perfectly steady.

"A man of my age can't waste time, you know."

There was nothing else to say to that, other than, "Direct me," and she headed the car down the dirt road through the long shadows and with the windows all the way down and the air conditioner blowing on high speed.

They sat at a rear booth in the café, which was of a sort long forgotten in the modern world of chain restaurants. It served home-style meat loaf and real mashed potatoes and had no place for a salad bar.

The waitress who came to their table was bold in her curiosity. She plunked down two glasses of ice water, said hello to Winston, then said directly to Claire, "Hi, I'm Fayrene. I own this place, and I've known this old coot forever." She regarded Claire with a look of expectation.

Claire got out, "Nice to know you."

And then Winston came in with, "Fayrene, you aren't old enough to know me forever. Now, we'd like two meat loaf specials and sweet ice tea. Claire here loves meat loaf, and I've told her yours is the best in the state."

While they ate and chatted, Fayrene kept a watch on them from behind the café counter, as if to make certain Claire wasn't about to rob the elderly man. This level of attention was quite handy, because when Winston needed catsup and Claire wanted lemon for her cold tea, all that was required was a glance toward the counter and the woman hotfooted it to their table.

In the way an older person could draw on memories from bygone years, Winston told of the town and some of his own history. He was quite obviously delighted to have found an audience for his tales. Likely most of his family and acquaintances knew it all and showed little interest. Claire was content to give him the interest, and she found an odd comfort in simply listening to him, and in the total adoration he plainly gave her.

Possibly it was this total adoration, or because he was a stranger and not someone she would ever see again, or maybe because she got very tired and melancholy while eating a dessert of hot strawberry pie a la mode, strawberries being a particular favorite and something she had on a couple of occasions shared in bed with Andrew, all of this encouraged along by a sad song plugged into the jukebox, but whatever it was, when Winston asked gently about her own life, she told him her history.

It just came spilling out of her mouth, more or less on the order of: "I was born right here in Valentine, at Grover and

Martha's house, but Mama hated it there, so she took me back to her home in Lou'siana when I was barely six weeks old. We lived with her daddy and aunt. My daddy came down to see us there. I remember him off and on, but he left before I started school, and we never heard from him again. I married my high school sweetheart, and we divorced a couple of years ago. I lost two babies before they were born, and the doctors say I won't ever have any. Mama died a year and a half ago, from pneumonia, but mostly I just think she never had liked livin' very much, you know?"

The entire time all of this was coming out, she imagined the image of her mother saying, *"How dare you spread the family linen out for this stranger!"*

Winston's reply to the last about her mother was a heavy, "Yes, I know."

She knew that he did know, in fact, as if she had known Winston all of her life. Maybe she wanted to have known him. Maybe she wanted him to be her father. She sure wanted to find something in this town and not have the trip come up so empty.

Claire forked up the last crumb of pie, thinking that sugar always caused her mood to shift downward and that maybe she shouldn't have had the dessert on top of the sweet cold tea. On the other hand, now that she had done so, she might as well go ahead and comfort herself with more. Sometimes, if she took in enough sugar, her mood would turn back up.

As she had already looked in the direction of the pie cabinet on the counter, Fayrene was on her way over with the pie before Claire had firmly made up her mind about another piece. Winston had more cold tea.

When Fayrene was out of earshot again, Winston said, "I seem to vaguely recall your father. I think he rode racehorses for Grover for a spell."

"When Mama died, I found a couple of pictures of him

in her jewelry box." She pulled the photographs from the envelope in her purse and passed them to Winston, who squinted through his glasses.

"Oh, yeah, that looks like Grover. He was a short man. Your daddy didn't appear to take after him in that. He wouldn't have been able to jockey those horses too long. And this is your mama? She was quite a looker. Like her daughter."

She looked at the photographs again, before tucking them safely back into her purse. "Thank you for your time, Winston. I've enjoyed hearing about my grandparents."

"Tomorrow, if you like, I could show you where they once lived. No house there anymore. Part of the land has a new housing subdivision goin' up on it. You might could check the land history, tax rolls and such, over to the county courthouse. You might could check the obituaries for when Grover and Martha died, see if your daddy is mentioned in them. And maybe there'd be some trace of your family history over at the Chickasaw tribe."

"The Chickasaw tribe?"

"Your grandmother's maiden name was Overton. That was my wife's name. Coweta was Chickasaw, on the rolls. In fact, it was her bit of land and house I live in, not from my family. She owned a half section out east of town, too. All of this land round here way back belonged to Chickasaws, and the traditional way was to pass it through the female line. Coweta left the house to our eldest daughter, not to our son."

Claire thought of it and saw her mother's Aunt Agnes hollering about her father. "Maybe I will. I don't know."

She drove him home, up to a big old Victorian house with a sweeping lawn and towering trees with shading branches.

"Thank you again, Winston, for your help and the lovely conversation. You should be on a welcoming committee for your town."

"It was my honor and delight."

The man had a way of speaking that cut to the heart. She touched his hand, then leaned over and kissed him, not on the cheek but on the lips.

When she pulled back, she saw his eyes fly wide in surprise. He stared straight ahead for some seconds, then said to her in a gallant fashion, "It has been a pleasure. I truly have fallen in love for the last time in my life."

He got out of the car and went up to the house, where Claire saw a teenage girl and a younger boy waiting for him on the porch.

In the distance, the motel's neon sign glowed yellow against the dusky sky. The Goodnight Motel. It was an old sign, but a nice name for a motel.

Then her attention was jerked to the side of the road, as she passed the old blue car that had earlier rudely passed her. It was sitting there, with its nose angled toward the ditch.

She pressed her brake, only to immediately let up and check her rearview mirror, for fear of having made another error in stopping short. Thankfully the road was clear behind.

Shifting her gaze again to the dilapidated car, she saw it appeared empty. She breathed a sigh of relief at escaping the decision of whether or not to offer assistance.

Coming to the motel, she slowed, her spirit sinking when she saw how old it was. Then she saw one of those cheap portable marquees near the road.

The place was for sale. *Vintage* was a much better word to use than *old* and *run-down*.

Patsy Cline had slept here?

"Oh well. I might as well, too," she muttered as she pulled into the driveway to the office and came to a stop beside three plastic pink flamingos stuck in the boxwoods.

Through the wide picture window she saw pink walls, and

a young couple at the desk speaking to a white-haired man in a Hawaiian shirt. She knew instantly that the young man was the driver of the battered blue car.

When she entered, the young man's head came round, and he gave her the once-over. She instantly estimated him as the sort who had considered himself far too smart for school and had quit in order to turn his talents to higher endeavors, such as stealing cars and knocking off convenience stores.

The white-haired man behind the counter said in a jovial fashion, "Welcome. I'll be with you in just a minute, ma'am…jus' soon as I get these young people set."

Claire nodded and stood to the side, perusing the room. While she couldn't help overhearing the conversation concerning exactly what to do about the young couple's broken-down car, she looked at the palm tree print draperies, the pink walls decorated with island maps and starfish and netting, and the two flamingo silhouettes on the wall behind the turquoise desk.

Just then her eyes met those of the young woman, a girl, really, who might have been no older than fifteen. Caught looking at Claire, the girl instantly turned her head, sending her long silky hair shimmering down her back. It was a striking shade of auburn, a color only nature and youth could provide. The skin of her arms and legs was very pale, like pink cold cream.

Claire noted that the girl stood just behind the young man's shoulder and did not take part in the conversation between her boyfriend and the motel proprietor. When the plans had all been settled for the couple to stay the night at the motel and for the white-haired man to give them a ride down to get their things out of the broken-down vehicle, the girl followed her hooligan out of the office, as if on a tow line.

Claire had to resist the strong urge to grab the girl and say, "Save yourself now."

Then the proprietor behind the desk was welcoming her again. "I'm Frank Goode, owner of this place. We aim to make you as comfortable as possible."

Her room was number one, in the duplex nearest the office, the little laundry and the cold drink machine. The door was bright turquoise, and turquoise shutters framed the windows. They needed paint, as did the eaves along the front.

Telling herself not to be too particular and to have confidence that even though outdated, the office had appeared perfectly clean, she entered the room and stood for a moment, inhaling the scents of Pine-Sol, aging wood and musty fabric. Hazy evening light fell through the sheer curtains and gave everything a soft patina—the wagon-wheel print bedspread, the two-toned veneer tall dresser, and the old air conditioner stuck in the far window.

Good Lord, she had made a wrong turn of about forty years.

Memory brought her gaze shifting to the bedside table, and there sat a little brown coin box for a bed massager.

In a flash of amazement and delight, she dropped her belongings on the bed and investigated the coin box. It took a quarter. Didn't they used to take dimes?

Quickly she dug the required coin from her purse and plugged into the box.

The bed began to emit a soft sound and to gently shake. Jerking off her boots, she stretched out over the wagon-wheel bedspread and gazed up at the shadowy ceiling, at what appeared to be a water stain, while the bed jiggled beneath her.

It was not much of a massage. More of a pleasant shimmy. She saw the faint pattern that the yellow neon motel sign began to cast onto the walls through the parted drapes. Her eyes fell closed, and her mind drifted back in memories. She

could see her mother and father dancing, eyes shut and holding each other close.

Why, it was Patsy Cline singing from the radio.

Chapter Eight

Shreveport, 1963

All through the summer when she was six years old, she would go with her mother to the Tall Pines Motor Court to be with her father. Usually this was weekends, but sometimes for three or four days. Her father never came to their house, where they lived with her grandfather, who Claire thought of as The Old Man, and her mother's Aunt Agnes, The Old Woman. Claire knew it was because her father *could not* come to the house, but she didn't know why. She did know not to ask.

Each time when they would get ready to drive to the motor court, her mother's Aunt Agnes would follow her mother around and make comments like, "When are you going to give this up? There's no future with that heathen," and just generally hound Claire's mother about going, while her mother would say little more than, "Please, Aunt Agnes, I'm going, so let's drop it…please…."

Claire recalled having a little plaid suitcase that she packed herself. She could never recall anyone helping her, as she could never recall anyone helping her do much of anything. The adults in her world were always busy doing more important things than paying her attention.

She would carry the little plaid suitcase past her mother's bedroom, where her mother packed and The Old Woman harangued, down the stairs and past the room where The Old Man sat with a book and cigar.

Each time they went to the motor court, Claire would pack her bag and go out to sit on the front porch step and wait for her mother. When her mother came, it would be flying out the door ahead of Aunt Agnes. She would take Claire by the hand, and Claire would feel her mother shaking the entire block and a half to where they stood and waited for the bus in front of the one store in Olivett that was everything—hardware, dry goods, drugstore and soda fountain.

Claire loved the bus ride, with so many interesting people and seeing the passing scenery, and she especially loved the motor court. She liked sitting on the stoop of the room and watching all the traffic going past on the highway, and she liked the lively music her mother listened to on the little radio in the room—Patsy Cline, Elvis, Roy Orbison—and how sometimes her mother and father would dance and laugh silly, or take her with them in her father's car with the red and white seats down the road to a drive-in, where they would buy Claire a strawberry milkshake.

Best of all, she liked that there were almost always children to play with at the motor court. There was one family with five children under ten. Claire's mother called them the gypsies. The family had arrived in a big gold station wagon with children hanging out the back and trunks piled on the top, and had taken up residence in a single room. Their mother fed the children peanut butter and jelly sandwiches out the door all day long. Claire would line up with them and be handed a sandwich, too.

A number of times Claire, quite unnoticed, would be gathered up right along with the other gypsy children, loaded into the car and driven off to the grocery store or Laundromat. On the occasions when she *was* noticed, she would be required to ask permission to go with the gypsy family, and her mother always said yes, with a wave of her hand, as if relieved to be either alone with Claire's father or with her recurrent misery. But most times the gypsy mother never even realized that Claire was with them, nor did Claire's mother give any indication that she had noticed her absence.

That was what had happened the last time Claire could recall seeing her father. She had loaded herself into the car with the gypsy children, all laughing and singing, and been carried along down the highway for the better part of an hour, until a stop at a gas station, when the mother took them all to the bathroom and discovered that she had one extra girl.

The woman got very upset, as the family was heading for Baton Rouge and visiting for a week. They had to turn around and take Claire back to the motor court, the station wagon swinging into the gravel lot, where Claire was lifted out bodily and left standing while the station wagon, worn-out shocks creaking, bounced out onto the road and sped away.

Quite annoyed at being booted out from the happy family, Claire headed for her parents' room, with hope of a strawberry milkshake. That was when she saw her father come out of the room. He had his battered suitcase in his hand. He went to his car, where the sun sparked off the chrome, tossed the suitcase inside, then shook his head and went back to the door. Claire saw his profile as he said something like, "I'm tired of it, Marie." Claire could not recall his exact words, nor what her mother said in return, but she did remember seeing desperation on both their handsome faces in the bright, hot sunlight.

Then her father got into the car and drove away, while her mother stood in the doorway and seemed hardly to breathe.

Claire never got her strawberry milkshake. The rest of the afternoon and into the night, her mother kept looking out the window. This was not unusual behavior. Very often this had gone on when they would arrive at the motor court and her father had not yet made an appearance. Her mother would play the radio and keep peering out the window and going to stand in the door.

Sometimes she would be called to the phone in the office because there weren't any in the rooms, and her mother would go racing out so fast that her skirt would snap and flutter.

But that night her mother was not called to the phone. The next morning Claire was roused out of bed at daylight, and she and her mother made the return bus trip back to the old people's house, where her mother went to bed for two weeks. They did not return to the motor court, and Claire had to quit asking when they were going to go, because each time she asked, her mother would moan and turn away.

Claire began going by herself to the Olivett store, with its soda fountain, where she dared to charge strawberry milkshakes. She was fairly certain she dared to do this because she was angry at the loss of the happy times at the motor court. The only one to ever mention her charges at the drugstore was Aunt Agnes, who told her, "You better watch your step, girl. I won't put up with heathen ways."

The drugstore milkshakes were never very satisfactory. No milkshake she ever had in her life tasted as good as those she had enjoyed sitting on the red and white back seat of her father's car, while her parents smiled at her and at each other.

Claire did not see her father ever again, and she didn't see the Tall Pines Motor Court again until she was seventeen and drove herself to Shreveport and searched and found the motor court. She drove into the lot and stopped and studied the place, which looked so much smaller and seedier than in her precious memories. She identified several of the rooms in which she thought she and her parents had stayed. She wanted to rent one, so as to get a look inside, but she was too shy to do so, and she told herself doing that was screwy, anyway.

She went down to the drive-in restaurant, which was still there, and ordered a strawberry milkshake. It wasn't the same at all, but the sort with vanilla ice cream from a machine to which they added canned strawberry syrup.

When she and Andrew had eloped, Claire had wanted to stay at the Tall Pines. Andrew had thought she was nuts, but he had indulged her. To his credit, Andrew had from the first indulged her in a lot of stuff. Of course, he generally made certain that she knew he was indulging her.

She finally got to see inside a room where she might have stayed with her parents, but this view proved mightily disappointing. It had all looked so much smaller and quite dreary. The room had only one window, because the air conditioner took up the back one, and she found a big roach in the bathroom. She had quite shortly wanted to suggest they leave and go to the nice Holiday Inn, but she had been too embarrassed to tell this to Andrew, who was totally intent on what they were supposed to be doing in the bed that sported a coin-operated vibrator.

She had many times since wondered what she had been thinking with wanting to have her wedding night in the place where her parents had broken up. She had probably doomed her marriage from the start. Probably she had picked up some sort of hex by staying at the motor court. Years later, back around 1985, she had happened to be driving past the area of Tall Pines, and she had looked for it, only it was gone, replaced by a gigantic mobile home dealership, with lots of colorful fluttering flags and big banners proclaiming instant home ownership.

Perhaps she should call Andrew, she thought, her gaze going to her cell phone on the small table. She would tell him about coming to a motel that still had a bed vibrator.

But she didn't move. She couldn't. She was held by the sweet rhythm of the bed and a reluctance that she couldn't quite name.

Sometime later, Claire awoke and went out to her car to bring in her overnight bag of clothes. There were three more cars in front of rooms with light showing around the windows.

As she dug out her travel bag, the yellow neon Goodnight Motel sign went out. She shut and locked the car, then looked upward at the night black sky alight with sparkling stars.

Awed and entranced, she walked out farther into the gravel lot, away from the lights of the buildings. The stars got brighter. They seemed so close, as if she could reach up and touch them.

A faint memory came to her. Her father's voice. "There's the Big Dipper, darlin'…and over there, that's the North Star, and…"

She could almost feel his breath in her ear. He had smelled of Camel cigarettes and sweat. His stiff shirt had been damp around his neck when he lifted her in his arms. She had felt that she was up so very high when he lifted her. As if she could touch the stars.

Abruptly turning, she went back into her room, where she bathed in the green and white tile bathroom that proved a surprise without mildew. She turned on the rattling window air conditioner, plugged another coin in the bed massager and settled herself in the vibrating bed. She wondered about many things: whether or not to call Andrew, and why she should have to consider the question, why he didn't call her, how the mechanics of a vibrating bed worked, if her father was out there somewhere, and how Lily Donnell was faring, wherever she was.

Chapter Nine

Sherrilyn came awake. Light shone in her eyes. It took her a minute to remember where she was.

It was the bathroom light. She saw it while still having most of her head covered with the pillow, trying to keep her ears warm. Denny wanted the air conditioner up high, causing Sherrilyn to use all the bedcovers plus the extra blanket from the closet.

She felt the pressure to go to the bathroom again, but she decided to remain snuggled down in the blankets and not let on that she was awake. If she hit the cold, she wouldn't be able to stand it. She would need to rush Denny out of the bathroom, and she didn't like to attempt to make Denny do anything. She would wait until he came back to bed, and then she would slip to the toilet. Maybe he wouldn't even realize.

Denny was aggravated at her for getting pregnant. He had wanted her to get an abortion, but she wouldn't do it. He had pushed her quite hard, and she had still refused.

This refusal on her part surprised her. She had held to no

abortion, even when, at one point, she had been afraid that Denny might beat her up. She had never flat out refused to do something for Denny, or for hardly anyone else. She could hardly stand for anyone to be displeased with her.

She thought that she might need to see a doctor soon, and she knew Denny wouldn't like it. He would complain about the money. Hoping not to get Denny any more annoyed with her than he already was, she had been tucking money back in order to pay for a doctor appointment and whatever the baby might need.

Sherrilyn was scared that Denny was going to get really mad at her. She didn't know what she would do if he did. She didn't know what *he* would do if he got really mad at her, either. Once she had thought he was going to drive away from a gas station and leave her, so she had raced into the bathroom and back out and thrown herself into the car when he already had it started and put into gear.

Thinking of how the pregnancy was a lot of trouble for Denny, she felt sick to her stomach. To counteract this, she told herself that everything would be all right, and blocked out all thoughts of a distressful nature in a way she had learned to as a child, when her father would get drunk and mean. She liked hearing the rhythmic noise of the air conditioner. Maybe she had to cover up, but she was glad the air conditioner was running, because the noise and the heavy blankets helped to block out the world. She faintly realized when the bathroom light went out, but by then she was drifting back into sleep.

When she next awoke, she jumped out of the bed and raced to the toilet. Afterward, she came quietly out of the bathroom, hopeful that maybe Denny was still asleep and she could slip back into bed without waking him. If he was awake, he might want to do it with her, and she really didn't think she wanted to do it. She worried about the baby and couldn't pay attention, and Denny got mad at her for that.

Then she saw that Denny wasn't in the bed.

She could see enough in the faint light of morning slicing through the crack in the curtains to tell that his side of the bed was empty.

Going to the window, she peeked outside. She didn't see him down at the vending machines. She remembered that the manager of the motel had said that free coffee and continental breakfast would be available in the morning. This meant doughnuts, and Denny absolutely loved them. That was how she had met him—she had worked at a Krispy Kreme doughnut shop. He would come to the shop three or four times a week and always when she was working. He gave her tips, too, even after they had begun dating.

Crawling back under the covers, she thought of how Denny had been really sweet for those first months. He would talk a lot about plans that he had for his own auto repair shop, even a chain of shops, and he would include her in the plans. He gave her flowers, and once, when he noticed that she needed new shoes for waiting the counter, he bought her a pair of Nikes. Just like that, he had showed up with them—and the right size, too. No one had ever done something so nice for her, not ever. She had cried.

Since he had gotten fired from his job, though, he had been angry. She could understand him being angry at the manager of the auto repair shop who had fired him, and even at the cops, who, just because Denny had a record, had hounded him about some stolen cars that he didn't know anything about. But she wished he wouldn't be angry at her. She tried and tried to please him, and nothing she did seemed the right thing. She hoped, when they got settled again and he got working with his cousin doing some sort of car sales in Denver, he wouldn't be so angry all the time, and maybe he would even be glad when the baby got there.

As the air conditioner droned on, she fixed her mind on

the sort of life they would have in Denver. She imagined a house, her own house. It could be just a little run-down place, but she would fix it up. She would have the baby, and maybe she and Denny would get married, and they would all be happy.

Pounding brought her up from beneath the pillow. Someone was pounding on the door.

She almost killed herself getting there. She thought it was Denny and that he had gotten locked out. He would be mad at any amount of time standing there on the stoop. Somehow it would be her fault that he had gotten locked out.

"I'm comin'," she hollered out, fumbling with the doorknob.

Jerking open the door, she found herself faced with a man in a khaki uniform, a man so big that her eyes came to his chest. She blinked, focusing on a shiny star on his shirt. *Oh, God, the sheriff.*

Her gaze traveled upward. The man nodded politely. "Good mornin', ma'am. Are you Sherrilyn Rhodes?"

She couldn't say a word.

He studied her. She felt naked in a tank top and panties, and all she could do was shake her head. Finally she got out, "I'm Sherrilyn Earles…not Rhodes." She was ashamed.

"Is Denny Rhodes here with you?"

"Uh…I…" Sherrilyn looked around at the bed, but even before she did, she knew Denny wasn't going to be there.

The sheriff came past her into the room and pulled the bedcovers all the way down, as if Denny had been small enough to hide in them. The motel manager, who had apparently been right behind the sheriff, stepped into the doorway.

The sheriff asked her if she knew where Denny was, and she said she didn't. Then she remembered about their car and said, "Our car…it broke down last night, and we were goin' to get someone to fix it this mornin'. He's probably lookin' for the garage."

She looked at the motel manager, hoping for him to back her up.

But the motel manager said, "Darlin', it's after eleven now, and no one has seen your young man. He's gone, and so is Miz Wilder's Mercedes."

Sherrilyn took this in.

"Excuse me," she said, and raced into the bathroom and shut the door.

She stood for several long seconds with her eyes squeezed closed and her head about to explode. Hearing voices in the other room, she put her hands over her ears and hummed. If willing herself to turn into vapor and slip right through the window screen worked, she would have been gone in an instant.

Then, as a thought hit her between the shoulder blades, her eyes flew open and she was staring at her nylon duffel bag on the floor on the other side of the sink.

"No…no…please, no." She threw herself down and un-zipped the bag. The zipper stuck on fabric.

Oh, no.

She got the bag open and saw the truth. Denny had been through it. Everything was tumbled, and she always packed very neatly. She kept everything rolled, because that was the way to prevent a lot of wrinkles. Her mother had taught her to do that when she had been a little girl going to a sleep-over, and she had never forgotten.

Tears blurred her eyes as she searched for the inside zip-per pocket on the end. A sort of hidden pocket. Maybe he had overlooked it.

But her money was gone, all that she had saved out, little by little, for the past six months of serving Krispy Kremes.

The money that would get her to the doctor, that would get her somewhere if Denny left her.

Denny had known about it all along. And he had taken her money and left her.

They took her to the police station. Everyone was really nice, but she was still scared and started to cry when the sheriff took her into his office. All she could think of was how embarrassed her mother would have been, and how her father and his wife would say she had always caused trouble. She never had been anything but trouble to everyone.

A woman with big blond hair like Dolly Parton showed up at the office door and demanded to know what in the world the sheriff had done to make Sherrilyn cry.

"I haven't done nothin'." He threw up his hands and stalked from around his desk. "You handle this. I'll come back when the tears are shut off."

Sherrilyn thought it was probably the good-cop, bad-cop routine, like in the movies, and that they were going to grill her and throw her in jail, although really, where else did she have to go?

The woman, who introduced herself as Lori, called Sherrilyn, "Honey," and gave her a tissue. Then she brought Sherrilyn a Dr. Pepper and a couple of aspirins and asked her if she was having her period. "Everything seems so much more awful when you're on your period."

"I think I have a bladder infection," Sherrilyn said.

"Well, that's awful, honey," the big-haired woman said. The next instant she took away the Dr. Pepper, took it right out of Sherrilyn's hand, went out and when she returned it was with a glass of baking soda in water that she made Sherrilyn drink.

Sherrilyn thought she might throw up, but quite shortly she began to feel better.

The woman asked questions and wrote down Sherrilyn's answers. Basically Sherrilyn's answers were variations of, "I don't know." She didn't know what time Denny had left; she didn't know anything about him planning to steal the car; she didn't know where they had been going, other than Denver. "We're from Houston," she said, starting to cry again. "He didn't like it there…."

The woman handed her a fresh tissue, patted her leg, and thankfully finally got to asking things she did know, such as her name and birth date. When it came to her address, Sherrilyn could only say, "I guess it's the Goodnight Motel."

Chapter Ten

"Your mother's urn?" The young deputy was reading the list of items that Claire had jotted down as the contents of the Mercedes. He cast her a quizzical expression and asked with some hesitation, "Do you mean an urn of ashes?"

"Yes," said Claire, who was attempting to make headway with the insurance company and had her cell phone to her ear. She could practically see questions float across the deputy's forehead, questions the insurance company was certainly going to ask, as well.

Why had she brought her mother's ashes on a vacation? Who would do such a thing? Not to mention the fifteen-hundred-dollar quilt Andrew had bought her for their sixth anniversary, and Aunt Agnes's small desk clock. She had never liked Aunt Agnes, but she had loved that clock as a child, and somehow having it seemed to triumph over the mean woman.

Across the room, the girl and the receptionist came out of the sheriff's office. The girl was clearly still upset. The receptionist pointed to the ladies' room, and the girl hurried toward it, clutching her shirt tight around her as if to hold herself together. She glanced across the room, saw Claire and then jerked her gaze away and ducked into the rest room.

Claire felt annoyed at the girl's reaction. It made Claire feel like she had too much of her Aunt Agnes's blood, and she did not think she had one smidgen of her great-aunt's cold blood.

She took out her frustration by clicking off on the insurance company's canned music that was playing in her ear. A check of the phone showed she had not missed any calls from Andrew. She had telephoned him twice, but he had not answered. She did not want to leave the news about the theft of the Mercedes on his voice mail. Even though he had lost the car in the divorce, Claire remembered how fond he had been of it when he had bought it, and that he had certain standards of care concerning vehicles. She felt that she had failed him somehow, and she really hated to hear what he was going to say about the matter.

"Okay, let's go over this information," said the young deputy. He was the same young man who had directed her to the Valentine cemetery the previous day—Travis Ford was the name on the tag pinned over the breast pocket of his shirt. He was handsome and the easy sort, who probably melted hearts all over. How she could tell that he wasn't married, she couldn't say, only that she knew. He was obviously intelligent, but in the way of so many men, he typed with an erratic hunt-and-peck-and-lots-of-errors method.

"No," she said, correcting her address, "it is 1504, not 1405."

"Oh."

He frowned deeply at the computer screen, and Claire had the strong urge to take over the typing in order to get finished before noon tomorrow.

Mostly she was hungry. Stress always made her more hungry than normal. All she had been able to grab since the discovery of her missing car were two doughnuts from the motel office. Now she was absolutely ravenous, and the only food in sight were two more dry-looking doughnuts. She kept eyeing those as the deputy kept correcting his typing errors.

Her gaze drifted again to the women's rest room door, which remained shut. The girl was probably thinking that her heart was broken forever and her life over. Claire had known this foolish feeling a number of times with Andrew. She felt it try to nab her now, as the memory of her picture album with all of the photographs of her and her husband passed across her mind. The picture album was riding on the floorboard of the Mercedes, unless Denny Rhodes had already tossed it in a Dumpster.

Fighting off the feeling, she got up and went for one of the dried-up doughnuts, but at her first bite, the young deputy let out, "Aw, these dang high-tech machines."

He had pressed a wrong button and thought that he had lost the form. Claire offered to help, and without an ounce of self-consciousness he said, "Ma'am, I'd welcome it."

Setting aside the crumbly doughnut, she found the form for him, and while she was engaged in this process, a man appeared in front of the desk. Claire suddenly looked up and there he was, gazing down at her and the deputy with sharp, narrow eyes.

Claire, realizing her intimate position hanging over the deputy with her breasts brushing his head and her hand over his on the mouse, jerked herself up straight, just as the deputy said, "Oh, hi, Dad."

He introduced Claire and his father, Larkin Ford, who nodded and extended his hand politely. Claire thought he was the man she had seen with the deputy in the field the previous afternoon.

The deputy gave his father a rundown on the theft of

Claire's vehicle. His father, obviously not all that interested, turned the subject to a discussion about plans to load cattle for shipment that afternoon.

It was likely unreasonable to expect everyone to let their own lives stop to deal with her stolen car. It was gone. Gone with the wind, and so, it seemed more and more, was her relaxing vacation. She began imagining returning to Shreveport. Possibly Andrew would not be regarding her so favorably after this happening.

Growing agitated at the prospect of having to tell Andrew about the car, she looked again at the rest room door, which remained shut. She checked her watch and looked at the door again. Maybe the girl had come out while she and the deputy were dealing with the computer, she thought, as she scanned the room and moved to peer into the sheriff's office. She didn't see the girl, and an uneasy feeling swept down her spine.

Just then a statuesque woman with iron-gray hair came through the front double doors. "Lunch!" she hollered out, as she brought a box around the counter and set it on the receptionist's desk.

"There's enough for you, too, Larkin, if you want a barbecue sandwich," said the big-haired receptionist, unfolding herself out of her chair.

The men headed in the direction of the food, but for some reason she wouldn't have been able to state, Claire was propelled in the direction of the women's rest room, where she knocked.

She didn't get any answer. She tried the doorknob. It was locked, as she knew very well it would be. A chill swept through her.

She looked over her shoulder and saw everyone else looking at her, as if they couldn't figure out what she was doing, but then the receptionist was coming rapidly to join Claire, who pressed her ear to the door.

"I hear water runnin'. Do you have a key?" She jiggled the doorknob, as if that was a help.

The receptionist knocked hard and called, "Sherrilyn, honey, are you okay?"

There was no answer.

Then, of one accord, they looked downward and saw water seeping out from beneath the door.

"A key?" Claire said again.

"I have one." The big-haired woman, who Claire suddenly saw as very capable, turned immediately and went to her desk. The men and the tall woman came over, the three of them gazing curiously from Claire to the door.

The receptionist called from her desk, "I can't find the blasted key. Travis, get that door open."

Instantly Claire saw the deputy's response and stepped out of the way, as the young man threw himself at the door.

Unfortunately he simply hit with a hard thud and sort of bounced back, then grabbed his arm.

Both men stepped together, as if to team up on the door, when the tall woman commanded, "Wait!" Unfolding something—a paper clip—she inserted it and poked it around in the keyhole, then turned the knob and opened the door, which now had water flowing rapidly out from under it.

There was the girl sprawled on the floor.

Claire was first through the door and down on her knees, feeling for the girl's pulse.

"She's alive...I think."

And then, when Claire lifted her head and silky red hair out of the water, the girl let out a moan.

Oh, dear God, please help.

Chapter Eleven

People gathered on the sidewalk to see what was going on with the ambulance at the sheriff's office. Julia Jenkins-Tinsley came hurrying up, pushing her mail cart, and Fred Grace kept inching down from his florist shop. Tate Holloway, putting out a hand to stop traffic, strode across the street from the *Valentine Voice,* with his boy, Willie Lee, at his heels. Belinda stepped out of the drugstore and hollered down to Vella, "What happened, Mama?"

Vella didn't answer, as she did not intend to carry on a hollering conversation, besides which, her attention was fixed on the striking blond woman who wanted to go in the ambulance, but tight-ass Newley Dodd of the emergency squad said that she couldn't, since she was not an immediate relative. He slammed the doors and took off.

The beautiful stranger stood there on the edge of the curb, watching the ambulance head away. "Someone should be there for her," she said to the air.

And Vella took it upon herself to reply, "Yes, they should. Come on, I'll drive."

The woman looked startled, but then she followed Vella, who led the way to her Land Rover, parked only three cars away.

"We're goin' up to the hospital," she called to Belinda, who stood in the drugstore entry.

"But, Mama, what's goin' on…?"

"Honey, you'll get it all in a minute from Lori," she said, with one foot in the truck. "I'll call you from the hospital. Make sure that nurse doesn't let your daddy fall out of his wheelchair."

She felt a little guilty at putting the responsibility of Perry off on Belinda, who never liked to deal with her father. But apparently she didn't feel guilty enough to stop her from running off. In fact, she backed from the curb at a more than normal rate of speed.

Glancing into her rearview mirror, Vella saw Belinda gazing after them with her hand on her hip, and farther down the sidewalk, Travis Ford was standing there looking after them as if he was left behind, which he was.

She caught up with the ambulance just as it reached the outskirts of Valentine. It was going without lights and siren, since the girl was not critical. "It's about thirty minutes to the hospital," she said to her passenger. "I'm Vella Blaine, by the way. I own Blaine's Drugstore." She stuck out her hand.

"Oh, hello. I'm Claire Wilder."

"I know. My daughter told me about you yesterday. She was at the soda fountain when you went off with Winston to the Little Creek cemetery. A beautiful stranger taking off with Winston is big news," she clarified at the woman's curious look. "And then I heard all about the mornin's trouble from Lori. There's nothin' that goes on in this town that most of us don't know it within an hour or so."

She liked the slow smile that came across the woman's face.

It showed a good sense of humor. Their eyes met, and it was almost startling the way Vella liked her instantly.

"So you came to town to look up dead relatives and ended up gettin' your car stolen."

"Uh-hmm…I'm on vacation. I wanted to see my father's hometown…I was born here, too."

"Well, my goodness, then you're one of us," Vella said, feeling as if she then understood her liking for the younger woman. "It's a shame about your Mercedes." She thought how she would just hate to have her Land Rover stolen. She loved her Land Rover.

After several seconds, the woman said, "I just ended up with the Mercedes in the divorce settlement. It was more my ex-husband's car. He picked it out, and he's going to be awfully upset about it being stolen."

"I should think that he wouldn't have anything to say about it, since you are divorced."

"Hmm…" the woman said in an agreeing tone that gave Vella a lot of curiosity about the ex-husband maybe not being so ex.

Then the woman said thoughtfully, "I never have liked it all that much. I was always worried about scratchin' it or somethin'." Her tone lifted. "It is fully insured. I'll probably get enough money to buy a car I really want." She was clearly struck with the fact.

After several minutes of riding along in silence, Vella asked, "What sort of vehicle do you think you want?"

"Oh, I don't know. I like yours. What is it?"

Vella told her it was a Land Rover and that she could go wherever she wanted in it, and haul gardening supplies and her husband, Perry, who was an invalid, and just about anything that she needed to carry.

"I don't haul that much," the younger woman said, frowning in a thinking fashion.

"What do you do?"

"Well, I was a legal secretary. I quit, though. I'm not doing anything right now."

"Hmm." Vella sized her up with a glance. "Maybe a sports car would suit you."

"Maybe…maybe a Mustang. I always wanted one of those. Or maybe a pickup truck. I had an old truck when I married my husband."

A Mustang and a pickup truck seemed worlds apart. Vella decided the woman was not a particularly decisive sort.

Vella herself had always been decisive, something that she considered one of her best assets, although Winston frequently told her that she was opinionated rather than decisive. She figured she was both. She certainly didn't like dithering around. Also, people seemed to lean on her to make decisions. Most people did not want to make their own decisions, and that annoyed her to no end.

"My daughter is a part-time personal shopping consultant," she said. "You might want to consult with her. She has a knack at pointing out what people really want."

Her own words illuminated the fact that Belinda was very much like her mother.

They ended up spending two hours in the emergency waiting room, which Vella had seen undergo four face-lifts in the past twenty years, if she was remembering correctly. It came to her that the reason she had so much experience in hospital waiting rooms was her advancing age and that of her relatives and friends. It was an exceedingly depressing thought and put a damper on the high spirits that she had experienced on the drive up from Valentine.

They drank coffee from a newly installed coffee bar that also had a tray of bakery cookies. Claire ate three of these out of a napkin on her lap, licking her fingers.

Vella watched her, intrigued with the contrast of elegance and earthiness. She noted that just about everyone who passed by took notice of the woman. Vella reevaluated her idea of Claire being beautiful. Her face was too round and flat to be considered beautiful, and she tended toward being a little heavy and soft by the current standard of lean and firm. She had the sort of full breasts that Vella herself had always possessed and knew provoked attention, but they were not the total draw, Vella did not think.

Both men and women who passed would give first a glance and then a second, intent look. A janitor came in and could hardly empty ashtrays because of looking at Claire. A disheveled-looking woman hurried up to the nurses' station, conversed there, and then came and threw herself down in a chair across the room. Quite shortly, the woman was pretending to look at a magazine, while her gaze kept straying in Claire's direction.

Vella, who at one time had herself elicited such attention, thought sadly how she had lost her hormones eleven years ago. She felt invisible next to Claire, who obviously did have a full supply.

They chatted about the possible course the jackass—Vella's term—would take with the Mercedes, the possible course Claire might take to continue on her vacation, the possible course of Sherrilyn Earles's somewhat pitiful life, as well as the girl's general lack of good sense but absolutely lovely red hair. Neither mentioned their private reasons for being in the waiting room on behalf of a girl neither of them knew from Adam's house cat.

Vella thought that her own reasons for being there were not all that virtuous; she was fascinated by Claire Wilder and was relieved to have a brief respite from her daily grind as caretaker to both an invalid husband and the family business, and generally a break from being the all-round responsible and powerful woman that she was.

They never did get to see Sherrilyn Earles, because the girl refused to see them. They did learn that she showed every sign of being anemic, that she had a bladder infection and that she was almost five months pregnant. They learned all of this by speaking with first one nurse, then another, and then the doctor, who made the assumption that Claire was Sherrilyn's mother. Claire, who masterfully did not correct the assumption, discussed at length what he recommended, which was for the girl to receive vitamin and iron shots and be evaluated by a psychiatrist for a short period there in the hospital, with follow-up outpatient therapy.

"I imagine she can be released in four or five days," he said.

As they stepped out of the hospital, Claire said, "I wonder where she's going to go after the hospital."

Vella felt lacking, because she did not have an answer to that question.

It turned out that they were both so taken up with the girl's situation that they didn't think about Claire's being stranded without a vehicle and with only one decent change of clothes until they were halfway back to Valentine.

"I can't deal with it right now," Claire said. "I am starving. I can't think."

"Well, that's one problem I can help with," said Vella with satisfaction.

She drove Claire to the drugstore, where she fed her two barbecue sandwiches, a bag of potato chips, a dill pickle and a large strawberry milkshake. She and Belinda sat there watching the striking woman put away that much food.

After that, Belinda was able to fix Claire up with two brand-new summer outfits that she had ordered from the Home Shopping Network and not yet worn. It was the most amazing thing that Belinda and Claire wore the same size.

Vella, looking from one woman to the other, could not picture it.

Then Vella drove Claire to her room at the Goodnight Motel, where she ended up staying and visiting with her for another hour and a half in which they sat around and drank Coca-Cola on ice from the motel machine, smoked cigarillos from a pack in Vella's purse, and told each other their life stories.

Vella knew there was plenty the younger woman left unsaid, although Vella was able to fill in with her imagination and years of experience. She put together a picture of a lonely but spunky little girl who had grown up too fast by having the responsibility of a weak mother and no father, and a lonely but creative, if indecisive, divorced woman who was still attached to her ex-husband.

For Vella's part, she talked as she had not talked to another woman in twenty years, since her best friend of that time had moved away to Australia. She confessed her deep loneliness and even revealed her profound disappointment at the early loss of a sex life with Perry, and how she still hankered after a potent male in her life.

She appreciated that Claire Wilder did not seem shocked or, worse, disbelieving. She also appreciated that Claire offered no condolences or advice, but simply seemed to listen attentively. In her experience, there were few people on earth who possessed such a listening ability.

She was so trusting of Claire, in fact, that she even told her about her flirtation and fantasies regarding her e-mail friend, Harold. She was bold enough to confess, "I have asked God to send me a man with whom I can really connect and share my life at this point. I don't know what that will mean for me, but God does."

Claire regarded her intently with her head tilted to the

side. "Why did you stay married to Perry, if you felt so lonely? Why didn't you get a divorce?"

"Oh, my heaven, I've asked myself that a million times. It seems like I was ready to leave Perry for at least the last twenty years of our marriage. But I just never did, for one reason or another. I guess for a while I wasn't certain divorce was right, but then I went on the idea that everything would be wonderful if I would work real hard and make Perry into all that he should be. Oh, I prayed and prayed for him to see the light, and while I was doing that, the time just went by. I threw him out once a few years ago, and that's when I had to look squarely at the situation and see that Perry was not going to change, and neither was I. We had ended up where we were, and we had something. A love and bond particular to us. I could accept that.

"I think, really, that it all worked out how God intended it to work out. Had we gotten a divorce, that would have been how it was supposed to work out, too."

"So you think that no matter what you do, you are doing the right thing? Don't you worry about mistakes?"

Vella laughed. "Honey, do you think you are powerful enough to mess up God's plans by some little mistake?"

Claire's answer was a shrug and a smile and to ask Vella if she might want some more Coke. Vella wisely didn't press the younger woman. A person's faith was something private. Winston was always telling Vella that she spoke too much of it and that she made things up as she went along. She admitted that she changed as she matured.

The sun was slipping down and the cooling scent of evening coming when Vella drove away from the motel, leaving Claire draped in the doorway, finishing her cigarillo. She smoked the thing quite well, considering she claimed never to have smoked one before.

On the drive home, Vella realized that she felt immensely

revived. She felt reminded that she was a woman with a life of her own. It seemed a sad commentary on her life that such an afternoon had constituted a refreshing retreat for her.

Then, upon arriving home, her mood began to slip downward, as she had to fight off the guilt for abandoning her husband for all those hours. She dismissed the night nurse and bathed Perry, then asked if he would like to watch *Mannix*. Perry had always loved *Mannix*. She thought his eyes answered yes. She turned it on, sat near him in the same living room where she had sat with him for forty-five years and rubbed lotion into his hands.

She thought of the young girl trying to drown herself in the bathroom sink, and all because of a man. Poor thing.

But in that moment of holding her husband's very still hand, Vella could understand how a woman might lose good sense. She knew she would have long ago, had God not enabled her to bear up and make the best of things.

She heard, in a whisper in her mind, *I will never leave you or forsake you.*

"I'm here, Perry. I won't leave you." Then she added to herself with a little worry, Well, if God allows me to stay. And who will look out for Perry if something happens to me?

Vella was a woman with such presence that Claire found her room impossibly empty after the woman left. She had thoroughly enjoyed their visiting. The difference between Vella and Gayla Jean, she thought, was that Vella was a fully mature woman. In her relationship with Gayla Jean, Claire often felt like an older sister. True, she *was* older than Gayla Jean, but she did not care to always be the adult one. She got tired of always being in the wise, mature role.

Since she could remember, even as a small child while growing up in a household with three adults, she had felt like the grown-up. At school the teachers had often made her classroom monitor, given her keys to offices and admittance to the teachers' lounge. After she had reached the age of thirteen, her mother had never had to write another check.

In Vella's presence, however, Claire felt an equal. It was a curiously freeing feeling.

She tried watching television, but unable to stand the confines of the empty room, she took her cell phone outside and sat on the stoop to watch the sun finish going down in the coral sky. June bugs hummed and thumped at the neon lights on the overhang above.

She decided to telephone Gayla Jean and get some boosting first, before trying Andrew. She punched in the numbers, then held the phone to her ear and gazed at the empty space where the car should have been.

"Oh, my gosh, Claire, I could just kiss you," Gayla Jean said the instant she heard Claire's voice. Then she made a kissing sound and laughed.

"What for?"

"Because of your example, I got my hair frosted, too. Honey, I am a bleach-blond woman, I have to admit it."

She gave a shout that caused Claire to move the phone from her ear.

"I feel like a new woman. I mean a *new woman!* if you get my drift," Gayla Jean said in a sultry voice, then giggled. "And Lamar is takin' notice! Ohmygosh, Claire—we are goin' out to dinner tonight, and it was his suggestion! Yes, he is draggin' his rear off the recliner to go out to dinner, and without the kids. I'm not certain we have done this since before Jeremy was born. In fact, honey, I only have a minute before we have to leave."

Claire, in the face of her friend's exuberance, felt hesitant to mention her own difficulty. She thought she should feel flattered that her friend liked her hair so much as to want to be blond, too, but she began to simply feel tired. She had called Gayla Jean to talk about her own stuff, not be drawn into talking about Gayla Jean's stuff. And she did not know how to explain her situation in thirty seconds or less.

While she was deciding about this, Gayla Jean asked her how she was doing, and "Where are you anyway?"

"I'm in Valentine, Oklahoma," Claire said. "You know, where my father was from and I was born." Then she blurted, "My car was stolen."

"The Mercedes?"

Claire wondered what other car Gayla Jean thought she had. She explained the situation briefly, and the entire time she was trying to do this, Gayla Jean on the other end kept up a running conversation with her children.

"Jeremy, you cannot watch *Halloween II*. No. It will rot your soul, and you'll wet the bed. I'm sorry, Claire, go ahead. I cannot believe you sound so calm after havin' your car stolen. What sort of motel are you stayin' in? Raquel, it is your turn with the dishes. Sarah, get out of there and stop devilin' her. Well, honey, I can't talk to you now...I didn't mean you, Claire...I meant Sarah. I'm comin', Lamar, just a minute. Lord, I can't get this shoe on."

All in all, it was a thoroughly disappointing and annoying conversation. When they hung up, Claire was left sitting there on the stoop in silence somewhere between relief at ending the somewhat confusing conversation, and acute loneliness and longing for the children she'd never had and the man and marriage she once had but had lost.

Seeking solace, she went down to the lighted cold drink machine at the corner of the office building. Bringing back a cold bottle of Coke, she sat again on the stoop to sufficiently build herself back up with sugar and caffeine, in order to feel capable of speaking with Andrew.

She dialed his home number. With each ring across the line, her urgency to connect grew stronger.

When he didn't answer, she tried his cell phone and got his voice mail there, too. There was nothing else to do but leave a message.

She said, "I'm in Valentine, Oklahoma, Andrew. I'd appreciate it if you would call me. It's rather important." Her tone wavered, as she wasn't exactly certain of her stance—ex-wife, good friend, or perhaps soon-to-be-new-wife, or simply just someone he used to know.

Why did she feel the need to tell him about the car? That they had even had a reconnecting conversation of a sort on the road two days previously seemed like a mirage. She had begun to seriously doubt his intentions, since he had not telephoned her over the following days, even after she'd left two messages.

She thought about their uncertain relationship in a progressively depressed manner as she continued to sit on the stoop, counting cars going past on the highway and studying the For Sale sign on the portable marquee.

Quite possibly she might have ended up sitting there all evening, hugging herself and crying, and maybe drinking all the Cokes in the machine, except a new male guest arrived and was given a room in the next cabin. When he saw her there, he—a rather attractive middle-aged businessman of some sort in short sleeves, loose tie and dark slacks—came over and attempted to flirt and draw her into having a drink with him, despite her cool manner.

Finally she said, "I am so not interested," went into her room, slammed the door shut and even drew the curtains.

She sat on the bed and cried, as any woman would who didn't know where she was in her life and whose car and precious belongings had been stolen and who was stranded at a third-rate motel.

Was this all God's idea? If it was, she didn't like it one bit.

★ ★ ★

"Claire?"

"Yes…I'm here." She sniffed and cleared her throat.

"You sounded funny…let me move. I'm at the Sheraton in New Orleans…there, can you hear me okay?"

"Yes, yes, I can hear you."

"I hope it isn't too late. I was in a meeting when you called. We're havin' major problems with the Walker Corporation mall project. I didn't listen to your message until I got back up here to the room."

"No…no, it isn't too late." Why had he not stepped away from the meeting to at least check her message? What if she had needed him desperately? She told herself he had no obligation to her, although he had given her the idea yesterday morning that he wanted to enter her life again.

As she was wondering if she wanted to point out his lapse in not checking her message, he said, "What's that noise?"

The bed vibrator. "What noise?" She got out of bed and moved to the chair.

"Nothin', I guess. It's quit now. So, you're in Valentine."

"Yes. I made it and found my grandparents' graves yesterday."

"Uh…good."

"And the Mercedes was stolen yesterday…well, last night." Was it just last night? It seemed like weeks since she had come to town.

"It was stolen?" His voice rose.

She gave an explanation, and he seemed to take it all rather well, after some assimilation, in which he repeated much of what she said. Then he asked, "Stolen?" and "It has antitheft—didn't you lock it?" and added, "They know who did it?"

"Yes," and "Yes," and "Yes. Well, they're pretty sure," she answered to each question.

"What are you going to do?"

She sighed. "Well, if they don't get the car back, I suppose I'll have to get another." Him asking the question annoyed her. She had called him for help on what she should do.

"Honey, they don't find Mercedes. At least not all in one piece. That car has probably already been taken apart and sold."

She didn't know what to say to that discouraging statement.

"How far are you from an airport?" he asked. "You could fly back to Shreveport."

"I don't know. I'll check. The motel manager will probably know."

"I can't get away from here for two more days, at least, or I could drive up to get you. If you can wait until Sunday, I'll come get you then. If I can get away from here. We're havin' some real problems with the contractor," he repeated.

To this she said instantly, "Oh, no…that's okay. I can get a car, I'm sure." He did not sound thrilled with the idea of having to come get her. She knew how he hated to be dragged away from his work. "If nothing else, I can get a rental. I just wanted you to know what happened, that's all." She felt silly now for calling him. And it was pure silly for her to want him to be thrilled with an opportunity to take off and spend time away with her.

"Hold on, the bellhop's at the door. I ordered a pizza." She heard his voice in the background, some noise, the door closing. "Okay, I'm back." He had a mouthful of food.

He said he couldn't do much from there, but that he wished he could be with her. She thought this was nice for him to say. She almost told him that she wanted him to come up, but she simply said in a very sane and calm manner that she would know more about her plans tomorrow. He told her to keep him posted.

"Well, I guess I'll let you go. I'm beat," he said.

"Yes, me too. Well, good night."

"Call me tomorrow."

"Yes...I will."

Claire set the phone aside, then wiped her hand on her pants leg.

What in the world did she want from him?

Whatever it was, she wasn't getting it.

From: Vella Blaine
To: <haltg@mailectric.com>
Sent: May 29, 1997, 11:45 p.m.
Subject: Troublesome Times
Dear Harold,

I am delighted to receive your picture! I don't think you look too different from the image I had in mind. You certainly don't look sixty-eight, though. More fifty-eight would have been my guess. And my goodness, a policeman. I confess to being quite impressed. I can understand how your Estelle was relieved for you to retire. I imagine a policeman's job is quite dangerous in a big city like Cherry Hill. You must have had to see things that would curl your hair.

We have crime here in Valentine now, too, I'm sorry to say. Nowhere is immune these days. My daughter's significant other is a career deputy with our sheriff's office, and he has more than once caught illegal aliens taking a back road through our county, and that can be a little dangerous. Generally the illegals are not dangerous, but the people transporting them are liable to pull a gun. People have guns around here. I myself have a shotgun. I have shot armadillos digging up my roses. A family of armadillos can make Swiss cheese out of a garden or yard. I've turned my ankle in their holes more than once. They are so annoying to shoot, though, because they jump straight up in the air when you shoot them. I never know if I hit or miss, until the critter falls over.

I hope that doesn't shock you, that I know how to use a shotgun on an armadillo.

And drugs, we're getting that problem now, out in the county, not in Valentine yet, thank goodness. Several months ago Lyle—that's Belinda's SO—busted up a drug ring. Actually, he didn't really bust it up. His car broke down, and he went up to a house to see if he could borrow a wrench, and it just happened that while he was doing that, the house exploded. The rascals had been making drugs. They scattered in all directions, except one who was knocked unconscious. Lyle had to apply first aid and get him to the hospital. The whole bunch were from up in Oklahoma City and had moved down here to do their dirty business.

Most of our trouble is caused from out-of-towners. Just last night we had a fellow from out of town steal another out-of-towner's car. He also took his girlfriend's money and left her stranded, and it turns out that she is pregnant. She got so wrought up about the whole thing that she tried to kill herself right in the sheriff's office women's rest room.

The poor thing didn't know that you can't drown yourself by keeping your head underwater, you just can't overrule your senses that way, and she tried to do it in the sink. She plugged up the overflow holes with toilet tissue and filled the sink and stuck her head in there. Well, you know her natural senses took over and caused her to jerk her face out, only then she like to have done the job anyway, because she hit her head on the faucet and knocked herself plumb out. Luckily she fell on the floor and not back into the water.

I don't know what they're going to do with her. She's up at the hospital now. No insurance, of course. Last we heard, the sheriff's office is checking to see if they can get hold of her family down in Texas.

Then there's that woman who got her car stolen. What do you do when you are on vacation and have your car and all of your clothes stolen? She is on a vacation all by herself. I cannot imagine it, but I have to say, I have been thinking of going off on a cruise by myself. One of those seniors' cruises. Have you heard of them? I would have to get reliable care for Perry in my absence, though, and that is a trick, isn't it?

I am attaching a picture of myself taken three weeks ago. The rain stopped long enough for me to stand outside with one of my prizewinning Chrysler Imperial roses.

Write when you can.

Your friend in caretaking,

Vella, in Valentine.

She attached the picture file, then gathered her gumption to send it. It was the best picture she'd had taken in years. Even Belinda said so. The lighting made her look at least ten years younger. Was that lying, God?

Well, for heaven's sake, You are right. Who would send an ugly picture? She hit the send button.

Then she clicked on the picture of Harold, took off her glasses and brought her face close to the screen to study the image. She had a quick fantasy about his sexual ability, which by his appearance would be strong. In fact, she had to close the picture of him and even turn off her computer to keep herself from looking at it again, because she felt hot desire begin to stir, and she could not face Perry in such a state.

Chapter Twelve

After he heard about the goings-on between Claire Wilder and the ruffian, Winston Valentine lay awake half the night beating himself up for moping all the day so that he missed everything. By morning, though, he'd come up with a new idea that sent his spirits rising.

He was out of bed before first light and shaving, splashing on the bit of Hi Karate that was left in the bottle that his daughter Charlene bought for him every Father's Day. He dressed, choosing to go ahead with a starched shirt, his newest pair of khakis and his good ostrich boots, which he had not worn in quite some time. Giving the left boot a hard tug, he about threw himself off the dressing chair. While he was catching his breath, he called himself every kind of fool in the book for his yearning for Claire Wilder.

What could he do with her?

He could look at her, see her smile, hear that danged fine sweet drawl of her honey voice. And all of that was a purpose to go on. He had an interest at last. Thank you, God.

He slipped down the stairs and to the kitchen with a minimum of creaks, many of those in his knees. With Marilee's night-lights all over the place, it was easy to go through the house, where he had lived since his dear departed wife, Coweta, had inherited it from her mother, Graceful Overton.

After over forty years, the house was called the Valentine home, Graceful Overton long gone and forgotten. The same as would happen with Winston someday. Just last week he had overheard a teenage girl at the IGA call it the Holloway house. It had unnerved him. There he was, standing in the snack aisle with the Lay's potato chips, seeing his own future demise and complete fading away.

The Holloway family had come to live with him in the house last year—Tate and Marilee and their son, Willie Lee, and niece Corrine, and now the new baby, along with an assortment of pets. The Holloways had needed a big home for the kids and animals, and Winston had needed someone to live with him and save him from having to listen to his daughter Charlene nag him about either moving in with her or going to the old geezers' home that she and her husband operated. As far as Winston was concerned, the arrangement was working out very well, although Marilee had proven to be about equal to his daughter in her nagging.

He made a pot of coffee and sat drinking and eating two brownies from a pan on the counter, until Corrine came in to get a cup of coffee for her aunt.

"How's Marilee this mornin'?" Winston asked.

"She said she is a fifty-year-old new mother."

"I thought she was only forty-three."

"She is."

"Ah, well, she'll make it." His Coweta had delivered their last in her forties. "Here, take her a chocolate brownie."

Corrine peered at him with sharp eyes. Nothing slipped past the girl, who had grown up fast with a wild, reckless mother, before coming to live with her aunt Marilee.

"Can you spare me the mornin'?" said Winston. "I need some help, on the quiet side."

With a speculative expression, Corrine, all of fourteen and thin as a rail, poured herself a cup of coffee that she wasn't supposed to have. "Aunt Marilee will ground me for good if she catches me gettin' you any more salty barbecue or Bama pies. Besides which, you might die." She drew out the word, *d-i-i-i-e.*

"I am not gonna die from barbecue or a Bama pie. And if you can slip those Snickers bars to Perry, who is half dead, you can sometimes spare me a Bama pie."

She blinked.

"I've seen you and Perry. He can sure enough communicate with you when he wants to."

"Not all the time, he can't. Just sometimes." She looked sad, and he regretted mentioning Perry. The girl had a special bond with the invalid man.

"I don't want a Bama pie. I need you to drive my car. I want you to take me out to the Goodnight Motel." He had been denied his license for two years, on account of not being able to see clearly. He might have tried driving himself, but he was afraid he would run someone down because of his poor vision.

Seeing the interest spark in her dark eyes, he got the instant idea that he was actually doing her a good turn, perking her up with an expedition. She cocked her head, studying him as he said they would take his Olds and go the back way, the same roads that she sometimes drove with Tate teaching her. "I can be teachin' you to drive."

She lifted the mug to her mouth with both hands, took a good sip and then gave a little grin. "Okay," she said, without asking him the why of it, which he had counted on. Corrine kept to her own business.

As she took her aunt's coffee and brownie up the stairs, he called softly, "About eight-thirty."

Thirty minutes later, the sun full and golden, Willie Lee helped him with raising the flags on the tall pole in his front yard. It was a ritual that Winston and his neighbor Everett had started a number of years ago. The entire town now expected to see the flags flying. He had lights on a sensor and could let the flags fly all night, but last night had looked like rain, so he had brought them in.

Across the street, the Northrupts' big U.S. of A. flag already fluttered lightly, and Len Northrupt stood on the porch drinking coffee. He waved to Winston.

Len was Everett Northrupt's son, newly divorced and staying at his parents' house while they were down in South America for a year, where Doris had dragged Everett to do missionary work. Len, who had recently retired from the Army, was a stickler for flag rules, and the first thing he did was quit flying the Confederate flag, even though Everett had it smaller and far below the Stars and Stripes. Every chance the younger man got, he argued with Winston about flying the Confederate flag, which just gave Winston more to live for.

Willie Lee, one by one and very careful to keep each flag from touching the ground, handed them to Winston—first the Confederate Stars and Bars, and then the U.S. Stars and Stripes. Together, old man and boy gave the raised flags a salute.

Afterward, Winston followed Willie Lee and the boy's dog up to the porch and sat in his rocker. Willie Lee brought Winston out a fresh cup of coffee and a sausage biscuit Corrine had made in the microwave.

"Is your mama up yet?" Winston asked.

Willie Lee shook his head. "She is ly-ing on her pil-low with Sis-tur," said Willie Lee, who was always very clear and literal in his speech. He was eleven now, but in his mind he remained six years old. Winston thought the boy had wisdom that wasn't tainted with knowledge.

"Well, you stay close around her this mornin' and keep her company. Help her out with Sister, okay? Here's a quarter."

The boy looked at the coin in his hand. "Why did you give me a quar-ter?"

"So you can put it in your pocket for when you need it."

"Oh."

"Wait. Here's a dollar. That ought to be enough for you to buy a double package of Twinkies when you go to the store with your mama, and you can share them with your dog."

Munro, Willie Lee's dog that was habitually at the boy's feet, gave Winston a look, and Winston winked at him.

The boy went back inside, and Winston drank his coffee, ate the biscuit and listened to the familiar sounds of his house and neighborhood coming awake. The day nurse for Perry, barely visible over the dashboard, drove past, heading for the Blaines' house. Len Northrup started mowing his backyard, appearing from behind his house, then being hidden again. Floyd Fisher came by doing his fast walking. Several more people, whose names escaped him but he recognized from their vehicles, drove past. Winston gave and received waves.

He knew most people on sight and was related to about half of them, having grown up and raised his own family in the town. The years had flown by.

He had two daughters and a son, Fred, the only one to carry on the Valentine name, and he had moved off to Palm Springs. For a while, Fred's wife, Helen, had been hankering to move into the big house on Church Street, but then she'd decided California was more her style, and Fred never could tell her no. They had returned for Winston's big blowout of a birthday at eighty-eight, but when asked about their next visit, Helen had said, "Over my dead body." Winston figured that if Fred couldn't say no to Helen, he couldn't kill her, either.

Just then the front door opened and Tate stepped out. He looked rumpled and a little confused, as any middle-aged man will who was trying to cope with a surprised middle-aged new mother and three children plopped on him.

"How's Marilee this mornin'?" Winston asked.

"Step lightly. She's singin' the 'I'm too old for a baby' song."

"Well, I don't think she can change her mind and send it back."

"Definitely don't say that to her." And off he went, casting Winston a wave, getting into his car and driving away to the *Valentine Voice* offices.

Winston checked his watch and decided he had better move his butt to the garage. When he got there, the garage door, a thick wooden affair, was heavier than he had expected. He stood there, and a few minutes later Corrine appeared around the corner. He hadn't even heard her coming. "Aunt Marilee is rockin' Victoria," she whispered.

"I don't think we need to whisper."

"Oh, yes, we do. Aunt Marilee can hear people just thinkin' about doin' wrong."

Winston experienced a jolt at the term "doin' wrong." Then he whispered, "Help me with the door."

They got the garage door up in relative quiet. The neighbor's stupid little collie began barking, but Corrine said the dog might serve as a distraction to any sound the car made.

Settled quickly behind the wheel, she turned the key and the Oldsmobile came to life. It purred softly. Fifteen years old and still a great car. She put the gearshift in Reverse and slowly backed out onto the street. Then she put it into

Drive and said, "Don't look back," and punched the pedal with her toe.

Winston grabbed the door rest and held on, hoping that he had not gotten himself into a fix he might regret.

They had a blowout going down Spring Road back of town.

"We are toast," Corrine said, looking at the flat left rear tire.

"With that sun, we likely will be soon," said Winston, feeling sweat begin to trickle. Months of rain, and the weather picked that day to be hot and sunny. "Help me get the jack out of the trunk."

"You can't change that tire."

"Lady, I'm not dead yet."

"You will be if you try to change that tire. Here, let me do it. Papa Tate taught me."

She wouldn't make a hundred pounds soaking wet. "You help me," he said.

They got the spare out of the trunk, and Winston had to sit on it and wipe his forehead with a handkerchief. Claire would likely be gone before he got there. He should have called. But he wanted to surprise her. He had it all mapped out in his head. He felt like a really foolish old man.

"Start prayin' for help," he told her.

"What?"

"I said pray for someone to come change this tire."

She cast him a doubtful expression, while he tried to get his breath. He was going to look terrible when he saw Claire. His shirt was smudged and about soaked with sweat.

Just then he looked past Corrine and saw a pickup truck approaching. He pointed, and Corrine turned, as he said, "I was prayin', what were you doin'?"

It was a white Dodge, and quickly he recognized it as belonging to Larkin Ford, the rancher who owned the land on either side of the gravel road.

Larkin was driving, and his son, Travis, leaned out the passenger window. "What's goin' on here, Mr. Winston? Have a flat tire?"

"No, son, we stopped and jabbed it a couple of times with a knife so we could sit out here in the sun until we got hot enough," said Winston.

Travis looked uncertain.

"Well, I guess we'll join you," Larkin said, as he got out of the truck.

Travis alighted, too, and went to telling Winston, "You know you aren't supposed to be drivin', Mr. Winston."

"I was teachin' Corrine."

Travis shook his head, grinning. "How old are you now, Corrine?"

"Old enough to see over the steerin' wheel, which is more than Teresa Betts."

Winston noted the flirty look she gave the handsome young man. She suddenly looked about twenty years old, standing there with her hand on her slim hip.

Larkin and Travis changed the tire together, and when they finished, Travis insisted on driving them back home. "You know I can't let you two go on drivin', Mr. Winston, now that I've seen you."

"Sure you can."

"No. I can't."

Winston was forced then to reveal that they were headed to the Goodnight Motel, and quite naturally Travis asked what he was wanting there.

"That's my business," said Winston, "and I can make it there just fine. Don't have far to go on the state highway, so don't you worry." He motioned for Corrine to get into the car.

But Travis insisted on knowing more, so it all had to come

out then about how Winston was taking the car to Claire Wilder. Winston made it sound like Claire was expecting him and would be driving him and Corrine home.

"Well, I'll just drive you over there, then," said the young man, much to Winston's annoyance.

Travis got in the driver's seat, Corrine slipped in beside him and Winston lowered himself after her, while Larkin followed in the pickup.

It was like a great cloud of witnesses, and unwelcome ones at that.

Chapter Thirteen

When Claire went into the motel office to get coffee and doughnuts, the owners, Frank in his Hawaiian shirt and his wife, Gertie, in a bright muumuu, greeted her with enthusiasm. It was quite a lot of enthusiasm, which Claire gradually realized was because they were extremely apologetic that her car had been stolen at their establishment.

"I'm real sorry about your car bein' stolen here," Frank Goode said a number of times, pulling a chair out for her and hurrying around to get coffee and two sweet rolls to place in front of her on the table. "I might should have been watchin' out for that fella. I've sure seen plenty of his type."

"You used to run with his type," Gertie put in, which caused Claire to look more carefully at Frank.

"Well—" he shook his head "—I didn't count on him bein' a professional. The sheriff said that boy worked as a mechanic in a sports-car garage and was suspected of stealin' those fancy cars before. Likely he had some sort of electronic gadget for gettin' through the car alarm. I am awfully sorry for not having spotted him for what he was. I just hate that your car was stolen here."

He went on in this vein until Claire said, "This coffee is delicious…this is just lovely…could I have one of those bananas, too?"

He brought her one of the bananas, and the act seemed to distract him from the subject of the theft.

His wife had disappeared, and she returned with a slice of country ham, apparently brought from her own kitchen in their apartment behind the office. Claire, a little amazed at the wonderful food, began eating. Then she noticed that the couple, sitting on the other side of the table, were gazing at her with anxious expressions that made her feel anxious, too.

"It's really all right about my car. You couldn't have known…and this is the best ham!"

She saw clear relief come over their faces. Perhaps they had worried she would sue them. So many people sued these days. She told them about the car having sufficient insurance and how she intended to buy a vehicle especially suited to herself, once she figured out what vehicle that was.

Gertie Goode, clearly more at ease, asked with avid curiosity where Claire was from and what had brought her to Valentine.

Claire replied that she was from Shreveport, was on vacation and had come to Valentine to see her father's hometown and grandparents' graves.

"Maybe you knew my father," she said with sudden hopefulness, running her eyes from one to the other. "John Tillman? He was the son of Grover and Martha Tillman."

Frank furrowed his brow, thinking. "No…no, I can't say that I did. Maybe, but I don't recall. And Gertie's from California."

Claire tried not to be disappointed.

Frank Goode was talking about how he had taken off for California in his youth and returned later with Gertie and his family to help his father with the motel. Now they were hoping to sell out and retire early to Florida. With some enthusiasm, Gertie brought out a brochure for a retirement community near Fort Walton Beach, where her sister already lived.

"I'm about ready to close this place and just leave it," Frank said with a large sigh, "but my father would roll over in his grave."

Gertie said, "He's dead, Frank. He can't roll over, and it wouldn't matter if he did, because we'd be all the way down in Florida."

"She's from California," Frank repeated to Claire with a dry grin.

Claire asked them about the advertisement of Patsy Cline having slept there and said, "My mother loved Patsy Cline."

Frank said that his parents had loved the country singer, too, and explained about having a possible Patsy Cline on the registration records. "We can't be sure it was her, but she did give a performance that night at the Cimarron Ballroom up in Tulsa, so it is possible. Back then, the Goodnight was a fine place for notables to stay," he said with shy pride as he retrieved a postcard of the motel and passed it to her. "That picture's from '79, but that's pretty much how the place looked in the beginning."

The postcard contained a detailed color drawing of the Goodnight Motel. Claire saw the place in all its glory, with the words *Sweet Dreams at the* in turquoise at the top of the Goodnight Motel sign that was in the forefront. The cabins were more sedately colored in white and black, the pool had both a diving board and a curved slide, and there were shade trees and picnic tables between the cabins.

Encouraged by Claire's questions, Frank leaned forward and explained that the motel had been one of the first of its kind during the motel boom of the mid-1950s. His parents had purchased it in the seventies. The motel had seen a number of periods of prosperity and decline, usually following the ups and downs of the oil business. He said that his father had early on attempted to keep the rooms as original as possible, and Gertie commented on Frank's mother's eclectic taste in furnishings, a comment that caused Claire, glancing quickly at the pink walls and flamingos, to grin.

"It was easier to have the *Sweet Dreams* taken off the sign when it was damaged in a tornado…what, Gertie? In '89?"

Gertie nodded. "That was the year that the cottonwood tree fell on cabin number four. I wanted to sell out then, but Frank wouldn't do it."

The pool was now covered, the chain-link fence around it rusting. Frank said the tile needed work and the pump had gone out last year, and in any case, it had not gotten enough use in recent years to warrant repairs. The original picnic tables had rotted away. Several years ago he had replaced them with two picnic tables from Wal-Mart, and they had both been stolen. The trees, cottonwoods, had all been cut down because of insurance requirements. The big tree at the end cabin was an elm and stayed, but he worried about blight getting the best of it.

As she listened, Claire looked out the window and ran her eyes down the row of cottages that stood like valiant old women beneath umpteen coats of peeling paint and roof patches, and then upward at the Goodnight Motel sign, showing its rust in the bright morning light.

"I'm more concerned about this place gettin' the best of us," Gertie said and pushed up from the table. "You've already had a heart attack, and I sure don't want to be left saddled with this place when you keel over."

Claire saw the worry on the woman's face, and the anger that came across Frank's. Thankfully, though, before she ended up in the middle of a marital fight, all of their attention was drawn outside to the arrival of a car and pickup truck.

"Well, I'll be dogged, that's Winston's car," said Frank, and Gertie put in, "That's Larkin in his new pickup. Huh. Wonder what's up."

Claire saw the deputy, Travis Ford, hopping out from the driver's seat of the car. For some reason, out of uniform and wearing jeans and a dark T-shirt, he looked older. He waved at her, and she gave a half wave in return. Then there was Winston, in a cowboy hat, getting out of the passenger side, followed by the girl who Claire had seen greet him on the front porch of his house. Travis went to take Winston's arm, but the elderly man shook him off.

The driver of the pickup truck was the man Claire recognized as Travis's father. He was staring at her through the windshield. She looked away.

Travis held the office door open for Winston, who was followed closely by the slim, dark girl. Winston, leaning heavily on his cane while trying his best to stand straight, came directly to Claire.

"And how are you, gal? I heard of the trouble." His eyes traveled up and down her, as if judging for injuries.

"I'm just fine, Winston." She hugged him and experienced a warmth welling in her heart at contact with this man who clearly adored her.

Then Travis was saying hello to her, and Gertie was offering everyone coffee and sweet rolls, and Frank was inviting them to make themselves comfortable.

To that, Travis said, "I'm headin' with Dad to work cattle. I just drove Mr. Winston and Corrine over here, because neither one of them is supposed to be drivin'. Mr. Winston lost his license, and Corrine hasn't yet gotten hers." He stood in a wide-legged fashion, with his arms crossed over his chest and eyeing Winston and Corrine like culprits.

Winston said, "I did not lose my license. I decided not to bother with it anymore."

Travis leaned around Winston and looked at Claire. "He said you would drive them home, Miz Wilder."

Claire, puzzled and taking note of Winston's tightening jawline, said, "Well, yes, I will—"

Winston broke in with, "I heard of your car being stolen and came to offer the use of my own."

"Oh. My. Well, thank you, Winston. That is so kind of you, but I…" Her first response was to decline the offer, which was her first response to any proposition sprung on her, as she rarely got into trouble saying no. But then, seeing his expression and having several notions pop into her mind at once, she said, "I appreciate the offer. I can then shop for some clothes…and I'd like to stop in to see Sherrilyn Earles at the hospital, too."

Quite suddenly she found that she wasn't stranded and lost at all. Suddenly she had a plan, at least for that one day. Her spirits rose.

"You are welcome to the use of my car for as long as you need it," said Winston in a gallant manner. "And Corrine and I will accompany you shoppin' and to the hospital. Corrine can direct you to the best places for women's clothes, and I will treat both of you ladies to lunch."

He introduced the girl, who had been standing slightly behind him but watching everything with her dark eyes. She was about thirteen or fourteen and on the edge of beautiful. Her smile was shy, and she didn't say anything, but she shook Claire's hand firmly.

Travis made his exit. "It was good seein' you again, Miss Wilder."

"Yes, you, too, Mr. Ford."

Their eyes met. His were the prettiest, smiling hazel eyes. He nodded at everyone and pushed out the glass door, sauntering with long-legged strides to the white pickup truck, sort of hopping into the passenger seat, where he cast her a wave that made her realize how she had been watching him.

Then she saw his father looking at her. She turned instantly, embarrassed at giving both men so much of her attention.

After her initial timidity at driving an unfamiliar vehicle—and a borrowed one, at that—Claire slowly relaxed and went smoothly along the road, green pastures and trees passing in a blur outside the windows. She liked the way she felt in the car. The hood was longer than that of her Mercedes, and it somehow made her feel fancy and even a little safer. She rather thought that if she hit something, there was a lot of hood to smash before she herself got smashed.

"Maybe I should get a car like this one," she said.

"It's a good car," said Winston proudly. "We might could work a deal," he added.

"The rear defrost is broken," Corrine said from the back seat.

Claire glanced at the girl in the rearview mirror.

"It's just a small thing," said Winston. "It can be fixed. I just haven't gotten around to it. We don't get much ice around here, anyway, and you don't, either, down there in Shreveport, do you?"

"No, not usually. We have had it…but I have a garage." Shreveport seemed strangely far away.

"It's ten years old and doesn't have cruise control," Corrine said. "You're probably used to that."

"Oh…well…"

"And a lot of the new vehicles today have dual temperature controls. This one doesn't have that. And you might really want a CD player. You can get compact disc players in most of the cars now, ones that hold multiple CDs, and the new cars get better gas mileage, too."

"Have you become a car salesman?" Winston tapped his cane on the floorboard.

"No…but we've been studyin' comparative shopping in economics class. And I will be gettin' a car to go to college. I'm lookin' into them. I'll probably be ready for a car that's three or four years old by the time I go to college. I don't imagine I'll be able to afford a new one." The girl spoke with an uncommonly adult and practical tone.

Claire, who had never bothered with an interest in vehicles but had left the matter to Andrew, listened to the girl talk about the particulars of gas mileage and cylinders and handling in a manner that compelled Claire to begin to study certain vehicles they passed in traffic and ask Corrine's opinions about them.

She was looking so hard at what Corrine called a cool SUV that she almost ran into a van in front of her.

"There's nothin' wrong with the brakes," Winston said with satisfaction when they got stopped.

The brightly lit mall was populated mostly by teenagers doing a lot of window-shopping and laughing and hanging on to each other. Those doing the buying were women of Claire's age, wives and mothers hurrying to get what they need. A group of older people did fast walking in tennis shoes, and the few really elderly people sat on the benches scattered near planters of greenery.

Winston sat on a bench, while Claire and Corrine shopped, returning to check on him in between stores. He had gotten annoyed at this and told them to just get their shopping done and quit worrying about him.

As Claire approached him this time, she saw he was holding on to his cane and had his right leg extended, as if it might ache. The bench was designed more for enduring traffic and the shenanigans of youth than for the comfort of elderly people. Malls in general were not particularly elderly-friendly. Neither was the world, she thought as she flopped herself down on the bench beside Winston.

"You haven't bought very much." He eyed her two shopping bags.

"These will do." She had ended up with several sets of underwear, a pair of walking shoes, a pair of pajamas from Victoria's Secret, and a pair of Liz Claiborne jeans, and a denim shirt and a silk shirt that looked like denim.

"I cannot replace the favorite accumulation of years in an hour and a half, and that's all the shoppin' I'm good for. I really dislike shoppin'," she said. "I probably couldn't even have gotten this much without Corrine's help. She's in the earring store."

"I've never met a woman who didn't like to shop," said Winston.

Claire had been thinking sadly of all of her favorite clothes, which were now probably dispersed among a myriad of assorted lowlife types. While considering the outrageous plan of calling one of her salesladies—Genevieve—and asking her to overnight some clothes, she noticed him regarding her with a mixture of curiosity and tender amusement.

"Winston, I wish you would quit lookin' at me like that." His looks made her feel irritated. How could she live up to them?

"Like what?"

"Like I'm beloved. You really don't know me at all. You certainly do not know me enough to love me."

She had thought he was simply being dramatic when he had told her he loved her. That he had wanted to impress her with his flamboyance. But he kept looking at her with such adoration that she began to think that he truly believed he was in love with her. The idea felt like an enormous burden on her shoulders.

Also, she wondered if she could have possibly made a

mistake in her judgment of his sound mind. After all, she really barely knew the man. Perhaps his stretching a story was more being on the verge of senility.

"It's wearing to have to live up to your adoration," she said, studying him with the new thought of the senility possibility. "I'm sure I'm going to disappoint you." She was certain it would disappoint him to know that she was wondering about his soundness of mind.

"I know a lot about you," he said with dignity. "I know where you're from and who your people were, and that you don't like to shop, and that you have trouble keepin' your eyes on the road when you're drivin'."

He grinned a wry grin. "And darlin', it isn't possible to disappoint a man of my age. How can you disappoint someone who enjoys nothin' more these days than lookin' at a beautiful woman?"

She studied his eyes.

"Do you think I'm a little off?" he asked, and she shifted her gaze away.

"No. But I think you may have flights of fantasy."

"I'm truthful, sweetheart, and unafraid. You are beautiful, and I like lookin' at you." He regarded her with sharp eyes. "Haven't men told you that you're beautiful?"

"On occasion. But there is one thing about beauty, and that is that it eventually fades. And then generally a man goes lookin' for someone younger and more beautiful. *You* are looking at a younger woman. A woman young enough to be your daughter. Why aren't you hankerin' after someone with beauty of your own age?

"My ex-husband certainly went looking for someone younger. Until a few days ago, he was set to marry a twenty-eight-year-old woman."

She felt the bitterness on her tongue, and saw a sharpness come into Winston's eyes. She felt naked.

After a moment he said, "I *would* look at someone my own age—if they didn't keep dyin' on me."

Her heart instantly went out to him, and she put her hand on his. "I guess we're a pretty picture," she said, pleased to bring a smile to his face.

Here came Corrine from the earring store, proudly sporting new dangling silver-tone fashion crosses from her earlobes. Both Claire and Winston examined the earrings with proper interest and appreciation. The girl glowed happily.

"Let's get Sherrilyn a pair of those," Claire said suddenly. "I think she had pierced ears. As a matter of fact, she had two in one, a stud and a hoop."

Leaving her bags with Winston, Claire and Corrine went off to the earring store, where they got Sherrilyn a card of earrings for people who had several holes in their lobes.

"My aunt Marilee won't let me have but one hole," Corrine said with a doleful expression.

"And I agree with her. One hole per lobe is all anyone needs, and more is bordering too closely on tacky. You might get to the age of forty and a position as Supreme Court Justice and find people suspicious of you because you have all these needless holes in your ears.

"But we can't help Sherrilyn about that now," she added. "I suppose we should be glad she doesn't have one in her nose." Although why it should matter to her where the girl had piercings, she didn't know.

From there, Corrine and Claire did a whirlwind of shopping for the unfortunate girl. With Corrine's teenage guidance, Claire chose things with abandon. Her credit card began to feel warm after all the handling; however, it was not at all taxing to shop for someone who couldn't put in an opinion.

She marveled that somehow she had come to be in a strange town, was now driving a strange car and shopping with people she had known for barely one day, one of them a man who said he loved her, and buying for a young woman she really didn't know at all, except mostly for the feel of the girl's wet and unconscious head lying in her lap.

While they were having lunch at a quiet little café, Claire was startled by a ringing from her purse. She pulled out her cell phone and was further surprised to see Andrew's number.

"Excuse me," she said to Winston and Corrine, who were gazing at her.

"I just wanted to check on you while I had a minute," Andrew said, and her heart swelled at the knowledge that he had called. That he had been thinking about her.

She told him that she was fine and feeling better about everything than she had the previous night. She kept her eyes focused on her water glass and was foolishly aware of Winston's avid attention. In fact, he made no pretense at not listening.

"Have you found out how far you are from an airport yet?" he asked.

"No, I haven't. I've been thinking that I might look at cars today."

"I thought you said you were goin' to fly home."

She was fairly certain she had not made a statement of that sort. "I think you mentioned that as a possibility. I'm still figurin' out what I want to do." She did not care for him pressing her at the same instant that she felt lacking for not being decisive about her plans.

He said, "Well, it's lookin' like I won't be able to get away from here to come up there to get you."

She told him that would be fine, that he didn't have to worry about it. She could take a bus or rent a car, and also that she was rather thinking she might continue on her vacation.

"Where are you gonna go?" Andrew asked.

"Oh, I want to look around here some more, and maybe I might head out west afterward. Maybe to see Roswell, New Mexico, and the Grand Canyon." She wasn't certain where that idea had come from. Possibly from seeing mention of Roswell on a morning television news program.

Andrew said, "You may have trouble rentin' a car to go out of state. Not all rental offices have cars for out of state."

Whenever Andrew didn't want her to do something, he would bring up all manner of discouragements. She responded by saying coolly, "I'll see. I have to go now. I'm havin' lunch. I'll call you when I know something more."

When she clicked off, Winston said, "Who was that?"

The irritation she felt for Andrew transferred to Winston. "Didn't anyone ever instruct you in matters of privacy?"

"Yes, but that's only for strangers you don't know," he said, "not for people who love you."

He said that right in front of Corrine. There was no telling what the girl's family would think of that.

Sherrilyn Earles had been moved to the psychiatric section of the hospital. They found the desk in front of the double doors manned by a tall, stout nurse who had no smiling ability and who took Claire's name, put in a call to someone, then told Claire without looking up, "She doesn't want to see you."

Claire gazed at the part in the woman's head for several seconds, then turned away to explain to Winston and Corrine.

"Can't you just give her the stuff?" Corrine asked.

Claire realized she was holding the two shopping bags. She returned to the big woman, who was now on the telephone. The woman held up her finger, and Claire waited. She peered through the glass doors, wondering which room was Sherrilyn's and having the fantasy of slipping past the woman and down the hall, imagining finding Sherrilyn and throwing the bags at her. In fact, she was quite annoyed with Sherrilyn for not agreeing to see her.

"Yes?" The woman had hung up the phone.

"Could you please give Sherrilyn Earles these things?"

The woman, frowning, took the bags and, looking through them, said, "Yeah. I'll give them to her."

As they walked away, Winston said, "I think it's all a lot of to-do for a girl who tried to use a little sink to kill herself. You have to know she didn't mean it. If they locked up everyone who threw a hissy fit, your aunt Marilee and your mama might be thrown in here," he said to Corrine, who laughed and hugged him.

Winston's home was a grand Victorian house, with a wonderful porch and a tall flagpole in the yard, from which waved both the Confederate and United States flags. Winston raised them each morning in a ceremony that often drew an audience.

"It's become an institution," said Corrine in her teaching manner.

It was explained to Claire that Winston had a son and two daughters and four grandchildren. Corrine was not one of these, as Claire had assumed, but in fact was no relation at all. She was a member of the Holloway family, who lived with Winston and clearly loved him as their own.

It seemed that everyone in the house revolved around Marilee Holloway, a woman with emotions that flickered lightning fast over her features. She continually carried around her new two-month-old baby girl, kissing her and caressing her, when she wasn't caressing her son, Willie Lee, or her niece, Corrine, or her husband, Tate. She was most definitely an affectionate woman. She even took Claire's hand straight away, leading her to the dining table and hollering to Tate to bring them some cold tea.

"You're in luck. Tate's makin' dinner this evenin'." Then the woman proceeded to boldly query Claire about her life, as if intent on making certain that Winston's affections, and possibly his wallet and physical state, were in safe hands.

Tate Holloway was a handsome man in his fifties. The children loved him, and so did his wife, plainly and completely, as he did them. He liked to tell a story, and he and Winston seemed to have a rivalry about telling stories to make everyone laugh.

The connectedness between all of these people was so strong as if to be humming in the air. Claire was both fascinated and overcome. She had to quit watching them, it hurt so badly in the empty place inside of herself.

In fact, she got so worn-out by having to manage strange feelings of sadness and want in the face of the happy and overflowing family that she was relieved when she could decently take her leave.

"Thank you for the evening…the wonderful meal. It's been lovely."

"No need to rush off."

"Oh, Winston, she's tired after such a day. Tate, fix her up some of those brownies to take with her."

"You keep the car as long as you need it, gal. Maybe tomorrow you'll want to go to the newspaper and check out the obituary archives for information about your folks. Miss Charlotte there can give you a hand, right, Tate?"

"You bet."

"Maybe."

At the car, she turned and waved at Winston, who watched her from the porch. She felt funny driving away in his car.

She drove slowly through the evening streets, looking this way and that, seeing people in their yards, or on the sidewalk, or through lit windows. Everywhere were couples and families.

When she passed Blaine's Drugstore and saw the lights through the window, she almost stopped, thinking of the possibility of a delicious strawberry milkshake and a friendly chat with Vella.

She felt much too vulnerable to present herself to another soul, though, and hitting the accelerator with a little more force than she'd intended, she sped the distance to the motel, where the marquee still proclaimed that Patsy Cline had slept there, and the yellow neon Goodnight Motel sign glowed like a welcoming beacon. And where tonight there were a number of guests, indicated by cars parked out front of the string of cabins. She evaluated each vehicle, thinking about what sort of car she wanted.

Then she was heading for her room in the first cabin, with the turquoise door and the flickering fluorescent light in the eaves. The familiar musty scent of the motel room welcomed her. She experienced a spark of happiness at having arrived at the room once again, but this was quickly followed by a letdown at being alone.

The room was freezing, so she shut off the air conditioner. The sudden silence was deafening. Quickly she turned on the lamps on either side of the bed, switched on the television, and then went into the bathroom to turn on those lights, too.

She retrieved her cell phone from her purse and checked to see if there had been calls she hadn't heard. None. Not even from the insurance company.

Why should Andrew call her again, considering her attitude of earlier that day?

She thought of calling him. *"I'm staying in a place just like the one where we stayed on our wedding night. Remember that, Andrew? Remember how you just loved the bed massager? This place has one, too."* Maybe that would bring him on the run.

"Be reasonable, Claire. I can't just up and leave. People want their buildings built."

It was a very unreasonable idea. She tossed the cell phone to the bed.

There came the sound of tires in the gravel lot. She looked through the window and saw a car pulling up in front of her room.

It was a Valentine police car, Travis Ford driving.

She opened the door and stepped outside, and experienced an interest that startled her as Travis sauntered forward all broad-shouldered and lean-hipped.

She told herself to get her head on straight. He had to be at least fifteen years her junior, for heaven's sake. Although he was a fine specimen of a man, and she a woman born.

He said he was just passing through and saw Winston's car. He inquired about how it ran, and she told him it did fine, that it had gotten them everywhere they wanted to go, to the shopping mall and restaurant and the hospital to see Sherri-lyn Earles. He said good to this and commented that Winston hadn't driven it for some time and likely it could have sticky valves or some such that Claire really didn't understand.

The entire time they conversed they looked each other over in a manner neither had dared to do while in the company of others.

"The sheriff found the girl's father down in Houston," he told her. "But he isn't inclined to help her."

"What will happen to her?" For a moment Claire forgot herself and stepped closer, coming to the edge of the stoop.

"The sheriff is callin' around, talking to state agencies. He'll find her a place."

"Well...that's good. I'm glad there will be help for her."

"We're here to serve the public." He eyed her. "Is there anything you need? Any way the sheriff's office might be of help?"

"I might be contacting you tomorrow, after I talk to my insurance company. They may need something more."

"Well, you don't hesitate to call." With the car door open, he paused and looked at her. "So you're stayin' around another day?"

"I think a couple of days. I've got to contact the insurance company again and decide whether to rent or buy a car. And I'm thinking, if I have time, to do a little research on my family." She felt a little embarrassed at her sense of inertia.

"Well, then…" He sort of looked at her with one eye. "Can I take you to lunch tomorrow?"

The question jarred her. "I don't know. I don't know exactly what I'll be doin' when tomorrow."

"Main Street Café, Blaine's soda fountain, or the drive-in Burger Barn. Your choice." He spoke in a coaxing manner.

"What about the pizza place?" She was flirting with him— *stop that!*

"Oh, ever'where has pizza. Not ever'where has the other three places. You can even get peanut butter and jelly at Blaine's."

"Okay." She was being daring. "I'll meet you at the drugstore. They have real ice-cream milkshakes."

"You like those, do you?" His smile was a lazy sort that could curl toes. Then, "Blaine's soda fountain at noon. See ya."

She watched him drive away, then went back into her room and shut the door with her foot.

It was just lunch. She wasn't having a wild affair.

From: Vella Blaine
To: <haltg@mailectric.com>
Sent: May 31, 1997, 5:15 a.m.
Subject: Family Ties

Dear Harold,

Goodness gracious, you had quite a stressful time yesterday. I'm so glad you found Estelle. You must have been scared to death. But it will serve no purpose to blame yourself, sugar, you are doing your level best by her. You are. You must remember that you are only human. Falling asleep of an afternoon is something very human to do, especially when you are run ragged caretaking a loved one.

And it all turned out all right. That is the important thing. You found her, and she was just fine. She did not even have to suffer the embarrassment of being buck naked walking down the street, because she didn't know that she was. She was in a happy place in her mind, and if those who saw her were offended, well, that is their problem.

I heard this on Oprah quite some time ago: What other people think of me is none of my business.

I have certainly had to adopt that attitude or go insane. At the very beginning of my marriage, my family, very strong Baptists, thought I never should have married a Blaine, because they were not churchgoers of any type. Today many people, including my aunt Doreen, who never wanted me to marry

Perry, think I should wait on him night and day, and other people think I should put him in a home, and others think that nothing I do is right. If I listened to it all, I would be put under.

Can you get someone to help you take care of Estelle? I know you said that she gets agitated with anyone other than you, but perhaps she would get used to someone in time. You haven't said—do you have children, or perhaps sisters or nieces who could help?

I have help of nurses, as I have said, and I do have two daughters that I could turn to in a pinch, though, truthfully I suppose that is an iffy proposition.

My daughter Belinda, who I have mentioned, has turned out to be a great help to me in the store. No one would have imagined this just a couple of years ago, I tell you. I'm proud of her, especially considering how far she has come in the gumption department. But the truth is that she only helps with her father when she can't get out of it.

My other daughter, Margaret, is a travel agent out in Atlanta. She has been home only once in the past five years. Margaret and I do not get on well. Perry never did get on with either of the girls. He was mostly afraid of them. Frankly, I often think Perry was afraid of me.

Still, the four of us are family, and that is an unbreakable tie in my opinion. I will watch over Perry with my last dying breath, and if one of my girls needed me, I'd be there in an instant. I believe that they would help me, too, somehow.

You know that young girl who tried to drown herself in the bathroom sink at the sheriff's office? I heard today that her one and only father says he doesn't want anything to do with her. He said that to the sheriff. He said, "She ain't my responsibility. I'm shuck of her."

I really cannot imagine it, and her pregnant with his grandchild. His own blood! Probably, with a father like that, the girl is better off up here at a women's shelter. That's what the sheriff is trying to arrange. She can't just be turned out on the street.

Well, you remember what I said about you being human. It is false pride to think you can do things above normal human capacity. You are doing wonderful by Estelle. She is lucky to have you standing by her, but it would serve no purpose for you to kill yourself doing it. She could end up in bad shape if you get incapacitated, you know.

It probably would be good to find some way of making it so that Estelle can't get out of her clothes the next time she escapes from the house. I cannot see as to how that could be accomplished, though. You need to be able to get her clothes off of her. Maybe alarms on the doors would give you more control, but I imagine you already thought of that, being a retired policeman.

You might want to put some aloe vera extract on Estelle's sunburn.

Write when you can.

Your friend in caretaking,

Vella, in Valentine.

She sat there a minute, looking at what she had written about thinking Perry might have been afraid of her. What did that say about her? Surely it wasn't true.

But it *was* true. Perry, big as he had once been, had sometimes skulked around and rarely disagreed with her. It had gotten on her nerves.

The truth was that she had been such an impatient person for most of her life.

Quickly, before she could read anything else she'd written, she clicked on the send button. Then she carried coffee fixed heavily with cream and sugar upstairs to Perry, who was awake. She sat and helped him drink it, hoping she was making up for all the years that she had been impatient with him.

Chapter Fourteen

The morning sun glimmered on the dark shingles of the spreading house, causing Larkin Ford to squint as he repaired the roof. The scent of sweet honeysuckle wafted faintly, hammer strikes echoed in the stillness, and every once in a while there came an impatient cry from the horse in the corral.

The window above him came flying up. "Good God, Dad, it's barely eight o'clock in the mornin'."

His answer, without a pause in the swing of the hammer, was, "It's gonna hit ninety-five today. I don't want to be up here doin' this four hours from now."

With one last strike at the nail, he looked up over the porch roof to see Travis, all prime male bleary-eyed and bare-chested, poked out the second-story window. Sometimes he was a little startled to see that his son had become a full-grown man, and this was one of those times.

He said with a little irritation, "Are you gonna let that spoiled mare of yours get all colicky because she didn't get that sweet grain at the hour she's used to?"

At that opportune moment, the mare let out a shrill whinny.

"Sally? Is she colickin'?" His son leaned farther out the window, straining to see around to the corral, an action that caused him to lose balance and pitch forward. Only some hasty gripping kept him from falling clean out onto the roof. He looked like a boy in his scrambling, and Larkin experienced a little relief.

He said, "I didn't say that. I just asked if you'd *let* her get all colicky at missin' her normal breakfast time."

At first Larkin was amused at his little teasing, but then he had the thought: Did his son think he would let the horse colic and not do anything for her?

He started to ask his son just that, but Travis, who was once more solidly back inside the window, was already going on with, "Damn it, Dad, would it kill you to throw her some hay…and to put off all the hammerin' for one hour? For once, when livin' in this house, I'd like to sleep past eight o'clock and not be woken up by you hammerin' or sawin' or startin' a tractor. Just one damn mornin'."

"Where's the dang window screen?" His son seemed to just then realize that he was hanging out the window.

"Got 'em down earlier. The hail tore 'em up pretty bad last go-round," said Larkin, who had been up since his usual four o'clock and started on chores since five-thirty, because he couldn't be still another minute.

He and Travis had a difficult time in the house, because he was an early bird and Travis a night owl, who often pulled night duty with the sheriff's office. Even on free nights, though, he often didn't get into bed until two or three in the morning. He would sit up for hours reading great thick books, usually biographies, or watching movies on television.

Muttering, his son disappeared, and Larkin hollered at him to close the window.

Moving the ladder, he removed more damaged shingles, then went down the ladder and back up again with new shingles and nails, carefully mending the roof of the house where he had grown up, as had his father before him.

From the high vantage point, he looked off to the west, over the nearest slowly pumping oil rocker and the land that rolled away to a line of trees marking a creek bed. He could feel the promise of storms in the hot and heavy air.

Larkin carried a cup of coffee to the doorway of the laundry room, where Travis was pawing through a basket of clean clothes. Doncia, who came weekdays, did the laundry but left it for the men to put away.

"What's your plan for today?" Larkin asked, sipping the hot coffee, which he drank even on the hottest days.

"Gettin' my oil changed…few other things."

"I'll help you change your oil quick and save you thirty bucks. Then you can help me with re-screenin' those window screens. That fiberglass screening just hasn't held up. I'm gonna replace it with aluminum."

"Sorry…can't. Got a lunch date."

It was Saturday. Travis often had a date on the weekend, although usually at night.

Travis found socks and looked up, saying, "And Larry Joe's runnin' a pickup special at the station. Twenty-one-ninety-five for oil and a filter."

"Must be cheap oil."

"Pennzoil," Travis said with high satisfaction as he loped back up the stairs.

Larkin felt out of touch with the times. Good oil change that cheap. Never heard of it.

His day stretched before him, long and hot and alone. He thought of Travis enjoying himself with a woman at lunch and felt envy, a feeling that he didn't like. He wondered what he himself would have for lunch. The idea of going in alone to the Burger Barn or café made him feel pitiful.

Quite suddenly he realized he was leaning back against the sink with a cup of coffee in his hand in the same manner that he had seen his own father stand a million times. The observation upset him so badly that he jumped away from the sink, sloshing the coffee right out of the cup.

From his shop, he looked through the open double doors and watched Travis, all dressed for town even to his best straw hat, cross to the barn and come out with a can of grain and flake of alfalfa that he carried to the gray mare, who was whinnying from the big corral.

The mare was eighteen and so fat she waddled. She was Travis's first very own horse from start to finish. He had been the first to touch her when she had been foaled, when he was ten years old. He broke her as a two-year-old and trained her for cutting competition, where he won enough to buy his first truck and fill a trophy case. He had sold five foals out of the mare for good money. Since returning home from the Navy, he spoiled her rotten.

A shadow appeared at the shop door. Larkin refused to look up from where he was working on a window screen, pretending to remain unaware of his son's presence. He didn't know why he did that, only that he felt defensive somehow. And he felt foolish because he had to wear his reading glasses. They made him feel old.

"If you'll wait until this evenin'," Travis said in an even voice, "I'll help you with those when I come home."

"That's okay…I'd just as soon get them done." *Don't put yourself out for me.*

The shadow lingered. "You know, Dad, you don't have to work yourself to death. Fayrene down at the café is always askin' about you…and so is Mona at the bank. It wouldn't kill you to take off and see a woman and have some fun for a Saturday. It *is* the weekend."

"Thank you for that notification." He would have died before looking up.

Travis, seeing the unrelenting set of his father's neck and shoulders, felt the frightening urge to punch him.

He said, "Well, you can work yourself to death, but that doesn't mean I'm gonna do it."

He turned and stalked away to his pickup. He might have heard his father call after him, but he wasn't certain, and in any case, he didn't want to reply. They would just get into another one of their fights.

Jumping into his truck, he roared the engine to life and head off down the driveway. He needed to move out, get his own place.

But what would happen to his father, if he left?

Working on the screens, Larkin kept hearing his son's suggestion: *Fayrene or Mona?* He wondered at his son's opinion of him.

Travis repeatedly treated him like he was so old, but he was only forty-six. He had been a wet-faced eighteen, shaving only on weekends, when he had gotten Karin pregnant, and barely nineteen when Travis had been born. Fayrene Gardner was at the very least ten years older than him, had been around the block more than twice, and ogled every male in long pants who came into the café. Granted, she was still a fine figure of a woman and smart in business, and Larkin thought a lot of her, too. That did not mean he wanted to spend time with her discussing the love lives of the rich and famous who were written up in the *National Enquirer,* which was her main staple of reading material.

And Mona Foust? Good God, and that was a prayer for his son's mental powers. The woman, bless her heart, had hair of a volume that probably wouldn't fit into his pickup truck, and was so ugly she should stay home anyway.

His son certainly didn't know as much as he thought he knew, if those two women were the only ones he could be suggesting for Larkin to consider. The truth of it was that plenty of available women, and a number of those who shouldn't be so available, flirted with him whenever he was out and about. It was two women to every man in this county. That had been written up in the *Valentine Voice.* He could tell his smarty-pants son a thing or two. Maybe he, Larkin, wouldn't have an idea of what to do with a woman once he got her, but by heaven, his son didn't have every single woman in their part of the state cornered.

He got wrought up enough over it all to cause him to mismeasure the fabric for two of the window screens and cut them half size.

"Aw, hell." He threw his cutting shears clear out the shop opening, then jumped up and down on the third window screen he had fixed, which looked far less taut than he wished.

Coming to a sudden halt in the middle of his temper fit, he saw his actions with amazement and dismay. He looked around to see the dog, Scooter, staring at him.

He straightened his shoulders, immensely relieved that Travis had not witnessed his meltdown.

With sudden decisiveness, he grabbed up the window screens, tossed them into the bed of his pickup truck and headed for R & D Glass and Screen up in Lawton. He wasn't so old and stuck in his ways that he couldn't start paying to have things done, no sir.

Heading out on the highway, Larkin thought that he might splurge and pay to have his truck washed and waxed, too.

Then, leaning over and checking himself in the rearview mirror, he swept a hand over his hair and thought boldly that he would go to the barbershop while he was up there and get a trim from Wynona Mathews, and maybe he would ask her to lunch. He often thought to do that, but had not thus far. Maybe he would today. He would at least return her flirting.

Chapter Fifteen

"**P**erhaps you thought that attempting to kill yourself would bring your father to show his love," the psychiatrist said.

"I guess," replied Sherrilyn, who really thought she had done it because she wanted to be dead.

Now that the psychiatrist had said it, though, she thought maybe she had been holding out a smidgen of hope about her father still loving her, despite all the evidence to the contrary. Now that smidgen was fully wiped out. That her father would not help in any way was about the biggest disappointment thus far in her whole disappointing life.

Mostly she was embarrassed at being so stupid. The guy in the ambulance had told her that someone could not drown themselves in a sink like that. Sherrilyn wasn't certain that was true. She had always heard that a person could drown in a teaspoon of water. She knew a person could choke to death on a bit of food, so she didn't see how it couldn't be possible to suck up water in a sink and drown.

During her second session with the psychiatrist, she got

up her nerve and asked him about it. "I always heard that a person could drown in a teaspoon of water. Is that true?"

He cast her a speculative look and said, "Do you believe it?"

She was the one who had asked him. "I heard it somewhere."

"Where do you think you heard it?"

"Well, I don't know. I just heard it." Man, he was annoying.

But he did cause her to wonder where she had heard it. The doctor was making a big deal about it, so she wondered if where she heard it was important. "Maybe my mother told me." She had heard it that long ago, so maybe it *had* been her mother.

"What else did your mother tell you?" he asked.

"About what?"

"About anything."

"You want me to tell you everything she told me? I forgot a whole lot. She's been dead just about ten years." She had already told him this and wondered if he listened very well.

"Do you remember your mother?"

"Yes."

"What do you remember about her?"

Sherrilyn thought. "She made great chocolate chip cookies...and she walked me to and from school. And I never had a baby-sitter. And I didn't have to go to kindergarten, because I didn't want to. Mama taught me lots of things at home." Those were wonderful memories. "She never spanked me."

He gazed at her when she stopped. She waited.

"What are some things that come to your mind that your mother told you?"

She looked at him.

"Did she tell you that she loved you?"

"Yes, she did. She told me that about a dozen times a day. My mother was a wonderful mother." She could claim that treasure, at least, and she wasn't going to let the psychiatrist run it down, either.

"Okay. What were some other things that she told you?"

She let her gaze roam around the room, at the framed official-looking papers on the wall, the books, his coffee mug that read, *I hate deadlines.* "Oh, stuff like to change my underwear in case I got in an accident on the way to school. Don't use someone else's hairbrush, I might get bugs. Don't read in the dark, it'll ruin my eyes. Don't go outside with a wet head, I'll catch cold. And never talk to strangers." She figured those were things that all mothers told their children.

He asked her if she believed all the teachings, and she said they sounded pretty practical, especially that advice about not using someone else's hairbrush. "I caught lice when I was in middle school from puttin' on another kid's hat. If you can get 'em from a hat, you can get 'em from a brush."

"The advice generally sounds worrying. Didn't your mother tell you some happy, funny things?"

Sherrilyn gave that thought and was stumped to not be able to think up anything of an especially happy nature, and she never did find out from the psychiatrist if it was possible to drown in a teaspoon of water. But after she went back to her room, she had vague memories of her mother.

Her mother had truly been a good mother and very careful about her. Her mother had lost a child before Sherrilyn had been born, and somehow Sherrilyn knew that it was her duty to be careful and not let anything happen to herself. Her mother used to hug her tight and say, "I'd just die if anythin' happened to you, sweetheart."

No one had called her sweetheart in such a way since her mother had died.

Until Sherrilyn was eight years old, her mother had watched over her and been there for her all the time. Her mother had been tender and constant, and Sherrilyn had a most wonderful life, until the day her mother had died from a brain hemorrhage while she had been making Sherrilyn a mayonnaise and tomato sandwich. They said her mother had been born with a defect in her brain, but no one had known, until she fell on the kitchen floor at Sherrilyn's feet, scaring Sherrilyn almost into hysterics.

Sherrilyn had been scared ever since, and now, thinking about it, she felt she had always been a little scared, like maybe she had known all along that her mother worried and that worry could kill her. That her mother mostly worried about Sherrilyn made Sherrilyn feel responsible for at least contributing to her mother's death.

She had very little memory of her father before her mother's death, but she sure did remember him after, because he got mean and nasty, at least to Sherrilyn. He had married a woman with two children. The woman disliked Sherrilyn and said that she caused trouble in the house. Sherrilyn had not been able to please the woman any more than she had her father, and when she was sixteen, she had been kicked out of the house. Sherrilyn had been doing her best not to cause trouble ever since, although she felt she so often failed at the endeavor.

It was because she didn't want to cause trouble at that very minute that she didn't scream at her roommate to quit snoring. Lying there in the dim hospital room, she wondered how many patients in the psychiatric ward went totally out of control because of snoring roommates.

"We can get you into Lilac House."

The social worker was a tall, big-boned black woman, with crisp short hair, perfect makeup and dangling earrings that only a big woman could wear.

Sherrilyn, who was shy of five feet four inches, and even at five months pregnant didn't weigh over one hundred and ten pounds, was a little afraid of large people, especially well-dressed and commanding ones. She almost huddled in the hospital bed, trying to hold on to herself while the woman mapped out her future.

"There are already ten women there, but they can make room for you."

Again she was an unwanted intruder. A trouble for someone.

"They'll provide room and board throughout your pregnancy. No smoking, no alcohol and no drugs." A hard look.

Sherrilyn wondered what there was about her that they would think she was the sort to do drugs. "Like, where am I gonna get money for drugs?"

The woman's expression didn't change. "And there won't be any men, either. You'll have to share a room with two other young women, but you'll have your own bed and a dresser for your clothes. You'll be assigned work around the house, and you'll be required to attend classes that will help you to get a job after the baby is born."

The woman paused and looked at Sherrilyn for a comment, but there didn't seem to be anything for Sherrilyn to say. She didn't have any choice. She knew right that minute that if she had not been pregnant, she would have been thrown out on the street to make her way the best she could.

"I've brought you information for putting the baby up for adoption," the woman said.

The woman held out several papers. Sherrilyn stared at them, and when she made no move to take them, the woman laid the papers on the bedside table.

"Look it over, Sherrilyn. My card is clipped on. You can call me anytime, and I'll be happy to answer any questions that you have. There are a lot of couples out there who can give your baby a good, solid home. A home that you haven't had," she added in a soft tone, touching Sherrilyn's leg.

"I'll be in touch with your doctor and be here when

you're released. Right now it's looking like maybe Tuesday. You're doin' good, honey. Keep eating."

When she was alone, Sherrilyn took the information about adoption, tore it in half and threw it in the trash.

Just when Sherrilyn broke down and decided to see what was in the bags the Mercedes woman—that was how she thought of the woman whose car Denny had stolen—had sent her, the woman showed up again. It was like some psychic occurrence.

She had dumped the bags on the bed and was looking at each thing that came out. There were two sleep shirts. She could sure use those. She had only had two nightgowns to her name, and they were dirty and ragged, forcing her to wear the hospital gowns. They made her feel sick.

There was a beautiful pink bathrobe. She held it to her cheek, it was that soft.

And dresses. A green one that was lame. She hated green. Everyone thought she should like it because of her hair color, but she didn't. The blue flowered one was okay. Sherrilyn hardly ever wore a dress. She had a couple of skirts but had started growing out of them. Right that moment she was wearing a large Houston Astros T-shirt over her jeans, which she couldn't zip up all the way.

There was a package of earrings. They were pretty cool.

And there was a *Seventeen* magazine. Sherrilyn liked to look through it and see the clothes and styles and hope that someday she might have just a few nice pieces, but the magazine itself was pretty expensive, so she didn't often get one.

There were two teenage novels. Sherrilyn thought they would be lame. Way too young for her, and besides, she didn't like reading all that much. She had been put in a remedial reading class at school. She had tried to keep going in school after she had left home, but she just couldn't work and go to school, too, so she had dropped out. She had been failing most every subject, except home economics, in which she excelled, because she had started at such a young age to take care of the house for her father.

She wondered why the Mercedes woman had given her all this stuff. There sure had to be some catch. Maybe the woman was some religious do-gooder.

Maybe she wanted Sherrilyn's baby.

This thought came as she held the flowered dress up in front of her body and did her best to see her image in the mirror above the sink.

At that particular moment, a nurse came poking her head into the room. "That's cute," she said. It was the young perky nurse, who was always smiling.

"I guess."

"Claire Wilder is here to see you. Wouldn't it be nice to have a visitor?"

Sherrilyn opened her mouth to say no but ended up saying, "Okay." She just couldn't tell this particular nurse, who had been friendly as all get out, that she refused to see the woman who had given her all the gifts.

The nurse looked really pleased and said she would show Ms. Wilder into the visiting lounge.

Sherrilyn stuffed everything back into the shopping bags and then looked in the mirror and down at herself, at the faded T-shirt and ratty jeans. Then her gaze moved to the shopping bags.

She had to give back the stuff. She was embarrassed to death to have the woman whose car her boyfriend had stolen buying her things, and besides, she didn't want to get mixed up with some religious do-gooder, or some woman who wanted to take her baby.

She felt stupid carrying the bags down to the visiting

lounge. She got mad at the woman for buying the things and making her feel stupid.

There were a number of people visiting in the room. Sherrilyn scanned the room, wanting to locate the woman as fast as possible and hoping nobody else noticed her there with the shopping bags.

The woman was standing in front of the couch. "Hello." She smiled and held out her hand, and then her gaze fell to the shopping bags that Sherrilyn held on to.

"Hi."

"I guess you know I'm Claire Wilder."

"Yeah…I know."

The woman was not but an inch taller than Sherrilyn, but she was a lot more curvy. She looked like one of the sophisticated women who sometimes cruised through the Krispy Kreme. They would come through the drive-through in their Caddies and Mercedes and BMWs, with their stylish hair, careful makeup and bright jewelry.

The next instant the woman surprised Sherrilyn by holding out a stuffed bear. "It was supposed to be in your things the other day but accidentally got left behind."

Sherrilyn didn't take the bear. Instead she dropped the shopping bags in front of the woman. "Thank you for all this stuff, but I really don't need you buyin' it. Here it is. Take it back." Oh, Lord, she sounded stupid.

"Why?" the woman asked.

"You just don't have to buy for me, that's all."

"I know I don't have to. I wanted to."

Then the woman sat down and plopped the bear in the top of one of the shopping bags. "If you do try on the clothes and find they don't fit, or you don't like any of them, you can return them. I left all the tags on them. They're from JCPenney, right over at the mall. You could take them back and maybe buy underwear. I didn't know your size, so I didn't attempt any of that. Or you can get the money, if nothin' else."

The woman wasn't taking the things back. And Sherrilyn thought about the money.

Slowly she sat, too. Almost before she had realized, she picked up the stuffed bear. It was dressed in a fancy hat and sweater.

"Thanks," she muttered, keeping her eyes on the bear. She could have shoved all the stuff back at the woman, but she really liked the stuffed bear. She had never forgotten the one she'd had as a little kid, one from the time of her mother. She had lost it out of her backpack when she had been sleeping in a park after her father had kicked her out. She had the really stupid urge to tell this to the woman. She kept her mouth firmly closed to keep from blurting out the story.

"So how are you doin'?" Claire Wilder asked.

"Okay." *Don't say anything about bears.*

They sat there, the both of them. The woman was staring at her, and Sherrilyn was staring at the bear and wishing she could think of something smart to say. She almost never knew what to say. She would listen and watch people and sometimes hear what she should say in a given situation, but this was a situation that she had never heard covered.

And then, "I'm real sorry about your car bein' stolen." There. She had gotten that said, and the urge to tell about losing her childhood teddy bear had passed.

"Thank you, sweetheart, but it certainly wasn't your fault. You weren't the one to steal it. And what could you have done about it?"

Sherrilyn watched the woman as she spoke, watched her tilt her head to the side and shrug, and the way her mouth seemed all full and soft.

"I don't know...nothin', I guess," replied Sherrilyn, who had been certain that somehow Denny getting away with the car had been her fault. Only suddenly, she realized that there had been nothing at all that she could have done about it. Probably she was lucky to have been in the bed and asleep. He would have been really mad if she had tried to stop him.

"I'm comin' out ahead, too," the woman said. "I'm going to get a brand-new car with the insurance money. And I'd say you're comin' out ahead, as well—you're rid of that jerk. You can do a lot better without him."

The statement crawled all over Sherrilyn. "Yeah, I'm doin' a lot better. I'm stuck in here in a loony bin, and when I get out, I get to go to a women's shelter, where they'll hound me about givin' up my baby until they find a way to get her."

She surprised herself by saying all that. She felt as if she wanted to smack the woman with the stuffed bear, and at the same time she realized the woman hadn't really said anything to deserve an attack. She felt even worse. She just couldn't seem to do anything right.

The woman gazed at her, and the sympathy in the woman's eyes made Sherrilyn want to die on the spot.

"What the hell would you know about any of it?" she said. "You don't know anything about me or my life. And I'm tellin' you right now—you can't be buyin' my baby with this stuff."

Out of the corner of her eye, she saw a couple of heads turn her way. Her face got all hot, and she considered getting up and walking out, but she didn't want to draw further attention to herself.

Claire Wilder said, "Well, you're right there. I don't know about your life. I can't, because I'm not you. But I sure know about being all by myself and not knowin' where I'm goin'."

Sherrilyn, shame falling all over her, kept her eyes on the stuffed bear. "I didn't mean that you could buy the baby with the clothes. I just meant that...well, that maybe you were one of those women who were desperate to get a baby."

Her anger was fading, and now she just felt stupid. That was the way her anger generally went. She would hold on to it, keep stuffing it back, until it blew up, and then she would feel all ashamed of blowing up and know she sounded stupid.

"Lots of babies are stolen every year. One time I saw on the news about a baby who got stolen right out of a shopping cart by a woman who wanted a baby…and there was a report on *60 Minutes* about how women went around pressuring pregnant women to give their babies up for adoption."

"You're right. There are situations like that, and you're smart to think of it."

Sherrilyn wondered if the woman was humoring her.

"And you're right about me and why I bought this stuff," the woman said. "I get all sappy about pregnant women. I lost two babies, and I can't ever have children of my own, just like those crazy women who steal babies. Because of that, I know how precious being pregnant is.

"But I am *not* tryin' to buy your baby. I just bought you this stuff because I wanted to do it, that's all."

Sherrilyn studied the woman, who seemed sincere, but who also seemed to pity her, and that was embarrassing.

"They can't take your baby, Sherrilyn," the woman said. "They can't make you do anything that you don't want to do."

"Oh, yeah, right. I'm here, aren't I? I didn't even want to leave Houston, but somehow I ended up doin' it. I end up doin' just about ever'thing that I don't want to do."

"Everything?"

"Well, okay so *most* ever'thing," she stated. "Except for gettin' an abortion. Denny wanted me to do that, and I wouldn't." She was really proud of that. "And I'm not givin' up my baby."

Chapter Sixteen

Shreveport, the married years

"*A boy for you, and a girl for me,*" Claire would sing to Andrew when she had first gotten pregnant. It was all so long ago and far away, and yet, sometimes, seemed like just yesterday.

She had gotten pregnant within two months of their marriage. This should not have been a great surprise. They had been like rabbits jumping on each other, having sex practically every day and twice on Sundays. In those days Andrew had had two things on his mind: getting his architect degree and sex, which he could have any time he wanted now that he was married. She wondered about this sometimes, the way he would be studying and suddenly look up with a hot beam in his eye and come after her. "I was just drawin' curves and seein' how I could fit them together," he said, making her laugh.

There was nothing like being young and in love and feeling all the newness and fire of passion. Claire had been a virgin when she met Andrew and, actually, until they had more or less gotten engaged. She had held out a long time, all caught up in the idea that good girls did not have sex before marriage. Now, when she looked back, she realized that the reasoning didn't seem to make sense. Somehow she had been controlled by so much fear of punishment. Aunt Agnes's constant criticism of her mother and her father had made a mark.

She had been truly fortunate to marry Andrew, who was several years older, more experienced, and not ruled by any idea of punishment for anything. Andrew had been, and still was, a man who believed the world was his own due. He had led her along in a loving and gentle manner into the wonderful discovery that sex was more than she had ever in her life imagined it to be. They had made love on the floor, on the table, on the counter, even once in the car in a public park, when they had almost been caught by patrolling police.

They had been devoted to each other, hungry for each other. Sometimes Claire would be so hungry for Andrew that she would cry and have to stop at a pay phone if necessary to call him and tell him so.

At first Andrew had not been happy about the pregnancy so early in their marriage. She surmised at the outset that he had not wanted to share her with a baby. But it had also been that he had been trying to get through school, and they were living off of Claire's salary.

Claire, though, had been thrilled. The lonely only child who remained deep inside of her thought that at last she would have a child with whom to play. A child to love and who would love her.

But then, at just past her third month, she had lost the baby. It had been a violent and dangerous loss, both physically and emotionally.

Andrew had cried. He had been sitting there beside the

bed holding her hand. When the doctor came in to talk to them and told them that the baby had been a boy, Andrew had laid his head against her and sobbed so hard that she had held her own tears in check so as not to upset him further.

"I'm sorry. I'm so sorry," she had said to him, stroking his silky hair.

Somehow she had felt to blame. Surely she had done something wrong. She had felt so well that she hadn't thought anything about moving furniture and being on her feet. The doctor said that didn't have anything to do with it, but she felt surely it must have.

"We'll have another one. I promise I will." The first week back on her feet, she had quit her job at the furniture store and become a secretary at Tri-State so that she spent a lot of time sitting down. Six weeks later, when the doctor said that she could have sex again, she had begun badgering Andrew morning and night.

But Andrew had wanted to wait to finish school before trying for another child. At first she had thought he was afraid that she might lose the baby, or that he might lose her, but gradually she understood that he worried that she might get pregnant again before he graduated. His eagerness for sex definitely seemed to wane, and sometimes he turned her advances away.

After he graduated, he wanted to wait until he got a really good job. That took several years of so-so jobs, until he landed at a top firm, but then he wanted to wait until he felt they were on firm financial footing. Andrew focused on his work and had only scattered interest in sex.

Finally, at thirty, by wonderful happenstance, Claire turned up pregnant again. She had been hesitant to tell Andrew, not certain how he would take it. He had been involved deeply with an enormous building project over in Houston, another steep step in his career. In fact, she had conceived on the only weekend in two months that they had spent totally alone and without interruptions from the building project.

"Well, I guess now's the time then," Andrew had said and smiled at her, although she had seen caution in his eyes. The next day, however, he had sent her two dozen red roses, with a card that said, "To my wife, the mother of my child." He had even gotten very interested in sex, as if Claire's pregnant state turned him on something fierce. It was wonderful, the sensual fashion in which he would approach her, a sort of worshiping and wanting combined.

Only she had lost that baby, too. A girl. Claire thought of her as Sweet June, because she had conceived her in June. Andrew had not cried. He had within a day gone out to build another hotel or something.

She had the painful suspicion within her that he had, after all, been glad they did not have children to draw his attention away from his work, and her attention away from him.

Unfortunately her attention for him never did return to full force. Her disappointments about her babies and the way her marriage was turning out floated around her like a perpetual shadow, locking herself inside and Andrew out.

Chapter Seventeen

After her visit with Sherrilyn, she had an hour and a half in which to look at cars before she had to head back to Valentine for her lunch date with Travis. She was annoyed with herself now for agreeing to the date and taking her focus off making a decision about a car. And also because she just felt a little silly about having a lunch date with what would be termed a *younger man*.

Some part of that annoyance, though, served to make her decide the instant she came out of the hospital that she preferred to purchase a car, rather than rent one. She had never found renting a satisfying endeavor. She always worried about something bad happening to whatever she rented—an apartment, a house, a carpet shampooer, and several luxury cars while on those few vacations that were really business trips. She would rarely drive those rented cars, so worried had she been about putting a scratch on them.

The entire time she drove Winston's Oldsmobile, she

drove with exceeding care and a whole lot of nervousness, worried that she might wreck it, or run over someone.

She looked at both new and used cars at two dealerships and gathered brochures, having short time for anything else, and then headed along the highway back to Valentine, mulling over her choices.

The only vehicle she had ever purchased on her own was the old truck she had bought when she was eighteen. She had grabbed it on a whim from a fellow student for five hundred dollars. Committing now to spending so much money on something that she knew relatively little about was unnerving. She thought of consulting with Andrew but quickly discarded the idea. Past experience had proven his tastes—and bank account—loftier than her own.

Perhaps she should consult with Corrine, and the more she thought of that idea, the better she liked it. She thought, too, of Winston's remark about possibly being willing to sell the Oldsmobile. She was, after all, now used to the car. If he would sell it, her looking would be over. Although, that action seemed like getting another car that someone else had chosen. She would be in the same position that she had been in with the Mercedes, driving around in a car that a man was terribly fond of and being responsible for it.

She was mulling over the situation when she became aware of the Oldsmobile slowing down.

Well, my goodness…she pressed the accelerator. The engine got louder, but the car did not pick up speed. In fact, it kept slowing down until it was going at a snail's pace.

She could not believe it! Hadn't she just been thinking of buying it? And what would Winston say? She pumped the accelerator frantically, but nothing happened.

Being in high gear with worry about being rear-ended, she directed the Oldsmobile to the side of the road, where it rolled to a stop. The left rear fender poked out too far into the road to suit her, but there was nothing she could do about it.

She stared at the steering wheel for half a minute, and then jumped into action with the hope the car was experiencing a momentary glitch that would right itself any second. For five minutes, she did things like test the accelerator, raise the brake pedal with her toe, check the emergency brake, move the shift lever into Park and back into Drive, turn the engine off and start it again, three times.

Still, the car would not move.

She lowered the windows on both sides and sat there with the engine running. Several cars whizzed past. She prayed for the car to start working again, more or less saying, *"If you don't want me to buy the car, all you have to do is tell me…. I won't buy it. I won't! Please don't do this…please."*

Then she turned off the engine and dropped her head to the steering wheel and gave out a little involuntary moan of despair.

It was at this point, as she was moaning, that she heard a sharply concerned voice through the window. "Are you all right?"

She shut her mouth.

Very slowly, she lifted her head and, through stray wisps of hair, looked at the person who had found her acting so silly.

It was Travis Ford's father, gazing at her in a scowling fashion.

"Scoot over, and I'll check it out." He opened the car door.

She sat unmoving. "The trouble is in the engine."

He kept looking at her expectantly, so she moved over, saying that she had been about to call for road service.

He slipped behind the wheel in the manner of a man who took charge. She gave him a quick study. He was handsome. His eyes were a startling blue in his tanned face. Flecks of gray in deep brown hair. Mid- or late-forties, maybe. Travis favored him just all over the place.

"Well, the engine starts."

"Yes. I've turned it on and off."

He shifted the lever. Twice.

"I did that, too."

He pumped the brakes.

"The brakes are fine. And the emergency brake isn't on."

He tried the emergency brake anyway.

He turned his head and gazed at her. "I'd say the transmission's gone out."

"Oh. That sounds quite serious."

"Pretty much. It'll have to be towed in." He was already pulling his cell phone from his belt and giving her direction. "Larry Joe'll handle it. I'll give you a lift into town."

"I have towing insurance with Triple A." Claire, intent on demonstrating that she could handle the problem, pulled out her own phone. "I was just about to call them."

He said, "You can do that, but it'll be a tow service out of Lawton, and they'll tow it to a garage there, since that's the closest. They'll charge you extra to tow it to Valentine, and that's where I imagine Winston would rather have it and where it will end up, because that's where Larry Joe's garage is. Larry Joe is Winston's grandson, and he's a mechanic."

"Oh. Okay."

As she watched him punch the buttons on his phone, she thought that she probably could have added a thank-you. She would say that at the first opportunity.

She thought to stay with the Oldsmobile, which was her responsibility, after all, and leaving it seemed to compound the error of somehow getting it broken down.

Larkin Ford, however, told her, "I already told Larry Joe that I'd be bringin' you in." He sounded like he was planning on towing her in. "It's likely that he'll have another person or two with him in the tow truck, and if he does, there won't be room for you."

He was a polite man. He held the door for her to get out of the Oldsmobile, and held the door of his pickup truck for her to get into the passenger seat.

A surprisingly slow driver, steering with his wrist hooked over the wheel in way too casual a manner to suit Claire, he did not seem inclined for conversation. Claire, who usually could take or leave it, found herself filled with a compulsion to chat.

"Do I remember correctly—your name is Larkin?"

"Yes."

"I'm Claire Wilder."

"Yes, ma'am, I remember. I met you at the sheriff's office."

"Yes. I just didn't know if you remembered." Did he have some attitude to be calling her ma'am, or was it politeness?

After another silent minute, she said, "Clouds are sure building to the southwest."

"Yep."

"You've had a lot of storms this spring, I've heard."

"Yep."

"Oh, look, it's raining over there."

His head turned to look. "Yep."

While she was thinking of something else to say, the rain started on them. Quite soon it was a full downpour that fell with such force over the pickup truck as to drown out voices. The windshield wipers thumped, and Larkin Ford turned the air conditioner up to get the fog off the glass. Claire worried about Winston's car.

Larkin Ford finally voluntarily said something. "Hope there isn't a tornado in this."

Ten minutes later, just as they neared Valentine, the rain stopped as if someone had cut off the spigot, and Claire found she could breathe again, as she watched the sun come out and shine over the rolling hills.

Larkin Ford slowed and lowered his window, and a truck coming in the opposite direction—a large and exceedingly brightly painted tow truck—also slowed. The two trucks came abreast and stopped right in the road. Claire glanced into the rearview mirror, checking if anyone was behind them. No one was.

Larkin Ford had been correct; the seat of the tow truck was too full to accommodate her. Behind the wheel was a young, sun-blond man, and next to him a young blond girl who could have been his sister, and Corrine, who waved and called hello. Then a fourth head popped up.

Why, it was Willie Lee, who hollered at her, "Hel-lo, Miss Cla-ire! I am help-ing to get Mis-ter Win-ston's car!"

"Hello, Willie Lee." Claire was foolishly delighted to receive the greeting. Then another head popped up—Willie Lee's dog.

Larkin Ford introduced the tow-truck driver as Larry Joe Darnell, Winston's grandson.

The young man smiled an easy smile that surely had the capacity to break female hearts of all ages. "Hello, Miz Wilder. I got ahold of Grampa, and he told me to tell you right off not to worry about this. Me 'n my help here will get it, no sweat."

Larkin Ford explained the location of the Oldsmobile to the young man, and the two spoke for a minute about the car's difficulty.

In parting, the young man said, "Grampa's waitin' on y'all down at Blaine's Drugstore."

And quite suddenly Claire remembered that someone else was waiting for her at Blaine's Drugstore—Larkin Ford's son.

As the truck sped into town, she looked ahead and even sat up in the seat.

By some peculiar coincidence, there was a parking place directly in front of the drugstore. As if he had been watching for her arrival, Travis came striding out the entry of the building the instant the pickup tires bumped the curb.

He met her at the passenger door with an eagerness that was a little disconcerting, with his father looking on. "Hi. Glad you made it." And over the hood of the pickup, he called to his father, "Thanks for bringin' my lunch date, Dad."

Claire felt her cheeks grow red.

Whatever Larkin Ford thought, however, she did not know. She did not look his way, but said a polite hello to Travis and then, seeing Winston, leaning on his cane, come out of the drugstore, she went to him, apologizing for somehow breaking his car. She explained how it had slowed down and not responded to the accelerator, and how she had succeeded in getting it to the side of the road, and how Larkin Ford had showed up and pronounced the transmission gone out. Allowing Winston to escort her inside, with Travis jumping to open the door, she made a great deal out of the story in a compulsion to draw attention from herself and Travis and their lunch date.

Winston told her, "Now, darlin', don't you worry about it one bit. That car has been settin' up and was bound to have a problem or two. I'm sorry for the inconvenience to you, that's all. I'm relieved that Larkin here came along when he did."

As he took Claire's arm, he thanked Larkin Ford for handily rescuing Claire—those were his words. "I'm mighty appreciative that you handily rescued her, Larkin," he said, as if the man had done him a personal favor.

Larkin Ford, who was trailing right along behind them, leaving his son to come last, said he was happy to have been of assistance.

Winston walked her to one of the drugstore's rear tables,

where Perry Blaine sat in a wheelchair. Winston introduced Claire to the disabled man she had only heard of from Vella. Claire said hello, and Perry Blaine opened his mouth, then closed it. He did seem to nod.

"He's pleased to make your acquaintance, aren't you, Perry?" said Winston.

Winston sat on her left, while Travis took the chair on her right, and Larkin pulled a chair up across the table and straddled it.

Claire looked around with some anticipation for Vella, in hopes to have the support of another woman among the men, but the woman was not in sight. Belinda gave her a wave but then returned her attention to the television mounted on the wall, which was featuring a shopping program, while the skinniest young woman Claire had ever in her life seen came over to take their orders.

Travis said immediately, "Put hers on my ticket."

Larkin Ford's eyes moved back and forth from her to Travis like one of those animal clocks with revolving eyes.

For the following twenty minutes, fortified by a sizable lunch of barbecue sandwich, potato salad and a strawberry milkshake, Claire was kept busy dividing herself between the men so as not to appear to give any one of them undue attention. Although why she would feel the obligation to do that, she couldn't have said.

Quite soon, however, she became worn-out and gave up her efforts to lead the luncheon conversation. She played her straw around in the milkshake and watched the men as they talked among themselves about the repair required for Winston's car—the excellent mechanic knowledge of his grandson, the price of cattle and the likely price of wheat in the coming weeks, and the discovery on a farm of a cultivated marijuana field that the sheriff was that minute busy burning.

In a fashion that Claire found fascinating, every so often

Winston would lift a cold drink, hold the straw to Perry's lips, and the man would take a drink. There seemed to be a silent conversation between the two old men. It was a display of friendship that touched Claire at her core.

Then there was Larkin. He was a guarded sort. He sat straddled on the chair, his forearms on the chair back, as if to not really sit with them. He didn't have much to say, speaking only when Winston asked him a question outright. He did almost smile now and again at some of Winston's humorous comments. It was a very reluctant smile, as if he was not one who smiled often and didn't want to be caught doing it, either.

The degree to which Travis physically favored his father was almost startling. The two did not seem at all of the same temperament, though. Travis was open and forthcoming. He sat forward, arms on the table, smiling often and obviously relishing conversing. He repeatedly cast Claire private looks and smiles, and regarded Winston with an open expression. But he barely looked at his father, who barely looked at him.

Growing more tired, Claire began to think of her alternatives for getting herself out to the Goodnight Motel. She had become a little desperate to get away to her room at the motel. She was ready to take a nap. Her car-less and relatively clothes-less situation loomed large in front of her, and she simply could not deal with any of it until she had some rest.

As she saw it, she could walk the distance—surely a mile and a half—in a temperature of ninety-five with a possible storm, or she could ask either Larkin or Travis Ford to drive her. She found it a dilemma to choose between the two men, for fear of what each might think, although why they would think anything, she wasn't certain.

Perhaps it would work to simply say, "Hey, which one of you fellas would like to give me a ride?"

While she was working herself up to do this, Frank Goode came in to get a to-go order of barbecue sandwiches to take back to the motel and surprise Gertie. Waiting for his order, he stopped at the table to say hello and chat for a few minutes.

When he started to leave, Claire stood up. "I'll ride back with you, Frank. Thank you, Travis, for my lunch and the delightful company. Thank you, Larkin, for rescuing me on the highway. And thank you, Winston, for your generosity and dear friendship."

Getting a little carried away, she gave Winston a parting kiss, and he beamed proudly. When the drugstore door closed behind her, she imagined him saying something like, "It's the prerogative of age, fellas."

Real Life

From: Vella Blaine
To: <haltg@mailectric.com>
Sent: June 17, 1997, 7:30 a.m.
Subject: Heart Pains

Dear Harold,

Yes, I have gotten your messages, and I'm sorry for the delay in replying. We've had a crisis around here.

First, though, I want to send my condolences on the anniversary of your son's death. I'm not surprised that Estelle had a poor and fretful day. Even if her mind is mostly gone, her spirit inside the body is alive and well and feels the pain. I can only imagine what Estelle suffered at the shock of her son dying so unexpectedly from pneumonia. We all expect miracles of medicine in this day and age. I have no doubt it may have contributed to her current state. I do believe that people can die of broken hearts, even if it takes a while.

I don't believe I am as close to my daughters as you describe Estelle as being to your son, although, maybe I am to Belinda but cannot know it while she is here with me. Reading your message caused me to give her a kiss, and I thought for a minute that she was going to pass out.

As for the crisis and why I haven't written, Perry had what they think is a heart attack and had to be rushed to the hospital. I was up there for two days straight and really was more wrung-out than I realized.

Perry is okay now. Well, as okay as a man can get who had a major stroke six months ago and is just falling apart piece by piece. The doctors think he had a mild heart attack this time, not another stroke. I asked why they couldn't *know,* but all they can do is hem and haw and order more tests. But really, all the testing in the world is not going to turn Perry's state of health around. Nothing short of the Lord Jesus working a miracle will do that.

It happened at the drugstore, praise God, because if Perry had been at home, he would have been with the dumb nurse, who likely would have been too involved watching taped episodes of *The Young and the Restless* and wouldn't even have noticed. Claire, who happened to be sitting alone at the table with Perry—I was working the pharmacy counter—saw Perry slump over.

I tell you, I don't really know what happened to me, but when I heard Claire call out and saw her wrestling Perry down to the floor and Belinda and Winston staring at me for direction, I just went to pieces and started bawling.

Belinda, she never can do anything in a crisis but stand there and have to be told to breathe, and Winston is ninety now and couldn't possibly handle Perry, who is still a big man. But he could and did get to the phone to call the ambulance.

Frankly, I never would have imagined that Claire could be so capable. She is proof that a person does not necessarily have to be of a decisive nature to be proficient in a crisis. She handled Perry, went to doing CPR, and he even came to by the time the ambulance arrived. By then I also had come to my full senses and took charge of a frantic effort to get Perry to the hospital.

But now I have to admit that I question my sanity with that effort to save his life. What am I saving it for?

Does that sound awful to you? It is just that Perry is here but not really here, and after this recent episode, he is a little less here. I am his wife, a married woman, but without a husband. This place in my life is not a place I ever thought about being. I guess no one does. If we thought about it, we would give up at the start. No one would get married. This is the "worse" part of for better or worse, but when you are young and set on getting married, with all of those starry-eyed dreams of it, you do not have one iota of what the real life will be like.

I read the other day that research shows that in the teenage years certain hormones give humans the bold idea that they are invincible. Well, if you ask me, God got that entirely backward. We need such hormones when we are old in order to deal with all life hands us.

Let me say thank the Lord for Claire. She has accompanied me to the hospital, watched over me all over the place, keeping track of my handbag, getting me coffee and making sure I eat and get rest. (After one trip to the hospital with her driving the Land Rover and me in my right mind, though, I couldn't stand to let her drive it again. I love my Land Rover too much.)

It is such a strange experience, having Claire's attentions. I have not been watched over in years. Actually, I cannot recall ever being watched over. I was the eldest of four children, and my mother used to say that from the minute I could walk, I took charge of her and Daddy and then my brothers and sisters as they came along. It shows my mother's nature that she let me do it.

This brings to my mind, Harold—who watches over and comforts you? Do you have a good friend nearby?

Well, I must end now. I've got to interview some new nurses. I yelled at that dumb one, and she quit.

With fond regards,

Vella

P.S. It is possible that Perry might also have choked on a piece of candy bar. We found a half-eaten Snickers in the seat of his wheelchair. That night little Corrine, a neighbor girl who is quite close to Perry, came down to the house, crying her eyes out, and confessed that she had sometimes slipped Perry a Snickers bar because she knew he loved them so much. Isn't that the sweetest thing you have ever heard? I told her not to worry one bit about it, and when Perry comes home, she can just feed him Snickers bars by the hour. I mean, why can't he have a Snickers? What's going to happen? He might get diabetes and die?

She ran her eyes back over where she wrote about her coming to pieces. She had not spoken of the episode with anyone, not even to Claire. Claire might have surmised, she thought, remembering the younger woman's attention. But she doubted that Winston or Belinda, either one, had any idea how thoroughly unhinged she had been. Even now, remembering, she felt a fresh wash of weakness.

She was getting old, she thought, her shoulders sagging as she clicked the button, sending the message.

Chapter Eighteen

Gertie was again pressing him about closing the motel and moving to Florida. She had gotten so worked up when her sister Peggy had telephoned the evening before that she had started smoking again, after having quit for a year and a half. Right then, leaning over the clothes dryer that he was working on in the guest laundry room, she put him in mind of a smoking dragon.

"We need to go while we still can, Frank. Peggy says the retirement village is fillin' up. Just three cottages left."

"I've told you that we'll close the motel if we have to. I've said that." He moved his head up and down until he could see the small screw he was looking for through his bifocals.

"That is what I am sayin'. Three cottages left, Frank. Do you hear me?"

"Yes, I hear you. But those are not the only cottages left in Florida, I don't imagine. What we need to think about is payin' for one. You seem to think we're gonna go down there and be on one big holiday. How are we gonna pay for any of it if we just walk away from this place?"

"We are in debt here, Frank. I'd rather be in debt in Florida. We can get jobs in Florida, where we won't have this motel sucking us dry." Puff, puff.

Finished with connecting the vent hose onto the dryer, he stood up behind it, rising with some difficulty because of his rotund belly. He hated that belly. He couldn't imagine how he had come to have it, any more than he could get used to having bifocals.

"What are we gonna do, honey? We're both closin' in on sixty, and one of us hasn't had a job in thirty-six years."

"Don't go tellin' me I haven't had a job, Frank Goode."

He realized he had said a wrong thing.

"I've kept a house, raised three children and you and my in-laws, and cleaned this motel. I can sure clean another motel…in Florida." Puff, puff. Gertie sort of grew when she got mad, and right that minute she seemed to get a foot taller.

He changed his tack to appeal to the soft heart he knew, or at least hoped, was beneath her crust. "Honey, we can't just up and close this place down right this minute. What would people do without it? And there's the Fourth of July festivities comin' up, and the Posey reunion after that, and then Valentine Days in August. And where're Mr. and Miz Tolley gonna have their summer date night away from MacCoy Green Acres, and Fayrene gonna get herself fixed up on Mondays…and little Miz Fairchild gonna go when Elliot's about to beat the tar out of her?"

The entire time he was bringing all this up, he began to feel more and more reluctant to leave the motel at all. But then he saw that his wife's face was not softening, and that she was, in fact, seeming to have reached his full height and even to loom over him.

"I don't care where they go, Frank. They can all look after

themselves. Nobody in town has lifted one finger to buy the place and keep it goin', so I guess that answers the question of how much anyone cares. And as for Nancy Fairchild, maybe if we weren't here, the woman would finally get some backbone and take up a fryin' pan and smack Elliot upside the head."

Her mouth went shut on that, and she gazed at him with expectation.

He tried to figure out exactly what he could say to her to please her, but it had to be something that wouldn't require him to commit to abandoning the motel, letting down his father and the town where he was born.

"Well, July Fourth generally brings in a full house. Maybe someone will show up who wants to buy this place."

She did not respond hopefully, so he put forth more on hard and fast money coming in, saying, "Then there's the Posey reunion. Five rooms rented, and some of the Poseys have paid ahead. That's money we'd have to give back if we closed up, so we gotta stay open through the end of July," he added in a firm manner.

She stubbed her cigarette with vigor in the nearby ashtray and said, "You have been singin' that same tune for the past two summers, and I'm gonna tell you somethin', Frank Goode. It is either you and this motel, or me and Fort Walton Beach."

Snatching up their little old Chihuahua, Felix, that was sitting on top of the washer, she stalked out the rear entry of the laundry room, letting the screen door bang about off its hinges.

Frank felt a certain panic. In all their thirty-seven years of marriage and several really bad arguments, Gertie had never before threatened to leave him.

He struggled to get his hefty frame out from behind the dryer with the intention of running after her, but just as he got out, Claire entered through the front.

He was embarrassed to think that Claire might have heard the argument, and in any case, he suddenly became deflated and lost the gumption to go after Gertie. Chatting with Claire right that minute presented a more attractive alternative, and besides, he would do best to let his wife calm down.

"Good afternoon, Miss Claire," he said, falling gratefully into his accustomed jovial demeanor. He liked being jovial. He understood himself then; confusion and anger simply mystified and frightened him.

He noticed that Claire wore a pink shirt emblazoned with entwined hearts that stretched over her ample breasts, and pink shorts, and carried a pink laundry basket. Frank loved Gertie, but he wasn't blind, and probably even a blind man would take note of Claire. She had a sort of essence that made a man know he was a man.

She asked him how he was, and he replied, "Oh, fair to middlin'. Dryer's cleaned up and ready." He slid the machine back into place with the satisfaction of a competent handyman, without any trace of a chastised husband.

"I imagine I could give my clothes a few waves in the air and they'd be dry," she said. "I can't get over how dry everything is now."

"This is 'bout regular for around here. I'd better start waterin' the bushes."

His gaze moved up her length of pale leg and the bit of her buttocks that poked out beneath her shorts as she bent down to reach into the laundry basket. He wondered why she was unattached, a woman like her. He wondered who the man was who had rung through the switchboard once since she had been here. Travis Ford had stopped by a couple of times that Frank knew of, and once Claire had driven off with him.

It occurred to him that he should have brought Claire up to Gertie. His wife liked Claire. How could they close the motel, with Claire still there? He would say that to his wife at the first opportunity.

Quite suddenly, at the sight of a good-size lacy bra, he turned away, thankful to have not been caught staring. He grabbed up a rag and attempted to look busy by tidying up in something of a fervent manner. His effort turned earnest, however, as he thought that he could please Gertie by cleaning the room. He could shine the windows, and his wife would be very pleased.

"You know, Frank. It would sure be nice to have the pool in weather like this."

He turned to see Claire resting her now empty laundry basket on her hip.

She said, "Maybe if you got it workin', you could open it to the kids in town and charge a small fee that would help with the upkeep. I remember when I was a kid, one summer my mother and I visited a motel down at Biloxi that did that. The activity of people all havin' fun at the pool might draw interest, you know. People might come out to stay just to have fun and cool off in this heat."

"Yeah...but there'd be insurance costs, probably more than anything we'd take in. We get a break in the insurance since the pool ain't open."

"Oh."

He scrubbed at the windowpanes and looked through the glass to the pool area, where the gate was padlocked and the pool covered with a fraying tarp. He felt a little angry at Claire for bringing up the subject.

He said, "The pool is like the rest of this place—old. People will put up with, even treasure, grand old hotels, but they like modern in a motel."

"Vintage has become quite popular," Claire said. "I have seen a number of vintage motels advertised in the travel magazines. Clubs like to have events at places like that. You know, antique car clubs and homemaker clubs. You could go through and really make this place just like it was in the fifties without much expense at all." Then she glanced over at him and said, "But I'm sure you know a whole lot more about it all than I do."

He refrained from telling her that was the exact truth, and that advice from the other side of the fence was awfully easy to give.

As if to prove his point, he got lots of advice from all over town later that day when he ran errands. When he stopped into MacCoy Feed and Grain and Ace Hardware to buy some window caulk, Adam MacCoy suggested Frank might want to paint the motel. "We got exterior on sale at fifteen percent off. Fresh paint can raise the value on real estate by as much as thirty percent."

"It's not the price that's the problem," said Frank, who thought Adam was doing pretty well to raise his own value by encouraging Frank into buying paint. "It's that no one is interested in runnin' a motel. It's a lot of work, you know." He snatched up his tube of caulk and left.

Then, at the post office, Julia Jenkins-Tinsley wanted to know why one of his kids didn't come home and help with the motel. Julia didn't even have children herself.

"I didn't raise my children to make the same mistake that I made," Frank told her. "My oldest is a designer for NASA, my middle one is secure with the telephone company, and my youngest is married to a farmer. I'd say they did well, and I'm not suckerin' them back in like my daddy did me."

Then, when he stopped in to fill the tank of the motel van, old Norm Stidham, retired and spending his days sitting in a chair out front of his gas station and giving his opinions to everybody and their neighbor who stopped for gas, suggested that maybe Frank should lower the price of the motel.

"We got it at lower than what it's worth," Frank told him.

"I might as well close it as to lower the price more. In fact, that's what I'm aimin' to do at the end of July."

"Well, I sure hate to see you do that," Mr. Stidham said. "Where's my kids gonna stay when they come to visit? We don't have room for all of 'em and their kids, too. No, sir. We need the Goodnight."

To that Frank said, "Everybody says that, but nobody wants to do anything about it."

"Well, why don't you just give it over to somebody to manage, like I did this station?" Mr. Stidham said. "None of my own wanted it, but Larry Joe here, he did, and he makes me a fine retirement."

"That might be an option…if I knew someone who was just dyin' for a twenty-four hour, seven days a week thankless job goin' broke."

"I hate to tell you this, Frank, but if that's how you're presentin' the motel, it isn't any wonder you can't interest a buyer."

His wife and everyone blaming him for the motel's decline and not selling was too much to bear. He told the boy pumping the gas that he had enough, shoved bills at him and didn't even wait for change, but drove on back to the motel, with an entire reel of the past and future rolling across his mind.

Back in his father's time, the Goodnight had been a winning proposition. People came, he and Gertie welcomed them and made them feel at home, and the money rolled in, enough to employ maids and handymen and even stand-in managers so that he and Gertie could slip off to Las Vegas on occasion. Enough to support the children and his own parents and see them cared for in an upscale rest home in their last years.

Frank wondered what was going to become of him and Gertie in their last years. He had the dismal vision of the motel boarded up, and him and Gertie shuffling around in their little apartment behind the office, warming their hands over the burners of the stove.

Gertie was right about Florida. They needed to go now, while they had the health to enjoy it and to make ready for the years to come. They were going to get old, and none of their children were nearly as attentive to them as he and Gertie had been to his parents. At least living in Florida they could be warm.

When he pulled up and looked at the pitiful state of the pool, he decided he would get it fixed. Maybe Claire was right, and anyway, maybe if the pool was fixed, Gertie would be mollified, as it would be like Florida.

He hurried through the office to their apartment in the rear to get the number of his cousin over at the plumbing and heating place, and to tell Gertie of his plan. He found her in the kitchen, removing pictures from the walls.

"I'm gettin' ready for Florida," she said.

After all his years of living, Winston was proud to say that there was no one living or dead whom he disliked. There were on occasion, though, a couple of people he might want to shoot. At that moment, Jaydee Mayhall was one of these people, because he was jiggling his leg up and down and tapping a domino on the table.

It was their weekly Tuesday game at the café. Winston was ahead, and that about ate Jaydee's lunch. Winston said a prayer of apology for being so happy about the fact.

"Did you die on us, Winston?" Jaydee asked, elaborately leaning down to peer up into Winston's face. Then he hollered over to the counter, "Fayrene, I think you had better call the rescue squad for Winston here."

Fayrene hollered back, "I'll tell you, Jaydee, after what happened with Perry last week, you are not funny."

Winston's response was to look over his reading glasses at

the younger man for several seconds, then ignore him and stare even longer at the dominoes.

"Damn it, Winston, will you make a move before we all turn to stone?"

"Well, yes, sir, I will." Winston put two blocks in place, while the two other players, Leon Purvis and Bingo Yardell, began to chuckle.

"I'd say you're gonna owe the dead man a hundred dollars pretty quick here," Bingo said, and gave a satisfied smile. Bingo didn't like Jaydee, either, because Jaydee was often making snide remarks about Bingo being a redneck.

Actually, poor Jaydee was a little short on people who did like him. As an attorney, local politician, landlord and general peacock, he had roused the downright ill will of a goodly number of citizens.

"There's blocks to draw yet," Jaydee said. "The game ain't over till it's over."

"You just live too fast," said Winston.

"I got a lot goin', if that's what you mean," Jaydee shot back. "And I want to play the game and not study it to death."

"Winston has a lot goin'," said Leon, playing two blocks. "Haven't you seen the young woman he's been with lately?"

Jaydee's eyes got sharp. "Yeah…who is that broad, Winston? A long-lost niece?"

"Jaydee, right there is the reason you can't hold on to a woman. Claire is not a broad but a woman and a friend gracing my life."

"Huh. I can keep a broad—it's when I marry 'em that I get into trouble." He leaned close to the table as Bingo made his play.

"Did I hear right, that she's from Lou'siana and was related to somebody 'round here?" asked Leon, who was about like an old woman for gossip.

"She is."

Jaydee was now studying the playing board with concentration. Winston could see the man was going to have difficulty with his blocks.

"How old is she?" Leon asked.

To this, Winston said, "One does not talk about a woman's age. However, in the interest of clarification and savin' time, as Jaydee likes to do, I'll say that her name is Claire Wilder, she is forty, divorced, and come up here from Shreveport on vacation and to see her heritage. She is the granddaughter of Grover Tillman and was born here. I've been showin' her the town."

"You better watch your wallet," Jaydee said.

"Make your play," Winston said.

Jaydee kept studying the board.

"Did you up and die?" asked Leon after a few minutes.

"Allll right, I pass."

Without hesitation, Winston played his remaining dominoes. "Pay up."

Jaydee frowned and shook his head, then pushed his chair away from the table. "I'm done with you guys."

"You owe me fifty," said Winston.

"All I have on me is a twenty. I'll catch you later."

"I'll take the twenty now and call it even," said Winston.

Jaydee, on his feet, dug into his pocket, pulled out two twenties and threw them down in front of Winston. "Here."

He then left the café in a huff, with Fayrene calling after him, "I'll put your coffee and chicken salad on your tab."

The men around the table chuckled and speculated as to how long it would be before the attorney returned to play another game.

"Tomorrow," was Leon's prediction, before leaving a couple of dollars on the table for Fayrene, who came by to sweep bills and change into her hand, calling them all, "Real big spenders, you fellas."

When they were alone, Bingo, gazing curiously at Winston, asked, "That woman…Claire Wilder," he said with a grin and careful pronunciation. "If she's the granddaughter of Grover Tillman, wouldn't that make her John Tillman's daughter?"

"Why, yes it would. Did you know him?" Winston looked the man over and estimated that Bingo and John Tillman would be close in age. Winston had asked around a little and not found anyone who had known or remembered the man, so he had quit asking. Actually, he had not really wanted to find anyone who knew the man. He rather liked to keep Claire's attention on himself and not have to share her with her father.

"Oh, yeah. He and I enlisted in the Army at the same time, and we both went over to Korea. After a fashion, he was my second cousin on my mother's side."

"Was? He's dead then?"

Bingo frowned. "Well, I don't really know. Last time I saw John was when his mama died. Sometime in the eighties."

"Nineteen and eighty," Winston supplied, pleased to recall the date on the grave marker.

Bingo nodded in thought. "He looked bad then. He came in this old rattletrap car that I was amazed ran. I guess John'd had some health problems ever since Korea. He got shot up pretty good over there and filled with drugs, then cut loose. Back then we were just 'sposed to come home from killin' and take up nine-to-five and goin' to church on Sundays."

"Oh, yeah," Winston said, knowing from his own experience and those of many friends now long gone. Then he prodded the man. "He came home for his mother's funeral."

"Uh-huh…and to sell the property. John did it all pretty quiet. He stayed out at my parents' house and didn't want anyone to know he was in town. He spent a lot of time in the barn, drinkin', 'cause my mother wouldn't let him drink in the house. I suggested to him that he might want to go to the VA hospital, but he said he had been and didn't want to go again.

"What I found out later was that he mostly didn't want Junetta and Rodney Carruthers to know he was in town."

"I remember Junetta," Winston said, and with a certain gladness. He had been a little upset because he had not any memory regarding John Tillman.

Bingo grinned. "I guess most men would remember her. John and her had this thing, and there'd been trouble with Rodney Carruthers over it. Carruthers attempted to pin a theft on John, which was why John had left town so quickly in the first place. You know, Carruthers did have some power, but the way I heard it, he wasn't too smart, and the truth of all of it come out pretty quick. Carruthers like to lost his job over it."

"When was this?" Winston was perturbed. He didn't remember anything about the incident, which would have been a big scandal, as Rodney Carruthers had been an owner in the bank. Winston had always known everything that went on in Valentine. He began to worry that his mind was going, with pockets of lost memories. Maybe there were a whole lot of lost memories, but how could he know, if he couldn't remember?

He suddenly imagined himself in the nursing home, sitting in a chair all vacant-eyed.

Bingo was saying, "Well…it would have been around '64 or '65. Summer, I think. I remember hearin' the story when I come home on leave and brought my first wife. No, maybe it was Star, my second wife…no, it was Jewel, my first wife."

Winston remembered then that during the summer of 1964, he had been traveling with his wife, Coweta, on the barrel racing circuit. He and Coweta had been attempting to keep their floundering marriage alive. Those had been hard years. Likely a lot had gone on around town of which he had not taken note in his preoccupation with trying to stay married.

He remembered Junetta Carruthers, though, so he supposed he was okay.

"When John came back to town, he said he didn't want to cause any more trouble," Bingo said. "But what I think is that John was embarrassed to have Junetta or anyone else see him in his derelict condition. Right after arrangin' for the sale of his mother's place, he left, and I never saw or heard from him again."

"I'd appreciate it if you wouldn't talk about this with anyone else," Winston said. "I wouldn't want a mixed-up story to get back to Claire, at least not before I have a chance to speak with her."

"No need for me to talk of it," said Bingo.

Winston was to meet Claire at the newspaper offices and get copies of her grandparents' obituaries. As he left the café and walked down a sidewalk already growing hot before ten o'clock in the morning, he imagined attempting to tell her about her father. It would be one thing to tell her about how he had been a hero in a bank robbery and died saving a child, or had joined the Secret Service and given his life for his country, or to save the life of the president, or maybe that he had gone to be a missionary in South America. But this sad and dreary tale of a man who had slid downhill would not be happy to tell or to hear. And it wouldn't be enlightening as to why her father had left her and her mother. Maybe it would be best to let sleeping history lie.

He had anticipated a lengthy time spent with Claire, going through stacks of old newspapers in search of the obituaries, which went to show how far behind the times he was. The *Valentine Voice* receptionist, Charlotte Conroy, handed over a manila file folder, saying, "I made several copies."

"You already got 'em?" Winston asked, annoyed.

"Well, it's no trouble. We have back to 1965 on computer."

Infernal computers, taking over the world.

"And I ran a search and found two articles from the sixties about horse races during the *Valentine Days* celebrations, where your grandfather's horse won," Charlotte added.

"Oh, thank you," Claire said. "What do I owe you?"

"No charge. We don't get that many requests for anything from the archives. Glad to do it." She returned her attention to her computer screen. Charlotte Conroy was a no-nonsense type of woman.

Winston followed Claire out into the heat. She was already opening the folder and looking at the pages inside.

"Want to drive out and get a burger and malt at the Burger Barn?" he asked, thinking of sitting alone in the car with her. One sure way he knew to please Claire was to get her something to eat.

"Hmm…okay."

He took her arm and guided her down the sidewalk toward where they had parked his car, which was once again running like a top. He had offered it for sale to Claire, but when Vella began making noises about maybe selling her Perry's Lincoln, Winston decided he would rather that. He wasn't in Perry's shape yet. He was halfway taking a notion to start driving again. Just to see if he could do that, he had that day driven the Oldsmobile down from his house and hadn't run over anyone or gotten caught.

Just then, here came Travis Ford hurrying toward them.

"The young Ford is after you."

"What?"

"'lo, Mr. Winston," Travis said politely before returning the full force of his smile to Claire. "Hey, Claire."

Claire and Winston both said hello. The young man brushed at his sweat-dampened shirt in a self-conscious manner and explained that he had been working horses and had just come to town for some quick errands. Winston thought he saw Claire perk up big-time with the mention of working horses. Probably it was the young man's virility coupled with the thought of horses. Drove women wild. With his wife and two daughters, and now Corrine, he had seen such reactions for all of his life. He himself used to use the working horses bit to attract women.

Travis said to Claire, "I was goin' to stop by the Goodnight on my way home and see you. The Little Opry starts up this Saturday night—it's just down the street here. It's music by local musicians and dancin'."

"Yes, I've heard."

"Well, I was wonderin' if you might like to go with me?"

"Oh. I…" She glanced at Winston, then said, "I would like to go with you, but I'm already goin' with Winston."

Winston didn't let his surprise show. He saw the disappointment flicker over the young Ford's face, but it was quickly replaced with his good-natured grin. "Well, I'll claim a dance with her, Mr. Winston."

"And I'll let you have it—one."

The young man grinned, then bid goodbye and loped off.

As they crossed the street, Winston said, "So, we're goin' to the Little Opry on Saturday night. Nice of you to let me know."

"We don't have to go," she said sheepishly. "I just wanted an excuse so as not to hurt his feelings."

"And you think goin' with me won't hurt his feelin's?" Winston's own feelings didn't do so good with that one.

"Not as badly as a flat-out no." She begged forgiveness with her eyes.

"I'm glad I can be of assistance," he said gallantly, "*And* I would love to go to the Little Opry with you, gal."

Claire took his arm, pressing close, and he patted her soft hand and inhaled her sultry perfume.

"I do feel it necessary," he said, "to point out that Travis is a fine young man. I wouldn't want to think you were lettin' his age interfere with any enjoyment the two of you could have."

"Winston, you are a most complex and baffling man!"

Her words and the way she looked at him made him feel quite pleased with himself.

"I'd rather go with you," she said.

"What you mean is that you feel safer with me."

After a minute, she replied, "There's such a blessing in feelin' safe."

And after another minute, he replied, "Yes, but is there life?"

On the way home from the airport, Andrew called Claire. He hadn't heard from her in a few days. He counted up and had the disconcerting realization that he had lost track of time in the midst of several trips to New Orleans. It had been four days since Claire had last called him.

Ringing came repeatedly across the connection, and he thought her voice mail was going to pick up, when a man's voice answered.

"Hello." It was a gravelly voice.

"Who's this?"

"Well, who's this?" said the gravelly voice.

"I'm sorry. I must have gotten the wrong number."

"Not if you were callin' Claire Wilder."

That was a surprise. "Yes, I was. Who's this?"

"Who's callin'?" The guy, whoever he was, was a wise-ass.

"This is Andrew Wilder, callin' my wife."

"I thought you and Claire were divorced."

"Just put Claire on." He felt foolishly helpless, wishing mightily to reach through the phone and strangle the guy.

"She's not available right at the moment."

"Well, what's she doin'?" *And why are you answering her phone?*

"She's placin' our order at the Burger Barn. But I can tell her you called."

"You do that." He clicked off and threw his phone in the passenger seat, knowing good and well that guy wasn't going to tell Claire. Fine. He'd call her again, when he got the time. Apparently she didn't need his attention.

Winston peered at Claire's cell phone, found the off button and pressed it, then laid the phone back down in the seat just where it had been before.

He watched as Claire stood at the order window, then received their food in white paper bags that glared as she stepped out from the shade of the overhang into the bright sun.

"Lord a'mercy, I'll bet you are about to roast," she said, slipping into the Oldsmobile. He loved it when her drawl got thick. It made him tingle so much that he thought he might actually be capable of an erection.

"No, I'm just fine," he said, a little disappointed as the tingle quickly faded. "I didn't have air-conditionin' in anything for the first fifty-five years of my life, and then we only had it in one room of the house."

"I thank God for air-conditioning," she said, then started the engine and blew the air conditioner full-blast as they drove over to the nearby park, where they ate their meal and perused the newspaper clippings in the shade of towering elms.

He never mentioned the phone call. He decided that a compensation of his age was the gumption to do the few things that he could and wanted to do.

Chapter Nineteen

Claire slept until nearly ten. The window air conditioner had the room so cold that, as had become routine, she got out of bed with the blanket wrapped around her, turned off the unit and opened wide the door to the fresh, if hot, morning air. On the step she found a thermal pitcher of coffee and covered dish breakfast on a tray—this morning cantaloupe, ham and sweet rolls.

This was the result of an unspoken agreement with Gertie. Claire tended to her own housekeeping chores, and Gertie began depositing a morning tray on her doorstep.

Leaving the door open, she sat at the small table in front of the window and ate her breakfast.

A minivan from Grace Florist pulled into the lot and came straight to Claire's door.

"Flowers for you, Miz Wilder."

"Oh!"

From Andrew! With high excitement she accepted the vase and carried them inside.

At that moment, her cell phone rang from her purse.

It might be Gayla, or even a wrong number, but she thought, looking at the flowers and imagining all manner of romantic scenarios, that surely it was Andrew. She had called him three times in the past week, and not once had he called her, not even to say if he had gotten her most recent post-card. So she had quit calling him, just to see how long it would take for him to call her. Today would be the fifth day. And today she got these lovely flowers!

She hurried to set the vase on the table, cast a, "Just a minute," to the delivery girl, and grabbed up her purse to dig for both the phone and the tip money, while catching her robe to keep it from flying open as the tie belt slipped loose. Trying to do so many things at once, she dropped her purse and everything spilled out. A wad of bills was in the mess. She gave this to the girl, thanked her, and flew back to her phone, which had quit ringing.

The screen, though, displayed Andrew's office number. Delighted, she quickly returned the call.

"Andrew? It's me—Claire." As if he wouldn't know her voice, or perhaps mistake her for Nina or some other woman who he might have taken up with since she left, which was something of an anxiety-producing thought, although a glance at the flowers renewed her spirit.

"I know. Your name shows up on my caller ID."

"Oh…that's right. I got the flowers…just now. That's why I missed your call. The delivery came just this minute." Gazing at the flowers, she felt deeply touched.

But Andrew said, "What flowers?"

Oh, dear. She was acutely sensitive to his tones, and she knew instantly that he was not joking and had not sent the flowers.

"Someone sent me flowers. Maybe Gayla. She knows I love flowers. She's been keepin' in touch. We've often sent each other flowers." She spoke fast, as she found the card and opened it.

The card read: *A token of my affection, love, Winston.*

Andrew did not ask who sent them, but a certain irritation that he had not been the one to send the flowers made telling him quite easy. "Winston Valentine sent them...you know, the elderly man who knew my grandfather. He's a very kind man," she added.

"That must have been who answered your phone yesterday."

His tone and words threw her into confusion. "Yesterday? You called yesterday?"

"Yes."

"Oh. I didn't know. And someone answered?"

"Yeah. He said you were at the Burger Barn?"

"Oh. That must have been Winston." Then, "He's elderly...and he just has his ways."

"Oh, yeah."

The line hummed.

"Did you call me about something special?" she asked.

"Just to see how you are."

"I'm fine." Again a long pause. "Did you get the postcard I sent last week?" It was something to change the subject, something other than asking: Why didn't you simply call back? Why haven't you sent flowers? Did you take back up with Nina or some other woman?

"Yeah. It was in my mail when I got in late last night— I've been down to New Orleans again."

"Oh. More problems with the shopping mall?" That would be why he hadn't called. When he got busy with his work, he didn't think of anything else. This was a sign of his responsibility, she reminded herself.

"Some. The structural contractor really doesn't have much experience."

"Oh, well…I'm sorry you're having trouble." What else could she say?

"It'll get solved. Did you get a car yet?"

"No. I really haven't had time. I've been busy helpin' Vella—but she's thinkin' that she might sell me her husband's car. It's a Lincoln." She said the make of the car with some hesitancy. Andrew was particular about his preference for fancy foreign jobs. "It's only two years old."

His response to this was, "What's goin' on with you, Claire?"

"What do you mean?" she got out after her initial surprise. She was at once angry at his demanding tone and gratified that she had rattled him. He had called her, and he cared at least enough to be irritated with her. That was something.

"Look—are you okay? This just isn't like you."

"What isn't like me?" She knew what he meant, but she wanted to hear him elaborate. She wanted him to be specific and not make her carry the weight of all the emotion by trying to anticipate what she needed to say to soothe and please him.

"You know—quittin' your job like you did. Just dropping out…and your hair…and then runnin' off to stay at some sleazy motel and gettin' the Mercedes stolen, and gettin' all involved with strangers for weeks."

What was wrong with her hair? He had said he liked it. And she had not *gotten* the Mercedes stolen.

Feeling herself shrivel in the face of his critical tone, she attempted to marshal logical thought.

"I came to see where my father's family is from—where I was *born*. I am on vacation, gettin' some rest…much needed, I might add. Vacation is a time when people go away and do nothing." She had come to see that she had been, at the outset of her journey, far more frazzled than she had imagined. Had she been able to get decent food delivery, she might have been in danger of lying in her bed for months.

"And I've made some nice acquaintances. People do that when they go on vacation, Andrew. At least, some people do—when they are not on a working vacation. And this motel may be old, but it isn't sleazy. It is charming and calming. Maybe it wouldn't be up to Nina Rennal's sophisticated tastes, but I happen to like it fine."

She wished she had not brought up Nina's name in such a way. The comment made her sound petty.

His sigh came over the line. She could imagine him, holding the phone and pacing, his expression that of long-suffering patience. She hated it when he took on that attitude.

"Okay—you sent me a postcard that says 'lookin' for real life.' What do you mean by that?"

Even though she was familiar with his attitude, it had its effect.

"I don't know." She slowly sat on the edge of the bed and raked a hand through her hair. "I read it on a bathroom wall a few weeks ago—'lookin' for real life.' It just seemed, well, an interesting thought." Her thoughts dammed up like water behind a thick tangle of clogging debris.

"I'm worried about you, Claire. You up and quit your job out of the blue, and now you've been up there for three weeks, haven't gotten another car, haven't seen about comin' home."

She gazed out the window at the road and the sign that now said in extra large letters: *Vintage Motel for Sale. Price Reduced.*

"What are you gonna do, Claire? How are you gonna make the payments on the townhouse? Takin' off for a week to see your father's hometown and gettin' a bit of rest is one thing, but this droppin' out and goin' off alone with no plans for when you're comin' back is…not like you."

He had an entirely different picture of her activities than was the fact.

"I did not up and quit my job out of the blue," she said.

"I had been thinking of quittin' my job for a long time. I was thinking about it way before we got divorced. I discussed it with you a number of times." She bit her tongue on saying, *remember?*

"I never wanted to be a secretary, Andrew. Never. And then one day I finally knew that I had to quit. That it was now or never."

Realizing her hand ached from gripping the phone, she changed hands quickly and tried to relax. "As for leavin' my whole life, I didn't really do that. Your job is your life, but mine never was. I left a house I never really wanted and a job I really disliked. I don't think I left much of anything."

And you weren't there. She stopped before saying this.

"You know, Andrew, me goin' off alone is not really any different than how I've always been. I feel like I've spent most of my life alone. Mama and Daddy didn't have any time for me, and after they broke up, Mama was there, but she really wasn't there *for me.* I spent my time bein' there for her. You and I spent most of our years working and meeting briefly each evenin'."

She stopped, rather surprised by her own words but knowing deeply the truth of it all.

"Do you really see us like that?" he asked.

To which she replied in an honest manner, "Yes. Pretty much, I do."

"We made two babies. That shows we spent time together. We went together since high school and were married for nearly eighteen years, Claire. We had some wonderful times. If you didn't, you pretended awfully good." The hurt in his voice touched her.

"I know that—yes, we had some wonderful, precious times." Her throat got thick. She didn't want to cry. She would not cry.

"I really did, Andrew. I'm grateful for what we had. And

I'm not placing any blame, but simply sayin' that I've mostly always felt alone. I certainly made my life alone the past two years, so goin' off alone doesn't seem all that strange to me. Where I have trouble is being with other people.

"You know, I can talk better on the phone than I can with someone in person."

This knowledge came in a sudden and clear thought, followed by knowing that she had such a hard time talking to Andrew, while he was the one she wanted to talk to most.

She was so intent on seeing this fact, as well as experiencing quite a bit of actual pain in the vicinity of her heart, and a great longing to reach out and touch him, that she barely heard what else he said, until he asked her when she planned on coming home.

"I don't know."

Truth. At once a relief and a risky thing to say. She sat up straighter. "I have sufficient reserves to be away for the summer. You don't need to worry on that account. I just need more rest, Andrew. I need time to figure out some things in my life. There's just been so much that's happened in the past couple of years…you and I…and Mama dyin'."

Please understand, said her tone. And attempting to present a plan in the manner that he was likely to find acceptable, she offered, "I may go on west for a couple of weeks. To see Roswell and the Grand Canyon. I've always wanted to see those places."

Then, impulsively, "Would you like to join me?"

For a breathless second, a balloon of hope filled within her that he would actually come. In an instant, she could see it all, the bright sun shining on them, hand in hand along magnificent rocky pathways. On neutral ground, away from their history and failure.

He said, "I can't get away now, Claire. I just can't up and leave. There's the problem with the mall, and a new project is comin' on board, and I'm likely to be the one to head it up."

His tone was sharp. She had asked for something he didn't want to give.

"Okay," she said.

He set in to impress upon her all the reasons why up and leaving his job was an impossible and unthinkable thing to do, and she said that she understood completely.

They left it like that, each saying a polite goodbye.

When she clicked off the cell phone, she sat for several minutes with the dawning realization that Andrew wanted her to come home. That was why he was harping at her. He had all but said it straight out.

She was briefly thrilled, but this was eclipsed by the question: Why couldn't he say it straight out?

He never had been able to say things straight out.

But that didn't mean she had to say them for him.

The morning when she had left her townhouse seemed much further in the past than three weeks. So much had happened. She had packed up and left her home, had a thrilling encounter with her ex-husband and then left him right there in the street, arrived in a strange town, had an old man fall in love with her, had her car and all her belongings stolen, tried to help an unfortunate young woman, made a good woman friend, begun flirting with a younger man, and helped to save a man's life. Oh, and there was breaking down Winston's car in there, too.

She had never in her life been so busy.

As she creamed her face and body, brushed her hair to softness, and applied makeup and perfume, her mind zipped back through the past weeks and onward back through the years.

The memories that came were unwelcome in her current state of mind, which had sunk down somewhere between anger and despair. What came to her was that she had spent most of her time trying to keep her mother afloat and following her husband around. She had put her life on hold with all kinds of fantasies about Andrew awakening to the fact that he was meant for her and her for him.

But now that such a fantasy actually seemed to be within reach, she could not find any feeling at all. It scared her, not feeling. An inertia seemed to have taken over her.

She mulled this state over as she slipped into a new set of black lace bra and panties (it was amazing what could be bought through Belinda's shopping service, she thought) and decided that a certain relaxation had come with the inertia. She no longer awoke several times in the night, wondering where she was and if she needed to do this or that. She had no job, no one to worry about pleasing, nothing that she absolutely *had* to do, only things she wanted to do, and these things did not have to be planned but could evolve with the day.

At last she had time to read, everything from *Women's Health* to *Southwest Travel,* and a compilation of C. S. Lewis—Blaine's Drugstore had quite a good magazine and book stand. She conditioned her hair, took hot, fragrant baths and long walks, looked at the stars, helped Vella, and chatted with all manner of strangers when she was at the hospital or went through the IGA.

She had slipped into what she imagined might be a manner lived by the "idle rich," except, of course, that hers was going on in a third-rate motel room with a sagging mattress, rattling air conditioner, and a divine forty-year-old bathtub with aged enamel—but a wonderful shape for reclining and absolutely no mold, because Gertie came every morning and sprayed all the tile.

Upon realizing that Gertie was doing this each morning, coming with her frosted pink fingernails protected in yellow gloves and spraying a Clorox concoction on the tile, Claire had offered to do it.

"I'll let you," said Gertie, handing over the spray bottle.

Claire had begun to bring her towels to the office and strip the bedsheets when she was ready, too. It was doubtful that the idle rich did such housekeeping chores, but Claire had her belongings—which she was gradually buying back up—spread all over the room and bathroom, and didn't want to have to move them out of the way of Gertie or the some-time housekeeper, Luna.

Also, she had formed an attachment for her room and the entire motel. She had begun to feel quite at home at the Goodnight. She even went so far as to buy lavender oil and ask Gertie to use it in the rinse water for the linens, instead of the brand of softener she'd been using.

"Lavender encourages sound sleep and sweet dreams," she told Gertie. "Maybe you could use it as a signature for the Goodnight. You know, make a new postcard…'lavender scented sheets on every bed for a good night's sleep…'"

She had many ideas for improving the motel. She loved to sit and think them up. It was a way to relax her mind.

Another reason she was relaxed was that she had thus far escaped having to make a decision about purchasing a car. She had been at the drugstore, drinking a strawberry milkshake and perusing automobile ads on the afternoon when Perry had suffered his attack, and since that time she had thrown herself into helping Vella and avoiding the decision about a vehicle.

Life in Valentine, at least in the summer, could be managed easily on foot. The walking distance from the motel to town turned out to be not nearly so far as she had first perceived, and in any case, the several times that she had started out to walk it, someone had come along to give her a ride. These were people she had met in passing at the drugstore or possibly the café, and she recalled faces but not names.

Each of them remembered her name, though, and said, more or less, "You're Claire Wilder, the woman Winston's been seein' and who got her car stolen, aren't you? And you saved Perry Blaine's life the other day, right?"

She felt as if an information card was circulating about her.

"That's how it is around here," Vella told her. "You are a new, unattached, good-lookin' woman in town. You're news."

The idea of being a subject of conversation and scrutiny was a little disconcerting; however, it did seem that everyone talking about her was an asset. She could cash a check or use her credit card with ease, and when she called up to order food, the person on the other end of the phone line invariably said, "You're out at the Goodnight, right?"

In Valentine, most anything that could be bought could also be delivered, and usually within twenty minutes. Even the IGA grocery store delivered, everything from deli meals, several organic and healthy choices, to Kleenex and cat food.

Claire ordered the cat food because she had taken to feeding a stray cat that lived somewhere around the cabins.

"People are all the time drivin' past and throwing cats and pups they don't want out the windows," Frank told her. "We sometimes have to call the city out to pick 'em up."

She suggested that, with an excess of cats, as a promotional device, he could provide a cat for any guest who might want one. She had seen this gimmick in a feature in a travel magazine.

All in all, she simply was not ready to run back to take up her life in Shreveport, even if she might possibly be taking it up again with Andrew. Not desiring life with Andrew was embarrassing and unnerving. She knew perfectly well that she was running the risk of him taking up again with Nina or another woman. What man would continue to be rebuffed, as she had rebuffed him?

Yet even so, she had to take the risk. She had to be certain in her heart of her direction in life when she returned. She wanted no more mistakes between them. She felt that surely she did want to take up with him, only she was momentarily confused. She thought that perhaps her condition was what she had heard termed burnout, and with a little more rest, the longing and desire for Andrew and a knowledge of what she wanted to do with her life with him, would spring forth.

They walked out to Vella Blaine's garage. It was an old wooden structure, about fifty years old and covered with blooming wisteria, while her very modern yard swept away from it, filled with carefully tended rose gardens and a magnificent rock patio. Vella said that she had not bothered with building a new garage because she so rarely took time out from her Land Rover to park it in a garage. Perry's Lincoln had not been parked in it, either, until he had suffered his stroke.

"Are you sure you want to sell it?" Claire asked of the car.

"Yes, I am. I'm going to sell it to someone, so you drive it a few days to see if you would like it." She put the keys in Claire's hands, then began opening one of the old wooden garage doors. Claire opened the other.

Sunlight shone on the trunk of a gleaming black car. Showroom condition.

"Perry finally traded off his old Lincoln for this one not long before his first small stroke," Vella said in a strained voice. "I urged him to get it. I thought maybe it would perk him up. Do you think that sellin' it is rushing him to his grave?"

"I cannot borrow or buy this car." Claire extended the keys.

Vella waved them away. "Oh, yes, you can. It is idiocy to let the car sit here and rot. I try to come out here and start it about once a week, but what with one thing and another,

I'm more and more forgettin'. I think it's been nearly three weeks since it's been started this time. I sure hope it turns over," she added, all but shoving Claire into the driver's seat.

"Are you sure you want to sell it? Maybe Belinda could start drivin' it?" Claire started to pop out of the seat.

Vella pushed her back down, saying, "I have given my daughter her apartment and a third of the store. I'm not givin' her a nearly new Lincoln. And if you haven't noticed, Belinda isn't exactly the car-maintenance type. She prefers a chauffeur—Lyle takes her everywhere she wants to go, which isn't hardly anywhere. She's as bad a homebody as her daddy. Why do you think she orders everything from the shoppin' channels? One time she took a notion to go on a ten-day Caribbean cruise, and she flew back home within five days.

"Now come on and get goin'. I want you to get it out of here while the nurse is upstairs shavin' Perry. Get buckled up. Perry never let anyone in this car that didn't buckle up."

That comment caused Claire to again want to abandon the car, but she was finding the seat could be adjusted perfectly to her body. A certain excitement came over her at the prospect of taking Vella up on her offer. If she could simply buy Perry's car, then she wouldn't have to go to car dealers and face making a decision on a model, and Vella said that Belinda, a notary, would handle the transfer of registration.

She suddenly wanted to say, "Oh, yes, sell me the car, I don't need to drive it," but since this seemed rudely pushy, she restrained herself.

Backing slowly from the garage, she gave Vella a little wave, then had to avert her eyes to the rearview mirror, as the woman's concerned expression made her feel anxious. So anxious, in fact, that she put her foot on the brake pedal, thinking that she could not possibly drive the car, much less purchase it.

Looking forward again, she saw Vella gesturing with both

hands, waving Claire out of the driveway. The woman appeared, in fact, as if she might start pushing on the hood if Claire stopped, so Claire backed on out into the street and headed away.

She had the good sense not to look in the rearview mirror.

She stopped into the florist and bought two small bouquets of daisies.

"They don't need wrapping. Please just tie them with a ribbon."

Then she drove out on the highway. Woo-hoo! It *was* good to have wheels again! A vehicle had never seemed all that important to her, but now, after not having one, she felt the great freedom of driving.

She pressed the accelerator and discovered that the engine could really get up and go. It had a CD player, too. That would take studying, but she turned on the radio without much of a problem. The speakers were grand. The window went down with just one slight press of a button, and the air conditioner had a mighty good fan. And there was a rear defroster. Corrine would approve of that. And a nice, comforting long hood in front.

Coming up on a slower car, she passed it with ease and a light toot of the horn. She liked this car! And it was being handed to her, and the sale would be good for Vella and good for herself. A win-win situation.

Then came the disconcerting thought: if she bought Perry's car, there would be no excuse for staying in Valentine.

She drove to the Little Creek cemetery and did something she had wanted to do from the first day—put fresh flowers on the sadly forgotten graves of her grandparents.

Laying a small bouquet of daisies in front of each of the markers, she offered up a prayer. It seemed a little silly, but necessary. Then she also said a prayer for her mother, whose remains were out there where only God knew their place. She hoped her mother would forgive her for being so careless with the urn.

"Mom, maybe I'll get you a grave site and headstone. Then I can bring you flowers." She was fairly certain her mother would love the flowers.

As she pulled weeds from around the bases of her grandparents' markers, it occurred to her that her mother probably would not approve of her paying her father's parents so much attention.

When she rose to go, she saw a man crossing the small cemetery, his hat in his hand. He stopped at a grave in the shade of a massive cedar tree.

It was Larkin Ford.

As she watched, he crouched in front of the marker. She moved to be able to see him placing flowers in the vase.

Curious as to whose grave he visited, she slowly walked toward him until she could read the marker: Karin Jeanine Ford.

As she was trying to decipher the rest of the words and dates, he rose and turned, seeing her.

He was clearly surprised.

"Hello," she said, and he responded politely to the greeting. She was pleased to see his surprise turn to curiosity.

She told him that she had been visiting her grandparents' graves, while her mind went ninety miles an hour on ways to find out the identity of the person he had come to give flowers.

"My wife," he supplied, gesturing with his hat.

"Oh." What did one say? "I'm sorry."

"It's been five years."

"You still bring flowers." They were lovely fresh flowers, daisies and carnations and little irises.

"Yeah, sometimes."

"This is the first time I ever brought flowers to a grave. My grandparents' graves just looked so forgotten. My mother was cremated, and I had an urn I sometimes sort of spoke to." She couldn't imagine why she felt it necessary to admit that. "But it was stolen with my car."

"I'm sorry," he said.

"Yes…well, it was pretty silly of me to have it with me, I suppose. I sometimes wonder what the guy who stole the car thought when he saw the urn…or whoever found it."

She chuckled, and he responded with his halfway grin, and this gave her the courage to ask how long he had been married.

"Since just after high school." He was uncomfortable again.

She told him she had been with her husband since high school, too. That they had been married for eighteen years but were now divorced for two years.

"I know," he said.

"Oh, that's right. I forgot about Travis." She wondered what Travis had told his father—had he mentioned their flirting? Had he made more out of it than it was?

"Travis didn't tell me. He hasn't said anything about you." It was as if he'd read her mind. He gazed at her intently. "You know…small town and people talk."

"Oh." She wondered what he had heard.

Just then a car filled with a family drove up. Larkin seemed to take this as his cue to say goodbye.

Claire lingered there in the cemetery in the shade of the big cedar with limbs swishing gently in the breeze. She looked at the tombstone of Karin Ford, who had lived only thirty-nine years. It said Beloved Wife and Mother. And Larkin still brought her flowers. It was such a beautiful thing that she got teary.

Winston said that summer had arrived and likely there would be little rain. Claire marveled that night after night there came stunning sunsets, all shades of golden and coral. Back in Shreveport, there had been so many trees that cluttered the sunsets. At times she missed the trees, especially the tall pines, but she liked being able to see the sky so big and wide.

Gazing through the window now at the sunset, she called Gayla Jean from the motel room phone, using her telephone calling card. She couldn't afford the high price of going over her minutes on her cell phone. She had begun to worry a little about money, about maybe being punished for the irresponsibility of quitting her job and spending all her savings on a motel and restaurants. It was like worry had come with Andrew's voice on the phone and stuck all over her.

Gayla Jean answered with her usual squeal and, "Well, how are ya, girl?"

"I'm okay. I'm havin' a pretty good time. I'm sleepin' in and just takin' it easy and just, well, being." She had recently read this term in one of the travel magazines.

Gayla Jean said, "I'm glad for you, honey. You deserve this vacation, and that's what I told Andrew. I think when he broke up with Nina, he expected you to come runnin'. Well, you have sure shown him."

"I'm not tryin' to show him anything." Was she?

"Well, you are just the same, and it's good for him. Men get too complacent. They let all the romance go. Have you possibly met some handsome man to have a romance with?"

"No. That's not why I came on this vacation." Larkin Ford and her meeting with him that afternoon popped into her mind, followed by Travis, who flirted with her, and Winston, who said he loved her. Why couldn't she have found so many men in Shreveport?

Gayla Jean was saying, "I know it wasn't, but I just thought you might have run into someone." Her voice took on a dreamy quality. "You know, like one of those romance novels or movies on the Women's Channel, the woman who meets the man of her dreams while on some trip to a foreign country."

"I'm not in a foreign country...and life is not like the movies," said Claire, feeling called on to point out the fact for her own benefit as much as for her friend.

"But the reason we watch them is because we want it to be. Romance is good for people. I'm workin' on it in my own life, too. Lamar and I are goin' to the Hilton for a night of love. We are attending a marriage enrichment seminar this weekend. I'm so excited. This will be the first time we have been off overnight without at least one of the kids. I bought a sexy negligee from Victoria's Secret, and I'm reading a book about pleasin' a man sexually. It is a Christian book. Did you know that the Song of Solomon is all about sex? I thought when it was talkin' about a garden, it meant a garden."

No, Claire said, she did not know that, and anxious not to hear any more about Gayla Jean's sexual endeavors, she said, "Did you get the postcard I sent last week?"

"Oh, uh-huh, we did. The kids have found Valentine on the map. Jeremy wants to know, though, when you are goin' out to Roswell. He heard you say you were goin' there, and the other day he saw a show about UFOs on television, and now he is all hot for us to go out there on vacation."

"What did you think about what I wrote...about havin' a good time lookin' for real life?"

"Is that what you said? I guess I didn't think anything...I don't really remember. You know, I haven't gotten a postcard from anyone in years. I can't even think of the last time I got a postcard. I guess I thought you were havin' a good time on vacation. Honey, I never realized how much pressure you were under, but Lord a'mercy, Mr. Dupree has Melanie in tears about every day. Did you mean anything more than that?"

"Yes...I mean no. I meant just what you said." She was

having a little trouble following Gayla's somewhat disjointed conversation.

"Oh, here's the card. Raquel put it on the refrigerator. 'Having a good time looking for real life. Wish you were here.'" There was a pause and then, "Valentine looks like a fun place, I guess, but I think I'd rather go to some romantic resort in Bermuda or Hawaii. I mean, if I'm goin' on vacation, I really want to go somewhere I can get away from my real life."

Chapter Twenty

She decided to drive up to see Sherrilyn at Lilac House. She wanted to see how the girl was doing, and Belinda wanted to send several boxes of items she had gathered for the young women at the shelter.

Claire was a little surprised at the generosity, and also at the items: silk shawls and satin robes, bedroom slippers, scented candles, perfumes, bath oils and fine lotions. She wondered if Belinda had gotten the shelter mixed up with a bordello.

"You've got some fancy things here," she said.

"Well, I didn't think it would be too practical to send street clothes, since I couldn't know sizes. QVC had a great week of sales on lotions, perfumes and candles, and Lori and Mama pitched in, too," Belinda said, tossing off her own generosity. "We need to do all that we can to encourage these young women to aspire to their highest. When they do, they'll take pains with their grooming, and when they look nice, they'll feel better, have more pride, and be productive wage-earners of society, not leeches drainin' off all our tax dollars. The

more women out there workin' their tails off, the more cus-
tomers we'll have. Plus, this is all advertising and tax-deduct-
ible," she added, pressing a gold Blaine's Drugstore sticker on
a bottle of lotion.

Claire must have revealed her astonishment, because Belinda said, "Mama thinks I don't know much, but I am runnin' this drugstore with a good profit."

She plopped the box she carried into the trunk of the Lincoln, dusted off her hands, and headed back into the drugstore with her ample hips swaying and her plastic
crystal-heeled sandals clicking on the pavement.

Lilac House was one of those old two-story affairs from
the turn of the century. It had probably gone through many
owners and fallen down to a rental before being bought at a
charity price and beginning, if not an upward climb, at least
a patching up.

Once inside, Claire saw that it was furnished in a generally warm manner with odds and ends. Glancing through
an open door into what might have been a study at one
time, she saw several computers and a shelf of books. This
gave her a bit of hope for the young women, several of
whom seemed the tough sort one wouldn't want to meet
in a dark alley.

Young women seemed to seep from other rooms and
swarm like bees, descending on the boxes brought in with
the help of Sherrilyn and the house mother, Ms. Seames.
With squeals and grabbing hands, and a couple of near fights,
all of the items in the boxes were dispensed and the girls disappeared, all except Sherrilyn, who stood there quite for-
lornly, holding only two things, a bottle of lotion and pair of
burgundy satin slippers that definitely clashed with her hair.

Claire was glad she had brought the girl some private items.
"For you," she said, handing over the large pastel green gift bag.

★ ★ ★

Claire followed Sherrilyn up to her room. "How many women are here?"

She was careful not to refer to them as girls—they were not girls but young women, though they appeared not to have gone much beyond twelve in maturity. She passed four bedrooms reverberating with high-pitched voices.

There was one bathroom. It would be a nightmare.

"Ten," said Sherrilyn, tossing her silky red hair over her shoulder. It had been cut, and not too straight. "And Mrs. Seames. Her room is downstairs. This is my room."

Claire followed her out onto what was an upstairs enclosed rear porch—a poorly enclosed porch—with a row of windows. There was a small dresser, a bed, and a nightstand. Some clothes hung on nails along one wall.

"It's awfully hot. Can you open a window?"

"That's why I leave the door open—to get some of the air-conditioning. It's pretty nice in the mornings, just gets a little hot by afternoon."

Claire wondered about the possibility of heat stroke or spontaneous abortion.

"You get used to it," Sherrilyn said. "I was in the front bedroom, but I asked to move out here. I don't like being crowded in with the others."

"I imagine I wouldn't, either," Claire said. "Open your present."

Sherrilyn shyly pulled the tissue paper from the gift bag and then lifted out a pair of maternity capris, a maternity blouse, hair clip and colorful underwear. After several encounters with the girl, Claire now felt confident to attempt choosing a size.

Sherrilyn held the clothes up in front of herself, and Claire said they would look very nice on her. The girl thanked her.

"Why are you doin' this?" Sherrilyn asked, the distrust again in her eyes.

Claire sighed. "I don't really know…except that I want to."

★ ★ ★

They went for a drive. Claire thought the girl needed to cool off for a bit and to be fed. She was still so terribly frail-looking. Claire knew that she herself needed to cool off and eat.

They went to a drive-in and had corn dogs and fries and Cokes. Claire suggested a healthy meal at a restaurant, but Sherrilyn was eager for the drive-in. While they ate, Claire let the Lincoln's engine run, with the air conditioner blowing. On the way back to the house, she stopped at a market and bought a bag of fruit and several packages of cookies.

When she asked Sherrilyn's preferences for both, Sherrilyn said in a gloomy manner, "It doesn't matter. The other girls are goin' to get most of it. We have to put it all in the kitchen and share."

Claire bought bananas and apples and six packages of the cookies, three of which she put into a separate bag. She carried this bag under her arm and up to Sherrilyn's room, stuffing it under the bed. "There, you can have a private nighttime snack," she said to the girl, who stood watching her with an uncertain eye.

Ten minutes later, as she was leaving, Ms. Seames asked to speak to her.

Following the woman into her office, Claire wondered if she was about to be reprimanded for hiding food in one of the bedrooms.

The house-mother launched into a rundown on Sherrilyn's situation, which was that Sherrilyn, not much more than a hundred pounds with a bowling ball stomach, was clearly on the losing end in a house with seven other girls who outweighed her by some twenty to fifty pounds, three others who were likely smarter, and all who were tougher. Two were decidedly meaner. How Sherrilyn had lived as she had and not gotten more street-smart was a mystery. While of normal intelligence and capabilities, she was clearly one of those people who were terminally naive, in the opinion of Ms. Seames.

At the end of this discourse, none of which came as a surprise, Claire said, "I'm not her mother. I'm not any relation, and these are private matters that perhaps Sherrilyn wouldn't like you discussing with me."

"Since you came today and brought her gifts, I'm assuming you are a friend…or that you at least care about her some," said Ms. Seames.

"Yes, I care about her. But I've only recently met her."

The woman was eyeing her severely. "The other day Tamara—she's the one with the stud in her lower lip—took Sherrilyn's stuffed bear. I made her give it back. She did, after tearing it apart. Sherrilyn responded to this by cutting her own hair."

Claire felt sick at the idea, and at a loss as to what to say.

Ms. Seames' expression said clearly: *I can tell you have some brains and means, and by heaven, you are going to help me.*

"What I'm saying is that Sherrilyn needs help. Personal help, and perhaps you can give it to her. Sherrilyn needs to learn how to live in the real world, and she needs to be convinced that it is in her and the baby's best interest for her to give it up for adoption. Very few of the girls who come through here ever manage to become capable mothers. They weren't mothered themselves. Those who do manage have family willing to take them in."

Claire gazed at the woman. "I'm here on vacation. I'm from Shreveport." Then, faced with the woman's determined expression, "I'll do what I can while I'm here."

Thank God for air-conditioning, she thought, and it was a fervent prayer as she turned up the system in the Lincoln.

Squinting, as she peered out at the road to Valentine, she

thought of the young women at Lilac House. Then her mind traveled back to childhood.

She and her mother had existed for years on the good graces of her mother's father and Aunt Agnes, two very cold and hard people. Aunt Agnes never let them forget that they were beholden to her for the roof over their heads. No wonder her mother had so often taken to her bed. But still, her mother had held on and done her best for Claire.

Quite suddenly it occurred to her that her mother had lived until she had become fully certain that Claire was sailing well and secure on her own.

She remembered one of the last conversations she had with her mother, who had been once again in bed.

"I don't have anything to leave you," her mother said. "It's hard for a woman alone. I wish you would make up with Andrew. Get him back and put up with things, Claire. So what if he doesn't come home much. He brings a paycheck, and you'll be glad for that when you're my age, livin' off social security. It's hard, Claire. Sometimes we would have starved, if one of my man friends hadn't of helped, or I hadn't had somethin' of Daddy's to sell off. It's all gone now. There's nothin' left for you."

Her mother could go on in this sad vein for an interminable time, so Claire had sought to cut her off. "I don't need Andrew's money, Mother. I have my own savings and retirement plans. I'm not rich, but I will be okay. Look."

She had shown her mother her investment portfolio. Her mother had been surprised, and then, Claire remembered, her mother had relaxed against the pillows and said, "Women didn't know about such things when I was young. Men did it all for us. Even Daddy did it for Aunt Agnes."

Her eyes came to rest on Claire, as if seeing an oddity.

Vella didn't cut her any slack in bargaining for the car. Claire, having done newspaper shopping for vehicles, felt the price was high by as much as a thousand dollars. Even so, to find such a car, to have it plopped down into her hands, made it a bargain.

She gave Vella a check, and Vella said that Belinda was a notary and would handle all the legalities. All Claire needed to do was stop by the drugstore to sign some papers, and to celebrate their deal, Vella invited Claire to the patio for a glass of cold sweet tea and shortbread cookies. What auto dealer could top that?

Vella stretched out in a cushioned chaise longue, while Claire sat at the table, the plate of cookies within easy reach. Vella asked about Sherrilyn, and Claire gave her a rundown of the visit and of Ms. Seames' strong suggestion that Claire help the girl by influencing her to give the baby up for adoption.

"I can agree that possibly giving the baby up for adoption would be best for the girl and the baby, but what's she goin' to have if she does that?" Claire took her third cookie, promising herself that would be the last.

"What's she goin' to have if she doesn't?" Vella countered. "The woman's right. The girl won't be able to take care of the child. They'll both end up on the streets."

"I know." The dismal thought had Claire eyeing the plate of cookies yet again. "I just don't think I'm the one to influence her in this." She told Vella about her first conversation with the girl and of how she told Sherrilyn that no one could make her give the baby up for adoption.

"I keep thinkin' that maybe I could take her back to Shreveport with me, let her live with me and have the baby, finish her education and learn a trade of some sort."

She admitted this somewhat wild idea with hesitancy, although, the more she thought of it, the more viable it became. Why couldn't she do such a thing? She had in the past day, since seeing the girl, come up with an extended fantasy of getting the girl a nice stylish haircut, having her teeth fixed, educating her about proper dressing and generally encouraging her upward in life.

Vella said, "That's one way to get the baby up for adoption—you take them both on."

Claire wasn't certain about Vella's tone, and she didn't like the implication of the words. "Someone needs to help her." She realized that she had taken a fourth cookie; it would be inappropriate to put it back now that she had handled it.

"Yes. I don't disagree. It might be good for both of you, really."

Claire tried to figure out which way the older woman was leaning on the idea. Then her attention was diverted by watching Vella slip off her shoe and examine her foot. Claire was a little amazed at the older woman's flexibility. Vella bent her leg and massaged her foot, showing quite lovely legs as her skirt fell back.

"I thought you had wanted to continue on to some place else for vacation," Vella said. "Didn't you say Roswell?"

"I did…but now I don't know. Now that I have the Lincoln, I guess I can continue on vacation like I had planned. Or go back to Shreveport." Claire fingered the cold glass of tea and gazed at the plate of cookies, thinking of the cookies that she had hidden under Sherrilyn's bed. The girl shouldn't have to hide cookies, nor should Claire teach her to do so. Claire should have taught Sherrilyn to stand up for her cookies.

Vella said, "I don't know why havin' a car should make you feel like you have to do either one. I think one of your problems is that you have been so responsible all of your life that you don't know how to have a vacation. The point of a vacation is to relax, wander around, do nothing. Not that you asked."

Claire agreed that she did not know how to have a vacation. "I never really had one."

She and her mother had gone a couple of times to the

Gulf in the summer, but Claire had spent a lot of the time looking out for her mother, being her mother's companion. She hadn't gotten to run and play much with other children, as her mother might need her to get aspirin, or put sun lotion on her back, or just be close by. Her experience with Andrew had been much the same. In her capacity as his wife, she had been attentive, and then there had been the obligation to entertain his business associates. She had experienced little time in her life when she didn't feel driven to do things.

"I guess I just feel obligated to do *something* to try to figure out my life and where I'm going. I really need to figure out if I want to take up with Andrew again. He isn't going to wait forever."

In fact, she might have already lost him. Every time she thought about that, her mind seemed to short-circuit and a big hole opened up in her chest.

"I think that you not running back to him in Shreveport should tell you something. And him, too."

This statement upset and annoyed Claire. "I don't think that's necessarily so. Running back to a person is no measure of how much you love that person. Maybe *not* running back to a person shows how much you value the relationship and want it to be right."

Upset, Claire took another cookie before she realized it. As she munched on it, her spirits began to slip downward.

"I guess it's true, though," she said.

"What's true?"

"What you said about my not racing home to Shreveport being telling. There's just so much involved. Maybe I'm more caught up in a dream than in reality. I had it for so long. I loved Andrew from the time I was thirteen and went to junior high. Heaven only knows how I didn't end up like Sherrilyn."

"You had a mother who gave you certain standards and pushed your education."

"Yes…yes, she did." Thinking of her mother in this light, she experienced a sharp and rare gratitude. Her mother had certainly given her standards. A few of them had been constraining and ridiculous, but her mother's regard for education had been a saving grace. Her mother had gone through almost two years of college before marrying, which said a lot for a woman of her time and place. Claire had always thought that one thing her mother had held against her father was that he was not of the same education.

"Do you still love Andrew?" asked Vella, still involved with examining her feet, stretching out her legs and putting her feet together as if measuring.

"I don't know. I'm all mixed up inside. I care for him…. I know that. Maybe I just don't believe in us as a couple anymore. It is the strangest thing. I have hoped and prayed for us to get back together, and now that I have the opportunity, I'm throwing it away."

She grabbed up the plate of cookies, now containing only three, and took them to the table on the other side of Vella, then returned resolutely to her chair.

"Oh, honey," Vella said, "none of us can figure out our lives or even know where we're goin'. What you have to do is pray to be shown, and then all you're given is just enough light for right where you are, so just accept that you're goin' to make a million mistakes along the way.

"You know, I never really knew who I was or where I was goin'. About the time I would figure any of it out, everything would change. I never in my wildest dreams imagined that I would end up a woman of some means."

Claire saw wonderment on her friend's face.

"I don't even know how I did it," Vella said, "but along the way, about the time I began to accept that my sex life was not going to revive with Perry, I started readin' financial magazines and investin'. It was someplace to put my energy. I could only dig in the dirt and plant roses during the day, and the nights were so long. And I started makin' money.

"I don't know where I'm goin' from here," she said, "but I don't worry about it anymore. I just go along for the day-by-day journey, trustin' God to lead me somewhere."

Claire admired Vella's confidence and faith and said so; however, privately, she felt that at Vella's age, with her life pretty much set, secure and behind her, the attitude was easy to put forth.

Claire's life stretched before her, sort of hanging by a thread in the wind. She had decisions to make. Was she going to end up being sorry her whole life for her erratic behavior at the present?

"A woman's forties are the hardest times of her life," Vella said. "If you can make it through to fifty, life gets really good. I think that was when I gave up trying to figure anything out, because I finally saw that I never had figured out anything that made a difference. Life goes on no matter how much you figure out about it."

Not finding anything that her friend said very hopeful, Claire eyed the plate of cookies on the other side of the lounge chair.

But then a bright thought occurred to her. "I am goin' with Winston to the Little Opry dance on Saturday night."

Her spirits rose at the thought that she had this commitment and need not make any decision about anything else until after Saturday night.

Then she noticed Vella's surprised expression. "Well, I hope Winston doesn't drop dead from all his antics."

This was not a comforting statement.

The obituaries from the newspaper provided the facts. Her grandfather had died in 1975 and her grandmother in 1980. The obituary for her grandfather stated, "...survived by John Tillman, son, of Valentine," but the one for her grandmother, Martha, said simply, "...survived by John Tillman, son." No mention as to where he lived.

Her father had been here, in Valentine, when Claire had graduated from high school. She wondered if he had known she graduated.

Shreveport, 1975

Her mother saw the graduation announcement Claire had addressed to her father, with an address simply of Valentine, Oklahoma. Claire had not meant for her to see it, had laid it down while she went to find her purse.

"What in the world?" Her mother gave her an incredulous look.

"I want my daddy to know I'm graduating." She braced herself for her mother's emotions and knew better than to add that she had a wild hope that, if he knew, he would come to the ceremony.

Her mother's response was a stony expression.

"Do you know his address? I could send it to his parents' house," Claire dared to ask. She had, for some reason, the idea that her mother knew her father's whereabouts. Maybe it was because of the way her mother acted every time Claire asked her anything about her father. Her mother would turn away, seeming to hide.

"I do not. I have not known where he was since the day he left us at the motel." Claire knew instinctively at that moment that her mother was lying.

Claire picked up the card and walked to the front door.

Her mother followed through the house, saying in that worked-up way she could get, "You might as well forget your father. He never looked back at us. And you better stop all your foolin' with that boyfriend of yours, too, 'cause he is way too much like your father. I'm the one who has stayed around, and you better take a look at that, little lady."

The last bit her mother yelled out the front door, and Claire knew that when she came home, she would find her mother in bed, where she would stay for three or four days. This had been exactly what had happened, except that her mother had dragged herself up to attend Claire's graduation, then gone immediately back to bed, leaving Claire to run around all night without guidance or possible help should she make any foolish error, such as many of her girlfriends had done, getting sick and drunk and having to call their parents to come and get them.

Claire never got to do any of that reckless sort of thing, because she had to be the responsible adult.

The graduation announcement had not returned to her, but she had never heard a word from her father.

The stars were just popping out, but the temperature still hovered around eighty-five. Moths fluttered against the buzzing and flickering fluorescent light above the Coke machine. Claire plugged in her coins—two quarters, a bargain in this day and age—and with a loud plunk, a cold Coke can dropped out.

Taking it up, she decided to say hello to Frank in the office. She really wanted to talk to someone. No matter what she had said to Andrew, she did get her limit of being alone. Also, Frank was a jovial sort; no deep conversation required.

He looked up from reading a newspaper spread on the counter and welcomed her warmly, offering to make her a cup of tea or fresh coffee. She showed him her Coke.

"So you bought Perry's car," he said.

"Yes. And I like it very well."

"I guess now that you have wheels, you'll be leavin' us." He looked sad at the thought, and this touched her.

"Not immediately. I'm goin' with Winston to the Little Opry on Saturday night, and Vella tells me I need more practice at resting and relaxing."

"Hey, we love havin' you here."

They talked about the heat and the Little Opry for a few minutes, in which Frank checked the clock on the wall several times. Claire asked him when he closed up, and he said that he did his best to keep the office open until ten o'clock.

"Gertie, she gets aggravated at me for not watchin' *Diagnosis Murder* with her," he said with a sheepish grin, "but with summer comin' on, we sometimes get late travelers, and then there's the Boris and Natasha regulars...." He trailed off and glanced at the clock on the wall.

"Boris and Natasha regulars?"

His gaze came back around, and he nodded with a half smile. "The fella's already here." He reached under the counter and brought out a notebook of cards, pointing to one, saying, "You bein', well, a friend now, I don't mind showin' you," and tapping his finger at the name on the registration card.

It read in very neat script: Boris Badenov.

"Like on the Bullwinkle cartoon?"

"Yep. He even wears sunglasses. And pretty soon now Natasha Fatale is gonna show up. She'll ask for a separate room. I always put him in ten and her in twelve, but, well..." His smile widened, and at her expression, he said, "The innkeeper business is pretty darn in'erestin'."

She wanted to know who they were, and he said he absolutely did not know but that they had been coming for the past year, usually on a weeknight, although a couple of times on Sunday.

And then there was Fayrene from the Main Street Café, who came about every other week on Monday to get away from her mother who lived with her. He said that sometimes Fayrene stayed a couple of days, not leaving the room. There were two traveling salesmen, one who brought different women to the room with him, and one who always left a little sample of his gift wares.

"Candles and candle holders, little froufrou lamps, baskets. Once he left a black nightie and a feather duster."

Claire laughed aloud and wished to get a look at the guy. She wondered if he had been the man who had approached her, but she didn't want to dismay Frank about it.

There was a couple who had met during an ice storm, later gotten married, and now returned each anniversary, and a woman who took refuge about four times a year from her husband, when he went on a bender and beat her up.

"We get whole families in here when they have their houses fumigated," Frank said, "or lose their furnace or air conditioner, or have storm damage. So, you see, I really hate to close up this place, but I don't mind tellin' you that I'm gettin' tired of the twenty-four-hour responsibility." Again he looked at the clock, which said five minutes until nine. "Natasha's late tonight. Sometimes she is."

"I can stay for the next hour and wait for her," Claire said.

"Nah…"

"All I need to do is register her, get the money and give her a key, right? I'll turn out the lights at ten and lock the door when I leave, if you give me a key."

"Well, yeah, but I don't want to—"

"Oh, go on in with Gertie. I really don't mind. I'm gonna wait to see Natasha anyway."

Acceptance swept his face before she finished speaking.

"I'll let you do it, and don't worry about a key. I don't lock it half the time anyway."

Claire stood behind the counter for a moment, then saw a tall stool pushed to the side. She pulled it over and sat down, and waited there, in front of the flamingo silhouettes, for Natasha Fatale.

Fifteen minutes later, a sporty-looking car—red, Claire thought, but couldn't be certain in the glow of the yellow neon lights—pulled up out front. A woman got out. She wore a short black trench coat, despite the eighty-five degrees, and a wide-brimmed black hat and sunglasses.

"Welcome to the Goodnight," Claire said.

"Oh." The woman paused just inside the door, then slowly approached. "Where's Frank?"

"He's already gone for the evenin'. I'm Claire. He instructed me. Room twelve, right?" She set the registration card in front of the woman.

"Uh…yes, thank you."

She watched the woman fill out the registration. *Natasha Fatale* in very accomplished script. Oklahoma license.

The woman paid in cash, and Claire gave her the key, saying, "Have a good evening. I'll be here another fifteen minutes, if there's something you need."

The woman nodded and left, walking in short strides in black spike heels. Claire watched through the window as the woman drove to the room and went inside.

At ten o'clock, she prepared to close up. She couldn't find the switch for the motel sign, so she left it lit, turned out the main office lights and left.

The soft summer night was inviting, and the thought of her lonely room caused her to stroll past the pool and wander all the way to the far end of the row of cabins. She kept a curious eye on Boris's and Natasha's rooms as she went. Music started up in the woman's room. Sultry jazz coming out on the warm night air.

Claire reached the dark expanse of grassy area at the end of the cabins. The moon was a bright crescent in the eastern black sky, and overhead stretched the Milky Way like so much glitter. It seemed close enough to touch. She put up her hand. She felt small and alone.

Whispers came across her mind: *Where are you, Daddy? Did you know I graduated? How are you makin' out, Lily Donnell? Are you findin' what you wanted to find?*

Some sound drew her gaze to the cabins. A dark figure was moving along, past eleven. The door of number twelve opened, and for a second a woman in a white negligee stood there; then the man's figure hid it, and the door closed.

Claire breathed deeply. Her gaze strayed to the Goodnight Motel sign, bright yellow against the dark. She gazed at it for a long time.

Then she walked slowly back to her room, where she turned the radio to sad country songs and plugged coins into the bed massager until she was rocked to sleep.

From: Vella Blaine
To: <haltg@mailectric.com>
Sent: June 20, 1997, 1:13 a.m.
Subject: Letting Go
Dear Harold,

It has been lovely to have so many e-mails from you telling about your hobbies. I don't know much about finches, other than I find them cheerful in my garden. The pictures of the birdhouses you've made came through very clear. They look like condominiums.

I'm glad you have your friend, Theo, such as he is. I guess I never really had many close friends, either. Winston Valentine has been about my closest, until Claire. I know what it is like to be the more intelligent and coherent in a relationship, too. My friendship with Minnie Oaks was of the same category. Since I've gotten so busy with the store and Perry, Minnie and I rather lost touch. I just stopped finding getting an ice-cream cone the highlight of my day.

Well, I finally did sell Perry's car to Claire. Selling it to her rather than some stranger made it a little easier, somehow. Like placing it in a friend's hands, although you know my opinion of her driving abilities. I halfway expected her to wreck it by now.

Selling the car was a big step for me, and I've been more than a little upset about doing it. Here I have gotten rid of one of my husband's belongings, and not just anything, but his car, and he isn't yet even cold in the ground. Well, he isn't even *in* the ground, but right upstairs in our bed.

And if Perry knew I had sold his car, if he were able, he might kill me. That is a fact, and even in his current twilight state, believe you me, I have taken every care for him not to find out that I have done away with his car. We never, ever took it upon ourselves to dispense with each other's belongings. I asked Perry about every piece of old clothes I ever gave to Goodwill. I let him go through his own clothes and other things. We kept separate lives in that manner, and he was so fond of that car.

Oh, my word, there I go writing *was,* rather than *is.* He is not dead. But he isn't really alive, either. And he sure is not ever going to be able to drive again.

All in all, though, I'm glad I faced that it was time to get rid of Perry's car. It is like I have let myself step ahead in life. Letting go of the past and reaching for the future, whatever that brings. There really is no other way to live.

I attempted to counsel Claire on her life this afternoon, but heaven knows, I don't have nearly the answers I put forth. I know this about life: it goes on and on and on, nothing new under the sun, yet somehow we all have to learn our own lessons by feeling around in the dark and doing the best we can with what we've got.

All for now, I guess.
Very fondly,
Vella

She was so tired that she didn't hesitate to send the message, although afterward she sat there thinking that she needed to break off with Harold. She was falling in love with him.

Chapter Twenty-One

Saturday evening, and the Little Opry drew people from three surrounding counties. Cars lined Main Street and had even begun filling the fire station and city hall parking lots. Both the soda fountain and the café were jam-packed, and people met in small groups outside of each, too.

It all sort of rattled Claire, who experienced a strange slice of possessiveness when she saw that their usual booth in the café was taken. She and Winston did manage to grab another one, just as the occupants left. Winston knew the people and pretty much hurried them along.

Fayrene plunked down two glasses of cold tea as she flew past. She and three other waitresses were running their feet off. Claire was fascinated, seeing people who looked to have come out of the West of her childhood mingling with the sort who could have jumped off the pages of a modern magazine.

"Who's that woman with Jaydee?" She needn't have whispered; her voice was easily covered by the din of chatter and the jukebox music.

"Oh, that's his last ex-wife."

"My, my." There was no back to the woman's dress, and not much front.

Belinda and her boyfriend, tall Deputy Lyle Midgett, came through the door. Belinda, quite made-up, looked around, turned Lyle with a manicured and many-ringed hand, and pushed him back out.

Then Claire saw Larkin and Travis Ford enter and stand looking around. Before she could suggest to Winston that they share the table, he had raised his arm and called to the men. Travis smiled and came straight away, while his father made his way more slowly, shyly answering greetings called to him.

"If you two want to eat before the Opry, you'd better sit yourselves down with us," Winston said.

Travis instantly tossed out a thank-you, dropped his hat on the hook sticking up at the end of the booth and slipped down quite happily beside Claire.

Larkin reached their booth, looked uncertain, then said, "Much appreciated," and sat more slowly on the seat with Winston, then got up to set his hat on the hook. When he returned to slip into the booth, it was in the manner of someone who wasn't certain that he would stay.

When the waitress came with Winston's and Claire's plates, Larkin and Travis chose the wise course of saying, "What they have." Within minutes, the girl returned with two more steaming meat loaf dinners.

Travis dug into his meal with gusto, in the manner of a man who had not had the guidance of a gentle woman for some time.

Claire's gaze met that of Larkin. He looked down and spread his napkin neatly in his lap. Claire blushed and found that she could not look his way another time through the entire meal.

Winston and Travis carried the conversation, talking about musicians who were to appear at the Opry, those who had appeared in times past, how and when the Starlight Theatre had become the Little Opry—saved by Jaydee Mayhall and one of the best things the man had ever done, and how he had now put in a new oak floor.

Throughout the conversation, Travis kept casting smiles at Claire and brushing his shoulder against hers at every opportunity. She found his attention adorable, gratifying, even; however, she felt a little awkward with his father sitting across the table.

A thoroughly silly inhibition on her part, she told herself. She wasn't going to do anything with Travis in public that she wouldn't do in private. She enjoyed him, and that was not a shameful thing.

Catching his eyes sparkling at her, she thought that she enjoyed him very much.

"I thought you said you were goin' on home?" Travis said.

And Larkin replied, "I changed my mind. Think I'll stay a while."

Claire heard the exchange as she walked arm in arm with Winston down to the Little Opry, with the Ford men coming behind. There was surprise on Travis's part, and something inscrutable in Larkin's tone. Had she not controlled herself and her manners, Claire would have turned around to study their faces.

Men and a couple of women lingered outside the doors of the Opry, smoking cigarettes, talking and laughing. Winston and the Fords stopped to chat, and Claire was introduced around. "She's visitin' from Shreveport," being repeated several times. Claire made polite hellos, while being distracted by her curiosity and peering through the open doors, seeing a great hall with white globes hanging from the ceiling and a stage area at the far end, where musicians were setting up and tuning instruments. Closer to the doors were long tables covered with white cloths, and between these children ran up and down. One of these was Willie Lee, along with his dog Munro, who played with a little curly-haired girl.

Spying Belinda and Marilee with her baby sitting at a table, Claire excused herself and went inside. "Vella didn't change her mind and come?" she asked Belinda.

"No. She's workin' over at the drugstore, and afterward she's gettin' right home to Daddy. She's decided she's not entitled to have any fun, with Daddy so sick. She's gonna punish herself a while because she thinks she should have prevented him gettin' sick last week, and for sellin' his car to you."

One thing about Belinda, she said exactly what she thought.

At the remark, Marilee, giving the baby over to Claire to hold, put in that selling the car was a practical idea and that her aunt was under a great strain, and they all needed to help out. She more or less told Belinda that she needed to do more to help her mother and father.

Belinda's response to that was, "There's only one of me, and my feeling guilty or killin' myself tryin' to do more isn't a help to anyone."

Claire smiled at Marilee's baby and thought how easy babies were to love. She thought of Sherrilyn's baby. How could she encourage the young woman to give up something so precious?

Little Victoria began to fret, so Claire handed her back. She got horribly rattled when a baby cried. She supposed she might not be a help to Sherrilyn, if that was the case.

Belinda, attention turned to the stage, said, "Oh, good, Reggie Pahdocony is gonna sing first. She sounds just like

Reba McEntire. That's a new guitar player with her. She dumped her lazy husband about six months ago," she said, leaning over toward Claire.

"They are not divorced," put in Marilee. "Leo's tryin' to get her to go to a marriage counselor. There he is over there."

"That may be so, but he came in the drugstore the past Thursday with June Fisher fallin' all over him."

Sitting between the two women, Claire became privy to a lot of the personal lives of half the people in attendance, learning which ones were married, which ones wanted to get married, which ones wanted to get un-married, and which ones were simply living in all manner of misery.

Jaydee Mayhall came up on stage, the lights went down and a spotlight came up, and he spent nearly ten minutes talking, before finally introducing Reggie Pahdocony. At the moment that the woman stepped up to the microphone, the people who had been waiting outside on the sidewalk began to stream inside.

"Well, there's Travis Ford," said Belinda, and Claire looked over as if she hadn't already seen him. "Brandy Lynn is here, too. Look over there. She's lightin' up like a Christmas tree."

Claire swung her eyes in the direction that Belinda indicated and saw a dark-haired beauty who might have done shampoo commercials. Belinda provided that the young woman was all hot to get Travis to the altar but that she didn't think Brandy Lynn could do it, because Travis was looking for someone a lot more like his mother.

While Claire tried to figure out how to ask what Travis's mother had been like without sounding as curious as she really was, Belinda said, "My gosh, as I live and breathe, there is Larkin Ford! This is the first time he's come to the Opry since Karin died. What is it now, Marilee—four years? Five?"

To that Marilee replied that she did not keep track of the

years of people's passing, nor of where Larkin Ford did or did not go. She was probably a little short sounding because she was trying to jiggle the fretting out of her baby.

Belinda, seemingly oblivious to Marilee's sharp tone, leaned over and said to Claire, "He and Karin used to come all the time to the Opry. Since she died, he has not even had a date."

"Now how do you know that?" said Marilee. "He could have had hot romances with women from Lawton or over to Altus, for all you know."

Belinda said simply, "I'd know. Sooner or later, I'd know," and Claire thought she probably would have.

"Well," said Marilee, rising, "since you keep track of every-one, when Tate takes a notion to come find me, tell him that I went to Jaydee's private office to nurse our baby."

"Will do," Belinda said in the manner of a self-contented woman glad to be of help.

The music started with Reggie Pahdocony crooning out the song "Fancy" and continuing on with Reba McEntire hits for another twenty minutes. This was followed by a bluegrass band, a young man who belted out delta blues, and a Texas swing group alternating with a modern country group. All of it was familiar music, to which most everyone could sing and dance with enthusiasm, although with the old hymns, dancing was replaced by clapping with the beat and singing under the breath.

As the evening wore on, the scents of women's perfumes mingled with that of a straining older air conditioner and smoke from people sneaking cigarettes, until they were run outside. Budweiser and Coca-Cola flowed from the dimly lit refreshment window, behind which women were kept busy pulling drinks from refrigerators, snapping off the lids and passing the bottles across the narrow counter. Adults wore themselves out on the dance floor, and children fell asleep across chairs.

Winston proved a masterful dancer, holding Claire lightly and pressing his dry cheek to hers. He swirled her around the floor in a manner that caused the crowd to part for them.

"I'm a product of the Big Band era, darlin'," he told her, clearly delighted to surprise her. She suspected that since learning he was to escort her, he had been secretly practicing. She imagined him dancing with an imaginary partner in the privacy of his bedroom. The idea so touched a deep place in her heart that she threw herself into doing her best to match his steps, being very glad that age slowed him a little so that she could keep up.

Quite quickly, however, Winston began handing her off for each fast-paced tune. First to Travis, who had been clearly and patiently awaiting his opportunity, and then a man she had met but could not recall his name, and then Travis again, followed by Winston once more, and then Larkin appeared in front of her with a raised eyebrow. By then she was so revved up that she danced with him without hesitation and indeed with a certain evident thrill.

From the first strain of the music, enthusiasm had kindled her spirit and warmed her blood. She danced the evening away as she had not danced since her wedding day, which turned out to be the first and last time she and Andrew had indulged in such thorough and sustained surrender to passionate dancing.

As she was to reflect later, perhaps there was merit to the idea that dancing could lead a person astray. Certainly it led to a lowering of inhibitions and a rising of passion, allowing one to behave in a familiar manner that one probably would not in other, less spirited circumstances. All of her ability, gained during childhood with her mother and onward into her high school and early college years, came back to Claire, and she swirled and swung her way between Winston, Travis and Larkin with the sweetest surge of high spirits and abandonment.

Indeed, Larkin and Travis soon so completely laid claim to her that the only other man to dare step in was Winston, to whom both men instantly and respectfully deferred.

At one point a rivalry erupted between the father and son, and Claire was handed back and forth between the two in so fast and furious a manner that she became dizzy enough to have fallen, had she been turned loose.

When Winston stepped in to claim her, she was thoroughly grateful to be saved and thought the rivalry ended; however, Winston proved to simply be another contestant, clearly intent not to be outdone by the younger men. He danced her up to the stage, where he beckoned over the fiddle player and hollered into the man's ear.

The songs Winston had requested were rousing renditions of the old classics, "Chattanoogie Shoe Shine Boy" and "Take Me Back to Tulsa," to which Winston danced Claire around with grace and gusto, and to the applause of Larkin and Travis and most of the other dancers, who moved back and made room.

At the last note of the music, though, Claire felt Winston give out. In an unobtrusive manner, she lent him her strength to get him back to a chair, all the way there praying as she had not prayed in years that if God would not let him die, she would get a hold of herself and be more thoughtful of Winston from then on out. She did not leave his side the rest of the evening and maintained that she was far too exhausted to dance anymore.

Travis and Larkin took up chairs beside and in front of her and Winston, where they spent the rest of the evening vying with each other in running back and forth to the refreshment window, bringing Claire a cold Coca-Cola, a small container of ice cream and a plate of cheese nachos, all of which she did eat, because she was starving after the great expenditure of energy.

"It was quite an evenin', gal. Quite an evening." Satisfaction echoed in Winston's voice. When Claire agreed, he said, "I thank you for it. I know I gave you a scare."

"Yes, you did." She was still a little worried. She would have helped him up the stairs to his house, but she didn't want to embarrass him. She breathed a sigh of relief when they reached the porch.

"I gave myself a scare…but it would have been a fine way to go out of this world. Yes, sir…dancin' with a beautiful woman."

"It would not have been very good for the rest of us," Claire said in a pointed manner.

"I'd do tonight all over again, given a chance." He winked in his mischievous manner that reassured her his vitality for life was still there, if tired.

Thank you, God, for coming through. We all need Winston.

Chapter Twenty-Two

Shreveport, 1970

Aunt Agnes came into the kitchen. She had on her black hat and carried her black patent leather purse. "I want all those dishes put away by the time I get back from church," she said, and Claire said, "Yes'm," then made a face behind the older woman's back.

Five minutes later, Claire's mother appeared in the doorway from the hall, hopping from one foot to the other, as she slipped on her favorite dancing heels. She wore a deep red skirt and dotted organdy blouse, and an eager flush. "Come on, honey…we're goin' down the road."

Her mother had just been waiting for Aunt Agnes to leave. It didn't matter that her mother's father was still in the living room; he was like a ghost, rarely speaking, always in the background.

Seeing an easy way to get her job done, Claire said that Aunt Agnes would be mad at her if she didn't finish the dishes, so her mother hopped in there and slammed things into the cabinet in two minutes. Then out the door they went, with her mother tugging her along.

Claire had seen it coming for days. Over the years since her father had left them, her mother would go along quietly and mildly for months on end, doing wash and hanging it on the line, following Aunt Agnes to church, working in the flower garden, and then would come the signs of discontent: perusing the classifieds for a possible job, purchasing new lipsticks, crying in the night, meeting the mailman and talking to him, fixing her hair for hours in front of the mirror.

Aunt Agnes would start in on her, and then one evening, when Aunt Agnes was gone to church or a missionary meeting, her mother would come out of her room dressed sexy and haul off down the road for Jake's Place, where she would dance for two solid hours, at least, leaving Claire to sit in a chair and watch her, or to lay her head on the table and pretend to fall asleep, while listening to adults whisper what a cute child she was.

Her mother often said that she didn't want to leave Claire home alone, but even as a young child, Claire knew that her mother wanted her presence for support and protection, too. With Claire there, her mother could dance all she wanted with men, enjoy their company, and even pretend while she was dancing that she was attached to a man, but at the end of the evening, she could use Claire as her excuse to go home alone.

Later, when Claire reached fourteen and fifteen, she would dance, too, although never forgetting to keep an eye on her mother. And always there was the unspoken knowledge that she could not, under any circumstances, outshine her mother's spirit.

On the way home, her mother would be relaxed and exceedingly gay, walking barefoot and swinging her shoes in her hand and marveling at the moon and stars, as if Aunt Agnes and what would happen when they reached home wasn't going to happen.

Aunt Agnes would be waiting in the kitchen and go at Claire's mother, calling her a heathen just like her run-off husband. Claire's grandfather would shut the doors to the living room, and Claire would slip off to her porch room and put her head between two feather pillows.

The next day her mother would appear sometime in the afternoon, dressed in a demure slim gray dress, wearing her string of pearls, and join Aunt Agnes in refusing to let Claire listen to rock and roll on the radio or to wear jeans outside of the house.

It was as if her mother was two different people, a woman warm and lively, and a matron cool and stodgy. Claire could not be sure which one was her real mother, and in any case, she had not wanted to be like either one.

Chapter Twenty-Three

Lying in the dim motel room, gazing up at the shadows cast by the outside yellow lights, Claire was filled with memories that brought waves of both gratitude and regret. She relived those days when, as a little girl, she would lie in the bed, watching through slit eyes, as her mother and father would waltz around the motel room at the Tall Pines Motor Court. How her mother would glow with life and delight when she danced! No wonder her mother had later taken comfort in dancing after losing her husband.

Maybe, Claire thought, dancing enabled her mother to break free of the imposed rigid confines of life according to Aunt Agnes, and even according to the deeply inhibited part of herself that seemed to hold her captive.

It was this woman, the one who could dance with abandonment, who had run off and married John Tillman, Claire thought with sudden enlightenment. No wonder her mother had been frightened by that part of herself. The demure and proper woman she had been raised up to be had likely been repelled.

A great sorrow for her mother, who had struggled between tumultuous emotional extremes, welled up within her, accompanied by strong regrets. *I'm sorry, Mama…. I just didn't understand. I love you, Mama.*

A soft peace stole over her, and she drifted off into sweet dreams, where she walked home from a dance with her mother, holding her mother's hand and laughing.

Winston and Tate talked in the glow of the single light above the kitchen sink; Tate leaned against the counter, and Winston sat at the small table; both indulged in a rare but satisfying glass of Jack Daniel's.

"There's nothin' like dancin' with a beautiful woman to perk a man up," said Winston.

"You were cuttin' the rug, that's for sure," said Tate, thankfully not scolding him for it, Winston thought. "And in fact, I didn't do so bad myself. I reminded my wife that she has a husband and not just an old man who gave her a late child."

"When you refer to yourself as old, what do you think that makes me? Wait your turn in this house."

Tate laughed at that and downed the rest of his drink, saying his wife was upstairs waiting on him to finish what he'd started on the dance floor.

But Winston said, "Before you go, I need your help on somethin'."

Tate regarded him with curiosity.

"I want you to see if you can find out the whereabouts of Claire's father, John Tillman. If he's dead or alive, or just anything about him that you can. Charlotte dug up the obits of his parents, if you need a starting place, but I don't want anyone to know that we're searchin' around, okay?"

"Well, sure. I have some people I can contact."

Winston had known he would.

Tate started out of the room, then stopped and said, "I'm awfully glad you didn't dance yourself into a heart attack tonight. I hope you don't get too carried away with that beautiful young woman."

To this, Winston replied, "Son, my heart was about ready to give up this past year, but the good Lord saw ahead and sent Claire to help me find my second wind. I believe I'm gonna be around here some time yet."

He was deeply touched when Tate gave his shoulder a warm, firm squeeze.

Tate went up the stairs, and as he neared the top, his spirit rose. Winston's second wind had somehow transferred to him. This was the way things went, he thought. The joy of life was contagious. Normally he could barely stay awake past ten o'clock at night, and here it was nearing one, and he was looking forward to making love to his wife in a way he had not done for a long time. He approached their bedroom door with both anticipation and trepidation, as he wondered if he would find her fast asleep.

Then he heard music.

He opened the door, and there was Marilee, in a white satin gown. The radio beside the bed played softly. Tate closed the bedroom door and strode to her and took her in his arms, slow-dancing with her in the moonlight that fell through the window, while she seductively unbuttoned his shirt.

Across the hall in her bedroom, Corrine heard her aunt Marilee's and Uncle Tate's bedroom door close. She turned on the light on her small desk, pulled out her journal and set to writing all about the Little Opry, where she had mostly been her usual unseen self, but where she had managed to have her first dance with Larry Joe Darnell.

She had fallen in love with Larry Joe before her thirteenth birthday. He was nine years older than she was, but someday she was going to marry him. She wrote all of her dreams down in royal-blue ink.

Down on Main Street, in her apartment over the drugstore, Belinda opened the door of her bathroom. Wearing her new red lace gown bought off the QVC channel, she struck a seductive pose in the doorway. Unfortunately, Lyle had the television going and his eyes glued on it. She had to call his name twice, the second time in a voice so loud that she was glad theirs was the only apartment in that area of the building.

His head finally came around, and he said, "What?" as if he didn't have a clue as to her intentions, which she knew he did not, because Lyle was a little on the simple and basic side. He was, however, very willing to please once she got his attention.

Three and a half miles out at the Ford ranch, in the house that sat beneath a glowing moon, Travis came home after sitting at the cemetery in front of his mother's grave and drinking a six-pack, one can after another. He came in to find his father working on account books, which was not a surprise. His father often sat over the account books in the middle of the night, as if wedded to them.

Travis told his father what he had been wanting to say ever since his mother had died.

He said, "If you would have paid as much attention to Mom as you do this ranch, you would have seen that she was sick in time to do somethin' about it. It's your fault she died."

Larkin, not knowing what to say, feeling that he never knew what to say, simply gazed at his son, absorbing the words and his son's pain as best he could. He didn't want to fail his wife in that moment, could almost hear her voice, "Now, Larkin, sometimes you just need to listen."

Before walking out of the room, Travis added, "Claire's mine, so you back off."

Larkin sat staring into dark space his son vacated and recalled his behavior of the evening, which was way out of character, to say the least. He felt a lot of regrets, mostly in connection with his son, but not enough to cover over the inner relief and hope he kept feeling. He thought maybe he was at last moving on from the loss of his wife. The idea scared him, and prodded him onward, too.

From: Vella Blaine
To: <haltg@mailectric.com>
Sent: June 22, 1997, 1:06 a.m.
Subject: Do you dance?

Dear Harold,

It's a lovely night here. Almost a full moon. Since you said you are a night owl, like me, I wonder if you have seen the moon. I saw it as I walked Claire outside. She was here earlier to talk about her good time at the Little Opry.

Did I mention the Opry to you already? It's a place where local musicians play in the summer months, and people go to dance. Claire got so wound up there dancing that she had to come by here and tell me all about it. She must have talked twenty minutes with barely a pause. It made me wish I had gone. Made me remember so many things.

You know, the rural country areas produce some fine musicians. I'll bet there are more musicians and singers from Oklahoma in Nashville than from any other place.

We in Valentine have our share. So many of them are older, though. Used to be that families made their own music in the rural areas. Just about every family had someone who could play guitar or fiddle, or maybe a piano in more fortunate families. They didn't have anything else to do, with no television and not many radios, either. My aunt's farm was twenty miles from any town, and she did not get electricity until the 1950s. When I would go stay there, my uncle and cousins would play guitars and fiddles and harmonicas, and we would all sing.

Do you dance? I don't think I would remember how now, after all these years married to Perry. I met him at a dance. He was all left feet, and he never really did get the hang of it. After we got married, he gave it up, like he gave up a lot of things.

But I didn't marry Perry until my early twenties, and before that I went to two years of college. I danced a lot. I remember dancing to Benny Goodman down in Dallas, and to Bill Monroe & His Bluegrass Boys up in Oklahoma City. I could really cut up the floor.

Vella suddenly realized that she was staring at the blinking cursor on the glowing monitor screen. She had lost herself in memories. She was greatly dismayed. More and more, she was seeing her own mother in her actions.

You know, Harold, we get to our parents' ages and start to find out that life is a wheel, and we didn't invent it. We're just goin' around ourselves. And there never is any reversing that wheel and going back. We all each only get one time around on this earth, and we leave so many things behind, only we don't know it at the time. We don't know it until it's too late. Fondly,
Vella

Without a thought, she clicked to send the message and to return to her memories.

Chapter Twenty-Four

Claire was awakened by the telephone. Where was she?

Ring…

Her motel room at the Goodnight…the clock read nine-thirty…it was freezing! She pulled the blankets around her and closed her eyes.

Ring…

Oh! Maybe it was Andrew.

"Hello?"

"Claire?" It was a familiar female voice. "It's me—Sherrilyn."

"Oh. Hello, Sherrilyn." The voice had been far too hesitant to be that of Gayla Jean. Claire experienced a profound disappointment that it wasn't either her ex-husband or her friend.

"I hope I didn't call you too early." The voice was even more hesitant.

"Oh, no…it's fine." Claire, experiencing a small alarm at the unsualness of the girl's call, tried to get her brain working.

"Mrs. Seames said any time after nine in the mornin' is acceptable to call someone, so, I thought it might be okay to call."

"It's just fine, honey. How are you this mornin'?"

"I'm okay," she said, not sounding okay.

"That's good to hear." Claire hoped the conversation wasn't going to continue in the present tedious manner.

Sherrilyn then said, "Well, the reason I called is that I have somethin' for you."

"You do?" Claire said, when the girl didn't continue.

"Uh-huh."

Claire waited.

"I…I have your mother's…urn. You know…her, uh, ashes."

There was a soft rain, and the windshield wipers beat in a comforting rhythm as Claire drove the highway to Lawton.

Sherrilyn had said the sheriff's receptionist, Lori, had told her about Claire's mother's urn being in the car. The story was that Sherrilyn, in the hopes of getting back some of her things—a picture of her mother, a pair of Nike tennis shoes, some other things—had telephoned a friend of Denny's in Dallas, who had given Denny the message. Denny had called her, and she had given her address—a post office box—to him, and he had mailed the urn along with her things, because he had felt terrible about having the urn.

Claire had strong doubts about the story. She believed that somehow Sherrilyn had succeeded in tracking Denny down, but she did not believe Sherrilyn had any post office box, and she sincerely doubted that a person of Denny's sort would be likely to either hold on to any of the girl's things, or even use the post office to mail anything other than drugs. It was far more probable that for his own purposes—maybe he was possessive about his coming child—he had come to see Sherrilyn. But why would he bring her the urn? The only reason Claire could come up with was superstition.

"Here." Sherrilyn met Claire on the porch and handed her the urn in a Wal-Mart sack.

Claire looked into the blue sack and saw it did indeed contain her mother's urn. She lifted off the top of the urn and looked inside, wondering if the ashes would still be there. They were, in their black plastic bag.

"This is quite a surprise. Thank you."

"Sure," the young woman said, sweeping her hair behind her ear. She apparently had suffered some further trauma, because her hair had been whacked off a little more. It was now to her shoulders. If she kept on, she might not have any left. Her lips were pale, her eyes with a dull cast. Claire would estimate her to be still anemic.

It was stupid to feel responsible for the girl.

"You want to go out for a soft drink and maybe a hamburger?" she asked.

Sherrilyn said that she did, although Claire would guess that the girl more wanted to get away from Lilac House than to eat, because she only picked at the hamburger and fries she ordered at the Sonic drive-in, where they ate with windows cracked slightly and the car and air-conditioning running.

Claire asked Sherrilyn how Denny had been when she'd seen him.

Sherrilyn gazed at her for a long minute, then said, "Okay, he was here. But he doesn't have your stuff anymore, and you have your insurance and a car you like a lot better. You said so."

"He stole from me, and from you."

"He brought me money when he came. Every bit and more of what he took. He wouldn't have taken anything from you if he hadn't been desperate to have a car so he could get a job. And you have plenty. You haven't missed anything at all."

"I don't think any of that is the point. He is a thief, Sherrilyn."

The girl turned her head, gazing out the window. Claire watched her for a moment, waiting. Then she looked out the windshield, unseeing, her mind running with options. She could tell the sheriff, possibly pry the phone number for Denny out of the girl, but what real good would that do?

Sherrilyn said, "You know, everyone steals from everyone. And the people who put themselves out there as so great are just stealin' in a way so's you can't see it."

There was an earnestness in her voice, a disillusionment that Claire didn't know how to address.

When Claire didn't say anything, the girl said, "He brought my stuff and your urn. He would have taken me with him, but he has just gotten another job and doesn't have a place for us to stay. But he's comin' back for me, because I'm gonna have his baby, and he cares about that. And I'm goin' with him. I'm not stayin' here and lettin' them take my baby from me. I'm not doin' it."

She set aside her half-eaten hamburger and looked straight ahead with a jutted jaw.

After a moment, Claire asked, "Would you like a milkshake? You really need to build yourself up."

Sherrilyn said no, but Claire was so upset she got one for herself. When she returned the girl to Lilac House, she didn't go in, but watched the girl, a small, skinny figure with her swelling belly, go up the stairs, a child carrying a child within her.

She really was not ready to return to her life in Shreveport. Each time she thought about doing so, about the townhouse and about taking up a job in a law office, which she knew she could easily find, she felt like throwing up. She could find no real reason for this. She did want to see Andrew, and she found she missed Gayla Jean and needed to call both, wanted to hear their voices; however, she didn't want to hear them ask when she was coming home. It was simply so much easier for her to have a relationship with them on the telephone.

Gayla Jean would most likely have said it was Claire's inner child who wanted the vacation to go on forever. Well, that was totally impossible, of course. No one could live on vacation forever. She was going to have to return sooner or later, and considering her bank account, it would be better to be sooner.

And perhaps she could rely on the telephone sort of relationship when she did return home.

She thought all this as she drove around the block, but when she came back past the big old house, with a lilac colored curb that she just then noticed, probably as it was wet with rain, she gripped the steering wheel with both hands and kept on going. She headed for the road to Valentine, but then she found herself going by the mall and turned in and went to the JCPenny store and looked at baby cribs.

Then she went down to the bookstore and ended up purchasing books on taking care of babies and on getting an education after dropping out of school. Down at the card shop, she bought a gift bag for the books and, at the last minute, a card.

In the Lincoln, she sat for some minutes staring at the raindrops on the windshield and thinking about returning to Shreveport and about the girl waiting for Denny Rhodes to return, and about what might happen if he actually did.

She took up the card and wrote: *Would you like to come and live with me until you have the baby and figure out what you're going to do?*

She drove back to Lilac House and pulled up to the curb, where she sat for a few more minutes. She must have sat there longer than she had imagined, because suddenly there was a tapping on the passenger window, and she looked over to see Sherrilyn looking in.

Claire pressed the button to unlock the door, and Sherrilyn got in with a rush of hot, humid air. "What do you want? Everybody in the house sees you sittin' out here."

Claire handed over the gift bag.

Sherrilyn frowned with a certain suspicion, her expression saying clearly: What's the catch now? She said, "I can't keep any more food in my room. The man who sprays for bugs found my cookies, and Mrs. Seames got all bent about it."

"It's not food."

The girl looked in the bag and said in a tired voice, "I don't want to hurt your feelin's, but I really don't like books. I'm just not that smart."

Claire didn't respond to this. She thought that if the girl didn't open the card, then she wouldn't say anything, would just drive off and would take another three weeks of vacationing, maybe drive clear to California.

The girl pulled out the envelope, cast a sideways glance at Claire, and then slowly pulled out the card and opened it, looking at it for a long minute, before saying in a breathless voice, "Yes…yes, I'd rather be anywhere than here."

In fifteen minutes, Sherrilyn had thrown her things together, and Claire had made explanations to Mrs. Seames, a woman wise enough to wish them the best, and the two headed back to Valentine.

They had nothing to say to each other on the drive. Claire thought she might have managed better if Sherrilyn had a telephone, in order that Claire might call her.

Sherrilyn rode slumped down in the seat and looking out the passenger window, and Claire drove along thinking in many different ways: *What have I done?* and *Maybe I could take Sherrilyn camping in the Grand Canyon.*

★ ★ ★

They were in the rear storage room of the drugstore, with the back door open and the sound of the rain falling gently. Vella was leaned back in her oak desk chair, smoking one of her cigarillos.

"It wasn't a hasty decision," Claire said, mostly to herself. "I've really been thinking about it from the first time I saw her in the hospital."

And Vella's comment on that was, "Sugar, I don't think you've ever made a hasty decision in your life." She dragged out *sugah,* in the way she had when making a point. "I do think that half the time, you don't know that you're thinkin' of doing something."

Claire thought that an accurate assessment. "I suppose I'm havin' a lot of fantasies, but I've had these ideas about how I can teach her to take care of herself and the baby, and get her teeth fixed and help her get an education. Encourage her upward...and help her to keep her hair."

Vella gave a soft smile. "Save her."

"None of us can really do that, can we?"

"No, but we sure do try, don't we?" Vella said, a hint of sarcasm in her tone. Then she added more gently, "It's a good thing you're doin', Claire. It is...*if* you don't forget that you are doin' it because *you* want to and need to do it. She didn't ask you to save her. And know that you're not God and can only do so much. And for heaven's sake do not expect one iota of thanks, and in fact, be prepared for her to be angry at you a lot of the time."

Claire gazed at her friend and shared a rueful grin. Then she rubbed her arms and looked out the door at the rain. "I don't know what Andrew is gonna say about this."

That was not true. She had a pretty good idea what his reaction would be.

Vella blew a long stream of smoke. "Do you care?"

Claire searched for honesty. "I guess I don't care more than I do about helping this child and her baby."

A certain acceptance and relief came over her. She had, without realizing it, as Vella had said, come to a decision about her relationship with Andrew. She was not pursuing it. She was done with pursuing Andrew, and the revelation crept over her that she had actually quit pursuing him the day she had left him standing in the road. She simply had not fully realized it and had kept calling him.

"I want to give you a going-away party," Vella said, dropping her feet to the floor with a suddenness and looking at her planner on her desk. "Can you postpone leavin' until Wednesday? I have to take Perry to the doctor tomorrow, and it'll take a day to get everything together, anyway. We'll have a barbecue. Marilee won't mind if we have it over there at Winston's house…."

She continued on with her plans, not waiting for any answer from Claire, who was thinking with some dismay of all that was going to be required of her, one of those requirements being returning to Shreveport and taking up her life on a regular basis.

"When do we go down to Shreveport?" Sherrilyn asked, as Claire pulled up to the office of the Goodnight. The young woman looked a little apprehensive. Possibly the motel didn't bring any good memories, but then again, apprehension seemed to be a permanent part of the girl.

"Wednesday morning. I want to get the car an oil change and lube job, and Vella wants to have a little goodbye party for us. Isn't that sweet of her?" She kept feeling the need to be perky in order to lift the girl up. This effort was taking a lot of energy, and she thought she might quickly wear out.

"I don't know any of those people."

"Well, you will meet them at the party," Claire said, although meeting people at a goodbye party didn't seem to make a lot of sense. "I'll get you the room adjoining mine," she told the girl and got out into the steaming heat.

Just as she approached the office door, Gertie came out. She carried an enormous tote slung over her shoulder, with a little dog poking out of it.

"Claire! I'm glad I got a chance to see you before I left. I've really enjoyed knowin' you, and if you're ever down in Fort Walton Beach, you look me up. I'll be in the phone book."

Claire, startled and confused, said, "You're goin' to Florida?" She noticed just then that the motel van parked a few feet away had a camper hooked to the rear.

"Yes, I am. I'm not waitin' on Frank another minute. I'm sorry that means the end to your breakfast trays. Frank isn't the best cook. Well…" The next thing, Gertie gave her a smoochy kiss on the cheek and strode to the van.

"I wish you well, Gertie!" Claire managed to say. And then she stood there, watching the van and camper drive up onto the highway.

Feeling a little alarm about Frank, she went into the office. It was empty.

"Frank?" Her worry grew. She was having this horrible fantasy about Gertie having gone berserk and killing Frank. Stranger things had happened.

To her relief, he appeared through the door to the apartment.

"I just saw Gertie. She said she's goin' to Fort Walton Beach." She had begun to think that maybe she had misunderstood the woman.

But Frank nodded and said, with a tight jaw, "Gertie doesn't want no more of the motel business. She even took the dog."

Chapter Twenty-Five

The key didn't work in the doorknob of the door connecting their two rooms, so Claire went to get Mr. Goode for help. While she was gone, Sherrilyn, curious, went over and jiggled the doorknob. It turned, and the door opened.

She looked at it with some amazement.

Then she stuck her head through the opening and peered into Claire's room. It smelled of a sweet fragrance, like Claire did. There were about a hundred bottles of perfume and lotion on the dresser. Sherrilyn experienced the urge to go over and use some, but fear of being caught doing something she shouldn't overcame the urge.

She saw that Claire wasn't very neat. The bed was not made, and there were clothes on it, and on a chair, and shoes strewn about, too. Sherrilyn thought that if she had Claire's money, she would be neater. In fact, even without money, she was neater.

A cell phone started ringing, and looking for the sound, Sherrilyn saw Claire's purse on the bed.

She suddenly got afraid of being alone in the vicinity of the purse, afraid that something might be blamed on her, and that Claire and the manager might even be mad that she had gotten the door unlocked, so she closed and locked it and sat on the bed until the two arrived. By then the cell phone had quit ringing. She didn't want to say that she had heard it.

Sherrilyn soaked in the bathtub in bubble bath that Claire had provided. She had not had a bubble bath since she was a child. Claire apparently had them with regularity; the woman went on about how the old motel bathtub was great for soaking, as if that was a major event in life.

The question of why the woman had taken her in went around in Sherrilyn's mind as she swished the water, making more bubbles. She figured it had to do with her baby and Claire not having one. When she'd called him, Denny had said Claire was being nice because she wanted the baby. He had even suggested that maybe Sherrilyn could sell the baby to Claire.

That he would suggest selling his own child made Sherrilyn really upset, but then he had said he was joking. Sherrilyn was pretty certain Denny had not been joking, but she understood that his desperation about money led him to think a lot of hateful ideas. Like keeping Claire's urn for an investment. When she had asked him what he meant by that, he had said, "Just an investment...just keep it, okay? Don't ask so many questions all the time."

Sherrilyn figured that he meant to have Claire pay for the return of the urn. He was probably going to be mad when he learned that Sherrilyn had given it back. But she had just had to do it. It wasn't right to keep the urn. Claire was right that Denny was a thief, but people like Claire did not know what it was like to try to survive in this world.

And maybe Claire did want Sherrilyn's baby, but that did

not mean that Sherrilyn was going to give it to her, she thought, rubbing her rounded belly that had really seemed to grow over the past week. It seemed as if it had just popped out.

"Sherrilyn?"

Sherrilyn jumped. "Yeah?"

"I'm goin' down to the office to get some coffee. I'll be back in a bit."

"Okay."

She heard Claire's door open and close, and then she had this fantasy about Claire not going to the office at all, but throwing things into her car and driving off, leaving her. Like Denny had done.

The idea caused her to sink far down into the warm tub of bubbles. She might have gone under, but she didn't want to chance burning her eyes.

She was just getting out of the tub when Claire's cell phone began ringing again. She thought about throwing on a robe and running the phone down to Claire at the office. She just hated a phone to ring and go unanswered. It could be an emergency. She wondered if she should have told Claire about the earlier call.

Thankfully the phone quit ringing, and Sherrilyn breathed deeply.

She used the entire little bottle of lotion Claire had given her, rubbing it all over in an attempt to take better care of herself, as Claire had suggested.

"You have to think of the baby, Sherrilyn. You want to give it a good start, don't you?"

Sherrilyn did. She really did. She loved her baby. She just didn't know how to do things.

One of her greatest fears was that she was going to mess up and make Claire mad at her, possibly mad enough to kick her out. She had to try really hard not to make a mistake, and to this end, she combed her hair carefully and dressed in the new nightgown Claire had bought her.

Claire still had not returned by the time Sherrilyn was finished.

Padding barefoot out of the bathroom, she crossed the room to the front window, where she peeked around the curtain.

Relief—Claire's car still sat outside the door, glimmering in the glow of the motel lights.

Oh, there was Claire...and the big fat motel manager talking out beside the office. The man sort of looked like Santa Claus.

Claire held a tray with cups on it. She had really good balance, because she held it with one hand while propping her other hand on her hip and doing a sort of turn on the balls of her feet. Having been a waitress, Sherrilyn knew that not everyone had such good balance when it came to carrying a tray. Sherrilyn herself could carry an entire arm of trays and still pick up catsup and mustard bottles with the other hand.

Dropping the curtain, she turned back into her own room and stood chewing on her bottom lip. Then she went to the connecting door to Claire's room, stood there for a second, then raced into the room and over to the bed, throwing the clothes there into the chair and making up the covers as fast as she could, thinking all the time that Claire was going to come in the door before she finished, but hoping not.

She fluffed the pillows and turned back the sheet, blanket and spread in an artful and inviting manner that she had seen in magazines, as if the bed awaited a person. She wished she had something to put on the pillow, like a flower. She found Claire's nightgown from the jumble of clothes on the chair and draped it nicely over the end of the bed. Then she switched on the bedside lamp, gave the sheet a last smoothing and hurried back to her own room.

All the racing around turned out for nothing, though. Before Claire came back inside, a car arrived. Sherrilyn saw this while once more peering around the edge of the curtain, and—*ohmygod*—it was that tall deputy from the sheriff's office.

She shut the curtain and her eyes, then opened both and peered out again.

She could not think of why he would come for her, but, as she remembered, she had not done anything wrong the last time the law had come and picked her up. She tried to hear their conversation but could not, only the sound of their voices. She tried to get her fingers to raise the window, but it was stuck.

As the two kept on talking, it slowly dawned on her that the deputy had not come for her. He was intent on Claire.

Then…the deputy kissed Claire. Just like out of a movie, out in the dark and with the motel sign shining on them, he took hold of her cheeks with both hands and bent down and kissed her. Claire still didn't drop the tray.

After that he got into his car and left. Claire stood there and watched after him, and then she just kept standing there, seeming to look up at the stars.

Sherrilyn tried to look up into the sky, too, but she couldn't, because of the eaves with the fluorescent lights. There were a lot of bugs in the lights. It was disgusting.

Then Claire turned and looked at the motel rooms, and Sherrilyn hurried to hop into bed. Pretending sleep, Sherrilyn heard Claire come inside and approach the connecting door. She felt the woman gazing at her. When she thought Claire had walked away, she opened her eyes a peek. Through the opened door, she saw Claire standing and gazing down at the neatly made and waiting bed.

Claire looked at the bed long enough to make Sherrilyn get a little worried as to possibly having done something

wrong. Then Claire sat on the bed, brought her hands together and hung her head.

After several long seconds, Sherrilyn realized that the
woman was praying. Embarrassed to be watching, she closed
her eyes.

Chapter Twenty-Six

Vella wished she had not volunteered to give a going-away party for Claire. She had made the mistake of assuming that Marilee would be available to help with the endeavor. Actually, she had in mind that Marilee would pretty much *do* the party. Her niece had the ability to put out a party as easily as opening an umbrella; however, that was before the baby. It turned out that Marilee had plans for meeting with some support group for older mothers that was forming at a church up in Lawton. It was a three-day affair.

"Oh, you don't want support. You want to go and brag because you've held up so darn well," Vella said, sounding off in her aggravation.

"Maybe that, too. I'll take boosting where I can get it," admitted Marilee, who didn't look a day over thirty-five, knew it, and was trying to hold on to it.

Marilee's preoccupation with the baby compounded Vella's despair about Claire leaving. Once upon a time, Marilee paid some attention to Vella, but that was gone as her niece's family grew and required her energies.

The more Vella thought of the party, the deeper her spirit sank at the prospect of losing Claire. Without Claire, there would be no one who attended Vella and did all those thoughtful things that Claire had done during Perry's crisis, and did still. Just the other day, Claire had brought Vella a miniature rose plant. It hadn't been her birthday or Mother's Day or anything, but Claire said, "Just because."

Vella felt childish, but she did so like Claire's attentions. Without Claire, she would be absolutely alone again, and in thinking of it, she did not feel that she could cope with a party. It was a taste of the same unable-to-cope feeling that had come over her the day Perry'd had his episode. The feeling of not being able to cope was more frightening than any actual event that could happen.

The entire notion about Claire was silly. Claire had been in their lives only a month, and Vella had survived before the woman came and would do so after she left. Besides, Shreveport was less than a day's drive away, which was what she told Winston when he looked all hound-dog about it.

"Shreveport is not on the other side of the world," she told him. "You can get down there in a few hours' drive."

"I can't drive," Winston said, as if offended, and clearly determined not to be comforted.

"Well, I can...or you can hire somebody. Or take the bus."

She had actually forgotten that he couldn't drive anymore. Being confronted with her lack of good sense and his increasing inabilities did not improve her mood.

It came to her mind, too, that there was the chance he could drop dead riding a bus; that had happened to a traveler on the bus that stopped in town the past spring. The driver had made his stop at the café and shaken the fellow to wake him, and the man fell over stone-cold dead. They both fell silent, Winston likely remembering the incident, as well.

Then Vella thought of Perry. There was not apt to be time that she could take from caring for him in order to run off to Shreveport. Even if she did, she wouldn't have a moment's peace, because she would worry the entire time that something would happen to him while she was down there.

In regard to the party, it appeared Vella had two choices: have the party at her own house, or cancel it.

After the better part of a day spent with Perry at the doctor's office, and then having to jump in and work the soda fountain counter for a late lunch crowd, she was wrung-out and ready for canceling the party and any other thing that required her effort. The entire time she made cold drinks and ice-cream sundaes, she tried to figure out a polite way to back out of the party, although she rarely let the thought of rudeness interfere with what she really wanted to do.

Before she could manage to cancel, however, other people, who had no business doing it, were already inviting people.

"I ran into Travis on my way here," Winston said, coming behind the soda fountain counter to help himself to a glass of cold tea. "He'd already heard about Claire leavin'. I invited him to the party tomorrow. I told him around seven."

"Well, that's nice of you. Why don't you just host the party and make all the arrangements, too?"

"What'd I do?"

"It is the hostess's responsibility to ask people to the party," said Vella. "And to set the time. If you're goin' to do it all, you need to hold the party, too."

At that point, Julia Jenkins-Tinsley, who had stopped in for a Coke just after closing the post office, spoke up. "Well, then you're gonna have to forgive me, because when Frank Goode came in to the P.O. to get a package earlier, I told him about the party. I figured you'd want to invite him, seein' as how Claire's been stayin' out at his place, and especially now that Gertie up and left him yesterday, and he's on his own."

Before either Vella or Winston could question this turn of events, Belinda, coming from serving a customer at the fragrance counter, said, "Oh, that's right, Mama. Frank was in here to pick up some lunch today, and he told me all about it. That would have been right before he went to the post office, Julia. Gertie got fed up with waitin' for the motel to sell, and she's gone on down to Fort Walton Beach to stay with her sister. I have never seen Frank so beside himself. I don't think he'd even combed his hair."

"Well, of course he is beside himself," said the postmistress in a quick manner. "He told me that he and Gertie had not spent a night apart since they had come here to help his father with the motel. Frank's gonna close the motel now," she added.

"Not immediately," Belinda said, speaking mostly to the postmistress, before turning to Vella and Winston. "He has paid reservations for the Posey reunion in the middle of July, and has to honor them. He's hopin' that maybe between now and then the motel will sell."

"Well, he told me that he's closin' up, and he sounded like he was doin' it soon as Claire and that unfortunate girl get out of here."

"Not until after the Poseys," said Belinda, squeezing that in before answering the ringing telephone.

Vella had gotten a tablet to begin a list for the party and was walking with Winston to a table, tossing comments about the Goodes back and forth, when Belinda hollered out, "Mama, there's a Harold on the phone for you from New Jersey."

Winston's head came up, and Julia swung around on her stool.

"Okay," Vella said, as naturally as possible. "Tell him I'll be there in a minute." She was not about to seem in a hurry and made herself take a few seconds to jot a quick list onto her tablet, then handed the list to Winston. "Here. You can at least give me a hand for your girlfriend's party. Take this over to Fayrene at the café and ask her to cater the dang thing. And for heaven's sake, don't invite anybody else but her." She walked toward the phone. "We don't need the whole town. I'll call up the few I want to be there."

Not taking a chance on Belinda possibly eavesdropping, she retrieved the cordless receiver lying on the counter and headed for her desk in the back room.

Belinda said, "You have a phone back there, Mama."

Vella did not reply.

She sat on the edge of her desk chair and took five seconds to compose herself. "Hello. This is Vella."

"Hi, Vella. It's me. Harold Gallagher."

His voice was deep and exactly what she had thought it would sound like.

"You know—Harold from Cherry Hill, New Jersey. This is Vella Blaine, isn't it?"

"Oh, yes. I'm sorry. It's just such a surprise." She snatched a Kleenex out of the box and pressed it to her damp temple, then fanned herself with it, as his deep chuckle came across the line.

He said that he liked her accent—*her accent?* He had a northern accent straight out of the movies. He told her that he had gotten the drugstore phone number from their Web site. That clever action seemed promising of an industrious nature.

He said that he very much needed adult conversation with an intelligent woman.

Vella, pressing her hand and the tissue to her belly and

scooting even more to the edge of her chair, said, "Well, how nice that you called me." Not a single word to say came to mind after that.

While Vella had no trouble writing to him, she found speaking a different manner. He, however, appeared to be a speaker. He led off about the weather, and that subject led to his wife's erratic behavior during full moons, and then Vella spoke of Perry's condition, after which things smoothed out enough for them to talk about themselves for another ten minutes. Vella had to listen very closely to him, though, because he talked at an incredible rate of speed.

When he said goodbye, he put in, "I'd really like to see Valentine someday, and you, too."

She wasn't certain what to say to this and came out with, "I'd like to see you, too."

When she hung up, she sat with her hand on the phone and imagined him coming to town, and herself having dyed hair and getting artificial nails. This fantasy quickly accelerated to them in bed with each other.

She jumped up from her chair, pressing her hands and tissue to her burning cheeks. "For heaven's sake!" What could she be thinking?

She heard a still small voice inside. *You have been praying for a man.*

Oh, dear, she thought, wadding the tissue and throwing it into the trash basket. She wouldn't know what to do with a man if she got him.

"Mama! Look!"

Vella was prepared to be aggravated by some new item on the shopping channel on the television hanging up on the wall beside the menu sign. Even so, she looked at the screen, where she saw a news report out of Wichita Falls. The drawings of two suspects flashed on the television screen, apparently made from descriptions given by the latest victim of a rash of car thefts in the area.

"Mama, doesn't that one on the right look like that Denny Rhodes—you know, the guy who took Claire's car."

"Well, it sure could be, I suppose."

"I'm gonna go tell Lyle." Belinda jerked off her smock. "He might need to get the word down to Wichita Falls about what happened here."

Vella pointed out that the theft of Claire's car had been a month ago, but Belinda said that did not matter and hurried out of the drugstore on a high horse of duty and curiosity.

Vella locked the door after her, then turned the Closed sign to face outward. With her fingers on the sign, she realized it was the same one they had used for twenty years, at least.

She did final cleanup behind the counter and put the bank bag of money into her large purse in the same manner that she had been doing now most nights since Perry's first stroke. Turning out all the lights but the one in the menu bar on the wall, she retrieved a glass of cold tea and slipped onto a stool at the end of the counter.

She lit up one of her cigarillos, blew out a stream of smoke, and sat looking back down the years of her life and having what her mother used to call a *come-to-Jesus-meeting*.

Chapter Twenty-Seven

At eight-thirty in the morning, the bright summer sun sliced over the trees behind the fire department and into the driver's seat of Larkin's pickup, where he sat parked in front of the Burger Barn, eating runny gravy and biscuits with a plastic fork out of a foam plate. He had not been able to be still at home but had not wanted to cause any noise that would awaken Travis. He felt the great need to somehow make things up to his son, or at the very least not do anything to escalate their current estranged situation. He knew he needed to speak to his son's accusation, but he and Travis had never spoken of such private matters. He didn't know where to begin. It was easier to wait for it all to blow over.

Just then, with a fork full of biscuit halfway to his mouth, he happened to look down the road to see Claire Wilder's car pull into the Texaco. She didn't stop at the fuel pumps but drove up in front of one of the yawning garage doors.

Continuing to eat, he watched her get out of the car—she wore a dark blue skirt that the breeze pressed against her form. Larry Joe Darnell came out to speak to her. She handed her keys to the young man and went inside the station.

Larkin took another big bite of his breakfast, wiped his mouth with the napkin, hopped out and threw the plate into the trash can, then drove down to the Texaco, pulling up in front of the pumps.

He told himself he would just get gas. He did not need to go speak to Claire Wilder.

There she was inside the station, he saw with a glance as he got out to pump his own gas, as he normally did. She sat in one of the ladderback chairs. She was alone. Old Norm Stidham didn't usually get down to the station these days until late morning.

His tank took barely five gallons, and then he had to go into the station to pay. He kept his head down, acting as he didn't know Claire was there. The bell above the door rang as he entered. He looked up then, straight at her. She was looking at him.

"Hello," he said.

"Hello." She smiled.

He felt a little silly.

"You wanna write up your bill for me?" Larry Joe called to him from the garage. He held up his oily hands.

Larkin gave a nod and said, "Sure," and went over to write up his own ticket, which would be billed to his monthly account, placing it on the spike where he knew it should go.

"Life in a small town," Claire said, when he turned around.

"I guess." He felt very country. City girl was written all over her.

He leaned back against the edge of the old counter, remembered his father and pushed away, stuffing his hands in his back pockets. "I hear you're leavin' us pretty quick."

She nodded. "Tomorrow mornin'." Then, "Vella's havin' a party…did she call you?"

"Yeah, she did."

"Oh…good."

"I don't know if I'll be able to make it tonight…. I'd already set up this thing with another guy."

"Oh, that's okay. It really was sort of short notice."

He didn't know what more to say and got nervous. He wished he could be more like his son, who could find something to say if he were dead.

Just then Larry Joe came through the door, wiping his hands on a rag. "Turns out I'm out of the oil filter for your car, Miz Wilder. I'll have to call down to the auto parts store, so it'll be a little bit longer."

"Oh."

"I could drive you back to the motel and deliver the car later, but I'll have to wait until my helper gets here, and by then, I could be finished with your car. Unless Larkin here would like to take you."

Larkin jumped. "Uh…yeah." Then he added, "No problem. I'd be glad to take you, Claire."

Her eyes studied him. He felt a little foolish with eagerness that he really didn't want to show.

"Thank you. I'll take you up on that."

He hurried ahead to open the passenger door for her. He didn't know if he should touch her to help her in, but she made it fine on her own, and he went around and slipped into the driver's seat.

He said, "Would you like me to drive you somewhere besides the motel? Do you need to get anything? Have you had breakfast?" He could eat another breakfast with her.

"I ate at the motel." Then, "But you know, if you wouldn't mind, I'd like to go out to the Little Creek cemetery. I want to take flowers out to my grandparents' graves and didn't get it done last night. If you wouldn't mind…if it isn't too far…"

"I'd be glad to," he said, and she hurriedly got out, saying she had the flowers in her car.

She ran into the garage, just like a young girl, and returned with two small artificial flower bouquets.

As he drove away from the Texaco, Larkin found himself glancing guiltily around for Travis's pickup.

"I'll just be a few minutes," she said.

"Take your time. I'm in no rush."

He watched her walk in the direction of her grandparents' graves. The wind snatched at her hair and blew her skirt against her thighs.

Then he walked to his wife's grave, where he stared at her name carved in the stone. It struck him that he couldn't even recall her face anymore.

He hadn't been able to do so for a long time, but he hadn't wanted to admit it.

He crouched down. Only two flowers from the bouquet that he had brought the previous week before remained in the small vase; the others had likely blown away. He started to pull out the dead blossoms, but then, his hand extended, he stopped and sighed deeply.

Maybe if he had paid more attention to her, things would not have gone as they had. But who would ever know? Maybe everything had happened just as it was supposed to happen. He had blamed himself in his grief, thinking that there should have been something he thought to do. But in the end, he had been helpless. He had done his best, and he was satisfied with that now.

With a sigh, he straightened, leaving the dead flowers to finish blowing away.

As his gaze crossed the engraved name once again, Karin's image flashed across his mind, full and smiling, as if to comfort him, just as she always had. Then the image was gone.

Turning, he walked away toward Claire and was there when she got to her feet, and, much to his surprise, stumbled, falling headlong into his arms.

Frank Goode talked to Gertie on the phone for half an hour, and she cried, but she would not relent and come home.

"I won't come back. You come down here," she said.

He went out to the garage in the back and pulled the black tarpaulin off his big old Harley-Davidson. Staring at it, he made plans for driving off-road, maybe out around Seep's Corner, which ran along the edge of a rocky drop-off into a deep canyon.

He might kill himself trying that, he thought.

Maybe he could somehow manage to run over himself as he worked on the bike. He had known a fellow who had managed to do that once right in front of Frank's face. The bike had been running, and it suddenly ran right off the stand and over the guy, breaking two ribs.

A couple of broken ribs would surely bring Gertie back home to take care of him.

But what if it didn't?

He considered this for a minute, then went to the workbench and opened the case of the electric circular saw. A chopped-off hand ought to bring her back.

"Mr. Goode?"

The voice startled him. He looked around to see a silhouette in the garage opening. It was the young pregnant gal.

"Yeah?"

"The dollar-bill changer isn't workin'. Could you give me some change?" She held out three ones.

"Go on and get it outta the register," he told her. "It ain't locked. There ain't enough in it to bother lockin' it," he added, taking the saw out of the case.

Sherrilyn stood there wondering if she had heard him correctly. "The cash register? You mean in the office?"

"Yeah," he said, not looking at her but lifting an electric saw out of the case in a rather disturbing manner that made her think of a horror movie.

Sherrilyn stood there for a moment, scratching one hot leg against the other. Mr. Goode didn't look very well. He hadn't shaved, and his hair was all oily and sweaty. There was an almost empty bottle of whiskey on the workbench.

She didn't want him to get angry at her for staring, so she walked away, but she turned and looked back to see him fiddling with the saw. She wished Claire would get back. She would know what to do about Mr. Goode.

However, this worry was shoved aside by her desire to call Denny on the pay phone before Claire did return, so she went around the building and into the office and over to the cash register.

A phone sat right there next to it.

She decided that she might get into more trouble with the cash register than she would making a long distance call from the office phone. She had a fear of being accused of stealing from the cash register, and she sure didn't want her fingerprints on it. Probably no one checked the phone records, though, and she would get to keep her money. She couldn't call collect, because she knew that wouldn't be accepted on the other end; she had tried and been told by someone with a Mexican accent, "We ain't takin' no co'lect nothin'."

Taking up the phone now, she moved back behind the partial wall and sat in the really neat rolling chair, where no one could see her if they looked through the windows. Probably Mr. Goode wouldn't come in, she thought as she dialed the number she had for Denny, but if he did, she would hang up quick and tell him she had been answering a wrong number.

When Denny finally got on the other end of the line, she told him how she was with Claire and going to Shreveport. She thought he would think that she had done well for herself and his baby, but he wasn't all that happy. He wanted to know why she had taken up with the woman. His attitude perplexed Sherrilyn, since the other day he had seemed to be in favor of her selling her baby to Claire. Sometimes Denny could be really changeable, though, and get her all confused. Before she could respond to him, he asked her about the urn. "You didn't go and give it back to her, did you? Is that why she took you in? Damn you, bitch!"

"No," she said quickly. "I didn't."

"Well, you hold on to it, Sherri. It can be your ticket, if she starts to have you arrested or somethin'."

"Why would she do that?"

"That's how rich chicks like her are. She can lose a piece of jewelry and blame you for it. Look, just calm down."

Sherrilyn had started to cry. She didn't normally cry so much, but she was exhausted, and really tired of being tired and blowing up like a balloon.

"Just don't let her see the urn," Denny said again, "and I'll get over there to get you real soon, okay? You can leave her the urn when I come get you. But right now, it can be worth somethin' to us. Just tell me where you'll be in Shreveport, and I'll come over there. Just give me the address, okay?"

"I don't know it yet. But I'll call you as soon as we get there," she promised, wanting to please him in some way. She was terrified to make him madder at her. Although she felt a little reluctant when thinking about him coming to get her. She thought she might like living with Claire, and that it would be good for her baby.

Just then she saw a pickup truck pull up underneath the portico. "I got to go...somebody just drove up." She hung up and replaced the phone near the cash register, thinking of how optimistic she had been before calling Denny, and yet how the conversation had not turned out at all how she had hoped. Their conversations never did. She didn't know what she kept doing wrong.

Peering around the partial wall, she was a little relieved to see it was Claire getting out of a shiny pickup truck. A man was driving. It was not the same man who had kissed her.

Now that calling Denny was past, Sherrilyn got to thinking about Mr. Goode. As the pickup truck drove off and Claire started for their rooms, Sherrilyn hurried out after her and said, "Mr. Goode said he wanted to see you." She didn't want to look stupid and say that she was worried the man had gone a little crazy.

Claire asked what Mr. Goode wanted, and Sherrilyn said she didn't know. "He's out back—in the garage," she said, hoping Claire would go right then, and thankful when she did. Accompanying her, Sherrilyn thought about what to say if Mr. Goode said he hadn't wanted Claire.

It turned out that no explanation was necessary, because Mr. Goode was clearly drunk as a skunk. Shortly after trying to talk to him, and him starting to cry and saying that he couldn't live without his Gertie, Claire sent Sherrilyn for the pot of coffee from the office, directing her to go in through the apartment, and to hurry. Mr. Goode had sat down on a bench, and there was no getting him up. After Sherrilyn brought the coffee, Claire told her to return to watch the office, in case anyone was to telephone or come in.

"What should I say?" Sherrilyn didn't like the idea at all.

"Ask them to leave a message. If someone comes in and needs somethin' right away, come get me."

Feeling a little better at knowing what was expected of her, Sherrilyn went off as instructed; however, she remained a little worried that Mr. Goode might be crazy drunk, like her father could get, and possibly harm Claire.

This idea grew in her mind as she rolled around in the office chair for five minutes, shooting herself across to the wall and back. Then, hopping out of the chair, she went back through the apartment, which she had now passed through twice—it was an old people's place, with a lot of gold and big flowers—and peered out the kitchen window to see Claire and Mr. Goode sitting in the garage opening, talking.

Mr. Goode no longer appeared threatening. He looked wilted. Claire was seated in a comfortable looking canvas chair. A fan on a stand had been produced from somewhere and was blowing Claire's hair.

No longer worried about Claire, Sherrilyn turned her attention to the apartment. She had begun to have to use the bathroom and wondered if it would be all right to use the one in the apartment. She didn't seem to have any choice. The bathroom was big, with separate bathtub and shower stall, and lots of images of pink flamingo birds on the walls.

One of the bedrooms had an enormous waterbed with a gaudy bedspread and smelled like Mr. Goode, and the other was a whole lot plainer than the rest of the house, with one of those really old looking nubby bedspreads.

Back in the kitchen once more, she noticed a sewing machine. She had enjoyed sewing things when she had been in school. If Denny married her and she could get a sewing machine, she could sew really pretty curtains for their house.

She went through cabinets just to see what was there and found a package of chocolate chip cookies. Taking out a handful, she carefully replaced the bag exactly as it had been. Returning to the office, she curled in one of the big chairs, where she ate the cookies while watching *The People's Court* on television, then fell asleep.

When she awoke, Claire was there, perched on the tall stool behind the desk and talking on the telephone to that old woman, Vella Blaine, who owned the drugstore.

Sherrilyn was a little afraid of the old woman. She was afraid that she was going to do something wrong around the old woman and hear about it, which was why she didn't want to go to the going-away party that evening. Not only would she not really know anyone, she feared she would do something wrong.

Just then she heard Claire say, "Well, I guess it isn't a goin'-away party anymore. You can't seem to get rid of me." And she laughed. Then she looked in Sherrilyn's direction and said, "Sherrilyn's awake, so I can tell her. I'll see you later. Bye."

"Tell me what?" asked Sherrilyn, who began to feel anxious about what she was going to hear. She was also stiff from sleeping in the chair and still in need of more sleep.

"Plans have changed," Claire told her. "We're not goin' to Shreveport tomorrow after all."

Sherrilyn was jarred out of thinking about going to her bed in the motel room and putting a quarter in the vibrator. She stared at Claire, who was saying, "I've made a deal with Mr. Goode, and we're goin' to stay here and keep the motel open, while he goes on to Florida."

She went on about how they were all set to stay at least through September, when the baby came, to see how things worked out, and how staying was a much better option, because it would be best for Sherrilyn to remain in Valentine in order to keep seeing the same doctors and all.

"I see a group of doctors at the clinic. I never have seen the same one twice," said Sherrilyn, who had experience with people putting the blame for things on her.

"Well, we'll get you set up to see the same doctor all the time," Claire said. "And stayin' here will be like an extended vacation," she added, which Sherrilyn felt was more to the fact of the matter.

Having anticipated a move to Claire's townhouse and a

new start on her life, Sherrilyn felt trapped in a situation over which she had no control. She had formed a mental picture of what Claire's townhouse looked like, what her life there would look like, and how she would look there. The old motel did not equal this fantasy one bit, besides which, she had told Denny she was going down to Shreveport and didn't want to have to tell him different. He would accuse her of not being able to get anything straight.

"Are we ever goin' to Shreveport?" she asked, beginning to think that Claire had lied to her all along, that maybe Claire didn't even have a townhouse in Shreveport. What did Sherrilyn really know about the woman, anyway? It was beginning to look as if she had made another huge mistake.

Claire turned to look at her, and Sherrilyn wished she hadn't been so presumptuous with her question and tried not to seem upset.

"Yes, I imagine we will," Claire said in a patient tone that grated on Sherrilyn's nerves. "I'll have to take care of my townhouse. But for now, I promised Mr. Goode I'd stay and see what I could do with the motel.

"And we aren't goin' to have to stay in the rooms. We're goin' to move into the Goodes' apartment back here. You'll have your own room, and we can fix it up a bit. We'll have a kitchen, television, everything. It'll be a really nice summer, like being on a vacation the whole time…and Mr. Goode is havin' the pool fixed, too."

She was obviously thrilled about the idea, and Sherrilyn was stuck with it. When she had fallen asleep, she had been on her way in life, and now she had awakened and was stuck once again.

Intent on keeping Vella sitting in her lounge chair, Claire went into the house for another pitcher of cold tea and plate of hors d'oeuvres, which Fayrene said were in the refrigerator. Fayrene had brought the food from the café, but obviously did not intend to serve.

Sherrilyn followed, an action that was getting on Claire's nerves. The girl had been stuck to Claire like her shadow ever since they had arrived at the Blaine house. Claire could hardly turn around for bumping into her.

Handing the girl the pitcher of tea, she said, "Take this on out and refill glasses. I'll be there in a few minutes with these hors d'oeuvres."

"I used to be a waitress. I can take both."

"Okay, then…" Claire handed the young woman the plate of hors d'oeuvres and helped her out the back door, promising to follow with coffee. "Be careful on the steps," she added.

She really needed to quit instructing the girl in such a manner, she thought. Sherrilyn had enough of a problem being timid, without Claire adding to it.

She put mugs on a wooden tray and took up the insulated coffeepot. At the screen door, she paused, gazing through the dusky screen to the scene on the stone patio.

The last rays of the golden sun were leaving the sky and full dark settling in, causing the string of colorful Chinese lanterns to glow brightly. Crickets and cicadas could be heard vying with the voices.

Claire's heart filled as her eyes moved over the faces of people she had not known until one month ago: Winston beside Marilee Holloway…Vella, with Perry nodding off in a large chair beside her…Travis talking to Sherrilyn…Tate Holloway and Corrine and Willie Lee talking to Julia the postmistress and her husband, who turned out to be the man who filled Claire's orders at the IGA delicatessen…Fayrene and Lori, the receptionist at the sheriff's department…and Belinda, too, with her SO, as Vella called him, Lyle.

Everyone had already heard the news of her staying and

taking over the Goodnight, of course. In fact, as a surprise, everyone had already been here when she arrived, and she had been greeted with applause, which had nearly brought her to tears. Winston had grabbed her and danced her around Vella's brick patio. She made him stop, whispering in his ear that she wanted him to save himself for the coming months and giving him a suggestive grin, to which he had responded, "You're a firecracker."

Travis had grabbed her next and danced her around, and then Vella had jumped in and danced with her, too.

Tate Holloway had started interviewing her for the newspaper, with Julia Jenkins-Tinsley listening to every word. Fayrene had suggested the idea of putting a Main Street Café menu in every room and offering discounts to the motel guests. This prompted Tate to volunteer free copies of the *Valentine Voice.*

Change and enthusiasm were contagious, Claire thought, looking at these people who had become dear friends.

"Need some help?" asked a familiar voice.

"What?" Startled, she turned and found herself looking up at Larkin Ford in almost the same fashion that she had that morning at the cemetery.

"I came through the front. Sorry to be late."

"I'm glad you could make it." My heaven, but he smelled good. And in that instant, she realized how disappointed she had been earlier at his not being there. "But it isn't a goin'-away party anymore."

"So I heard." A real grin bloomed on his face, as he gazed at her in that intent fashion that he'd had that morning.

Then his gaze shifted, and he looked beyond her, his grin fading. Reaching around her, he pushed open the screen door.

Turning to step through, Claire saw Travis on the bottom step. His eyes went from Claire to his father and back again. "Do you need some help?" he asked her.

Feeling that she had to provide something for him, in order to equal out letting his father help with the door, she gave over the insulated pot of coffee and said brightly, "Thank you so much."

She watched the two men for the rest of the party and noticed that they did not say one word directly to each other.

"The baby's movin'." Sherrilyn, with an expression somewhere between alarm and wonder, put her hands to her belly. "It really is. You want to feel? It's right here…here."

She grabbed Claire's hand and pressed it to the spot. Claire, who was somewhat stunned to see the girl smile and further surprised to have the girl grab her, prepared to fight off the envy that so often attacked her in the face of other women having babies.

But the envy was far overwhelmed by the wonder of feeling the thump in Sherrilyn's belly, as well as the life alight on the girl's face. At that moment the girl was proof that all pregnant women were beautiful.

As Sherrilyn got into bed, she chattered, saying more and in a happier tone than Claire had ever heard her speak. She talked about how the girls at Lilac House had said they felt their babies move way earlier than Sherrilyn now did, and that she had thought that she had felt it move a lot of times before, but now she was certain.

Then she stopped talking and a stricken expression came over her face, and she averted her eyes downward.

"What's wrong?" Claire asked, sinking down on the edge of the bed. The girl's expression had changed so drastically that she was a little alarmed.

Sherrilyn, a mask of indifference once more in place, shrugged. "I was just gettin' carried away. I forgot about you havin' lost your babies and all."

Claire said gently, "It is wonderful for you to enjoy being pregnant."

The girl's gaze came up slightly, and she rather peeked at Claire, who pulled up the covers and smoothed them over the girl's legs.

"I can still get a little sad about the loss of my babies," she said. "But my sadness is not a reason for you to temper your excitement at this special time in your life. You have a right to enjoy this gift. And besides, I enjoy watchin' you. I'm glad for you. It helps my sadness."

Sherrilyn peered intently at Claire with a curious expression. "That old woman—Vella—she said that you didn't know any of these people here before you got your car stolen."

"Oh, I knew Winston. I met him the first day, when I came to town and stopped into the drugstore…and Belinda, too."

"You know a lot of people now."

Claire smiled. "Yes, I do. I was originally born here, and I think that makes a difference to some people. This was my father's hometown, and that's what originally brought me here. I was on vacation and just thought I would stop in to see where my father grew up. I was only going to stay one night, and I imagine I would not be here now, with you, if my car hadn't been stolen."

She deliberately didn't mention Sherrilyn's boyfriend as having stolen the car, not wanting to see the girl sink back into the dark place inside herself.

"It's funny how things work out, isn't it? I stopped to see my grandparents' graves, and to just see where my father had lived. A sort of connection with him. He walked out of my life when I was a child, and I've always wondered about him."

"My mother died when I was nine." Sherrilyn's gaze darted downward, and the shadows once again came across her face. Claire noted the girl's very long eyelashes. "My dad was mad afterward. Then he got remarried, and his new wife said I caused too much trouble." The shadows deepened.

"Their loss," Claire said quickly. She was trying to think of something else to say when Sherrilyn's eyelashes fluttered up and the girl fixed Claire with a questioning gaze.

"Did your mom remarry?"

"No. There was just me and my mother. We lived with my mother's father and aunt for a while, and then just me and Mom, until I married my high school sweetheart. I became a legal assistant, and he became an architect. After eighteen years of marriage, we got divorced. I lived a few years on my own, pining my heart out for him, until one evening I read something on a rest room wall. It was one of those lightbulb moments, you know, and I thought that I just had to change some things or I was about to die. Anyway, I packed up and went off on a trip to see what I might find."

She saw she had captured Sherrilyn's attention, and the darkness on the young woman's face had thankfully been replaced by curiosity. "What did it say on the wall?"

"It said, *On my way, just passing through, looking for real life—wish her well, this Lily Donnell!* And I thought, well, there's a woman with a good idea. And that I surely wasn't gettin' any younger."

Eyes widening, Sherrilyn scooted up on her pillow. "I read that same thing on a rest room wall."

"You did?"

"Uh-huh. I did. I'm not lyin'," she said with earnestness. "It was in black magic marker, right by the mirror in a rest room at a truckstop in Fort Worth. I remember, because I liked the name Lily Donnell. I liked all the Ls."

They gazed at each other.

Claire said, "Well, for goodness' sake."

They laughed together and started wondering just who was this Lily Donnell and making up stories about her.

★ ★ ★

Hearing tires crunch on gravel in the parking lot, Claire peered out between the draperies and saw a car pulling up in front of number five.

She realized that she was thinking of the rooms in the same manner as Gertie or Frank would speak. "Number five left us a tip," and "The number ten regular has a new after-shave that stinks a long time."

A salesman type of man got out of a gleaming sedan and went to the door of the room and through it. Claire's gaze moved on to note that while she had been laughing with Sherrilyn and then getting ready for bed, guests had arrived to stay in numbers six and eight, too. One was in a big rig truck. This made her think of how many trucks she had seen pass by on the highway. Not a whole lot, but some. Perhaps she could come up with something to entice more into the motel.

Clicking off the light, she opened the draperies and curled in the chair to gaze out the window at the Good-night Motel sign.

She had made a deal to become a partner in the motel, with option to purchase, and was staying in Valentine. The opportunity had just fallen right into her lap. But it wasn't a hasty decision, because it had been there in the back of her mind all along.

She had mostly known that she didn't want to return to her life as she had known it. And trying to return with the responsibility of Sherrilyn put her almost into a panic. What did she know about helping a troubled young woman? Staying in Valentine afforded her wise people who could help.

Vella said that Claire knew, from her own experiences, a lot about what Sherrilyn needed, yet still, she was awfully grateful to be given this chance to have support from Winston and Vella and even Belinda. In Shreveport, she would have been pretty much on her own. She was seeing this clearly for the first time. Andrew was not likely to spare attention from his work, and Gayla Jean was her only true woman friend and had her own family and interests.

For the first time in a long while, Claire felt a sense of excitement about what she wanted to do. Taking care of Sherrilyn and the motel. Renovation of both a human spirit and a building.

She closed her eyes as a profound gratitude swept her. Thank you, God. It seemed somehow that she was managing a renovation in her own life. She felt a sense of direction at last.

Chapter Twenty-Eight

She had wondered if Frank Goode might back out of their deal in the light of a new day and sober mind.

He did not. He was ready. "We're on…let's get 'er done," he said with evident excitement.

Vella and Winston attended as witnesses, and both Claire and Frank signed the agreement Claire had drawn up and printed from the motel computer. The motel was in her hands, with specified financing from Frank, through September, when a final decision and sale would take place, with the agreement of both parties.

Vella and Winston had both wanted to purchase the motel outright and hire Claire to run it, but Claire liked this idea best. Much better a trial period, giving both Frank and herself room to change their minds. This course let her catch her breath.

"This course postpones your need for a firm decision," said Vella, not altogether approving.

"Yes. All decisions do come in the correct time," replied Claire, holding firm.

At midmorning, she stood beneath the office portico with Vella, Winston and Sherrilyn, waving off Frank Goode, who happily roared away on his shiny black Harley, towing along a shiny black trailer, into the heat waves already simmering off the blacktop.

Claire watched him until he disappeared and then ran her gaze along the row of duplex cabins, noting the dated design, the places where the paint was noticeably peeling, and the spaces that needed shade from trees. She felt excited and overwhelmed at the same time.

Winston produced a bottle of champagne, and they all went into the office to make toasts out of foam cups. While they were doing this, a van with Goode Heating and Plumbing plastered on the side pulled up. Frank had been true to his word and employed plumbers to make the repairs on the pool.

The plumbers introduced themselves as Frank's cousins, Bubba Goode, whose looks pretty well matched his name, and a much younger and smaller man, Reynolds Goode. Watching them through the window as they went to uncover the pool, Claire suddenly grabbed the box of letters from beneath the counter and strode out to the mobile marquee.

Those in the office watched her from the window as she took down the previous For Sale sign and put up:

Under New Management
Welcome
Enjoy sweet dreams with vintage vibrators

As she was returning to the office, there came Vella in a rapid stride toward her.

"Sugar, I think you had better go back there and make it say *bed* vibrators."

Shreveport

Gayla Jean punched in the number of Claire's cell phone and listened to the rings come across the line. She was about to hang up when someone answered. She didn't recognize the voice. "Claire?"

"No, this is Sherrilyn. But Claire's right here. Hang on a minute."

"Oh, hi, honey. This is Gayla Jean—Claire's ex-sister-in-law. Has she told you about me? She's told me about you. How're you doin', sweetheart? Are you still anemic? That can just make you feel so bad. I've been anemic a couple of times. The doctors watch me now, because of it."

"Uh—no, not too bad now."

"That's good to hear," said Gayla Jean, who thought the girl was a little slow in answering. Possibly she was a little slow mentally, so Gayla Jean spoke more deliberately. "You eat lots of steak and eggs. That's what I do when my blood's down. I'll have steak for dinner this weekend. I'm throwin' you two a welcome back dinner. Well it won't be welcome back for you, I guess, since you haven't been here. It will just be a big welcome."

"Uh, yes, ma'am." The girl said "uh" a lot. "Here's Claire."

There was some noise, and Claire came on the line.

"I was glad to speak to that Sherrilyn," Gayla Jean said. "Maybe it's the cell phone, but she sounds about ten years old, and a little mousy."

"Yes," Claire said.

"Oh, that's right, she's right there. She didn't hear me, though, did she?" Gayla Jean, who knew her poor habit of talking loudly at times, felt horribly ashamed that she might have offended the girl.

"No, honey, she didn't."

"Oh, good. Well, where are you guys? I saw on my caller

ID that you had called. I just missed you, because I got in to
the office way late today. I took Raquel to get her learner's
permit this mornin'. Lordy, but I felt old, Claire…and then
first thing when I got in, Melanie rounded us all up to do an
intervention on Mr. Dupree. We had to go in there and each
of us tell him of episodes of his temper tantrums that we
remembered. It was not pleasant. Six people tellin' him how
he got all manic and turned red and said awful stuff, and that
was supposed to make him willin' to go to anger management therapy. All it did was get him to break a ruler on his
desk and fire Melanie. He couldn't fire anyone else, because
none of us actually work for him, not to mention he
wouldn't have anyone to do the work.

"Melanie certainly isn't as timid as she once was. She said
since he fired her, she was goin' to get unemployment, and
she plans to file a complaint for harassment. She's goin' to law
school at night, too. She says you were her inspiration, Claire.
She wants to thank you, and I've invited her to your welcome
home dinner this Saturday night, if that'll work for you."

"Well, Gayla Jean, that's what I called about. There's been
a change in plans, and we're not comin' home just yet."

"You're not comin' home? Honey, what in the world is
goin' on?" Gayla Jean sank back in her desk chair, suddenly
exhausted from all the emotion of the day—her baby girl
growing up and getting a driver's license, and people all
around her going crazy.

Claire told her about being handed the opportunity to
manage the motel at least until September. "It will be best
for Sherrilyn, and it will be good for me, too. It's like being
on a long holiday."

Gayla Jean, momentarily speechless, heard a certain tone in
Claire's voice. A certain lively note that she had not heard in
a long time. Maybe never. She asked, "Have you told Andrew?"

"Not yet…and please, Gayla Jean, don't tell him before I do."

"I would not do that, honey." She felt a little hurt. "I do know which things to tell and which things not to." She was just a little tired of Claire and Andrew, who were determined to stay apart. She had done her best, and there it was. No one could blame her for not trying.

"Right this minute," she said, "I'm ready for takin' a long vacation myself. I've got a teenager to get through drivin' and into college, and one spendin' a fortune in braces and another makin' a career out of the principal's office. You know, the Murrays, who headed the marriage enrichment seminar, go away for the entire summer each year. They have done that for years. Used to be, Mr. Murray would travel from his job in Shreveport down to Galveston, where Mrs. Murray and the kids stayed at a cottage. Lamar's boss sends his family off to Eureka Springs for six weeks. Six weeks! We take a puny week and spend it goin' to see my mother down in Mobile. I am really sick of that, but Lamar and I each only get two weeks vacation.

"I told Lamar that he and I could become marriage enrichment leaders and go away for weekends to fancy hotels several times a year and have it all paid for."

Something came to her and she made certain to tell Claire before she hung up. "Claire, honey, you might should consider having the motel host a marriage enrichment getaway weekend."

When she got off the phone with Claire, she called up Lamar and said, "Well, Claire is not comin' home after all. Don't tell Andrew, though."

"I won't."

"That means we'll have this weekend free, honey. Wouldn't it be great to go down to New Orleans and stay at one of those fancy places in the French Quarter? I need to get away, Lamar. How 'bout you?"

He said instantly, "You got it, darlin'. And I'll bring pizza for supper tonight, too." Lamar had learned many things from his wife, although he wisely didn't spout off about them.

After she hung up, Gayla Jean pulled her marriage enrichment study book out of her desk and began reading. The difficulty with the entire world, in her opinion, was that people did not pop out of the womb knowing how to relate to other people. They had to learn it from others, who were supposed to know how to have a decent relationship, but unfortunately, most other people did not know, either. So all manner of pitiful and mean ways of behaving to each other were passed around, like the flu. Her daddy used to say that he learned at the school of hard knocks, and then he would whack one of his children upside the head. What kind of loving behavior was that to learn? She didn't think there was a place in the Bible where Jesus taught people by whacking them.

Gayla Jean had early on in her marriage known that she needed help and applied herself to learn. In high school, she had been voted Miss Congeniality. These days she read books and watched all the *Oprah* television shows that featured psychologists telling about how to improve a marriage. She had improved herself, and she knew a thing or two.

As she read over the marriage enrichment book, she felt a welling of desire to help other people learn the principles of being happy and having a happy marriage. She saw herself as a perfect marriage enrichment leader, although if Lamar was to be a marriage enrichment leader, too, he had to get more regular with church. That was going to be trickier to accomplish than getting him to go to New Orleans, where he got to eat himself silly at wonderful restaurants.

She would stop and buy a new black nightie on the way home. One could always get more flies with honey.

Andrew was in another interminable but important meeting when his cell phone rang. Doodling on his yellow pad, he didn't realize at first that a phone was ringing. He was pre-occupied with thoughts about his life, which seemed in a big knot. Then he realized that the client representative had quit talking and looked up to see the man staring at him.

In an instant, he saw that all six pairs of eyes around the table were staring at him and realized that it was *his* cell phone ringing. He had forgotten to turn it to silent.

"Sorry," he said, digging for the phone, which was deter-mined to stay in the pocket of his sport coat hung over the back of his chair. At last he got it out and punched the but-ton to silence it.

Everyone's eyes shifted back to the man at the head of the room, who resumed speaking. He was a representative of a corporate client that had retained Andrew's employer, Ren-nals & Associates, to design a small but lavish gambling ca-sino. "A jewel of a casino," was the idea. The man had flown in from California just for the day and was meeting with the top architects at the firm.

As a senior architect, Andrew was up front, while Nina, a niece of the president of the firm, was still in the junior ranks and sitting at the rear of the room. Andrew could see her reflection in the tinted floor to ceiling windows. He felt silly because of the phone incident. This was the first time that he had been required to be in a room with her. He was su-premely thankful that Nina was still in the junior ranks. This limited his contact with her. If he kept himself out of town or in his office when he was in town, he could go days with-out running into her.

He didn't know what he was going to do if he got back together with Claire, and Nina rose up into the senior ranks, which she was bound to do, since her uncle, Bart Rennals, headed the firm. It was highly likely that sometime in the future, he would have to work on a project with her.

He sneaked a peek at his phone, now lying on the table. The caller had been Claire.

He was both excited and annoyed. It was the second time this morning that she had called. He hadn't been able to answer before, because he was getting ready for the meeting, and he couldn't talk to her now, either, he thought with irritation.

Settling himself back into his chair, he determinedly focused on the client. He was in the running to head the group that would design the casino. Despite the fiasco of his relationship with Nina, her uncle had not held it against him. Andrew felt called on to do everything he could to make things up to Bart Rennals and to stay in the man's good graces.

His eyes slid over to look at the phone again. He saw he had a message.

He glanced over to the concentrating profile of Bart Rennals.

Another five minutes, and Andrew found himself surreptitiously palming the phone and getting to his feet. While doing his best to appear a man in need of a bathroom, he slipped out the door, catching sight of Bart Rennals's frown as he went.

What in the world was he doing?

He strode down the hall and to the men's room, punching the buttons to recall Claire as he went.

Someone answered quite quickly. "Claire? Can you hear me?" There was a lot of interference noise, and he had this small panic that he would be cut off from her. He moved over to the windows.

"Are you there, Andrew? Can you hear me?"

"Yeah."

"Oh, good. You're clear on this end."

Andrew checked his watch and wondered what had gone wrong in his brain. If Claire had not called him, he wouldn't have gone so crazy, so he was mad at her. "You called me? I'm in a meeting.... I stepped out and need to get back."

"Oh. I'm sorry." That sat there a minute, and then she said, "I had no way of knowin' you were in a meeting. I left a message."

Her tone annoyed him. "I didn't check. What did you need?"

"Well, we can talk about it all later, when you have time. Right now I just need to tell you that I won't be home today, as I'd planned."

"You're not comin' today? What happened?" He had been thinking that this would happen. He had told himself it wouldn't, but now here it was.

"I can tell you later, when there's more time."

"Just tell me now, Claire. Give me the short version."

"No...I..."

The connection was breaking up again, and he realized that in his agitation, he had walked away from the windows. He moved back to them. "What did you say?"

There was a pause, and she said, "I've decided to stay and manage the motel—the Goodnight—through the summer."

He looked in the rest room mirror. "You are *what?*"

"I have the opportunity to stay here and manage the motel, and I've decided to do it. I've committed to stay at least through September. And if I like doing this, I may buy the place."

"God, Claire."

"I know it seems odd, even crazy. But it's a great opportunity to have a paid vacation." Her voice had a laugh in it.

He leaned against the windowsill and listened to her tell him something about the guy who owned the motel needing to go to Florida, so Claire had taken over managing the place temporarily, but with an option to buy. She said staying gave her an opportunity to see if she would like owning a motel, and the girl she had picked up the opportunity to stay with the same doctors until she had her baby.

Had he even known the girl was pregnant?

Her voice dropped lower, so he had to listen hard. "I'm finding something here, Andrew. Something I lost a long time ago. I'm only just now coming to see this. I don't know for sure if I'll buy the motel, but I do know I'm excited about giving it a try. I need this time here."

"Time?" He thought, Away from me? But he didn't say that, because he was afraid of the answer. "Time for what?"

"For trying out what has come my way."

"What are you goin' to do for a living while you're tryin' this out? Are you goin' to get paid for this? Are you goin' to make enough to keep the townhouse?" The damn thing didn't come cheap. He knew that well enough. "Do you know what you'll lose if it's repossessed?"

"I'm okay. I have enough in savings, and I'll make enough here to cover expenses."

Her tone remained firm. He couldn't get her with that. Claire knew money; she always had.

"I was lookin' forward to you comin', Claire. I miss you." The words popped out.

There was a pause, and she asked, "Did you plan a party or a dinner for me comin' home tonight? I hope I didn't mess up your plans."

"Uh…no. No, I didn't. I think Gayla Jean said something about havin' a dinner this weekend." He suddenly felt lacking.

"Yes. I spoke to her already."

Again the line crackled.

Then Andrew said, "What do you expect me to do while you're up there, Claire?"

"I don't expect anything from you, Andrew. This is something I have to do for myself, my life. I'm not doin' this to hurt you. I never meant that. I care for you, and I want you to be happy, and I want to be happy, too."

In that split second, he saw his life with her and all at once his failures and regrets.

"Do what you want, then," he said, then clicked off the phone and drew back his arm, almost throwing the device into the plate glass mirror.

Breathing deeply, he deposited the phone into his pants pocket. Then he closed his eyes, feeling like a childish ass for hanging up on her. He thought to call her back, but he couldn't. He wondered what was happening to him.

He had thought he had gotten through all this craziness when he had divorced Claire and started on what seemed a new life. He had thought he knew exactly what he wanted. Only things had not turned out as he had imagined. He had found himself in more of a mess with Nina, a woman almost young enough to be his daughter.

Gathering what good sense he could find, he stepped to the mirror, adjusted his tie and smoothed his hair, and told himself that women were nothing but trouble. He wasn't going to sit around waiting for her. He had a good career and lived just how he wanted to live.

When he returned to the meeting room, the doors were open and people streaming out. Nina passed him, looked at him, then turned her head to speak to a colleague. Andrew retrieved his things. He was on his way back to his office when Bart Rennals hailed him in the hall.

Andrew followed the man into his office, where his boss asked him if he thought he might want to head the casino project, saying in his deep and soft, old-fashioned Louisiana drawl, "I haven't made a decision, you understand. I'm jus' askin'."

Andrew stood there looking at the man so long that the older man's white eyebrows rose.

"I need some time off," Andrew said, speaking through a constricting throat. "I have some personal matters that need attending. I was thinkin' that I could finish up with a few problems on the mall, then turn it over to McCawley and take a few weeks off. I haven't had a vacation in nearly two years," he added.

Bart Rennals nodded slowly. "I'll have to give the project to Farrell."

Andrew nodded. "I know."

"Okay, then," the older man said quietly, and Andrew left, knowing that he had just given away a chance at partnership, and perhaps his entire future with the firm.

But he found, strangely, that in that moment he did not have a regret for the decision. He felt more relief and a certainty that he was doing exactly what he needed and wanted to do for the first time in a long while.

From: Vella Blaine
To: <haltg@mailectric.com>
Sent: June 25, 1997, 10:31 p.m.
Subject: Confession
Dear Harold,

I'm sorry I haven't written in several days. I've really been busy since I spoke to you on Monday. And also, I've been doing some thinking.

I need to tell you that I lied about my age. I am really 68, well almost 69. It has been hard for me to face getting older. Then, with taking care of Perry and the store, I just don't have much time or energy left for anything else. I don't think it's a very good idea for us to get any more familiar with each other, so I'm not going to write anymore. I hope you understand.

Vella

Her hand hesitated. She didn't wish to sound so abrupt. Winston always told her that she had little tactfulness.

But she was what she was, she thought, and clicked the send button. It was done.

She was too old to think of romance.

Twenty minutes later, as she pored over the account books, the computer chime alerted her to a message. She was surprised to see that it was from Harold.

Furtively, she clicked on the message and read: *I'm here, when you want to write. No strings. Unconditional.*

Oh, my, what a man. He could actually spell unconditional.

Chapter Twenty-Nine

It wasn't that anyone could complain about lack of cleanliness or nonworking lights, faucets or air conditioners. Everything in each of the rooms was in working order, and all but the last two cabins were perfectly clean and sanitary, if a little musty and threadbare in places.

Claire had stayed in old elegant hotels in both New York and New Orleans that were equally, or even more, musty and threadbare. The difference was that they were proud of their datedness.

The problem with the Goodnight was the lack of that pride. There was an aura of abandonment, a forlornness, as if Gertie and Frank had left it a long time before they had finally driven away.

"It's sort of pitiful," Sherrilyn murmured, when they investigated the two last cabins, numbers nineteen and twenty. These had been cleaned and then shut up for some time, judging by the cobwebs behind the draperies and the musty smell.

Real life, Claire thought. That was what was needed.

"Open those windows."

She and Sherrilyn went from cabin to cabin, room to room, flinging open windows and turning on the radios beside the beds.

Claire began to toss out ideas—lavender soap in the bathrooms, lavender sachets for the pillows. The rooms needed a different paint scheme. The thing to do was to begin with one room at a time. Definitely get the Main Street Café menu, because it would go along with establishing a vintage theme. And a listing of phone numbers for all the local eating establishments, since Claire well knew the availability and pleasures of food delivery. Maybe, just maybe, a few regular guests. In the cities, people lived in hotels. Why not in Valentine?

"You could put in a couple of whirlpool tubs," said Sherrilyn, who slowly began to get into the spirit. She had been looking at Claire's stack of travel and vacation magazines. "See…like this. 'The Red Heart Cabin at the Falling Springs Retreat in the beautiful Ozarks,'" she read off the page, then tapped her finger on the picture.

Claire, who had just set two plates of sandwiches on the table in the kitchen of the apartment, liked the idea immediately and said so. "But let's choose one thing we can do today. Just to give us a start."

She saw Sherrilyn shoot her a curious look, possibly because Claire had used the terms *we* and *us*. It seemed to Claire that the moment she had made the offer of her support and the young girl had accepted, the two of them had become partners for the road ahead, wherever it led.

Sherrilyn really was a most agreeable partner, saying yes to anything Claire proposed, which was probably as it should be. They chose the project of putting lavender soap in the bathrooms. Belinda had enough bars of soap on hand, so Claire instructed Sherrilyn to drive in to the drugstore and pick them up after lunch.

"Me? Drive?"

"Oh, I'm sorry...I just assumed you could drive." She was rather amazed to think that the girl couldn't drive.

"I can." Sherrilyn bit her bottom lip. "I was just surprised that you'd want me to...in your car, I mean."

Claire looked into the girl's green eyes. "Unless you want to take the motel pickup truck, but it's a stick shift."

Sherrilyn shook her head. "I don't know how to drive a stick."

"Then take the Lincoln."

A half an hour later, she watched the girl drive away, a small figure behind the wheel of the large car. Here was one big benefit to staying in Valentine—the drugstore was less than two miles away, with the highest speed limit at thirty-five miles an hour.

And then the idea jumped into her mind: *Would the girl return?*

Well, of course she would. Even if she was of an unstable and naive nature, she was not totally stupid.

Claire went to the bedroom and set her mother's urn atop the waterbed headboard, then decided she didn't like that and moved it over to the dresser, where Gertie had left a lone half-empty bottle of fingernail polish.

"Mama, I know this room isn't quite your style—it isn't quite *my* style—but, well, I'm glad you're back." She paused. "I'm really okay, Mama. And I love you. I wish I could have told you that better while you were really here."

She thought her mother might like that she made the effort to talk to her.

By evening of the first day, they had moved their things into the apartment, thoroughly cleaned numbers ten and twelve, and added pillows to give four to a bed, in preparation for Boris and Natasha, whenever they showed up. They had also decorated the lavender soaps with lavender ribbon and arranged them with a specially folded washcloth in each bathroom. Claire was thrilled with how they looked next to the sinks.

"Your townhouse must be a real pit for you to choose this motel over goin' back there," said Sherrilyn, and then ducked her head in the habit she had after giving voice to an opinion.

"My townhouse does not have a bed vibrator, or pink and black tile in the bathrooms."

"Well, neither does this apartment," Sherrilyn said in a small voice, after several seconds.

True. Claire was very sorry to have to move from her motel room bed with the vibrator to the waterbed in the Goodes' room. She had never cared for a waterbed; however, she felt strongly that Sherrilyn, in her condition, needed the firm mattress of the apartment's second bedroom.

That first evening, Claire set out a plate of cookies that she had gotten from the IGA. She thought it would be a nice touch to give each guest two cookies on a small party plate with the room key. And a copy of the *Valentine Voice,* too.

Then she and Sherrilyn sat behind the counter in the office to await guests. They watched the small television, cars driving past on the highway, and the sun setting in dramatic streaks of orange and coral.

At eight o'clock, Sherrilyn went to take a bath. She returned a half an hour later to report that the Goodes' bathtub, of the new Fiberglas-surround variety, was a "pain in the butt." Rubbing her backside, she complained that the tub had no reclining slope.

"Anyone come yet?" she asked.

"No. Not yet," Claire replied. "I think it's because the sign isn't on, but I can't find the switch." She had looked all around the counter area.

Sherrilyn made a thorough search around the area, too, and then all around the office. They ended up calling the number for Gertie in Florida, but no one answered. By then it was getting quite dark.

Travis Ford stopped in, and the first thing he asked was why the sign wasn't on. Claire, by then not in a very good mood, explained about not knowing where the switch was. Travis searched, too, and found the switch in the kitchen, which Sherrilyn thought was so very smart of him.

So the sign was on. They each looked out the window, as if fully expecting cars to just rush into the parking lot.

Then Sherrilyn disappeared into the apartment, leaving Claire alone with Travis, who moved a step closer and gazed at her with a decidedly attentive expression, to which her femininity naturally responded.

Oh, my, oh, my! She took a deep breath and reminded herself of the gap in their ages and all things of good sense.

"Would you like coffee and a cookie?" she asked, moving away and giving herself something to do.

He grinned, took a cookie and bit into it while keeping his gaze on her.

They drank half a pot of coffee and ate half a dozen cookies, while he told her about his times in the Navy and how he had come home at the death of his mother.

Claire could not resist asking about the woman, and he replied that his mother had died of uterine cancer. He spoke briefly of her, of how he had been an only child and that his mother had doted on him. Claire heard the love in his voice. She recalled Larkin putting flowers on the woman's grave. Karin Ford must have been a loving woman.

Travis's phone beeped. A call about a family disturbance out at a farm. Putting down his cup, he kissed her cheek before she knew what he was about and took off.

Claire felt a mixture of relief and loneliness at his departure. As the clock ticked away and no guests appeared, she was glad that no one was there to witness the lack. Winston called, and after him, Vella, and both asked how many people had stopped in for the night.

"None…yet," she said, wanting to keep things on a hopeful note.

Occupying herself with the useful activity of investigating the counter and desk area, she found a plastic sign on the shelf beneath the counter that read: *For after-hours check-in, press buzzer.*

Sherrilyn found the buzzer right beside the door, and the hook for the plastic sign.

It seemed amazing that Claire had not noticed the sign or the buzzer, considering the weeks she had been living at the motel. She had Sherrilyn go into the apartment, and she pressed the buzzer.

"It works!" Sherrilyn reported.

Claire stayed in the office until the large clock on the wall above the pink flamingos—those were going to have to go— read ten o'clock. Then she hung the sign for the buzzer in place, turned out the lights and went to bed in the Goodes' waterbed that sloshed every time she rolled over.

In the morning she could hardly get herself out of it. She decided she did not need to hurry, because there were only herself and Sherrilyn in the entire motel. With this thought, she became quite disappointed and depressed, and lay back down and went back to sleep.

She was awakened by a incessant buzzing and Sherrilyn shaking her. "Claire…Claire. That man—your friend—at the door."

"You mean Winston?" Claire asked, taking hold of Sherrilyn's hand to be pulled out of the sloshing bed.

"No, not that old man. That other guy… Here…here's your robe."

Claire, thinking of Travis and wondering why Sherrilyn didn't just let him in, went out to find Larkin at the front, pushing the buzzer and looking through the glass door with a worried expression.

"It's almost eight o'clock," he said, when she let him inside. "I thought somethin' might have happened."

"It did. We slept in."

"Ah…"

"If you'll make the coffee, I'll be back in a few minutes." She was embarrassed to be in her bathrobe in front of him, with the way he was looking at her. In her haste to return to the apartment, she bumped into Sherrilyn, who was peeking through the cracked-open door.

While dressing, she had an idea. Anxious not to let Larkin get away, she hurried out of the Goodes' bedroom, putting on her sandals as she went and hollering at Sherrilyn to get ready to make breakfast. She raced back to the office, where she found Larkin just then filling one of the mugs with the coffee that he'd made.

"I'm glad you're still here. I need your help, if you've got some time. I'll have Sherrilyn fix you some breakfast, if you will do me a favor."

She was talking about as fast as Gayla Jean.

With Larkin's muscle, they drained the Goodes' waterbed and moved it over to room number one, where Claire had spent the previous four weeks, and brought that bed and vibrator over to her bedroom in the apartment.

Quite happy to have *her* mattress bed and *her* vibrator back again, Claire said, "Now we can advertise a special waterbed room."

"You think someone will want that?" asked Larkin.

"The twenty-something crowd will." She was suddenly aware of Larkin's gaze intense upon her and how they were talking about beds. That they had, in fact, been around beds all morning.

Then Sherrilyn said, "Not if they would have seen you tryin' to get out of it this mornin'," and let out the first true giggle that Claire had ever heard come from her.

There was a second metal building beside the workshop in the rear. Frank had said it was storage for the motel. A musty heat smell wafted out when Claire threw up the door and stood there with Sherrilyn, looking at possibly four decades' worth of old furniture, storage boxes and junk.

"Don't come in here," Claire said to Sherrilyn. "I'm sure there's bound to be brown spiders. Maybe snakes." Heaven knew what all.

"Look at this lamp! It's a cowboy on a horse." Sherrilyn came in anyway.

"Why in the world would anyone keep these?" Claire asked of the old mattresses stacked on one side. They were the old cotton-batting mattresses, and cotton was hanging out in wads, where mice had been stealing it.

"I don't know, but there's a couple more. Yuk…I think that's mouse turds."

"Don't touch anything. I don't want you catchin' somethin'."

"This lamp's okay. Let's take it and see if it works."

"Good Lord."

"What is it?" Sherrilyn came to peer over Claire's shoulder.

"I do believe it is a file cabinet with all the records from the 1970s."

Then, tucked behind the file cabinet— "Oh, look. Two floor lamps!" One had a cowboy at the top, a mate to the tabletop one Sherrilyn had spied earlier.

There were three metal patio tables in pretty good shape. There were umbrellas for the tables, but they were rotted. There were luggage stands that could be fixed, and sets of fancy oak drapery rods, and a large framed picture of the motel from when it was newly built.

"It was fine for its day," Claire said, displaying the picture to Sherrilyn.

Sherrilyn pointed. "Look, the sign said 'Sweet Dreams at the Goodnight Motel.'"

"Yes...it did."

And there, all the way in the back, behind an old headboard and coated with years of dust and grit, they found the missing part of the motel sign.

Claire sent Sherrilyn to the pool for help from one of the Goode cousins, and she returned with Reynolds—"Just call me Rey"—in tow. Claire wondered why Sherrilyn had not gotten the bigger Bubba, as Rey stood only half a head taller than Claire and was skinny as a noodle.

The young man proved an amazement, however, because as soon as he and Claire had the *Sweet Dreams* sign out of the storage shed, he lifted it by himself and carried it over to the workshop.

Claire admired the vintage piece. The neon glass was mostly shattered, but the metal was all there, if bent a little in places. Surely, surely, it could be repaired, she thought, energetically dusting it off with a rag.

She turned to call to Sherrilyn and saw that the young woman was busy directing Rey, who was bringing objects out of the storage shed as she instructed. From all appearances, had Sherrilyn asked him to totally empty the shed and wash it out, he would have done so.

Travis stopped in again at dusk. He said, as he poured himself a cup of coffee and slouched his handsome body against the counter, that he was just going on duty and that he would be working each night through the weekend.

Claire, who was already a little anxious because again there were no guests, wondered what she was going to do about Travis and his attentions. It might have been easier, she thought, if she didn't like his attentions so much.

Her thoughts were drawn away from this difficulty on sight of a dark sedan pulling up in front of the office. A guest! She was further thrilled when out of the car came a tall man wearing a black slouch hat and black trench coat.

Travis shifted up straight, and his expression became attentive, as if to get ready for possible criminal activity. Claire laid a hand on his arm and murmured, "A regular." She felt smart saying that.

The man entered the office briskly and with his head down, the brim of his hat concealing his face. When his head came up, so did his eyebrows.

"Hello," Claire said, giving a welcoming smile while taking note that the man's legs were bare down to his loafers. Probably that was the only way to survive the heat of the trench coat in summer.

"Uh...hello." The man shot a quick, uncertain gaze at Travis.

"May I help you with a room?" asked Claire.

"Yes. A single. Uh, number ten, if it's available."

"Yes, sir, it is."

As the man filled out the registration card, he inquired about Frank. She told him about Frank and Gertie having retired to Florida, and introduced both herself and Travis.

"Welcome to the Goodnight, Mr...Badenov," she said, and without laughing. "We're glad you stopped in."

She gave him a small basket containing the Wednesday edition of the *Valentine Voice* and a number of luxury toiletry samples procured from Belinda. Although, thinking of the man's reason for coming, perhaps a bottle of wine and two glasses would have been more appropriate. She made a mental note to consider this idea for the future.

Travis did not appear to recognize the man's name and costume as being reminiscent of a childhood cartoon. He watched the man drive over to his room and voiced concern that the man was a stranger to town, and that Claire was alone with that sort coming along.

Claire, who did not enlighten him to the man's playacting, said that it was generally people from out of town who needed a motel room, and that she was not alone. "Sherrilyn is a holler away back in the apartment."

In fact, Sherrilyn had been with Claire until she had seen Travis drive up, when she had disappeared back into the apartment. Sherrilyn was shy around everyone except Claire, and now Rey.

Assuring Travis of her complete safety—"Did Frank or Gertie ever have a problem they couldn't handle?"—Claire ushered him to the door.

Travis had been gone no more than five minutes when another car drove up. Another guest! And this one appeared to be in something of a hurry. The car came flying from the highway and stopped with a jerk at the front door. A woman jumped out. Her clothes and hair were in disarray. She was middle-aged, needed to touch up her roots, and was clearly in a state.

Rather than come to the desk, she sank down into a chair, saying that she just needed to catch her breath. Claire brought her a glass of ice water and wondered if she might want to call Travis back again. On closer look, she saw that the woman was perhaps her own age; she just appeared older.

The woman smiled weakly. "Thank you." She sipped the water, then said, "I'm right glad the motel hasn't closed up. I don't know where I would go."

Claire introduced herself.

"Glad to meet you. I'm Nancy Fairchild."

The woman who Frank had said came to escape her husband, Claire thought, but she wasn't about to ask to make certain.

The woman paid with cash from a deep pocket in her purse. Claire gave her a welcome basket along with her room key, and the woman's eyes widened. "Well…well, now," she repeated, looking uncertain.

"There's no extra charge," Claire said.

"Oh. That's nice. Thank you." Then, stopping at the door, she said hesitantly, "I don't mean to be a bother, but can you give me a wake-up call at six o'clock? I'm afraid I'll miss the alarm, and I've just got to get home to fix Elliot's breakfast."

"Six o'clock. No trouble." Claire made a note.

Ten minutes later the telephone rang. It was Nancy Fairchild. "I think someone forgot and left a pretty soap in the bathroom here at my room."

"That's compliments of the motel," Claire said.

"It is? You mean for me?"

"Yes, ma'am."

"Oh." Then, faintly, "Thank you."

Sherrilyn was in the office, showing off her freshly painted toenails, when Natasha arrived for her tryst with Boris. Sherrilyn was so captivated by the woman in the black coat and sweeping brimmed hat that she forgot to disappear into the apartment.

"We hope you enjoy sweet dreams here at the Goodnight," Claire said, handing the exotic woman her gift basket.

The woman slowly took the basket, gave a graceful nod and the barest hint of a smile, went out to her car and drove down to number twelve.

"Do you think she's a spy?" Sherrilyn asked in a hushed voice.

Obviously the cartoon had been missed by an entire generation of younger people. "What would she be spying on in Valentine?" Claire asked.

At ten o'clock she shut off the lights in the motel sign. She read the note for Nancy Fairchild's wake-up call. Six a.m. Oh, dear.

But there were three guests, she thought with satisfaction, and hope for great success in the future, no matter that she was fairly certain she had already spent any money made this one night on soaps and baskets.

Larkin stopped in while she was attempting to hang the old picture of the motel, now all shined and with the chunk out of the frame repaired. She wanted it hung above the desk space in the office, to give her encouragement and focus. She intended to bring the motel back to its original state.

"Here…I'll do that," he said, taking the hammer from her hand. "You stand back and do the spottin'."

Wiping moisture from her forehead with her arm, she was for it.

"A little to the right…a little more. Now back to the left…down a hair. To the left…no, back to the right."

"Do you want to get out a graph and chart?"

"Oh, just put it there."

Larkin put the hook on the wall, and together they hung the picture. She thanked him, and he asked, in a flirtatious manner that she had not imagined he would employ, if he had earned a cup of coffee. He stayed to talk for thirty minutes in which each of them kept looking the other over for possibilities.

She was still deep in considering Larkin's possibilities when Winston showed up, driving himself.

"I wish you wouldn't keep doin' that. I might have to rat on you," she told him.

"I'm not a child," he said, clearly annoyed.

"Then don't act like one." She felt badly. She knew he missed seeing her every day, but she had things to do now. She didn't know how to tell him this without hurting his feelings and making him feel old and discarded.

He said, "Don't you have things to do?"

"Well, yes." Had he read her mind? "I have rooms to clean and patio furniture to paint, and a lawn that needs mowin'."

"I'll handle the lawn," he said and reached for the telephone, dialed and spoke to someone he called Muddy, and engaged this person to come mow and trim. After that, he told Claire to go do what she had to do. "I'll watch the desk for you."

"Sherrilyn will be here in a few minutes. She went into the grocery store. Besides, there isn't likely to be anyone coming in the middle of the day. And if there is, I have the buzzer here."

"Never can tell…. I'll stay. Do you have some cold tea?" With his cold tea and a travel magazine in hand, he shooed her away.

He ended up staying through until early afternoon, which allowed Claire and Sherrilyn to work on the rooms without keeping an eye on the office. And he also took two reservations.

She was amazed. "Two reservations?"

"Yep. There's a carnival comin' to town next weekend for Fourth of July, you know."

"No, I didn't know." She had, in fact, not been paying attention to the approach of the holiday but simply trying to learn what needed to be done during these first few days.

"Well," Winston said, quite happily, "neither did my cousins from over in the western part of the state. But they do now, and they thought it'd be a good idea to stay in town."

"You bribed them."

"I just made a suggestion. They're lookin' forward to vis-itin' with family hereabouts."

Claire gave him a kiss of appreciation and received his adoring expression in return. She thought how little it took to please some generous people.

She insisted on driving him home, and Marilee returned her to the motel, along with a plate of brownies. During the drive, she and Marilee worked out a pool day each week for Marilee's special needs children's group of ten children. The group would pay twenty-five dollars a time for the privilege of using the pool.

That evening Travis surprised them with a pizza for sup-per and stayed to help them eat it. After he left, Claire thought about how the daylight hours separated father and son's visits. She wondered what might happen should both men show up at the same time.

Chapter Thirty

She sat at the desk area in the office, in the glow of a green shaded lamp that she had rescued from the storage building, going over the expenditures and accomplishments of the past four days.

Four days seemed so short a time for her to feel as at home as she did. And a short time to have spent so much money. And a long time to have rented no more rooms than had been rented.

With tonight's guests—two truckers, a rather disheveled, angry man, and Mr. and Mrs. Tolley having a date night away from their senior residence—they had rented a total of nine rooms in the past four days. Her spirit slipped downward as she balanced income against outgo.

A salesman had come by, given her a catalog for motel supplies and stayed the night, leaving in the morning with an order for feather pillows and foam pillows, four for each room, and new bedspreads, towels of the thicker variety, and coffeemakers for each room.

Bubba and Rey finished the pool, and it sparkled beneath the bright sun. There was no bill; Frank had some sort of agreement with the cousins.

Claire asked if they could build her a shade pergola at one end of the pool area. "I'm a plumber, not a builder," Bubba said, but Rey said he could build anything. He took Claire's requirements, then returned that evening with a trailer of supplies and another cousin, Shorty. The two men set to work until dark and returned the following morning to be plied along until they finished by Sherrilyn and pitchers of cold sweet tea.

To go with the patio tables, which she had painted a fresh white, Claire bought umbrellas and chairs from MacCoy Feed and Grain, which had a fully stocked patio and garden department.

Researching past utility bills, she worked to factor in the expenses. As she calculated her dwindling savings, she tried not to hyperventilate. Reminding herself that one had to spend money to make money, she looked up at the old picture of the Goodnight in its glory.

Just then Sherrilyn came through the apartment door, carefully carrying a tray. "I made tea." She spoke with the shy eagerness of a child hoping to please. Since her discovery of a fancy china tea set in the back of a cabinet, she had delighted in having little tea parties. "Jasmine tea…it was new at the IGA today. And I brought you a piece of pie, too."

"Thank you. This is delightful."

The girl beamed. She had let Claire even up her hair and now had it pulled back in a clip. Her cheeks were rosy in her pale face. Possibly she had gotten too much sun while supervising Rey and Shorty, and surely she had gotten a good dose of feeling her womanly power with Rey. Both had benefited her.

Claire, her eyes slipping back over to her account books,

sipped the tea and wished mightily that it was black, but she didn't want to discourage the girl from experimenting and widening her world.

"I could get a job waitressin' evenings at the café," the girl said with suddenness. "Fayrene said she could use me on Friday and Saturday nights. That would help with money."

Claire was startled and deeply touched. She also wanted to say the correct thing.

"Do you want to do that?"

"Well...I could." Sherrilyn's gaze shifted downward.

"Yes, I know you could. I've seen you carry things—my goodness, you do have balance. I don't know many people who can do that."

The girl smiled with a hint of pleasure.

"But we are fine, sweetheart. Really. I have a substantial amount of savings. While I cannot keep this up indefinitely, I am okay until September."

She saw a certain relief flicker across the girl's face and was struck by the knowledge that Sherrilyn had little concept of security.

"Your main job right now is to take care of yourself and your baby," Claire said. "Besides, if you're waitin' tables at the restaurant, who's gonna cook for me?" The girl really was a good cook.

A smile flashed across Sherrilyn's face for an instant as she looked Claire straight in the eye, and then she lowered her gaze and turned away. Very often, when the two of them had what could be termed a moment of connection, the girl would seem as if she couldn't stand it and have to hide.

Claire stepped outside, and the soft night lured her out beneath the stars. She went to the pool. It shimmered pale aqua with deep light below and a glow falling from the Goodnight Motel sign. The sight brought immense pleasure.

She looked back at the cabins, where a few lights glowed but all was quiet.

Taken by sweet impulse, she slipped off her Keds and, quietly, not wanting to cause attention, eased into the pool.

Oh, my, oh, my. The water was cold. Yet glorious. It bubbled around her ears as she allowed herself to sink to the bottom, where her feet touched the rough surface. Pushing off, she shot up, broke through and gasped for air. Every cell of her body seemed to laugh with delight.

When was the last time she had been swimming? Before she and Andrew split up. Almost four years ago, during that working vacation in Jamaica, when Andrew had not been able to get away to swim with her. She had spent the entire week disappointed and angry. She very foolishly had pouted around the hotel suite, even though Andrew had encouraged her to get out and tour with a couple of the other wives.

Memories of the past drifted across her mind as she swam the length of the pool and back again. She had often been foolish and wasted what could have been good times, because she had been asking Andrew for something he could not give her. Perhaps, in a way, she had been asking him to make up for all the attention she had missed out on from her absent father and uncertain mother.

She had been searching for all those years, and maybe she was at last finding what she needed. She was seeing herself and finding a purpose for her life.

Lying back in the water, she kicked herself along, gazing up at the Goodnight Motel sign. She had, she realized, finally learned to enjoy her own self. And how surprising to suddenly feel closer to God.

Pausing to tread water, she looked beyond the motel sign, peering to find several twinkling stars. She had a sense of God smiling on her.

★ ★ ★

Giggling and feeling like a child, she entered the apartment through the back door, rather than drip water all the way through the office. "The pool is great," she said.

Sherrilyn was on the telephone. She said, "I guess you have the wrong number," and quickly hung up.

There was something on the girl's face. "It was just some drunk who dialed the wrong number," she said, averting her gaze and carrying a plate from the table to the sink. "It was the second time, too."

Claire stepped to the laundry area for a towel. As she dried her hair, she thought that Sherrilyn had not even questioned her about getting into the pool.

It had been Denny on the phone. She just knew it had been, and she felt a wash of disappointment and alarm.

It was a Sunday afternoon thing that happened all on the spur of the moment.

Claire had finished tidying up the rooms after the guests had left and had sat her weary bones down for a telephone chat with Vella, whom she had not had a chance to speak to in days.

Upon hearing about the pool being operational, Vella said, "Oh, I used to love to swim. I was on the swim team in college." Then, in a wistful tone, "You know, I almost put a pool in when I redid the yard. I wish I had."

Immediately, Claire said, "Come for a swim this afternoon.... I'll call Winston."

"Let's barbecue hamburgers," said Winston. "Do you have a grill?"

"Well, I don't know.... Sherrilyn, do we have a grill?" There was one on the back patio, it turned out. Gas, Sherrilyn reported. It had wheels. They would move it to the pool area. Winston would bring Corrine and Willie Lee, and Vella would drive them all.

This was exciting! Claire had not entertained in years, and with that thought came a sudden and clear view of her life.

She had been a hermit. Even before her divorce from Andrew, during those years of struggle to keep the marriage, she had been withdrawing, hiding from people and refusing to invite them into her world. As she had failed with Andrew, she had become afraid to have friends. Afraid they would guess her flaws and failures. After the divorce, the friends she had shared with him had gradually dropped away, until only Gayla Jean had remained, with R.K. simply providing male influence now and again. He had wanted to get closer, but she wouldn't let him. Even when Gayla Jean would ask her to dinner or on a shopping expedition, Claire would not accept.

Now, with high and determined emotion, she grabbed a piece of paper to make a list of groceries needed for the day of welcoming friends.

Then she looked at the telephone.

Yes, she would do it, rather than leave the occurrence to chance, which would surely not turn out well. And what if one or both happened to drive past and see festivities at the pool and wonder why they had not been invited? It was best to issue an invitation to both men and face them together.

She dialed Travis first, having his cell phone number already in her automatic dial. He answered with some surprise. Asking Travis anything was easy.

"Hey, cool. I'll be there, Miss Claire," he said with eagerness in his voice, just as she had known he would.

Ford, Larkin was the listing in the phone book. She dialed and prepared what to say. The ringing sounded five times. Her spirit dipped, and then suddenly there was his deep voice.

"Hello."

"Hi, it's Claire. The pool's repaired, and I thought…that

is, we sort of…" She was so silly, stammering. Why couldn't she just get to the invitation? She got to it. "Winston and Vella are bringin' the kids…we're barbecuing hamburgers…would you like to join us?"

Silence. Lord only knew what he thought. Well, his thoughts were his business.

At last he said, "Sounds good. 'Bout what time did you say?"

So they were both coming. By inviting both Ford men, she would be making plain the fact that she valued them as friends.

Yes, it was true that she found both men attractive. What red-blooded woman would not? No shame there. However, she was not up to any sort of intimate relationship with a man.

Lord knew, she was finally just getting an intimate relationship with herself.

Corrine and Willie Lee brought friends, and soon the splashing and laughter of five young people filled the pool. When Claire said, "Munro, don't you want to play, too?" Willie Lee's little dog hopped in and swam around for a few minutes, then came up the wide concrete steps at the corner and shook all over the adults.

Vella amazed everyone when she removed her terry wrap. She was in a bathing suit and was stunning, with the form of a youthful woman. She dove into the pool and swam the length with long strokes and the perfect form of an expert swimmer, while the young people respectfully moved out of the way.

Winston, wearing a Panama hat, sunglasses and a thin, white short-sleeved shirt, sat in a chair in the shade of the pergola and supervised Claire, who prepared to grill hamburgers and hot dogs for the first time ever in her life.

Sherrilyn had offered to do the job, but Claire didn't want the young woman to get overheated. She coated Sherrilyn's creamy skin with sunblock and made her wear a wide-brimmed straw hat and timed how long the girl sat in the hot sun at the edge of the pool with Rey, who showed up on the pretext of checking the pool for problems and immediately accepted the invitation to stay and moon around at Sherrilyn.

Travis showed up five minutes ahead of Larkin, answering the question that had arisen in Claire's mind of whether the men would tell each other and possibly come together. If he knew his father was coming, he didn't give any indication.

"A housewarmin' gift," he said, and at first Claire thought he meant the cooler full of canned drinks that he'd brought, but then he opened the cooler and pulled out a container of red-ripe strawberries. He wore knee-length khaki shorts and a tropical print shirt, topped by a straw cowboy hat and his easy grin. When he removed his shirt in order to take a swim, Claire had to turn away from the sight of his tanned, hard body.

Claire had begun surreptitiously looking for Larkin from behind the safety of her dark glasses, when he drove up and parked behind Travis, who clearly was surprised.

Larkin sauntered to the pool area. He wore his usual attire: jeans, boots, hat and sunglasses. The only concession to the heat and the day was a pale short-sleeved shirt. He had also brought her a gift. A blooming prickly pear cactus that he had dug up from somewhere and put in a pot.

He said, "I saw a prickly pear in the picture we hung the other day over your desk. It was planted at the base of the sign." He gestured to where boxwood bushes now clustered around the bottom of the Goodnight Motel sign.

She gazed at him, amazed that he would notice so small a detail.

Then she saw his gaze shift to the side. Travis was getting out of the pool. The two men did not greet each other. Larkin turned away to pull a chair up next to Winston and begin a conversation. Travis moved a chair over beside the grill and plopped himself into it, while Claire once again dropped her dark glasses down to hide her eyes and made a business of flipping hamburgers.

"Claire?"

"Hum?" She did not wish to open her eyes. The sun, two juicy hamburgers and two scoops of Vella's potato salad, along with uncountable potato chips and three tall glasses of cold sweet tea, had lulled her into a stupor. Stretched out in a patio chaise longue, she was relaxed and happy, no longer worrying about Sherrilyn getting sunburned, or Winston's reaction to a couple of beers and the heat, or whether or not Larkin and Travis spoke to each other or attempted to flirt with her.

"Claire, sugar, I think you have a motel guest," Vella said, her voice also reflecting a certain languidness.

"Sherrilyn can handle it."

Reluctantly she opened her eyes a slit in order to locate the young woman, whom she had not seen for some time.

She saw Winston nodding in his upright chair and snoring lightly. Larkin hid behind the Sunday edition of the *Valentine Voice*. The children, barred from swimming on full stomachs, were tossing a Frisbee on the lawn, and Travis, devoid once more of a shirt, was playing with them. For a second Claire was distracted by the sight of his lithe body, which she happily watched from the secrecy of her dark sunglasses.

Then, noting Travis's head turn toward the office, Claire shifted her gaze in that direction. She saw first the silver car gleaming in the late-afternoon sun.

A Jaguar?

And there was a man, tall, slender, brown wavy hair, standing beside the car and looking from the office to the pool.

Claire started coming up off the chaise longue, as Vella said, "Sugah...from your description, is that your ex-husband?"

"Yes...yes, it is."

Chapter Thirty-One

Should she kiss him?

She did not, but avoided what might have been a kiss by going into his embrace, all the while terribly conscious of the attention of those at the pool area.

His shirt was silk, and he smelled of rich cologne. The image of him standing in the road when she had left came to her.

"What are you doin' here?"

"You invited me to join you."

She looked into his beautiful eyes, struck by how handsome he could be.

"But you said…oh, let's get out of the sun." And not in direct sight of the pool.

She led him into the shade of the entry portico. She wished she wasn't all sweaty and smelling of charcoal smoke. And, ridiculously, she felt that she might cry.

Her gaze strayed past him, and she saw Winston and Vella standing at the end of the pergola, where they could watch.

"You said you couldn't come…you said you were too busy." She pulled her hand from Andrew's.

He met her gaze. "I decided that I could make some adjustments." He paused, his eyes shifting away. "I dropped the project and took some time off."

"Oh."

She was stunned.

His gaze came back to hers with purposeful intent of the sort she recalled from years ago. "I came to see you."

He really had come. This was real.

"I'm…I'm stunned."

"Could you be glad, too?"

"I am. I *am* glad you came." She had to do something with him. She looked through the glass door and saw Sherrilyn, at the desk, with Rey beside her, both of them staring.

Taking his hand again, she led him inside. "Andrew, I'd like you to meet Sherrilyn Earles…my partner."

Sherrilyn's eyes jumped at that term. She managed to say hello, and to shake the hand Andrew politely extended. One thing about Andrew, he was always most polite. He also shook hands with Rey, who went on at some length about Andrew's Jaguar being the first one he had ever seen in real life.

Claire, who kept feeling as if she had to *do* something with her ex-husband, told Sherrilyn to give him the key to room number two. She would have put him in her old room, which was about the best of all, except now it had the waterbed.

Then a second thought. "That is, unless you had planned to go on up to Lawton. You might find accommodations more to your liking up there." She would not be ashamed of the Goodnight. But she was practical, knowing Andrew's tastes.

"I'd planned on stayin' here," he said instantly, then added, with a twinkle in his eye, "I look forward to tryin' out that vintage bed vibrator."

"I'll take his bags," said ever-helpful Rey. "If you'll just un-lock your trunk."

Andrew declined the offer of help, and Rey looked a lit-tle disappointed.

To make up for this, Claire asked the young man to go ahead and put ice and cold drinks in the room, and to turn up the air-conditioning. While the job did not involve the exotic automobile, it was a service, and that seemed to make the young man happy.

Now, what to *do* with Andrew? She could not simply shove him into his room until everyone left. He would have to be introduced, obviously, as Winston and Vella were still standing there, gazing at the office.

"We've been having a barbecue," she told him, "in honor of the newly repaired pool. Come…I'll introduce you to everyone." She could not resist adding, "I imagine you'd like to meet Winston."

"Oh, yeah. I'm sure I'd like to meet Winston," he said in a low tone, his hand tightening on hers.

Everyone was waiting, not even bothering to hide their curiosity. Except Larkin, who drove away just as Claire and Andrew reached the pool area.

Vella was the last to leave, and alone, because Travis had al-ready taken Winston and the children. "I'm goin' home to take a cold shower and lather on the aloe vera." She slipped into the driver's seat, then paused. "You are gonna tell me all about what's transpirin' between you and your ex, aren't you?"

Claire laughed. "Yes, when I find out."

"Well, sugar, his comin' all the way up here says a lot."

And so it did.

"I'm all…well, I don't know about this. Say a couple of prayers for me, will you?" Somewhere along the way, Claire had formed the opinion that Vella had a hotline to God.

"I always do," Vella said in so tender a manner that Claire's throat swelled.

She stood and waved her friend off, then turned, sweeping the row of cabins with her gaze, noting the cars—four of them—and one big Peterbilt hauler. A total of six rented cabins, one of those rented to a family of four who had come to town to visit relatives and stopped when they saw the pool was open. At that moment the family was entering the pool gate, and cries rang out: "Mama…Daddy…hurry!" The children raced ahead with eagerness. And there, standing in the doorway of his room, the trucker watched, as if maybe he, too, might join in. These sights gave good satisfaction. This night represented definite progress for the Goodnight.

Then her gaze moved, finally sliding over to look at the silver car parked in front of the turquoise door of number two. The golden rays of a setting sun struck the bottom of the door.

She thought of Andrew inside. He had come, and deep inside there was a spark of gladness at this fact.

With purposeful strides, she went to shower and dress for the occasion, which required the curling iron and a full, natural-appearing makeup job, and several spritzes of Beautiful perfume. Whenever a woman met with an ex-husband, she should do it looking good. Possibly, she thought, as she applied lipstick, her somewhat disheveled and harried appearance when he had waylaid her on the road out of Shreveport had been the cause of her choosing to drive on out of town. She certainly had not felt at all up to conversing with him at the time.

What if she had made a different choice and stayed that morning? Would she ever have left? The idea was a little disconcerting. She would not want to have missed out on the past weeks, there at the Goodnight, and the people she now knew as friends.

She checked herself in the mirror. Slim-fitting denim capris and a sleeveless, off-the-shoulder summer blouse and dangling silver earrings all said *woman*. A fresh pot of coffee and the best cups and saucers from the cabinet on a tray said competent, thoughtful woman. Or so she hoped. There never was any telling how someone else might view one. What mattered was that these things expressed her own views.

She rehearsed knocking on the door and what she would say, what he would say, what she would say. She had quite a good conversation with herself.

But she did not have to knock on the door, because Andrew was sitting on the stoop in the plastic chair, giving all evidence of having been waiting for her. He watched her come with the tray. She walked deliberately and saw in the way that he rose without taking his eyes off her that she had captured his male attention. She was satisfied that her effort on her appearance had been well spent.

"I brought coffee. I remembered that you like a little brown sugar in it," she said, quite pleased with herself. "Is it still too hot for you to drink it outside?"

"It's not nearly as hot here as down home—but we could sit inside, if you would like."

"No…no, I like the evenings. The sky is so big here." Right that moment the western horizon was like a postcard, the sun setting as a fiery ball in a turquoise sky, as if all for them and their meeting.

He readily agreed and then brought out a chair from his room for her. "I trust I have the manager's permission to bring out a chair?"

"Yes, thank you."

There was an air of eager-to-please about him in a way that he had not displayed for years. Her mind sped back in time to when they had first met and dated, when she had yet been a teenager. For a brief moment, the years fell away.

His gaze met hers, and they smiled at each other.

Gales of laughter rang out from the pool. The trucker was there now, too, sitting in a chair and watching the family at play. Claire got excited by the sight and said, "We just got the pool in operation. I think it's goin' to help business."

"That's good," he said.

They glanced at each other and looked away. Again silence fell between them, for nearly a full minute. The yellow lights above came on, and cicadas and crickets began chirping as the evening settled in.

Andrew said that he knew he had taken a chance coming out of the blue, that he hoped he hadn't too inconvenienced her. She was uncertain about how to respond and finally said, "It's fine," which didn't seem quite polite. She was having too many emotions at once to be able to identify them. And then she had one of alarm, wondering if she had possibly been assuming things that she should not assume. Perhaps he had come about some legality, although she couldn't imagine what that could be. Perhaps this entire time, even when he had intercepted her leaving that morning, they were not properly divorced. That could have happened; she had seen this in movies and actually read of circumstances in her legal training.

While she was thinking these disconcerting thoughts, he said, "I'm sorry I hung up on you during our last conversation."

She had forgotten all about that phone call. This did not seem to be a complimentary admission.

"No apology needed," she said. "I didn't take offense, and I'm sorry that my decision to stay in Valentine for the summer disappointed you."

Another pause came between them, and she considered repeating how she just had to do this thing with the motel, and that it wasn't anything *against* him.

But she refrained; she didn't think the repetition would be helpful. And besides, it *was* a little against him, she supposed, as, in staying, she had chosen the Goodnight over him.

While they drank their coffee in silence that was not exactly companionable, she prodded herself to ask him straight out about his reason for coming.

"Andrew…"

"Claire…"

They each spoke at once, then stopped and chuckled.

He raked a hand through his hair, then leaned forward with his forearms on his knees.

Her heart melted. "Why did you come, Andrew?"

He breathed deeply, then said, "I said it on the phone. I miss you." That sat there for long seconds. And then, "I miss *us,* Claire. I just feel that we never really finished it between us. Now, when I look at it, it's just plain stupid, our breaking up. And I want to see if there could possibly be anything left. I want that chance, if you think you might, too."

Tears sprang to her eyes as the past two years of hoping and dreaming came at once across her mind. Now, you come to this? *Now?*

"Is it too late?" he asked.

"I don't know," she replied in a hoarse whisper. She would not lie to him.

He looked down at the ground.

Staring at the hair curling at the back of his neck, she said, "I'm here until September. I gave my word. It's something I want to do."

Andrew kept on looking down at the ground. She really wished he would look up at her now.

"How long did you plan on stayin'?" she asked.

"I took an indefinite leave from the firm."

"You did?"

His head came up, and he gazed straight into her eyes. "Yes."

"Well," she said, after taking that in, at least as much as she could in that moment, "if you want to stay, maybe we can see about us."

She had tears in her eyes that she made no effort to hide.

He reached for her hand. She was deeply touched to see that his eyes glistened, too.

When she returned to the office, Rey was still there, attending to Sherrilyn, sitting beside her and watching a movie on television. Apparently he was going to need instruction about visiting etiquette.

"I think it's time you went home now," Claire told him. "It's past time we closed up the office."

"O-kee, Miz Wilder," he said, in his instant accommodating manner. "Thanks for the hamburgers this afternoon. I'll see you all tomorrow," he promised Sherrilyn just before loping out the door.

"Doesn't he have to work tomorrow?" Claire asked.

"Oh, yes, but he said he'll get over here in the afternoon. He said their plumbin' jobs are a little light right now, and he doesn't much like workin' with Bubba, anyway."

"Ah." Claire, who had experienced a slice of worry that Rey might be another of the irresponsible low-down sort of fellow Sherrilyn had previously gotten involved with, was relieved.

"So, are you still gonna stay here?"

"What?" Claire looked up from wiping up the coffee area to see Sherrilyn regarding her closely, with that anxious expression again.

"I just thought that with your ex-husband comin' up here and all, maybe you were thinkin' of goin' back with him to Shreveport."

"Well, I'm not. We're here until you have the baby. After that, we'll decide what we're goin' to do." She wanted to be helpful with using the term "we," although she could be assuming a lot in regard to her and Sherrilyn's relationship.

"Okay. Good. I'm gettin' used to here now." It seemed Sherrilyn was assuming along much the same lines. A moment later, "I told Rey that maybe you would hire him as a part-time handyman."

"Well, I don't know if we can afford to keep a handyman on hire, even part-time."

"He'll work cheap, and we're gonna need someone. Fayrene Gardner called over a little bit ago because her bed vibrator had quit workin'."

"She did? Why didn't you come get me?" Claire prepared to go see what she could do. Fayrene was in number four. Possibly she could be moved to number ten, since Boris and Natasha weren't likely to show up.

"Oh, Rey fixed it. He told her on the phone to try givin' the box a couple of good bangs, and she did that, and it started workin'. See—he's a pretty good handyman."

Claire didn't suppose she could argue with such logic.

She was keyed up. Even the bed massager didn't seem to soothe her. Thank goodness for Vella, who answered on the second ring and said that she had been waiting, having coffee and smoking a cigarillo.

Claire relayed the conversation with Andrew. In speaking of it, she remembered his expressions and body language, and realized that in every way he was as uncertain as she.

"I don't know how I feel about it. I don't seem to be in love with him. He asked me if it was too late, and I think it may be, but that makes me so sad, so maybe bein' sad about it means I don't want it to be too late, so it isn't really. But whenever I think about what gettin' back together means, I think about us livin' in the townhouse, or maybe some other house—we would really need a bigger house, with Sherrilyn…."

She went on in this confusing vein, finally ending with, "I just do not seem to know how I feel, and that does not seem like I love him."

"Sugar, you loved him when you didn't slam the door in his face," Vella responded, in a somewhat impatient tone and with a sound to indicate her blowing a stream of smoke. "Love isn't a feeling. It is somethin' you *do*. It's a choice. So is gettin' married to someone. You can have all this passion for a man, but that might not be love. Do you want to love Andrew in the way of loving a partner? Do you want to join your life with his and love him on a daily basis, through sickness and in health? I can tell you *that* is the love of marriage."

Claire frowned. The questions were not helpful. "I don't know," she said, feeling rather determined to stick with that answer. In fact, she felt it her right to stick to that answer. She did not have to know at that moment, if she didn't want to.

"I suppose that's why he's come," she said. "I guess he feels like he didn't end it with us, but you know, I did. Until now, when he brings it up."

Later, after hanging up from Vella and plugging a quarter into the bed vibrator, she lay there thinking, *Now* he has come?

Now, when she had accepted that their relationship had died because they had both let it go.

Mainly because *she* had finally let it go by driving away and leaving him standing in the road. Before that, long before that, Andrew had let it go. He had let it go when he decided to have a relationship with Nina.

At the time of their divorce, when she had agreed it was best and had very willingly signed her name to the divorce papers and shaken Andrew's hand amicably and walked away determined to start fresh, she had not truly let go. She had been lying to herself and to Andrew. In her heart, she had not been able to let go. She had kept holding on for years, wrapping herself round and round

with a string of fantasy dreams of reconciliation, until—
until that evening when she had read Lily Donnell's message of life and had driven away from Andrew's
apartment, where he had been with Nina, and gone home
to throw herself into her cold and lonely bed. That string
of fantasy dreams had been snagged and had ever since
been unraveling, as she had been letting go of her con-
trived life with him by a hundred small decisions, over
days and hours and minutes, of choosing things other
than connecting with him.

Vella was right about it all being a choice. Claire had made
the choice, and now here she was having to make it again.

She plugged another quarter into the bed vibrator. Then
she had the thought that it was silly to have to put quarters
in her own bed vibrator. Surely the machine could be made
to work at will.

The next morning, Fayrene, who had forgotten and still
had an eye mask pushed up on her forehead, complained at
length. "That bed vibrator quit workin' again in the night. It
quit just when I was finally gettin' ready to drop off to sleep.
I have insomnia, which is why I come out here in the first
place, 'cause the vibrator helps me sleep. If I wanted a regular bed, I could go on up to one of those fancy motels in
Lawton. I wanted to stay out here another night, but I can't
do that without a reliable bed vibrator…and you *advertise* one
right on your sign."

Claire apologized profusely and offered a free night's stay
in another room. "I'll put you in a double room. Two double massaging beds, and that way, if one quits workin' you
can move to the other bed."

Fayrene's eyes lit up, although she was careful to display
only grudging acceptance.

As soon as Claire finished settling Fayrene, she went out

to the mobile marquee, where she changed the advertisement to read Welcome! Free Smiles And Coffee.

That didn't seem to promise more than she could deliver.

Chapter Thirty-Two

After almost a month away from the motel, his family heritage, Frank finally got courage enough to call Claire from Florida. Claire had telephoned his sister-in-law's phone number and left messages, wanting to know where this or that might be found, and also politely inquiring about how Frank and Gertie were getting along. Gertie had sent one postcard that Frank knew of, but mostly she had left Valentine and the motel in the same manner that she had left California all those years ago—without a backward glance.

Frank had relayed messages back to Claire but had been too hesitant to personally speak to her. He had dreaded hearing that she was going to close up and leave the motel, although by all reports—his one daughter who lived near Valentine had called him once, as had Gerald Overton from the bank—business had picked up. His daughter had reported, "Mama's flamingos are gone. I drove in to check, and sure enough, the flamingos are gone from the bushes *and* from the wall in the office. They are *ga-own*. I said that Mama would have a hissy, that's what I told Claire. She said she saved the flamingos, back in the storeroom, if y'all come back, but I told her Mama ain't comin' back…she is *ga-own*."

Frank didn't tell Gertie about the flamingos. He didn't think she would do more than blink, but he saw no need to take a chance, now that she was so happy.

At first he had suffered occasions of homesickness for the motel, and then, when he heard from his daughter and Gerald, he had suffered from homesickness and jealousy at once. Pretty quickly, though, those unsettling episodes had faded under the shining days spent in an RV park on the sunny Florida Gulf Coast.

He and Gertie had decided to try RVing before settling into a cottage, he reported to Claire on the telephone. They had rented first, then gotten a good deal on buying one. Frank was earning right fine fixing RV engines and contraptions at the parks, and Gertie had fallen into a job of writing her own column for two RV newsletters, where she recommended parks with the best deals, places to eat and shop, and all manner of goings-on for the RV communities.

"How are things up there?" Frank finally asked, with a little trepidation. He knew he would have poor feelings if things were not going well, and if things were going really well, his feelings might even be more poor.

"We're doin' pretty well," Claire said. "We're so glad the pool is fixed. Thank you for sendin' your cousins, Frank. Now, I have to admit—that pool can be work. I can see why you were not wild about it. I've had trouble with the ph and the filter, and I broke down and got a pool service. The guy is givin' me a great deal. I'm enjoyin' it, and Vella comes every couple of days for a swim, and that is such a help to her in relaxing. I think that pool made a difference over the Fourth of July weekend. We were almost full from Thursday through to Sunday. A strong heat wave came through, and there was some problem with electrical overload out the east end of town."

"Electricity problems always did help us out," Frank interjected. He thought Claire was talking faster than she used to, or else he had slowed down.

"It did. We got three families who couldn't stand bein' without air-conditioning in here for two evenings, and a fourth for one. And then the PRCA rodeo was bigger than normal, at least that's what Travis said. Anyway, we did really good with all that. Oh, and a fellow who had traveled in for the chili cook-off set his trailer on fire and had to come stay here.

"After that, it was pretty quiet until the Posey reunion, when we were full for another three-day weekend. And we've booked another reunion for the middle of August— the Stidhams. Mr. Stidham wanted the entire motel for a weekend, but I told him I had to save three rooms, at least."

"You don't say? A Stidham reunion," Frank repeated, sending a look to Gertie, who cocked her head, listening even as she typed out her column on the table in the RV kitchen.

"Yes, and there's been a few more inquiries. I think if we had some sort of meeting room, we could book more events, like women's retreats and antique auto clubs, that sort of thing. Boris and Natasha are still comin'. In fact Boris told me to tell you hello, if I talked to you. And Nancy Fairchild spent most of the Fourth of July weekend here, and after seein' that she insisted on makin' her bed and cleaning the bathroom each time, I asked her if she wanted to come to work as a maid. She works for us Thursday through Sunday."

"You don't say."

"Yes. And I am glad to have her, because it was too much for me, all the cleanin'. Tell Gertie that I don't know how she did all that she did…and you, too."

Frank appreciated Claire's kind words. "Well, it was a job, but we enjoyed it while we did it, and now I guess it's our turn to rest and relax." He glanced over at Gertie and saw her cast him one of her I-told-you-so nods.

Claire said, "I found a bunch of paint in the workshop, and we've been paintin'."

"Paint? I don't recall…"

"Oh, it was in a cupboard. There were a couple of dried up cans, but most of it was good. We've painted the eaves, and some other places. My ex-husband is up here for a while, and your young cousin Rey comes a lot, and they're both givin' us a hand. I don't want Sherrilyn paintin', or even cleaning the rooms, because of fumes, so she minds the office. She's doing very well. She actually has round cheeks now."

"You don't say."

He listened a bit more to how she rented the pool out for Marilee Holloway's special needs kids and occasional pool parties, and how she had found two of what appeared to be brand-new vibrating beds in the storage building.

She offered to send him pictures of things, and he thanked her, even as he thought he would not look at the pictures. At least, not right away.

When he got off the phone, he said to Gertie, "Let's head on across to Atlantic Beach for a bit. It'll be cooler over there on the ocean for the summer, and we can come back to the Gulf in the winter."

She would drive the RV, which she loved to do while wearing her blue plastic sunvisor, and he would come behind on his Harley. He was going to ride that bike as long as he was able, and when he sold it, he would buy them a top-of-the-line RV, he told Gertie, and they would spend the rest of their days in Florida on permanent vacation.

"You've earned it, sweetheart," he told her, and kissed her in a manner that he had not kissed her in years.

Claire Wilder was making an even better topic than when she had first come to town. Winston heard various stories of

how she had either connived the Goodnight Motel away
from Frank and Gertie Goode, or had given them a wonderful relief, depending on who told the story. Norm Stidham's story was that he had given Frank the idea to turn the
management over to Claire, but not too many people were
interested in his story, because he talked so much.

There was no doubt that the Goodnight Motel was being
spiffed up, and everyone was approving of this. "Claire Wilder has done this town a service. We need that motel," Tate
Holloway said with satisfaction one evening over dinner. As
editor of the *Valentine Voice,* he worked hard to keep the town
on the march of progress.

Tate ran an article on the new and improved motel—front
page, no less, with pictures of both the original and the present. It was pointed out that he might have done such an article while Frank was still there. Tate countered that it was
the sprucing up of the motel that made the article timely,
although he did feel a little badly, so he ran Frank's picture
and pointed up the heritage of the place.

In that article, as well as in two ads that Claire ran, the availability of a waterbed room was listed, and of course the fact
was brought out and waved around a whole lot, again either
to approval or disapproval, depending on a person's persua-
sion of mind. Belinda had made it her business to tell Claire
of the gossip, when she rented the waterbed room for a
night's stay for herself and Lyle.

Claire, who had something of an innocent turn of mind,
was embarrassed about the talk and ran an ad that highlighted the pool as family fun, but some people weren't
going to let the waterbed talk die. And of course there was
still the gossip about Claire being the woman who Winston
Valentine was spooning around with—Winston himself encouraged this report—and who had been dancing with both
Larkin and Travis Ford that night at the Opry, and now had

an ex-husband who had come to town in a flashy, "Jag-u-war," said Deputy Lyle Midgette, who liked to say the name of the car, so that other people would know that he knew a thing or two.

"It is Jag-war," Belinda corrected him each time.

"The man on the commercials says Jag-u-war, and he's from the country where the car is made. I've heard him," Lyle finally defended himself one day at the drugstore, in a rare display of stubbornness followed by quickly asking Belinda for picante sauce for his nachos, in a patent effort to distract her.

"I've heard a commercial for it, too," said Belinda, who would not be distracted even as she put the picante sauce on the counter in front of her significant other. "The dealership that sells 'em up the road in OKC just says Jag-war."

"It's not the same commercial," Lyle tucked in there. "Can I have a couple more hot peppers?"

"Whatever it's called, Larry Joe has already worked on it twice," put in Julia Jenkins-Tinsley, who sat on the opposite end of the row of counter stools. "Norm Stidham said it shouldn't go to just any mechanic but one licensed just for those cars." Undoubtedly, she wasn't about to attempt to pronounce the name. "But you know Larry Joe can work on just anything. Norm said that Andrew Wilder was real particular but paid Larry Joe well. He's pretty wealthy."

"Well, I imagine he is wealthy," said Belinda. "Only people with money can drive a Jag-war."

Julia took that in for several seconds and said, "I guess he's livin' out there to the Goodnight now, too. He's gettin' mail there."

This got Belinda's attention. "What sort of mail did he get?"

Winston listened to the exchange from where he sat at a table, working the newspaper crossword puzzle. He reflected that more and more people ignored him, as if he was not even present. Such was the fate of the elderly. Or perhaps it was simply because he was always sitting there, which brought him back to the fate of the elderly. He supposed he was glad to be able to sit somewhere.

Julia was saying, "He got a letter from that architectural firm where he works, or at least did work before comin' here, and a big manila envelope. Felt like maybe there were a couple of envelopes inside of it, and it had a return address in Shreveport, same person who sometimes writes Claire cards, usually with decorated envelopes. A Gayla Jean Wilder. Must be a relative."

"Well, yes, obviously," said Belinda in that superior tone. Then, "I wonder if he's decided to stay. I can't imagine bein' able to drive a Jag-war, and takin' up livin' at the Goodnight." There were murmurs of agreement, and she added, "I heard Claire tell Mama that she and Sherrilyn are signed up for childbirth classes up at the hospital, so they aren't headin' back to Shreveport anytime soon."

Julia leaned closer to the counter, and her voice dropped, so that Winston missed a lot of what she said. "Nancy Fairchild said…Claire…her ex…not livin' together. He's still in his room, and she's…with Sherrilyn. Nancy…dancin' around the office…paintin' it together. He's done all this paintin' and… I've seen them…eatin' at the café and drivin' somewhere. But…Nancy says, they are…"

Winston got up, slamming his newspaper down on the table. "Oh, for heaven's sake. If you're gonna talk, let's get it straight. Claire's ex-husband came up here to settle some matters that are strictly between them two. Claire is enjoyin' managin' the motel and is doin' a good job of it. And Lyle is correct—there's an advertisement on cable television where some foreigner says Jag-u-war."

Three pairs of eyeballs stared at him as if he had risen from the dead. He grabbed up his newspaper and stalked out.

The trio left behind at the drugstore fountain were quiet for a full minute, as if waiting to make certain Winston didn't come back.

Then Julia could not control herself from asking, "Did your mother tell you that Claire and Sherrilyn have started comin' to church?"

"She may have mentioned it," said Belinda, who hated to admit she didn't know something.

"Well, they have. They've been there the last two Sundays, and sit up towards the front, too, right behind the pastor's family. There's a few who aren't too happy about Sherrilyn comin' and sittin' right up front like that, but Pastor Smith covered it with a sermon about love."

She let that sit there, before adding, "Claire's ex hasn't come with them. Although, I imagine somebody has to stay and manage the motel on a Sunday mornin'."

Then, "I'm not talkin' about people... I'm just statin' facts."

Winston was enjoying the luxury of cold sweet tea and front porch sitting, the extreme pleasure of which seemed to belong to the elderly, when Tate arrived home.

"We've located John Tillman," Tate said. He handed Winston a piece of paper, then threw himself down in the porch swing.

Winston unfolded the notepaper, upon which was printed the name, date and circumstances of death and place of burial.

"I know that wasn't the sort of answer you were hopin' for," Tate said.

"Well, I don't know what I was hopin' for. Just an answer for her, I guess." He had wanted to be her hero, he realized; he had wanted to be the one who brought daughter and father together in a storybook ending.

"You don't have to tell her. I imagine that if she had wanted to find him, she could have searched herself...or hired someone to do it."

Winston nodded and said that he knew. The fact was at that moment larger than life for him, as he remembered Claire on that first day he had met her and taken her to the Little Creek cemetery to see the graves of her folks. She had shied away from further searching, only doing things that Winston pressed on her. Perhaps it was a lot easier for her to imagine her father alive. To hold on to the dream that he might one day come and tell her that he loved her.

Winston wished that he had never butted in on the situation. However, he had done so, and there always did seem to be a reason for things that came to pass.

He poured Tate a glass of tea from the pitcher that had just been waiting for someone to come along and share. The two men sat on the porch, commenting on the true pleasures of life in a small rural town. Tate had lived elsewhere, places like Houston and Atlanta and even New York City for a brief time, and could make definite contrasts. Winston had only been away from Valentine during the war years. That was enough, he said, to know what he had going at home.

Travis was atop a young colt, pushing him into a walk, when he heard someone call a greeting. It sounded like Claire's voice, and, surprised, he turned to look. The colt took advantage of the unguarded moment and attempted to buck. Fortunately, Travis reacted quickly, got the colt pulled around and was able to dismount without making a fool of himself in front of Claire.

Leading the horse to the corral fence, he waved and welcomed her as she crossed the yard. He was excited that she had come to his house, could hardly believe his good fortune, and thought she looked great in slim pants and a knit top that displayed the fullness of her generous breasts, which he could look at fully from the distance and not be caught.

Closer, and her beautiful smile and eyes shone out from the shade of her wide-brimmed vaquero-style straw hat.

"I see you've learned to wear a hat in the sun," he said.

"It is a definite help, if I want to keep my skin."

He told her that he wanted her to keep her skin, and she smiled.

They exchanged conversation on her compliments to his ranch and questions about the young horse. Then she commented on not having seen him for a couple of weeks, and he said that he had been on leave from the sheriff's office in order to handle the ranch while his father had been traveling. He was not going to say that he didn't feel he needed to be hanging around her so much, with her ex-husband at her elbow.

"I noticed that I haven't run into your father anywhere for a while," she said. "Where's he been travelin'?"

"He went down to Houston to check on buyin' a new bull, and then down to Fort Worth for a paint horse show. You just missed him this mornin'. He's gone over to the sale barn. He's been buyin' up some new breeding stock."

Was that disappointment that flickered in her eyes?

The question was not one he wanted to entertain for more than an instant. He preferred to delight in her unexpected visit.

He invited her up to the house, out of the sun, for something cold to drink. She admired the wicker chairs on the porch, and he told how the chairs were antiques that his mother had found and refurbished.

"She was always antique huntin'…. Would you like some ice water? I think that's about all we have." He felt inept at entertaining a visitor.

He chose the better glasses, and rinsed and polished them

before he filled them with ice and water, then carried them carefully to the porch.

When he handed her a glass, the thought occurred to him that there had not been a woman, at least one who counted, at the house to use the glasses and sit in a wicker chair since the death of his mother.

This thought hit him somewhat hard and seemed to linger as he backed up and leaned against a porch post.

"I'm sorry to miss your father," she said. "I wanted to talk to both of you, to ask about the possibility of buyin' or leasin' that acreage of woods behind the motel. I've been told it's y'all's land."

He said that it was, as best he knew. She explained her plans, which were all about making a nature trail with benches for meditation and bird watching for guests at the motel. She had the idea of offering retreat packages for groups like the Methodist Women and the Valentine Rose Growers.

He responded that he thought it likely his father would have no objections. "Dad'll be back this afternoon, and I'll tell him to call you."

That bit of business concluded, he quickly floundered around for something to say in order to extend her visit. They talked about the heat, and in trying to be polite, he did the really stupid thing of asking about her ex-husband, and she replied, but it was an awkward moment.

She then remarked again on how lovely she thought the chairs were and that she intended to look for some for the motel. She recalled similar chairs on her grandfather's front porch, back in the early sixties. She talked on at length about summers "down home," as she called it, and digging crawdads in the ditch and being the first in their community to get a television. It was all in the vein of how his father could talk sometimes, he thought, feeling a certain sharp clarity that he shoved aside and went to talking about things he had done as a kid in the summer, things not so different. Yet, somehow, he found himself talking a lot about his mother.

Later, when he walked her to her car, he had the fleeting urge to attempt a kiss. Something in her eyes stopped him.

What stopped him, he realized later, was seeing the fine lines at the edges of her eyes and a steadiness in her gaze. It was the power and strength of her womanhood that overwhelmed and humbled him.

There was tangled inside of him the spirit of a boy and the wisdom of a man. Like pieces of a puzzle falling into place, the wisdom of the man came to understand that the fantasies he had been having about Claire had been the fantasies of a boy. Those had their place, but following that boy was getting to be lonely. He was not a boy anymore but a man who needed to make some changes in his life.

Shortly after noon, when he came in and found his father microwaving burritos, he told his father about Claire's visit. "She drove up right after you left," he said, watching his father closely and noting the surprise on his face the minute he initiated a conversation. They had not been much on speaking terms during the past weeks, since that night when Travis had said the words that he had wished a thousand times since to retract.

He told of Claire's desire to purchase or lease the wooded property, commenting that it appeared she had long-range plans for staying.

To that his father nodded and kept his gaze downward, making a great to-do out of testing a burrito's temperature by burning his fingertip as he said, "We're not usin' the area. Lease or buy, whatever you and she think is best. I'll leave it to you to handle the deal."

"Yeah, well, I think you'd better handle it."

His father's gaze came up.

Travis said, "I've decided to take that job Red Pettijohn offered me last winter. He says it's still mine, if I want it. He's got quite a few head of horses to get ready for the fall sales. He said he's likely goin' to want me to fly out to California next month, and Kentucky the month after."

His father blinked and stood there staring at him in a way that caused Travis to have to look away. He tried to form an apology for the hurtful things he had said that night weeks ago, but what came out was, "It's time I got out of here."

His father gave a sad smile and sort of shook his head. Then he said in a broken voice, "Son, this is your land, too, and we got a lot of it. There's room enough for both of us."

"I know, Dad...it's just I gotta go for now and do some things on my own."

He and his father looked at each other, and then his father reached out and hugged him.

Chapter Thirty-Three

Andrew dealt with the dead air-conditioning unit in the way he had dealt with one three days earlier—by dropping it into the Dumpster and then making a fast trip to the Home Depot, where he purchased a brand-new one.

He had just finished setting the new unit in place in room number seven when Claire came in and, not noticing that it was a new one, thanked him for repairing it and went on at length about how good he was with fixing things.

Under such compliments, he didn't see any need to tell her that he was not fixing the units. He did not want to risk falling in her esteem. He had at one time been able to impress her, but somehow, doing so had become hard. What she wanted was mostly a puzzlement to him.

She went into the bathroom with fresh towels, and he picked up the few tools he had used. He went to the bathroom door just as she was coming out, and they stopped short of bumping into each other.

"Oh…" She laughed.

"I just wanted…"

They gazed at each other. It was time. It was past time. He leaned toward her, watching to see if she came up to meet him. She did, and they kissed. He wrapped his arms around her and put everything he had into the kiss. When they broke away, he opened his eyes to see hers come open wide and stare at him.

He tried to read her expression, but he couldn't, except maybe to see surprise. Her gaze drifted downward in a manner that was hardly reassuring, and he searched for the question that was about to explode in his mind.

But then they were interrupted in the inevitable manner they were always interrupted. The phone beside the bed rang, and Claire sort of pushed him out of the way and went to answer it, while he stood there, resisting the urge to jerk the phone out of her hands, studying her profile and listening to her say, "Yes, Sherrilyn?… Okay…tell him I'll be right there."

She hung up and said, "It's Winston. He's driven out here again. I guess I'm goin' to have to talk to Tate and see if he can get him to quit drivin'. He has somethin' to tell me, though, and I have to go on over…."

He went to the door and watched her as she hurried across the parking lot to the office. Hurrying away from him again, he thought.

Then he took up the tool bag, closed the door to the room and went around back of the cabin to get the box the air conditioner had come in, which he squashed and fit into the Dumpster. Then he gathered up trash to throw in on top of it, just in case Claire happened to look in.

After that, he returned to his room, walking past his car and seeing it was once more covered with fine dust because of the gravel parking lot. The car had never been exposed to so much dust. They did not have dust like this in Shreveport, which was a civilized part of the world that used concrete. He had driven the Jaguar out of Shreveport, of course, but always on properly paved streets and highways. Likely the dust from the motel's lot was going to generate problems that would plague the expensive vehicle in years to come.

With those unhappy thoughts, he went into his motel room, because he couldn't think of anything else to do right that minute. Winston's car still sat outside the motel office, but going over and kicking it would be a really stupid thing to do. Being jealous of an old man was foolish beyond measure.

He checked his cell phone to see if there had been any messages from McCawley at his office; in the first weeks after Andrew had left, McCawley had called and sent faxed information, needing Andrew's advice nearly every other day. That had somewhat irritated Andrew, but now he was irritated that McCawley had not called since the previous week, and neither had Andrew's secretary, Selma. Likely everyone at Rennals and Associates had forgotten his existence.

He stared down for some minutes at the drawing he had been working on for the renovations Claire and he had come up with for the motel. That was something they could talk about, whereas how each of them felt still went unsaid.

Was she as frustrated as he was?

He reached out and swept the drawing pad and pencils from the table, sending them halfway across the floor. Then he stalked out to his car and headed away to the car wash, driving fast through the motel lot, past the car belonging to the old man.

The car wash was a do-it-yourself job, which further annoyed him. He kept a rag in the trunk to wipe off the water so it wouldn't spot the finish and ended up buying all the towels in the dispenser to go over the windows to his satisfaction. And just to be plunking in the money and pulling the knob, for some strange reason. He ended up with five extra packaged towels to carry around in his trunk.

When he returned to the motel, the old man's car was gone. He hoped Claire had not gone off with the old man again. He wanted to talk to her. He *had* to talk to her. He had to know her response to the kiss, which really had not seemed like a response at all. But maybe he was wrong.

Aware that he had fallen into a bad mood, he was careful with his tone in speaking to the girl, Sherrilyn, who was at the desk. Claire had once said that Sherrilyn said he spoke sharply to her. Andrew didn't think he had, and he didn't want to be accused again.

"No, she didn't go off with Winston," the girl told him. "She's in her bedroom…but she doesn't want to see anyone."

He wondered if the term *anyone* included him. He didn't think that could be the case, but it annoyed him that he couldn't be certain. While he worked this out in his mind, Sherrilyn spoke again in a confidential manner that got his attention.

"The reason Mr. Winston drove over here was to tell her that he found out her daddy is dead. He's been dead fifteen years."

Sherrilyn felt a little sorry for Andrew in that minute. He sure didn't seem to know what to do. She sympathized, because she didn't know what to do, either. Claire had been upset a couple of times about things around the motel, and that always caused Sherrilyn to want to do something to make it right as quickly as possible. She always felt helpless and a little frightened when Claire got upset about anything. Claire just always seemed to be in control, and if she wasn't in control, then no one was.

Sherrilyn saw in that instant that Andrew felt as unsettled as she did, and this insight made her not so in awe of him.

"Would you like a sandwich?" she offered, in the manner

of a woman who has already learned that food fixes a lot of things with men. "I can make you a really nice sub. Our IGA deli delivery came just this morning."

He shook his head, then said that he would come back in an hour or so and check on Claire. She watched him go back out to get into his sporty car and drive away fast enough to throw gravel when he headed up onto the highway.

Staring after the car, she thought of how classy and cool he was, like one of those characters on *The Young and the Restless* or *The Bold and the Beautiful*.

With this thought, she changed the channel on the television and turned up the volume, although just then the telephone rang, so she had to immediately lower the sound again.

"Goodnight Motel," she answered, with rare confidence. She had been watching Claire's manner in answering the phone and practicing when alone.

"Sherrilyn, it's me, Denny."

After a moment of surprise, she said, "I'm sorry…Sherrilyn is busy right now and can't come to the phone." She did her best to have just a bit of a Mexican accent.

"I know it's you, Sherrilyn."

"This is not Sherrilyn. Would you like to leave a message for her, *por favor?*"

"Sherrilyn, cut it out," he said in his mean and nasty voice that caused her to hang up the receiver almost before she realized she had done it.

Next, she quickly turned off the phone's ringer and stood staring at the phone while caressing her swelling belly with both hands.

From inside the apartment came ringing. She went to the two extensions and turned off their ringers, too, hoping that the caller was indeed Denny, not someone who wanted to rent a room.

★ ★ ★

Claire decided in the night that she had to go see her father's grave. She was up at dawn and calling Winston, who she knew would already be awake, to go with her. He readily agreed, of course.

She did not realize that she had not thought once of asking Andrew to accompany her until she told him of her plans. At that moment of seeing the expression on his face, she knew fully her error. And yet, she could not change her mind.

He just gazed at her and did not suggest coming.

She then made a big deal of asking him if he would mind watching after Sherrilyn. "I'll be gone a good part of the day, and she hasn't been alone with the motel that long before. I worry that some emergency could happen, with her pregnant. It would help to know that you were with her." She wanted to point up what a help he could be by staying.

"Sure," he said.

She thanked him, started out, then came back and gave his cheek a quick kiss.

It was a full two-hour-plus drive to Oklahoma City, then they still had to locate the cemetery and then her father's marker, which was nothing more than an engraved square laid flat in the ground. It was the general marker provided by the Veteran's Administration.

Claire and Winston hardly spoke during the trip. It was not an awkward silence; it never was an awkward silence with Winston, who said that he had lived long enough to say pretty much all he needed to say on most subjects and had come to value silence. And also, he slept a great deal, waking when she stopped for gas and bought him an Orange Crush.

During the long time to think, Claire admitted the truth to herself of why she was relieved that it was Winston who accompanied her rather than Andrew. If Andrew had come, she would have spent a great deal of time worrying about exactly what to say to him to keep things from being awkward between them. And when they found her father's grave site, no doubt Andrew would have wanted to hang around, whereas Winston knew enough to leave her and go sit on a bench in the thin shade of a sparse tree.

She had stopped at a store and bought flowers. The only thing to do with them was to lay them on the small square with her father's name. After five minutes of gazing at the square, she turned and walked to Winston and told him she was ready to go.

So they left and headed back home, stopping before they left the city to get lunch at the Cattleman's Café, where Winston used to eat twenty years before when he had been a cattle broker and come to the stockyards on a regular basis. He talked a little bit about those times while he ate a steak and Claire did little more than idly munch on French fries.

Just before reaching Valentine, Winston said, "I'm sorry I butted into your business. I was wantin' to be your hero. I got so caught up in that business and imaginin' a good ending that I didn't truly think of this happening. Then, when I found out, I thought it was right to tell you, rather than keep it hid. Maybe that was the wrong choice. I'm sorry."

Anger that Claire had barely realized was there slipped away. "You did right," she said, finding her throat thick. She had wanted to cry at the grave and couldn't, and now she couldn't risk crying while she was driving and having to watch the road. "It hurts to know that my daddy will never come ridin' up on that white horse, like I dreamed about since I was a girl. But I guess at least now I know that for the past fifteen years he *couldn't* have come, even if he had decided to."

It was small consolation and made up out of smoke and mirrors, but she needed it right now. She even imagined him getting to heaven and being really sad that he had not ever even sent her one word. She wondered if he had tried and her mother had kept it from her. This was something she had considered since childhood and regretted not having asked her mother, before her mother died. It could also have been a mail delivery error. Letters went astray all the time.

She told all of these assumptions to Winston, who said that any one, or even all of them, could have happened.

She let Winston off at his house and then drove home to the motel. It was midafternoon, and the sign on City Hall gave the temperature as ninety-eight degrees. Even so, she lowered the windows, and with the air vents blowing cool air on her neck, the sweetly familiar scent of dusty hot pavement came through the window.

She realized with a suddenness that the scent reminded her of childhood, of both the Tall Pines Motor Court and Olivette. It brought sadness, and she couldn't figure out why she liked the scent, except perhaps that when she had been a child, she had still entertained a lot of hope about things being different.

As she drove along Main Street, she thought of her father, who had at one time walked and driven the same street. He never had come to find her before he died, and likely never would have. He had not cared that he had a daughter. That was the truth of it. And yet, she remembered him when she was a child, buying her a strawberry milkshake and showing her the stars.

She had come to Valentine looking for much more than a fantasy father, she thought. She had come looking for that little girl who she had been before he had walked out and her mother had been crushed by heartache. She had needed to find the child who had known how to savor something as simple as a strawberry milkshake, and who enjoyed playing with rowdy children, and who dared to jump into a car with a stranger and head off on an adventure.

She had found that child, she thought. Although she was not quite certain what to do with her.

The Goodnight Motel sign came into view, and she slowed to turn in the driveway. Andrew's car was parked in front of his room, and there was a dark sedan in front of the office. Unwilling to face people straight away, Claire followed the narrow driveway around to the rear of the apartment, stopped the car and turned off the engine, then sat there, feeling as if she could not move to get out.

She would need to speak to Andrew. She couldn't put it off any longer, except maybe long enough to have a nap. She was too exhausted to talk sense. She wished and tried that minute to cry, but could not.

Frustrated, she got out of the car, slammed the door and went into the apartment, where, as she set her purse on the counter, she heard a scream and then loud voices. *Threatening voices.*

Claire had already started across the room when there came another piercing scream. "Sherrilyn! I'm comin', Sherrilyn!"

She raced across the kitchen and into the living room, where her gaze met the black eyes of a squatty young man poised for a moment in the office doorway. Then he was gone into the office, and Sherrilyn was still screaming, and there was all sorts of hollering and crashing of furniture.

Claire reached the door of the office to see Sherrilyn shoving the rolling television in front of her with one hand and saying, "No. It's Claire's."

The *it,* Claire saw with amazement, was her mother's urn, which the girl clutched against her swollen belly, protecting it from Denny Rhodes and the squatty black-eyed young man.

Suddenly a loud honking started outside. The squatty young man hollered, "Get the bitch, man," and produced a knife.

"Give them the urn, Sherrilyn! Give it to them!" Claire strode directly between the girl and the men, who were taken by surprise at the action, thus giving Claire time to grab the urn and thrust it at Denny Rhodes.

"Take it and get out! Get out!"

The two men set out to do just that, but at the same moment that they headed for the front door, Andrew came flying through it. He launched himself at Denny, who was in the lead, tackling him to the floor. The black-eyed young man retrieved the urn that went rolling and ran out the door.

Then suddenly there came a thunderous blast, and the explosion of the rear window of the sedan parked out front. The car horn—the emergency beeping—continued, and Claire, prepared for more explosions by holding Sherrilyn's head sheltered in her shoulder, was amazed to see Vella, wearing a flowered floppy-brimmed hat and her white swimsuit cover-up, come into view. She carried a shotgun.

"He's runnin' down the road," Vella said breathlessly as she came through the door. "Call the sheriff."

From: Vella Blaine
To: <haltg@mailectric.com>
Sent: July 30, 1997, 12:15 a.m.
Subject: Adventures in living
Dear Harold,

I give thanks for you having continued to send me notes, to stretch out your hand in friendship, even when I rebuffed it. I did read them, every one. I read where you said you just had to have somewhere to write, and tonight I find myself in the same position. I find that I am especially grateful for your hand of friendship. There was an occurrence in our town today that brought home to me the preciousness of understanding hearts who listen when we need to talk, as I do now, in the dead of lonely night, when the few surrounding me in whom I can trust are busy sleeping, and I am powerfully stirred.

The thief who stole Claire's car the past May and left his girlfriend to try to drown herself in the sheriff's bathroom sink came back to town today. He came after a little computer disk that he had hidden in Claire's mother's urn. He had tucked it underneath the plastic zipper bag of ashes. Who would have thought of that? I call him dumb, and he really is, but that bit was clever. Did you know that a body's ashes are often put in a plastic zipper bag? That way you can keep them, or simply open it up if you decide to scatter them. Or maybe so you can scatter half and reseal it to keep the other half.

Anyway, the urn had been in the car, when it was stolen by Denny Rhodes—that's the scumbag's name. Then last month sometime, he gave it to Sherrilyn to keep for him, only she gave it back to Claire. She didn't know anything about the disk, of course. It contained a list of contacts and accounts for an auto theft ring down in Texas. Denny Rhodes had stolen it, obviously in a brainless and misguided moment to which characters of his sort are prone, when he had believed he could use the disk to protect and advance his position as a professional auto thief. When his employers found out, of course, they put him straight and sent him up here to get the disk back, accompanied by an associate for insurance.

Unfortunately the associate did not prevent the scumbag from further brainlessness, when Sherrilyn defied him and told him that he could not have the urn, that it belonged to Claire. Being quite naive of mind, the girl thought he just wanted the urn for meanness, which is not too odd an assumption. Rather than explain that he wanted only what he had hidden, the idiot got all forceful and insisted that he was going to make her give him the urn.

How I got into it was that I had gone to the motel to have a swim. I've been doing that every few days, and it's proven such a help to soothe my spirit. Perry is having very restless nights, bless his heart. I had just driven up to the pool and was hauling out my tote bag when I heard a horrible scream. Sherrilyn has a particular scream. Then I saw it right through the big office window—Sherrilyn and that Denny Rhodes and the other tough, and all of them yelling and screaming, and Sherrilyn running around.

I immediately went for my shotgun, which was in the rear of my Land Rover. While I was doing this, Claire was getting into it in the office. Then Andrew came driving in, and I told him Sherrilyn was being robbed, which was what it looked like to me. He raced ahead of me, just straight on into the office.

Frankly, that is still a surprise to me. Andrew Wilder had not struck me as a particularly heroic sort, but one never knows what someone will do in a threatening situation. He threw himself right in there and tackled Denny Rhodes to the ground.

What I did, when that other scumbag came racing out the door and started to get in his car, was to haul off and shoot out the back window. That scared the fellow bad enough that he lit out on the run.

I remain a little horrified over my violent reaction. All I could think about, in that instant of hearing those screams and seeing the two men and recognizing one as that thief, was that Sherrilyn was pregnant, and nothing but a slip of a girl. And I had no idea what they might have done or taken from Claire and Sherrilyn, and for some reason, I had it in mind that the bugger might get a gun or something from his car. I simply did not want him to get in the car and away loose on the town. Although, I ended up sending him loose. Luckily, he was caught quite quickly in town. Deputy Midgette came on him at the IGA trying to start a car and offered to help, but then, as the deputy was helping him, word of the loose criminal came over his radio, and he managed to apprehend the fellow, who was all tuckered out, because he simply was not used to walking and running.

What has me a little unnerved is my reaction of being ready to shoot. I've thought about what might have happened had I missed the window and shot the fellow. I was so upset for hours, but it has gradually come to me that I wasn't likely to miss what I aimed at. I took lessons and was top in my class. I have a license for my gun and can shoot the tip end of the tail off a possum, if I want to.

Now that I'm finally settling down from all this shock, though, Harold, the big thing that I'm coming to understand is that my life is not over. There's a lot of juice left in me, and plenty of reason to hope for new adventures ahead.

Why, I'm an independent, healthy woman with dear friends, who I love and who love me. Taking care of my husband in his last days is the charge God has given me, and I'm perfectly suited for that. I have strength enough to take care of Perry, and if he has strength enough to go on in such a patient manner as he does, can I do any less? And I have been given the help of friends for this task. What are any of us here for, if not to make life easier for one another?

I came back to the drugstore and kissed Belinda, and she liked to have fainted.

Again, thank you for your friendship.

With love,

Vella, in Valentine.

After she pressed the send button, she had to sit and fan herself because of having a hot flash such as she had not experienced in quite some time. Telling the story had brought out all manner of emotions. She supposed, though, that she could not expect to go shooting out car windows just to get a power surge. In fact, she had promised the sheriff to confine her shooting activities to the gun range.

Chapter Thirty-Four

In the middle of the night, Claire got up and went to check on Sherrilyn. The girl was sleeping soundly. Claire looked at her for a long minute, then wandered out to the office and gazed out the window at the cabins stretching in a line.

She saw Andrew coming out of his room with two suitcases. She watched him put them into the trunk of the Jaguar, then return to the room.

If he wanted to slip off, she would not spoil his plan. She had sensed that he had been ready to go for days but unable to say so.

There would be many things about the frightful incident that Claire would never forget, and among them was Andrew coming to the rescue. He had actually come running with gritted teeth and emitting a "Grrrrr." She didn't tell this to anyone, as she felt he might be sensitive about it, and each time she thought of it, she started to laugh.

The reason Andrew had not been at the motel at the time

the two thugs had showed up was that he had gone to Home Depot to get an air conditioner to replace yet another one that had broken that morning. Claire had been highly annoyed upon hearing this, after having asked him to stay with Sherrilyn for the express purpose of being on guard for an emergency; however, all she had to do was remember his fervor at coming to their defense, and her heart melted all over her chest.

Padding quietly through the apartment, she went to the kitchen, opened the refrigerator and stared at the full shelves: banana nut bread, fruit salad, a plate of ham and cheese chunks, fried chicken, potato salad and chocolate cake.

The violent incident of the previous afternoon had stirred up the same behavior as that of a funeral or a family reunion. People came, and they brought food.

For hours into the evening, they—including many people that Claire didn't think she had ever met—had come to find out the details, to offer consolation and express outrage, and to chat with old friends at the impromptu gathering.

Claire had been overwhelmed by how many people came to tell her that they were glad she was okay, to shake her hand and even to give her hugs. She had thought Marilee Holloway might not turn her loose.

Poor, shy Sherrilyn had somehow felt at fault for the entire thing. Despite all of Claire's reassurances, the girl had fled to hide in the apartment. People kept asking about her, and when she did not appear, a rumor started that she had been hurt. Rey heard this, when he first heard the news of the assault. He came running in a clear panic.

After Rey arrived, Sherrilyn sat with him on the couch in the office. Gradually, after so many people stopped to tell her what a brave girl she was, she began to smile and nod and be able to answer, "Just fine," when anyone inquired as to how she was getting along.

"Woo-ee!" said Tate Holloway, with that certain sparkle in his eyes that a journalist could get when there was good copy. "This town has been lively since you came, Miss Claire. And I guess you're home folks now."

Andrew overheard this comment. Claire saw his head swing around, and his gaze struck hers for an instant, before her attention was diverted by Travis and Larkin Ford coming in the front door and straight over to her.

She thought of it all now, while sitting at the table in the quiet of the night, picking all the fresh strawberries out of the fruit salad.

She recalled Sherrilyn's determined stubbornness to protect what belonged to Claire, and her own protectiveness of Sherrilyn and the baby, and Andrew's display of heroism, and Vella in her swimsuit cover-up that bared her elegant legs while she carried a shotgun like a backwoodsman.

She remembered the chilling look in the black eyes of the man with the knife, and the sound of the gun, and then the arrival of the sheriff, at which point Sherrilyn immediately began crying. Claire had thought the big sheriff was going to come undone at the tears, while he could lift Denny Rhodes by the collar with one hand.

And then Claire herself had started to cry when she saw Winston. She had gone to him and cried all over him, and he had patted her back.

In the light of these experiences, the heartbreak over her father, which had seemed so painful and gigantic, had faded to be of scant importance. Suddenly she saw her life as so full and rich with people who loved her and whom she loved. In that moment she knew exactly what she had, and what she wanted, as clearly as she could feel her own heart beating.

Andrew did not leave in the night. Early the next morning Claire saw the Jaguar still parked outside room number two and imagined him inside, trying to think up some good excuse to head immediately back to Shreveport, while not appearing to break off from her. To be of help, she called and invited him to breakfast.

"Is there any of that Coke salad left?" he asked, coming into the kitchen through the back door.

"Yep. I saved you some." She had remembered his fondness for jellied Coke salad.

"You did?" He gave her a look of pleased surprise, and then averted his eyes.

Sherrilyn shared breakfast with them. Her awe of him had turned into something close to hero worship. She put his Coke salad in a crystal dish and poured his coffee in what she considered a better cup.

Together around the table, the three of them rehashed the events of the previous day, until they got around to the subject of Claire's father. Andrew asked if she was going to have her father's remains moved down to Valentine. She told him that she was not, that her father had been where he was for fifteen years, and she saw no need to dig up something buried that long. "Let the dead bury the dead," she said, to which Andrew looked puzzled but didn't say anything.

After they finished the meal, Sherrilyn made a big deal about leaving them alone. "I'm goin' to clean those two rooms we rented last night. I'll be gone more than an hour, so you two are on your own."

Claire drank her coffee and looked at Andrew, who kept looking down at his plate.

Finally Claire started it off with, "I thank you, Andrew, for all you've done. Words just can't say how thankful I am."

He looked up then. "Well, I'm sorry I left Sherrilyn yesterday. I just didn't think anything like that was going to happen."

"Of course you didn't. Who would have?" She laid her

hand on his. "But what I was referring to was your comin' up here to Valentine. I thank you for all you've done here…and mostly for giving us time to work things out. I always felt as if we did not get things worked out between us at the time of the divorce. I think we have now."

He nodded, as if a little uncertain. "I guess that's it, then. We gave it a good shot." Relief blossomed across his face.

"We gave it a *great* shot."

Then, on safer, free ground, he said, "I screwed it up when I let you go."

"No. You didn't. It happened, I think, back at the very beginning. I don't think I married you, but who I wanted you to be, and you did the same with me."

She suspected he didn't understand any of that, but she continued anyway.

"This is me, Andrew. I love this dusty, two-bit town, where if you don't get cable TV, you have to put foil on your rabbit ears. But you can get the best strawberry milkshakes in the land and see the stars easily on a clear night. I like the people, even the ones who would shoot off a shotgun if she felt it necessary—maybe especially her. And I adore this funky motel. I really do."

It seemed so funny, the way she felt about the motel. But real and honest. She laughed at the knowledge that seemed so precious, while Andrew shook his head.

Claire stood squinting in the hot sun beside the Jaguar, which was again coated with fine dust.

"I really don't know what I'm gonna do without you," Andrew said, looking a little confused and worried.

"Yes, you do. You're gonna build great buildings." She set them both free from her mothering him and him leaning on her.

He looked more confident. Then, "Here. Maybe you

can use these." Andrew handed her a roll of plans. "I drew up some of the changes and additions you said you wanted."

Plans for the motel, from Andrew Wilder, one of the premier architects in Louisiana.

"Oh, Andrew. Thank you." She felt a tinge of guilt. "I wish I had something to offer you. I don't suppose a free lifetime pass to come to the Goodnight Motel would be much."

"Oh, you never can tell. You know, I do rather like that bed vibrator." He was stepping toward his car, eagerness to be gone all over him.

He kissed her cheek, told her to take care of herself and promised to call. He gazed at her for a moment, as if expecting something from her.

But she had nothing to offer, other than a reassuring smile. She waved him out of sight and knew it was highly unlikely he would ever call.

Larkin and Travis bid goodbye at the Texaco, hugging unashamedly. Afterward, Larkin had to blink away tears as he watched his son drive off.

"If you had as many youngun's as I do, you'd be relieved he was goin'," Norm Stidham said.

"Probably," Larkin said, and took comfort in the mundane tasks of filling the fuel tank and checking the oil in his pickup truck.

Just then Andrew Wilder's silver Jaguar came speeding up to the pumps on the other side. Old Norm Stidham was getting out of his chair, but Larkin called, "I'll get it," and stepped over to fuel the sports car.

"Thanks," Andrew said.

"You bet," Larkin said, looking through the Jaguar's window and seeing a couple of duffel bags inside.

Norm had come out from his chair anyway, to talk to the man about the previous day's exciting events.

"Too exciting for me," said Andrew Wilder. "I'm headin' on back down to Louisiana, where I can live in peace…and never get off a paved road."

Larkin looked up to see the man looking straight at him.

The architect in the silver car headed one way out of the station, and Larkin in his pickup truck headed the other, driving to Grace Florist, where he purchased a large, colorful bouquet. His late wife had taught him about how to approach a woman.

When he pulled up in front of the Goodnight's office and looked through the wide window, he saw Claire at the front desk. She saw him and waved.

Holding the flowers behind his back, he went inside.

"I just saw your ex-husband at the Texaco."

"You did?"

"Yep. He said he was on his way back down to Shreveport."

"Yes." She was studying him.

"Travis left this mornin', too. He's goin' to work a while down in Texas. Got a real good job brokerin' horses all over the country."

"All over the country?" She frowned. "I imagine you'll miss him."

"Yes, I will. But he needs to make his own way. He can't stay around and try to hold my hand his whole life."

He had begun to grin, and she did, too. He felt a little silly with the flowers behind his back, but he didn't know how to bring them out to her.

"So, are you gonna miss holdin' your ex-husband's hand?" he asked.

"No. We're done with that. Although he did leave me these great plans for the motel."

"Oh, he did?" He looked down for the first time to see

that she had architectural plans spread on the counter. He felt thwarted from his endeavor to impress her. Flowers didn't seem much next to building plans.

Then, remembering, he cleared his throat. "I hear we need to do a little business on the five acres out back." He swung the flowers around in a flourish. "I'm sure I can make you a good deal."

With delight, he saw her surprise.

"Oh, Larkin." She took the flowers as if they were precious jewels.

He gazed at her and thought of the long years of drought behind him. He could not believe his good fortune.

Then she advised, "I have got a motel and a young girl with a baby on the way. I do not know if I want to deal with a relationship with a man on top of that. I really don't know if I ever again want to get into a permanent relationship with a man."

She wanted things understood. She did not want any guessing.

"I'm a man to appreciate an honest woman," he said.

"Good," she said, pleased, and her eyes were clearly appreciating him, too.

From: Vella Blaine
To: <haltg@mailectric.com>
Sent: September 16, 1997, 12:15 p.m.
Subject: He's arrived!

Oh, Harold, that digital camera that you sent for my birthday sure came in handy this morning! Here's the first picture of Raphael Ryan Earles, with his gallant mother and thrilled godmother, ten minutes after he dared to pop into the world. That happened at 4:05 a.m., just after we got Sherrilyn to the hospital—I drove, thank God, as I had to go like the wind. We thought for a few minutes that Claire was going to end up catching the little tyke in the rear of the Land Rover.

He weighs in at 6 lbs., 5 ozs. Isn't he the tiniest thing? What is with young people these days, naming children so strange? Sherrilyn may have insisted on naming him Raphael, but I'm calling him Ryan, which is a normal, perfectly sound name. That girl mostly sways in the wind, but every once in a while, she will dig in her heels, and that's what she has done on this name business. She says a person follows their name, and Raphael is the name of a great painter, plus it means God has healed, and she wants her son to be healed of having a father like Denny Rhodes.

Got to go—Winston's in here passing out cigars.

Love,
Vella

Dear Harold,

Here are the pictures from little Ryan's dedication at church today. In this first one Rey is cut off on one side because Belinda took the picture so that I could be in it. I'm the grand-godmother, which seems the closest I will ever get to being a grandmother, as Margaret says she has entered early menopause, and Belinda says having children is too messy.

The second picture is Pastor Smith presenting little Ryan to the church family. The Ladies Circle Number One provided those large lily flower arrangements. The picture of all those ladies surrounding the pastor and little Ryan is the Ladies Circle—the woman with the orange hair is Inez Cooper, who was so righteous about Sherrilyn not being married but having a baby. Ryan has won her over, as you can see from her sticking her head up near him.

The third picture is one I took of the pastor with Ryan and the godfathers. That's Rey in this one—the scrawny fellow in the too-big suit next to Winston. I think Rey being godfather is a hazardous situation. If he and Sherrilyn break up, things could be awkward. Claire feels Winston—he's the white-haired one—can cover this as grand-godfather, but that's still pretty hazardous, given Winston's age.

Life is generally a hazardous proposition, though, isn't it? When I think of all the hazards we all face from the moment we come onto the earth, I am reminded that life is stubborn about going on.

I give thanks for you continuing on, dear friend.
Love, Vella.

From: Vella Blaine
To: <haltg@mailectric.com>
Sent: November 3, 1997, 4:15 p.m.
Subject: Partners

My dear friend—Again, many thanks for the camera. Here's a picture of Claire and I signing the papers, effectively becoming partners in the Goodnight Motel. I'm the financier of the outfit, Claire is the manager, and Sherrilyn sort of boosts us up. We are going to give old Jaydee Mayhall a run for his money in this town.

Oh, Belinda took the picture, and that's why I'm almost cut off. She took three shots, and this is the best of them.

Hugs from Valentine.

Vella

From: Vella Blaine
To: <haltg@mailectric.com>
Sent: March 23, 1998, 11:22 p.m.
Subject: Friends

Hi, sweetheart. It's been a long, cold winter, especially for you, I know. I thought you might enjoy these pictures. Sherrilyn took them. She's becoming quite the photographer.

The first is we godmothers with our beautiful godson. I'm learning to call him Rafe. It's rather a strong name.

And there's me demonstrating how the new meeting building can open out onto the pool. It's the grandest thing this town has ever seen. Claire has already booked two wedding receptions for May and June.

That is Larkin with Claire holding Rafe. Do you know she told me that she and Larkin have not so much as kissed? She says she is a little afraid to kiss him, because it might end up being like the fire that burned down Chicago. I told her that she is not getting any younger, and that she needs to enjoy the life and blessings she has been given.

Here is yellow forsythia on the south edge of the *Welcome to Valentine* sign. In just a few weeks, there will be roses blooming.

You might want to consider coming out to see us, Harold. You've had a hard winter in grieving over Estelle, but spring down here has come again, as always. You could relax at the

Goodnight and enjoy the warmer weather. No expectations on my part. Just friends. We all need our friends.

Love in that special way,

Vella

P.S. I wish I would have had the camera handy yesterday afternoon. Sherrilyn came running out of the drugstore rest room hollering, and I thought maybe she had seen a snake or something, but what was the funniest was Winston jumped up and sort of made fists.

I asked him later what he had been thinking, and he said that he thought maybe they were under attack, like what had happened back last summer at the Goodnight. What I think is that he has all this time felt left out of what happened and doesn't want to be left out again.

Anyway, Sherrilyn was only making a fuss about having seen some fresh writing on the ladies' room wall that got her and Claire all excited. It was something like *Lily Donnell was here*. It seems as if Claire and Sherrilyn have seen the woman's notes in other bathrooms. They quizzed Belinda for quite some time about having possibly seen the woman, but Belinda had no idea. Sherrilyn made me promise not to paint over it the next time we paint.

That's us from Valentine.

Your friend,

Vella

Chapter Thirty-Five

A large truck with a crane stopped at the edge of the highway, and a large lumbering sort of man came through the office door.

"We got your sign and are ready to set it in place, Miz Tillman."

Not wanting to be termed the ex-Mrs. Wilder for the rest of her life, Claire had returned to her given surname, a move she was especially grateful to have made when Andrew ended up marrying Nina after all, back in December.

With some excitement, she stuffed Raphael into a sweater, lifting him and savoring the sweet baby smell of him.

She was enjoying the wonderful situation of being a second mother. She got all the fun and joy, and rarely had to stay up nights. Right then Sherrilyn was off at the junior college in a special study class for the GED, and Claire resisted the urge to call the girl on her cell phone. As important as the sign restoration was to Claire, it was not more important than the girl's diligent efforts at education. From the moment

Sherrilyn had given birth to Raphael, she had become in-
fused with the sort of mothering spirit that was determined
to provide the best for her child, which meant that she set
out to provide for him an intelligent and knowledgeable
mother. Claire was awfully proud of her.

Carrying the baby outside, she stood with him, both of
them blinking in the bright sunlight, and watched the crane
on the back of the big truck lift the panel of curved neon
into place. Three and a half months earlier, the old *Sweet
Dreams* panel had been sent all the way to Dallas for repair.
Now it was home. It swayed gently as it was maneuvered into
its original position at the top of the sign by guide wires and
strong arms. Then the men went to work connecting and
securing, and eventually the large foreman flipped a switch
at the base of the sign, turning on the light.

Claire peered hard, but in the bright sunlight, with the
azure sky above, she could not see the neon light. The man
up on the crane called down that it was working, though.
She watched the sign for a long minute after the workmen
had left. She was still standing there, near the mailbox, when
the postman came by in his little postal van and handed her
the mail.

Carrying a now dozing Raphael back inside, she deposited him into his swing and went through the day's mail.

There was a padded envelope addressed to Mrs. Claire
Tillman Wilder, as if the person who had sent it was not certain of her name. The return address was an M. Williams, in
Bakersfield, California, and all of it hand-addressed. From
time to time small companies or independent salespeople sent
her brochures and sample items for the motel. That was what
she expected to find when she turned up the envelope.

Something wrapped in tissue paper fell onto the counter.
There was a letter with it, handwritten. It said,

I heard you own the Goodnight now. I was going through some old stuff I brought back from my mother's house the past winter and found this wallet. I guess my stepbrother had it from your father. They were cousins on the Overton side. Thought you might like to have this. Regards, M. Williams.

She unfolded the tissue paper. The wallet leather was powdery and coming off on the paper.

It had belonged to her father.

Gingerly opening the wallet, she found inside a ragged driver's license with a faded picture of a rather ragged-looking middle-aged man. Not at all the face of the man she held in memory. But the name on the license was John Tillman, no middle initial, the date of her father's birth.

She gazed again at the small photograph. Yes, she saw the resemblance.

Looking at the sad image made her so sad herself, and unnerved, that she almost closed up the wallet.

But curiosity had her now.

With gentle fingertips, she continued pulling things from the wallet, a worn social security card for John Tillman, a membership card in a carpenters' union, two torn bits of paper with numbers and addresses but no names scribbled on them, and a tattered quote cut from some publication. She carefully pressed it out flat and read, "Hard things are put in our way not to stop us, but to call out our courage and strength."

She ran her eyes over the much smudged piece, noting a clear fingerprint on one edge. She caressed the fingerprint, thinking of the worn hand that had put it there.

Then, there at the last, a small, worn-edged photograph.

Her breath caught in her throat as she gazed at the image of herself as a child, aged five or six, sitting on a concrete step. Not laughing, just looking at the camera.

She stared at the picture for long seconds in which her eyes began to tear. Then she looked into the wallet and found one more thing, cut down, folded, and compressed by years: her graduation announcement.

At this, she put her head down and sobbed.

He had carried these reminders of her in his wallet. He had cared about her after all.

That night, just at dusk, Vella came with Winston. Larkin came and brought champagne. Belinda drove out with Deputy Lyle, and Julia Jenkins-Tinsley and her husband, Juice, just happened past and saw them all standing out looking at the newly refurbished motel sign in all its glory.

"I did not recall the *Sweet Dreams at the* bein' in blue," Julia said.

"It's turquoise," said Belinda. "And I remember it."

"I think it got wrecked and taken off when you were real little and probably don't recall," Julia said.

"Well, I do."

Sherrilyn, handing around glasses of champagne from a tray, put in a compromise. "It's on the old postcard. It's a little more turquoise now, bein' new, and probably doesn't look just the same, Miss Julia. Don't you give Raphael champagne, Mr. Winston," she added sternly.

"The nut does not fall far from the tree," Vella said in a low voice to Claire, who saw Larkin had heard and was grinning.

"To the Goodnight," Larkin said, speaking in a rare move as leader and raising his glass.

"To the Goodnight," everyone repeated.

Then Larkin added, "And to Claire, who one day came drivin' down this road and right into town and brought a lot of good things with her."

"To Claire!" everyone said with enthusiasm, while Claire breathed deeply and felt mildly embarrassed.

Winston then had to throw in a toast. "To all of us," he said with a mischievous grin.

After the toasts offered for the Goodnight's good rise, everyone gradually left, until Claire and Larkin were alone in the spring evening and the glow cast by the gold and blue hues from the neon sign.

"I really love this sign. I think maybe I wanted the entire motel for this sign. Isn't that silly?"

"I guess no sillier than the way I love my truck…or my barn with the blue roof."

Their exchange struck her as silly, too, and she laughed. He put his arm around her and drew her against him.

He was warm, his body hard. Just ever so slightly, not wanting him to notice, she turned her head toward his chest, in order to catch the scent of him, which at the moment was faint virile cologne, cotton corduroy, and warm male skin.

She looked up at him. The hues from the neon sign painted the side of his face. He gazed at her with that question in his eyes. Such a patient, warm and promising expression.

Almost before she realized that the time had come, she threw herself onto him in such a manner as to take him somewhat by surprise, but only for an instant, before he laid claim to her with a kiss that fulfilled every fantasy that had come across her mind and then some.

"Oh, Larkin…" Her head was swirling, and she had to hold on to him.

"Come here, woman."

He kissed her again, and while they were doing this, there came faint music from one of the rooms. The two broke the kiss. They gazed at each other and smiled, as the deep voice of a romance song came across the soft night.

They began to dance, there in the glow of the Sweet Dreams at the Goodnight Motel sign, in the manner of a man and a woman who had lived and knew that from now on is all that mattered. They each came with baggage, and the wear of years and people of the past. But they came with the knowledge and experience of forgiveness and the love that it brings.

A large golden-brown sedan, of some years but well kept, took the exit ramp from the toll road and came to a stop at an intersection with the state highway. The driver, a man with a careful manner and a face that could support the sunglasses favored by highway patrolmen, read the green highway sign that said: Valentine 10 Miles, with an arrow pointing to the right.

He turned right and followed the ribbon of blacktop that snaked through rolling hills scattered with cattle, mesquite and clumps of trees.

Seeing the Welcome to Valentine sign, with golden forsythia waving in the breeze, appear on the right, he slowed the car, looking ahead for the expected Sweet Dreams at the Goodnight Motel sign.

The sign came into view. Below it, near the road, was a rather surprising sign.

Patsy Cline had sweet dreams here
You can too!

He directed the car into the drive and stopped in front of the office. A young woman with a baby on her hip was just walking around the corner. She greeted him as he got stiffly from the car.

"Welcome to the Goodnight," she said in such a friendly manner that he thought maybe she knew who he was. He knew her and almost called her by name, but then felt reluctant to be so forward. Although people in this part of the country struck him as being naturally forward people.

She held the door for him, but he reached above her head and took hold of it, saying, "After you." He had certain standards. It wasn't right for a young lady to hold the door for him.

There was a woman at the desk. He recognized her instantly. She was prettier than he had expected. She smiled at him, too, and said, "Welcome to the Goodnight." The greeting appeared to be a popular tradition.

"Would you like a room?" she asked.

"Yes, I believe I would." He wondered if he should reveal himself, but she distracted him with another question.

"Single or double?"

"Oh, single," he said, in a very faint doleful manner, although he saw the woman's eyes flicker up to him as she passed across the registration card.

She busied herself at the computer while he filled out the card. When he finished, laid down the pen and pulled out his credit card, she returned, making a comment about the weather and that it was tornado season and there was a possible storm coming that night, but that the motel had shelters.

Then, "Ohmyheavens! Harold? Are you Vella's Harold?"

He nodded. "I came a few days early," he barely got out, as she introduced herself as Claire, then called to the young woman, "Sherrilyn! Harold's here!" and came around the counter to envelop him in a big hug. The next instant the girl with the baby on her hip reappeared and was hugging him, too.

"I'll call Vella...no, let's surprise her. No, I'd better call her. I don't want her to faint or something."

She made the call, hung up and called for someone named Nancy to come mind the front desk. Then they piled into his car and directed him into town, which looked exactly as he had imagined, and to Blaine's Drugstore and Soda Fountain, which was exactly as he had imagined many times, and where he saw immediately an old white-haired gentleman sitting at a table with another old man in a wheelchair, and he knew exactly who they were.

Claire took his hand and brought him forward. He was glad to have stopped at the motel first and to have gained these escorts. It would have been harder, even for him, a man toughened by years on the police force, to have come into this cold.

"Well, by golly, you're here at last," was Winston Valentine's greeting, and then he introduced him to Perry Blaine in the wheelchair, who blinked at him and nodded in a great gentlemanly manner, then smiled like a child upon being presented with the baby by the girl.

And then there was a tall, magnificent woman coming toward him. The rare sort of woman with whom a man never dared trifle.

"Hello, Vella."

"Hello, Harold." She held out her hand and shook his in the warm way of using both her hands. "Welcome to Valentine. We're so glad you've come!"

Everyone gathered around the round granite black-topped table. He ended up next to Perry Blaine, and when Vella and her daughter served up shakes and sundaes in celebration of a guest, Harold helped Perry eat his sundae and felt useful again.

"How long are you stayin' in our fair town?" Winston asked him.

"Oh, a couple of weeks," Harold answered. "Just thought I needed a little vacation."

"Uh-huh," said Winston, with a speculative grin.